An Irish Doctor in Love and at Sea

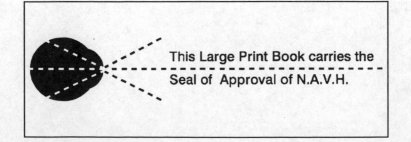

This Large Print Book carries the
Seal of Approval of N.A.V.H.

An Irish Doctor in Love and at Sea

Patrick Taylor

THORNDIKE PRESS
A part of Gale, Cengage Learning

GALE
CENGAGE Learning·

Farmington Hills, Mich • San Francisco • New York • Waterville, Maine
Meriden, Conn • Mason, Ohio • Chicago

GALE
CENGAGE Learning

LIBRARY OF CONGRESS CATALOGING-IN-PUBLICATION DATA

Taylor, Patrick, 1941-
An Irish doctor in love and at sea / by Patrick Taylor. — Large print edition.
pages cm. — (An Irish Country novel) (Thorndike Press large print core)
ISBN 978-1-4104-8298-3 (hardback) — ISBN 1-4104-8298-7 (hardcover)
1. O'Reilly, Fingal Flahertie (Fictitious character)—Fiction. 2. Physicians—Fiction. 3. Country life—Northern Ireland—Fiction. 4. Large type books. 5. Medical fiction. I. Title.
PR9199.3.T36I763 2015b
813'.54—dc23   2015033090

Published in 2015 by arrangement with Tom Doherty Associates, LLC

Printed in Mexico
1 2 3 4 5 6 7 19 18 17 16 15

To Dr. James "Jimmy" Taylor,
squadron leader, RAFVR (Ret.),
and
all those of his generation who at huge
cost fought and overcame great evil

•

At the going down of the sun
and in the morning
we will remember them.

Ne Obliviscaris. Lest we forget.

My father, "Jimmy" Taylor, MB, RAFVR

AUTHOR'S NOTE

Real life is not monochromatic. It is painted from a varied palette. In ancient Greece, drama, the staged representation of life, was represented pictorially by two masks: one smiling, Thalia, the muse of comedy; and one crying, Melpomene, the muse of tragedy.

This book, number ten in the Irish Country Doctor series, is home to both.

It continues in part to follow the fortunes of the doctors and the villagers of Ballybucklebo in the mid-1960s. It answers questions from readers of earlier works about the futures of the well-known characters, and introduces newcomers to the story. This is Thalia's half of the book.

I hope you will enjoy the goings-on, and if anyone tries to sell you Woolamarroo quokka herding dogs (and many thanks to Jill Evans, friend and author of *The Time Traveller: The Development of the Great Dane,* for invaluable advice on doggy miscegenation and reproduction), please remember, forewarned is forearmed. But if you still go ahead, I'm sure Donal Donnelly could as well get you a *really* good price on the Giant's Causeway and the Mourne Mountains.

While Donal may take a liberal interpretation of the truth, I always strive for accuracy. Scenes here set in the Dublin and Ulster of the '60s, and the medicine of the time, are as realistic as memory serves and ordnance survey maps and my old medical texts from my student and trainee days allow. I should tell you that back in Ireland, Davy McMaster did run a bar in his farm at Lisbane when I was a young man. Lars and Fingal go there. Many's the hot Irish I've had at Davy's after a day's winter wildfowling on frigid Strangford Lough. Today it is an elegant roadhouse, the Saltwater Brig. Dorothy, my partner, and I went back to it in September 2014 when we were in Ulster for the fiftieth reunion of the Queen's University medical graduating class of '64.

In the author's note in my last book, *An Irish Doctor in Peace and at War,* I made a solemn promise that I would conclude the adventures of Surgeon Lieutenant Fingal O'Reilly, RNR, and his bride-to-be, Deirdre Mawhinney, during the Second World War. I have kept that promise. This part of the book has its dark moments, and is Melpomene's — and I make no apology.

Fingal and Deirdre together spend time in

Gosport in England, where Fingal has been seconded for anaesthesia training to the Royal Naval Hospital Haslar. Later, Deirdre goes home to Ulster and Fingal returns to his battleship HMS *Warspite* in the Mediterranean in 1941. (All battle scenes there are taken from the writings of eyewitnesses, to be found in the books cited below.)

Haslar naval hospital opened in 1753, three years before the outbreak of the Seven Years' War (1756–1763). During that war, 1,512 sailors were killed in action, but there were 133,700 other losses — most died of disease. The need for such a facility was obvious.

In describing the anaesthesia of the '40s, I owe a great debt to Doctor Roger Maltby, an old friend from Calgary who provided a rich source of material about the techniques. He also put me in touch with Surgeon Commander Mike Inman, RN (Retired), who read and corrected my naval descriptions in *An Irish Doctor in Peace and at War*. Mike Inman introduced me to a remarkable man, Eric Birbeck MVO, Royal Victorian Order (for service on HMY *Britannia*). Eric served in the Royal Navy Medical Branch for forty-four years, retiring as a senior chief petty officer. After retirement, he then became an anaesthetic technical officer in the British Civil Service. Eric, as the chairman of the Haslar Heritage Group, has been associated with Haslar for more than fifty years and has provided me with invaluable source material (see later). Last September, he walked me through the old hospital and took me to see the places in Hampshire like the Crescent, Alverstoke, Gosport, the Paddock, and the Gosport/ Portsmouth ferry that you will visit in this book. There really is a pub called the Fighting Cocks, and it was nicknamed "the Pugilistic Penises" by the staff of Haslar. As if that were not enough, Eric has read every page of the manuscript and kept me right on matters of naval custom, naval medicine, and the workings of Haslar hospital. The book and I owe him a very great deal. Thank you, Eric. The accuracy is his. The errors mine.

I have chosen to populate both stories with both real and fictional characters. The real people in the Ballybucklebo story are doctors and one bandleader. Graham Harley, a superb clinician and mentor, taught me and fostered my interest in human infertility. "Buster" Holland delivered my daughter Sarah. Nigel Kinnear was Regius Professor of Surgery at Trinity College Dublin. Sir Albert Liley's contribution to the treatment of Rhesus isoimmunisation revolutionised its management until a vaccine against Rh positive red cells was developed, making the disorder a thing of the past. Ron Livingstone was a classmate and later a distinguished academic Canadian obstetrician and gynaecologist. Teddy McIlrath became a consul-

10

tant radiologist at the Royal Victoria Hospital, Belfast, in 1965. Bill Sproule was a classmate at both a private school and when we were trainee obstetricians. And Charley Whitfield, who also taught me, was Regius Professor at the University of Glasgow. They have all served medicine with great distinction.

Clipper Carlton's Showband, a seven-piece dance band from Strabane, was fronted by Fergie O'Hagan and played at dance halls and functions. Dorothy and I danced to them in the late '50s.

There are many real people in the 1940–41 story as well — at Haslar, on the Takoradi run, on *Warspite* in the Mediterranean, and playing parts in '30s and '40s medicine.

At Haslar, two admirals commanding, Surgeon Rear Admiral T. Creaser, and his successor, Surgeon Rear Admiral A. B. Bradbury; the matron, Miss M. Goodrich; the chaplain, John Wilfrid Evans.

On the Takoradi run, Squadron Leader Ludomil "Effendi" Rayski, a gallant officer who had been commander of the Polish air force before Poland's defeat by Germany. Rayski escaped from his native land to fight for the Allies.

In the Mediterranean on HMS *Warspite,* Admiral A. B. Cunningham; Commander Sir Charles Madden, executive officer; Commander Geoffrey Barnard, fleet gunnery officer; Commander B. J. H. Wilkinson, fleet engineering officer; Admiral Henry Pridham-Wippell, who so ably commanded the out-gunned British cruisers at Cape Matapan that he was knighted. He subsequently survived the sinking of the battleship HMS *Barham* in November 1941. Patrick Steptoe, medical officer on HMS *Hereward,* who was sunk with his ship on May 27, 1941, off Crete, became an Italian POW, and after the war went on to advance laparoscopy (and teach me the technique). Steptoe was one half of the team with Professor Sir Robert Edwards, Nobel Laureate, that produced Louise Brown, the world's first test-tube baby.

In medicine, Professor Robert Macintosh, who headed the first-ever British academic department of anaesthesia located at Oxford University; and Sir Archibald McIndoe, who revolutionised the plastic surgical treatment of burned aircrew.

And in other theatres, Douglas Bader, the legless fighter pilot; and Captain Edward Fegen RN, VC of HMS *Jervis Bay,* who gallantly held off the German commerce raider *Admiral Scheer* so his convoy HX-84 could try to escape.

It is with great admiration and deep respect I have chosen to be as true as I can to the parts each played in real life that I have borrowed to give my story authenticity. I am using them too as a metaphor for everyone who served in World War II, a conflict that sadly is now slipping from memory even though the year of publication of this work, 2015, marks the seventieth anniversaries of both VE and VJ Days.

Their being and actions are matters of history. Any dialogue has been put in their mouths by me, with the exception of Admiral Cunningham's speech after the evacuation of Crete (see below). The rest of the characters peopling these pages are the progeny of my overheated imagination.

When it comes to being accurate, may I make a few more general observations about the wartime story and in a scene back in Ulster?

I have modified time reporting from the civilian clock I used in *An Irish Doctor in Peace and at War.* While for simplicity of understanding it has been retained in pure narrative, in battles reported by Tannoy, the military twenty-four-hour clock is used, as it would have been in real life.

I note on page 35 that the RAF, at the height of the Battle of Britain on September 15, 1940, had claimed 182 (185 according to other sources) enemy planes destroyed. Postwar records set the actual figure at 75. In all such matters as food rationing, motorcars, radio programmes, songs, films, and women's fashions of the day, I have used archival sources, usually accessed on the Internet. The remarkable Takoradi ferry route was in service from 1940 to 1943 and functioned as I have described. I have seen the Battle of Britain Memorial Flight that is mentioned in chapter 34. It was flying over Duxford, which was Douglas Bader's station during the Battle of Britain. It is comprised of two fighters, a Supermarine Spitfire and a Hawker Hurricane, and one Avro Lancaster bomber. To watch those venerable veterans and listen to the snarl of six twelve-thousand-plus-horsepower Rolls-Royce Merlin engines brought tears of gratitude for the heroic young men who flew them in battle and the determined young women who ferried them from factories to airfields. Particularly impressive is that seven men made up the operational crew of a Lancaster. Its ferry pilot flew single-handed — and there were no power-assisted controls.

There is one other important character in this book. HMS *Warspite,* "The Grand Old Lady." For completeness, may I tell you that once returned from America fit again for battle, she served with valour against the Japanese in the Indian Ocean in 1942–43 before being transferred to the Mediterranean, where, in September 1943, supporting the Salerno landings, she was struck by a primitive German air-launched guided missile. After being patched up again, she fought in 1944 as a floating battery supporting the American landings on Utah Beach on D-Day.

She was sold for scrap in 1947.

In conclusion to the explanations, and in fairness, having boasted of my attempts to be accurate, I must also confess to some small deceptions made for dramatic purpose. HMS *Touareg* and HMS *Swaledale* did not exist. I conjured them. Nor was there any air raid on Portsmouth on October 1 as it is described in chapter 10. Portsmouth did suffer sixty-seven attacks between July 1940 and May 1944. I apologise to the people of that fine city, which, apart from lesser raids, endured three catastrophic assaults on August 24, 1940, January 10, 1941 (alluded to in chapter 42), and March 10, 1941.

As you may know, for many years I was involved in medical research. Old habits die hard. For those of you who wish to read more deeply into the background to this novel, I have consulted:

Ballantyne, Iain. *Warspite.*
Birbeck, Eric, Ann Ryder, and Phillip Ward. *The Royal Hospital Haslar: A Pictorial History.*[*]
Birbeck, E. *The Church of Saint Luke Royal Haslar. An Appreciation.*[*]
Birbeck, E. Numerous reprints describing medical procedures, staffing, and working at Haslar.[*]

[*] Denotes material provided by Eric Birbeck

Bungay, S. *The Most Dangerous Enemy. A History of the Battle of Britain.*

Clarke, R. *The Royal Victoria Hospital Belfast. A History 1797–1997.*

Cunningham, A. B. C. Admiral of the Fleet and Viscount Cunningham of Hyndhope. *A Sailor's Odyssey.* (The words of his speech after Crete are taken from his dispatch cited on p. 462.)

Gardiner, J. *The Blitz. The British Under Attack.*

MacLean, A. HMS *Ulysses.*

Monserrat, N. *The Cruel Sea.*

Plevy, H. Y. *Battleship Sailors.*

Prysor, G. *Citizen Sailors.*

Richardson, J. B. *A Visit to Haslar 1916.**

Tarrant, V. E. *Battleship* Warspite.

Watton, R. *The Battleship* Warspite, which contains her marine architectural drawings. Her sick bay really was on the main deck, the wardroom on the upper deck aft on the port side, and the four-gun six-inch batteries on the upper deck abaft A and B turrets.

Wade, F. *A Midshipman's War. A Young Man in the Mediterranean Naval War 1941–1943.*

Poems quoted: "In Flanders Fields," Lieutenant Colonel John McCrae, M.D.; "For the Fallen," Robert Laurence Binyon.

I hope this note has helped to explain this

work, and the glossary at the end of the book defines some of the more arcane aspects of British service usage and regional dialects, including those from both ends of the Emerald Isle. They are here to give you, the reader, more insight into it — and, I trust, more enjoyment of the pages that follow.

PATRICK TAYLOR
Salt Spring Island
British Columbia
Canada
October 2014

1
A Party in a Parlour

The Dublin coddle had been cooked to perfection and Doctor Fingal Flahertie O'Reilly had not been able to resist the sherry trifle for dessert.

"That was very good," he said, looking wistfully at the few smears of cream, custard, and strawberry jam on his otherwise empty plate. "I think I'll have a second . . ."

Kitty O'Reilly grinned. "Fingal, my love, you're already having a bit of difficulty getting into your gear. Don't forget, we have a formal black tie dinner tonight. You want to look your best for me, don't you?"

"Of course," he said. "For you? Anything." And while he seemed to say it in jest, one look into those amber-flecked grey eyes told him that inside he really meant it. He beckoned to the waitress in the familiar little restaurant on Dublin's Leeson Street, asked her for the bill, paid, then rose and helped Kitty to her feet. "How do you fancy a stroll, bit of a leg stretch? Work our lunches down?

19

It's not too far back to the Shelbourne Hotel even if we go the long way round."

"Love it," she said, "for old times' sake." She took and squeezed his hand. "Remember I used to have a flat here on Leeson Street thirty years ago?"

"I do," he said, preferring not to recall too clearly that night, in 1936, when she'd told him that he'd put his work ahead of her once too often, and that as a couple they were finished. "And I remember," he said, "walking you from your hospital on Baggot Street to get to that very restaurant we've just been in."

They were turning onto Wilton Terrace, on the north bank of the Grand Canal, both relishing the walk in the crisp, late-September air, heading in the direction of Mount Street. The lawn that bordered the canal was dotted with widely spaced trees. He looked across the expanse of grass to the narrow waters and the reed-lined bank of the far shore. "It was a Sunday, I think," he said. "We were coming along the other side of the canal, and we stopped for a bit of *craic* with an old boy who was repairing the retaining wall. He and I smoked our pipes, as I recall, while he told us the history of An Canáil Mor."

"And then," she said, "you chatted with a bunch of stark-naked kids from the Liberties, swimming in the canal. Remember how hot it was?"

. . . wherein the good old slushy mud
seagulls did sport and play . . .

He sang a snatch from "Down by the Liffey
Side," perhaps not entirely appropriate for
the canal, but overhead real gulls soared and
made harsh, high-pitched *gulla-gulla-gulla*
screams on a breeze that brought the Dublin
smells of traffic exhausts and mudflats of the
nearby great river at low tide.

"One of the gurriers was a patient, and you
gave him a bag of sweeties, and he called you
'the Big Fellah.' I could see how you were
respected in the Liberties because you cared
for your patients, and I loved you for it." She
walked closer to him and he put his arm
around her waist. "I've always loved you, Fingal," she said.

He hung his head. It was, he felt, superflu-
ous to echo the sentiments like a moonstruck
sixteen-year-old. He knew he did and she
knew and that was what mattered. As they
passed under the bridge carrying Baggot
Street, he couldn't resist saying, "A lot of
water has run under the bridge since then
—"

"That," she said, "was a terrible pun, Fingal O'Reilly, or whatever —"

"It was a metaphor —"

"Right. A metaphor, a terrible metaphor,
but a true one."

They were all alone under the bridge.

She grasped the lapels of his tweed jacket and kissed him. They parted and walked on, holding hands. "I love you and I love Dublin where we met," she said. "Strumpet City, Dirty Dublin, Baile Átha Cliath — the town at the ford at the hurdles."

O'Reilly smiled. "Me too."

He pointed to where a barge, brightly painted, engine putt-putting, diesel smoke belching from its funnel, butted blunt bows west heading for the midlands of Ireland. "Horses pulled most of them when we were youngsters here," he said, and thought, But you can't turn back the clock.

In its passing, the vessel chased a flock of mallard. The birds, sunlight shining from the drakes' emerald heads, flared, rose together, then circled, setting their wings, and pitching back into the canal with much ploughing of watery furrows, squabbling, and tail pecking.

"I've always loved ducks," he said. "Maybe it's time to put my gun away, but I'd miss Strangford Lough so much."

"And so would Arthur Guinness, the great lummox. He is a gun-dog, after all."

"You're right," he said, pulling her up the steps by the next bridge to Mount Street Lower. "Do you know I once assisted a gynaecologist in a private house here. He removed an ovarian cyst right in the woman's bedroom. My old boss, Phelim Corrigan, gave the anaesthetic."

"Such different times," she said. "Surgery's all done by specialists in hospitals now." She swung their hands in a wide arc. "Here we are. Merrion Square. Do you remember when we stopped to listen to a man haranguing a crowd of Blue Shirts about the Spanish Civil War?"

"I do. And I remember you insisting we stay to listen," and a few weeks later going off to Spain, my Kitty, he said to himself. My own fault, but it had hurt like hell. "And when you'd heard enough, we called for Bob Beresford, who had a flat here, and the three of us went to the horse races." O'Reilly's heart ached doubly for the lost years that might have been spent with Kitty, and for his long-dead friend. He said nothing for a while, remembering. Remembering.

Today, and indeed the rest of this weekend, was certainly a time for memories. In a few hours, he and Kitty would get into their best bibs and tuckers to attend the opening cocktail reception and welcoming dinner for the thirtieth reunion of their 1936 medical school class at Trinity College. But those were fond memories, happy ones, and he recalled a snatch from an ancient English folk song he'd had to learn at school,

Begone dull care, I prithee begone from me

"Right," he said, "time to get back to the Shelbourne. We'll cut across Merrion Square, nip along Merrion Street Upper, and take Merrion Row to Saint Stephen's Green. I'd like a nap before we have to start getting ready for tonight's festivities."

"Come on then," she said. "I do want you rested, and I'm really looking forward to seeing you in your naval uniform. I'll never forget the sight of you in it at one New Year's Eve formal dance when we were both students."

And Fingal O'Reilly, who hated formal dress, would for her sake struggle into his number one uniform in lieu of a dinner suit and black tie, ready to forge more memories of happy times together.

O'Reilly clapped as the applause grew for Sir Donald Cromie, plain "Cromie" to his closest friends, who had risen in his place at their table in a private dining room of Dublin's Shelbourne Hotel. He jangled a fork on an empty glass, and the high-pitched sound rose with the buzz of conversations and laughter, and the clink of cutlery on china, to the white-plastered ceiling, there to mingle with a cloud of pipe, cigar, and cigarette smoke.

O'Reilly winked at Kitty, who smiled back.

God, but he loved that smile. He surveyed the other graduates from the Trinity College School of Physics, class of '36, and their spouses who had assembled for the opening cocktail party and banquet of their reunion. Sitting round linen-draped tables, most of the men wore sombre dinner suits, their satin lapels shiny, and the ladies added bright counterpoint in their evening gowns or cocktail dresses. The opposite, he thought, of dowdy ducks and flamboyant drakes like the mallard he and Kitty had seen earlier on the Grand Canal.

He looked back at Kitty. Her sleeveless empire-line dress of shot emerald green silk was punctuated by a corsage of deep pink moth orchid that his brother Lars had grown in his own greenhouse. She sported matching pink satin opera gloves, and her hair was cut in a pageboy style to frame her face. Kitty O'Reilly was, in his opinion, by far the most elegant and desirable woman here. And he wasn't the teeniest bit biased.

He grinned at the thought and tugged at the collar of his Royal Navy mess kit dress uniform jacket, with his medal ribbons on the left breast. He should have been wearing miniature medals, not just the ribbons, but for very personal reasons he hated his decorations, one in particular, but no one here would care that he was in breach of regulations, and it had been a long time since he had left the navy. He'd have been a damn sight more comfortable in tweed pants and a sports jacket, but the conventions must be observed. Kitty liked him to wear the damn monkey suit to formal occasions, and there was nothing O'Reilly would not do to please her. Two other people were similarly dressed. A fellow O'Reilly had barely known was in the full kit of an RAF squadron leader, medical. One of the women was in the dress mess kit of an officer in the Queen Alexandra's Royal Navy Nursing Service, with whose nursing sisters he had worked closely in Haslar hospital in 1940.

"Settle down, now, settle down," Cromie said, and the hum of conversation and clapping began to fade. "I know we've all got a lot of catching up to do, but first I must make a few announcements."

O'Reilly knew he should turn and start paying attention, but his gaze lingered over the little crowd. Thirty-five years ago the now middle-aged doctors had begun their medical studies as fresh-faced youths and a few lasses. As Donal Donnelly, Ballybucklebo's arch schemer and mangler of the English language, might have said today, "Back then the world had been everyone's lobster." O'Reilly shook his head. A lot had happened in those thirty-five years. He still had a full head of hair and wore his half-moon spectacles only for effect, but spectacles and thinning hair, if not bald pates, were the order of the day now. Charlie Greer, once a flaming redhead, now looked like a tonsured monk, with only a fringe of remaining hair. Used-to-be athletes had grown chubby, and he knew for a fact that he wasn't the only one wearing a cummerbund to hide the reality that the top button at his trousers' waistband was undone.

He thought about where their careers had led his classmates. Some were senior in their chosen fields here in Ireland. Others had made the pilgrimage back here from the United States or British Commonwealth countries. Fair play to them all. He hoped they were as contented as he, the principal of a general practice in the drowsy County Down village of Ballybucklebo, where season ran into season and little disturbed the harmony of life. He would be getting back to work on Monday, and as far as he knew, he'd not left anything that young Doctors Barry Laverty and Jennifer Bradley could not deal with.

He shook his head. Thirty years, the last twenty in Ballybucklebo — but his life had not been all peace and quiet since he had qualified as a doctor.

"Now wheest, the lot of you," Cromie said. "Wheest, and that includes you, Ronald Hercules Fitzpatrick."

The man in question, who, as had been his wont back in their student days, had barely uttered a peep all evening, at least managed a smile as laughter rang out. His gold-rimmed pince-nez shone and his large Adam's apple bobbed rapidly above a winged collar, one size too large, and a clip-on scarlet bow tie. His neck reminded O'Reilly of the grinning ostrich with a large lump halfway down its neck. The bird and its irate zookeeper, whose pint the animal had swallowed, glass and all, had been one of a number of classic posters advertising Guinness stout.

O'Reilly waited for the laughter to die.

Cromie said, "I hope you've all enjoyed your dinner as much as I have . . ."

O'Reilly patted his tummy. Gazpacho, sole almondine, iced champagne sorbet, beef Wellington, roast potatoes and seasonal vegetables, baked Alaska, and an assortment of cheeses and crackers had been complemented by chilled Pouilly Fumée, a Chateau Mouton Rothschild, and Taylor's port, 1941. He had declined the latter in favour of a glass of John Jameson's Irish whiskey. "Certainly was a nice snack," he whispered to Kitty, who made a mock frown and said, "Fingal, behave yourself."

". . . and so we've to thank the other members of the organising committee. Gentlemen, please rise: Charlie Greer and Fingal O'Reilly."

O'Reilly stood and smiled at his other male tablemate. Charlie, now a senior neurosurgeon at Belfast's Royal Victoria Hospital, was the man who had given O'Reilly his bent nose during a friendly boxing bout back in 1935. Together they had played rugby football for Ireland. Now Charlie had a comfortable potbelly and was an amateur, but internationally recognised, expert on the works of Mozart. His wife sat beside Cromie's. As girls, the two women had attended Cheltenham Ladies' College, a very exclusive school in England, an institution that aped the then-common boys' public schools' tradition of handing out nicknames. O'Reilly had known Mrs. Greer as "Pixie" and Mrs. Cromie as "Button" for so long he'd forgotten their real Christian names, if indeed he'd ever known them.

More cheers and a voice calling, "Looks like Tweedledum and Tweedledee to me."

O'Reilly caught a whiff of delicately scented tobacco from someone's cigar as he waited for quiet. Then he interrupted Cromie in a thick Northside Dublin accent. "Lord jasus, there's one in every crowd that wants to be the centre of attraction. If your man Edgar Redmond there was at a wake, he'd not be satisfied unless he was the feckin' corpse, would you, Edgar?"

More laughter.

O'Reilly nodded to himself. His old adage, *"Never, never let the patient get the upper hand,"* was equally applicable to heckling colleagues.

"Thank you, Fingal, for those few kind words," Cromie said, "and to quote Michael Collins, who, upon returning to the same hustings whence he'd been arrested while making a political speech and subsequently jailed, remarked, 'As I was saying when I was so rudely interrupted . . .' "

More laughter, and a voice saying, "Nice one, Sir Donald."

Cromie made a small bow. "Thank you, Sid. Now we of the self-appointed organising committee hope you enjoyed your meal. We are delighted that so many could attend. We'd particularly like to acknowledge Hilda Bronson, whom most of you will remember as Hilda Manwell. Now please hold your applause or we'll be here all night. Please stand, Hilda."

A petite, middle-aged woman, completely grey-haired, but still as trim-figured as ever, wearing a short, floral-patterned, satin evening frock with a flared skirt, rose and smiled all round the room.

"Hilda and her husband have come all the way from Sydney, Australia, to be here, and it was a letter from her last year to Charlie Greer that got the ball rolling for this get-together. Thank you, Hilda, on both counts." Cromie, ignoring his own instructions about applause, began to clap, and everyone joined

30

in as she, O'Reilly, and Charlie regained their seats.

"Now," Cromie said, "tonight is not the time for speechifying, but there are a few housekeeping chores I must attend to. I'll keep it short. The bar here will remain open until eleven tonight. Breakfast is informal tomorrow so take your pick of the dining rooms in the hotel, but we must convene in the lobby by nine thirty. It's no distance to the college where it all began thirty years ago. We will walk there and have a series of lectures."

Fingal did not need to pay attention. Hadn't he helped the lads plan the whole weekend of reception and a dinner tonight, talks tomorrow morning, so expenses could be defrayed against taxes, luncheon with your friends to be arranged individually, a free afternoon, a formal dinner tomorrow evening in the college, and a farewell breakfast in a private room in Bewley's on Grafton Street on Sunday morning?

He closed his eyes and in an instant could see himself all those years ago, sitting through dull, dry, droning dissertations on anatomy and physiology, hours spent in the formalin-reeking dissecting room, histology laboratories, the drudgery of the preclinical years. The excitement of walking the wards, seeing and treating patients, knowing at last that he'd been right, that medicine had always been his destiny. Years lightened by fun in pubs — Davy Byrnes or the Bailey, both on Duke Street; the Stag's Head; Neary's on Chatham Street — rugby matches, boxing, dances in a floating ballroom; movies like *The Thin Man* with William Powell and Myrna Loy, *Captain Blood, Top Hat;* meeting a grey-eyed student nurse — he smiled at Kitty — and losing her because of his own stupidity.

O'Reilly heard Cromie say, "And our guest faculty member at the dinner tomorrow will be the surgeon Mister Nigel Kinnear, who taught us, saw distinguished war service before returning to teaching, and who next year will be installed as Regius Professor of Surgery."

Prolonged applause.

Nigel Kinnear had supervised O'Reilly's trembling hands as he performed his first appendicectomy back then. And in those five years he'd laid the foundations to learning his trade and seen the growth of a lifelong friendship with Cromie and Charlie and —

"Mister Kinnear will give the first Bob Beresford Memorial Oration. Bob made the supreme sacrifice in 1943."

Bob Beresford, gentle gentleman, O'Reilly thought, and bowed his head.

What little subdued conversation there had been, died.

"I'd like us to rise and be silent for a minute in remembrance of Bob, Jean Winston, Archie

O'Hare, and Phillip McNab, who sadly are no longer with us."

There was a scraping of chairs on the hardwood floor as everyone rose.

O'Reilly bowed his head. He'd known the other three, but Bob Beresford had been the fourth of the Four Musketeers. Dear Bob, probably the best friend Fingal had made in his life. He glanced at Kitty and saw how she was staring at him, concern in those grey-flecked-with-amber eyes. She'd known Bob, known him well, before the war, but it hadn't been until much later that both she and Fingal had learned of his death at the hands of the Japanese a year after the fall of Singapore where he had been serving in the Medical Corps in 1942. Bob had died looking after the sick and dying though mortally ill himself. "Greater love hath no man than this, that a man lay down his life for his friends." John 15:13. I miss you yet, Bob, O'Reilly thought, and felt a lump in his throat. He was grateful for Kitty's reassuring squeeze of his hand.

"Thank you," Cromie said, "and before you take your seats may I simply remark that I've finished the chores. I'd suggest that now the formal part of the evening is over, you all circulate and renew old acquaintances, but before that I'd like you all to raise your glasses and drink with me, 'To absent friends.' "

"Absent friends," came from the crowd as

from one voice, none more heartfelt than Fingal Flahertie O'Reilly's.

Conversation and laughter began again slowly and then grew in volume. "I'll be damned. Sticky actually passed his speciality examinations?" he overheard someone say. "I don't believe you. Sticky . . . ?"

It was a nickname O'Reilly knew was often given to Maguires in Ireland, just as Murphys were always called Spud.

"He was so dense we didn't think he could pass wind when we were students. He just managed to struggle through medical school."

O'Reilly chuckled, as did the storyteller's audience.

"He didn't just pass. He took a gold medal, was having a stellar career when the poor divil had a stroke. He survived but . . ."

"Aaah, that's sad," a woman's voice said.

Indeed it was, O'Reilly thought. Sticky had always been a great class jester, a kind man. Fate could be very unkind. He was aware of someone at his shoulder and found himself towering over Hilda Bronson. "Hilda. Lovely to see you. Hilda Bronson, meet Mrs. Kitty O'Reilly."

"It's plain Kitty," Kitty said.

Hilda grinned. "We met at the graduation dance all those years ago," she said. "I thought then you seemed much too good for a great lummox like Fingal O'Reilly."

O'Reilly chuckled. "You always did call a

spade a bloody shovel, Hilda."

"Us few women had to among all you men," she said. "Now meet my other half, Peter Bronson."

O'Reilly was offered a paw as big as his own, and damn nearly as powerful, by a tanned man who said, "G'dye, mate," in an Ocker Aussie accent as thick as Kinky's champ.

"Bonzer meeting you. Hilda says you played a bit of rugger."

"Don't let those two get started, Kitty," Hilda said. "When he's not running a law practice, my Pete eats and breathes rugby football. Now the Greers and Cromies have moved on, why don't we sit with you two for a minute? My feet are killing me in these damned stilettoes."

The gentlemen held the chairs for the ladies, then joined them.

"If memory serves, you were to play for the Wallabies on their '39 tour of the UK and Ireland, but the bloody war got in the way," O'Reilly said.

"Huh," said Peter Bronson. "I joined the Royal Australian Air Force, flew Beaufighters, even though my new wife," he smiled at Hilda, "wasn't too pleased."

"I'm sure Kitty wasn't either about you in the navy, Fingal," Hilda said, nodding at O'Reilly's uniform.

O'Reilly waited.

Kitty, always the soul of tact, said, her voice quite level, "I'm afraid I'd gone off to nurse orphans in Tenerife during the Spanish Civil War when Fingal was called up . . ."

He knew there had been more to it than just nursing. Tenerife had left Kitty with a ghost, and one that must soon be confronted. O'Reilly tried to make light of it. "Careless of me letting her go, I know."

"Fingal and I didn't get married until last year." Kitty smiled at him. "He's a slow learner."

"But slow and steady wins the race," O'Reilly said. "I'm a very lucky man." And to hell with convention, he bent and kissed Kitty while in his heart he knew his first wife, Deirdre, looked on, smiling.

"Good for you, O'Reilly," Hilda said, then her voice softened, became wistful. "Pete never talks about the war."

"Neither does Fingal," Kitty said.

"But I reckon you had an exciting one, cobber," Pete said. His voice was level.

O'Reilly frowned. "Oh?"

Peter pointed to a blue, white, and blue medal ribbon on O'Reilly's jacket to the extreme right of the ones for the Africa Star, the Atlantic Star, the 1939–45 Star, and the War Medal. "No need to talk about it, but the Pommies didn't hand out Distinguished Service Crosses for collecting cigarette cards or winning the egg-and-spoon races." His glance fell on O'Reilly's rank insignia, then Peter held out his big hand, which O'Reilly took. "I'm proud to meet you, Commander O'Reilly. Very proud."

O'Reilly lowered his head, and while he should have been flattered, he could only nod while in his mind whirled pictures of those still-vivid war years, some memories faded to pallid shadows, others indelible, his for life.

And for all of them he had this old uniform with its little pieces of coloured ribbon to indicate where his bronze stars and a silver cross should hang. And, when he let them surface, memories, a host of memories, memories of a journey that had begun on a British battleship in Alexandria Harbour in late 1940. But those were not for tonight. Tonight was for fun, but — O'Reilly took a deep breath — Kitty wasn't alone in having a ghost from those years. His, like hers, would always be there.

2
MIGHTY THINGS FROM SMALL BEGINNINGS GROW

There were naval uniforms everywhere when Fingal opened the door of the second-class compartment and climbed down from the Southern Railways train in Portsmouth Harbour Station. He felt weary, travel-stained, and pale-faced — his Mediterranean tan long faded on the more than two months it had taken his troopship to reach Liverpool from Egypt by way of the Cape of Good Hope.

Apart from three U-boat scares, the voyage had been uneventful until the crossing of the Bay of Biscay in the midst of an equinoctial gale. The ship had pitched and rolled for days and he had yet to regain his land legs.

He adjusted the sling of his gas mask holder and lugged his suitcase along the platform. It was crowded with cap-wearing petty officers and naval ratings, their circular hat ribbons bearing the motto HMS but not the names of their ships. They were heading for the vast Portsmouth naval base. Fingal was on his way to the Royal Naval Hospital Haslar in Gosport across the narrow strip of water to the west that connected Fareham Lake with the Solent.

Hardly anyone in the station was in civvies. Wartime travel, he knew, was discouraged. The platforms had been dotted with "Is Your Journey Really Necessary?" posters. Despite his tiredness, he smiled. There was one trip he hoped would be necessary. No. Bloody well vital. If he could arrange it, and she was willing, his fiancée, Deirdre Mawhinney, was going to be facing the rigours of getting from Belfast to Gosport. Because while Fingal might be going to study anaesthesia at Haslar hospital, he had another important reason for being here. Marriage to the most wonderful girl in the world. For that opportunity he'd have crossed Biscay in a canoe — without a life jacket.

He passed the locomotive, still leaking steam from its pistons, the coal smoke from its funnel stinking the crisp late-September air. According to a *Daily Mail* he'd picked up en route, today was Thursday, the 26th.

His railway journey of nearly three hundred miles had been interminable. He'd changed trains twice, once in London's Waterloo Station and then at Woking, and waited none too patiently as his train was rerouted around bombed tracks. He'd found the blackout unnerving too, after the bright lights of Alex-

39

andria. What Winston Churchill was calling "The Battle of Britain" for control of the air over southern England was in full swing in the autumn of 1940. As the train approached London, Fingal had seen some of the devastation.

Fleeting images of a bedroom with neat floral wallpaper, fully furnished and not a piece out of place — but with the front wall missing. Whole streets of terrace houses flattened and charred with some gables left standing like carious teeth jutting from infected gums. A lonely spire — all that was left of a church — pointing an accusing finger at the uncaring sky from whence the destruction had come. A double-decker bus upended with its rear wheels leaning on an upstairs windowsill. A geyser erupting from a shattered water main and a tattered teddy bear floating along a gutter.

Everyone was in this war now, not just the troops. And it was getting worse. Already he had read the slogan "London can take it," and been proud of the British. And it wasn't all a one-way street. On the nights of September 21 and 22 the RAF had bombed Berlin and on the 24th and 25th Berlin and Hamburg. He knew the news had cheered the civilians, but he could not bring himself to feel that it "served the bastards right"; he only felt pity for the innocents on both sides.

Judging by a pall of smoke over Portsmouth, the city and its massive naval dock-yards had not escaped unscathed. Under a lowering sky, a northeasterly wind carried a stink of burning very like the one he'd smelled after the second battle of Narvik, back in April. A worry he'd had since the fall of France in June resurfaced. Would it be right asking Deirdre to come to this place?

"Give you a hand with that, sir?" A uniformed porter touched the peak of his cap. The man looked about sixty-five, but then all the young men would have been either called up or working in industries vital to the war effort, like coal mining and steelmaking. Even now, unmarried women were being encouraged to work at what had been traditionally men's jobs, in shipyards, on the land, in munitions factories.

Fingal stopped and set his case down. "I'm going to Haslar hospital," he said. "Can you direct me?"

"I certainly can, sir, but let me take your case and get you through the ticket barrier and down to the pontoon for the ferry. I'll give you directions for when you get to the other side."

"Carry on," Fingal said, happy to be relieved of the weight, but feeling guilty that an old man should be burdened.

Once on the quay, the porter said, "Right, sir. The boat won't be long. It's a steam chain ferry and takes about fifteen minutes to get across. When you get to the other side you'll get off on High Street. You can get a taxi, 'cos the bus takes forever, but you'll have to go all the way round Haslar Creek through Alverstoke and back along the creek. It used to be a short walk across the bridge, but the navy took the middle section out so motor torpedo boats could go further up the creek to the repair facilities."

"Thank you." He slipped the man half a crown, far too much, and settled down to wait.

The ferry had deposited Fingal, a few civilians, and a couple of sailors on the Gosport pontoon. He yawned and his stomach gurgled. The last thing he'd had to eat had been a stale cheese sandwich in Woking station, washed down by something masquerading as tea.

On the short ferry ride he'd seen a number of submarines moored at their base at HMS *Dolphin* and more of the bomb damage to the dockyards and the city of Portsmouth. Barrage balloons hovered over the dockyards like a school of dead fish with distended swim bladders. And once again he'd wondered. Was it wise to bring Deirdre here? Would it be less selfish to ask her to stay in Ireland, try to get leave, tie the knot there, and be satisfied with a short honeymoon before going back to this bloody war?

The wind bowled dry brown leaves along the gutters. A grey destroyer butted through the Solent, heading for Portsmouth. Gulls screeched above and the smell of the sea that had been a constant in his nostrils for months was no less strong back on the shores of home waters. At least there was no trace of the all-pervasive stink of fuel oil that had been one of the hallmarks of the battleship HMS *Warspite,* his last ship.

A vehicle came around a corner and Fingal wondered if it was a taxi. He'd never seen anything like it. The chassis and body were those of an ordinary motorcar, but on top a deep, open, rectangular box projected a foot from the edge of the roof in every direction and was filled with an enormous inflated balloon held down by a network of ropes. He stepped into the road and held up a hand.

The thing pulled up and its driver dismounted. He was an older man with a massive Old Bill moustache — probably, Fingal thought, a survivor of the trenches of the First World War.

"Need a cab, guv?"

"I do, but what in the name of the wee man is that yoke?"

The driver laughed. "Petrol's rationed, sir. Very hard to come by."

And Fingal knew why. He'd seen tankers torpedoed in the mid-Atlantic, knew the cost in the lives of merchant seamen of getting fuel to England.

"But you can run motorcars on coal gas." He sniffed. "You can get a niff of it now."

Fingal inhaled. The smell took him back three years to the Aungier Place Dispensary and the tenements of Dublin, where much cooking had been done on coal gas ranges. "Ingenious. But does it work?" he said.

"Like a charm," he said. "Just don't be lighting no cigarettes. Gas can go 'Whooom.' Not nice."

Fingal chuckled. "Fair enough. Royal Naval Hospital Haslar, please."

"Right, guv."

Fingal subsided into the backseat, too bloody tired to care about the smell of gas, the stubble on his chin, his travel-stained uniform. "Cabby?"

"Yes, guv?"

"What's the Blitz been like here?"

"Well, sir, early on in August, the Jerries hit the Portsmouth dockyards and knocked out the Chain Home station in Ventnor on the Isle of Wight in one big raid."

"Chain Home?"

The driver held his index finger along the side of his nose. "Very hush-hush. Part of an early warning system that lets us send up our fighters before the Jerries get here, and our fighter boys've been kicking the living day-lights out of the Hun. Our lot got Ventnor fixed in no time, too.

44

"The poor sods in the naval base and Portsmouth have been hit hard. But so have civilians. On the twenty-fourth of August, Princess Lake Road Cinema in Portsmouth was hit during a matinée. Eight kiddies were killed. Poor little blighters."

Fingal gritted his teeth. Deirdre here? He blew out his breath.

"Ain't been so bad on the Gosport side, though," the driver said. "We're going through Alverstoke now."

Fingal watched as the cab drove along a street where one side was a long curved row of white terrace houses.

"That's the Crescent, sir. Officers from Haslar have quarters and married quarters there."

Do they, by God? Fingal thought, and the driver had said Gosport hadn't been too badly bombed. He must find out more. "What about the bombing here in Gosport since August?"

"Sirens go off now and then, but it's usually another raid heading inland or for Portsmouth proper. Sometimes a bomb or two falls on Gosport, but compared to places like London or Liverpool we get off pretty lightly." He chuckled. "I don't often admit to any good feeling about the Jerries, but I will say this. Three days after the Luftwaffe lost a hundred and eighty-two planes at the hands of our RAF, they sent a bunch of Stukas to

45

attack HMS *Siskin,* the naval air station here in Gosport. Took guts, but it was bloody silly. The RAF have a fighter station at Tangmere about twenty-five miles away. Not all the Stukas went home, believe me, sir, and they didn't do much hurt on the ground. I reckon the worst is over. The Luftwaffe haven't seemed so keen to come our way since then. And anyway, guv, if His Majesty and the queen and the two princesses are refusing to leave Buckingham Palace even though the bloody Boche bombed it when the royal family was at home, I reckon we can stick it out too."

Fingal nodded. It did sound as if Gosport was relatively safe and that the worst of the bombing was over.

If Deirdre was willing to risk it, he would send for her. She could be here in a few days. Damn the Germans. That "London can take it" attitude resonated. Why should he and Deirdre, why should anyone, surrender to any man or any nation? He'd just have to find somewhere in the country for her to live, or maybe in quarters in Alverstoke. And in not many weeks she'd be Mrs. Fingal O'Reilly. He relaxed now the decision was taken.

"This bit's called Dead Man's Mile," the driver said as the cab passed a high redbrick wall, " 'cos the funeral processions used to go along here from the hospital to the cemetery."

That's a cheerful idea, Fingal thought.

"We're here, guv." The taxi stopped outside a gateway in a high iron railing, the impressive redbrick gateposts covered in a creeper.

Fingal peered ahead. Through the gateway he could see the front of a massive redbrick building which faced Haslar Creek behind him. He dismounted and walked to the back of the cab where the cabby was unloading Fingal's suitcase.

The man pointed to a pair of iron tramway tracks leading from a jetty, through the gateway, and under an arch in the main building. "Used to land patients from Portsmouth at the Haslar Jetty and trundle them in wheeled carts along those lines, all the way to the hospital. Back in the 1850s a bunch of sailors from a Turkish ship in harbour were treated for cholera in Haslar. That's why folks from Gosport are called 'Turkers' and the town 'Turktown.' "

"Really? Thanks. I'll remember that."

"Lots of history here, sir. That'll be one and six."

Fingal gave the man a florin.

The taxi spluttered off, leaving behind a cloud of noisome fumes, and Fingal stared at the immensity of the three-storey wings stretching away from either side of the central four-storey block.

What the hell did the future hold once he'd passed through that gateway and into Royal

Naval Hospital Haslar? He shrugged and picked up his suitcase.

He knew he didn't look much like, to use a term belovèd by the navy, an "efficient" naval officer. In fact, the dim mirror in the train's lavatory had confirmed that he was a mess, or as they'd say back home, like something the cat dragged in. He'd done his best to shake as many creases out of his uniform as possible, dabbed the stains from his tie, and set his cap on straight, but his shoes needed polishing and his chin felt like a stubble field.

Now that he was finally here, Fingal knew he must make a good first impression when he reported for his new posting. It might be quite a while before a humble lieutenant got another chance to speak with the commanding admiral, and Fingal wanted to ask what he'd have to do, if anything, to get the navy's permission to marry.

He was stopped by a Metropolitan policeman who'd said, "Identification, if you please, sir."

Once the officer was satisfied, Fingal had followed the tramlines running from the front gate between two rows of deciduous trees, their leaves turning to autumnal brown. He now paused before an archway that pierced the central building, a four-storey affair with three oversized windows spanning the middle two floors. A further set of three small windows were crowned by a massive, triangular pediment of pale stone bearing a coat of arms and ornately carved heraldic figures.

A five-foot wall of sandbags surrounded the entire structure, presumably so that if caught in the open during an air raid, staff could at least try to shelter from splinters and blast.

He set his suitcase down and fumbled in his inside pocket, withdrew an envelope containing his orders and a sealed confidential report. He reread his orders instructing him to report to the Surgeon Rear Admiral T. Creaser, M.D., KHP (Honorary Physician to the King), RN.

Fingal hefted his case in his left hand, clutched his orders and report in his right, and strode under the arch and into the tunnel. A uniformed sick berth attendant coming the other way came to attention and saluted. Damnation. The compliment must be returned. Fingal stopped, set his case down, and did so.

"Can I help you, sir?"

"Please. I'm looking for the office of the medical officer in charge."

"Come with me, sir." The man picked up Fingal's case and marched along the tunnel, through a doorway on the left, along a short corridor, and halted in front of a closed door. "In there, sir, and the admiral is in." He returned Fingal's case.

"Thank you," he said. "Carry on." And as the man saluted and left, Fingal knocked on the door.

A voice from inside said, "Come in."

Encumbered by his case and the orders, Fingal managed, at the expense of crumpling the envelope and papers inside, to open the door. He stepped over the threshold into a small, simple room. The floor was of polished wooden planks, the walls painted white. A central fireplace was surmounted by a massive coat of arms flanked by wooden plaques embellished with rows of names in gold lettering. He guessed they were the previous commanding officers.

A middle-aged man, on his cuffs a broad gold stripe surmounted by a narrow one with a curl, sat behind a kneehole desk positioned sideways to a window. He frowned as he scrutinised Fingal, then shook his head. The expression on the man's face was one of sadness, resignation.

Fingal could practically hear the admiral thinking to himself, Oh well, there is a war on, and whoever this is he's Royal Navy Reserve, not regular navy. We must make allowances.

Fingal came to attention — the navy does not salute indoors — and leant forward to proffer his orders. "Surgeon Lieutenant O'Reilly reporting for —" He got no further. A small rug under his feet slid on the polished wooden floor and Fingal pitched forward, ramming the envelope at the admiral as a fencer might deliver a lethal epée thrust to the heart.

Admiral Creaser rapidly moved his head and upper body to one side to avoid the blow.

By the time Fingal had grabbed the desk, arrested his forward movement, and managed to be standing at some semblance of attention, the admiral was once more sitting upright, not a hair out of place. "Now, Lieutenant O'Reilly," he said, holding out his right hand, "shall we try this again?" Not the faintest of smiles played on his lips, and his voice was stern.

Fingal handed over the envelope and orders.

"Hmm," said the admiral after he'd read both the sealed and the unsealed documents. "Hmm. Interesting." The senior man looked up. "Stand at ease."

Fingal did.

"There's a chair. Be seated and take off your cap. You should have before you came in."

"Thank you, sir." Fingal sat and took off his cap, well aware that he needed a haircut.

The admiral glanced up and, by the look on his face, seemed to be registering the same thought. "I see you are being sent here to learn anaesthesia and trauma surgery. We had a signal about you so we've been expecting you," said the senior medical officer. "Our next course will start on Monday, September

51

the thirtieth, so you're a couple of days early. That's good. We appreciate punctuality here."

Fingal said nothing.

"I've read your confidential report from Richard Wilcoxson. He's a very good man. Fine judge of character." The admiral cocked his head sideways and pursed his lips. "Richard says you are a first-class physician. Perhaps you get a bit too involved with your patients — but you are young yet —"

"I'm almost thirty-two, sir."

"If I want information, O'Reilly, I'll ask for it."

"Yes, sir." I hope I'll never get old, Fingal thought, if it means not treating patients like human beings.

"Richard also says that you are more interested in your trade than naval customs and dress, not shy about questioning a senior's decisions if you think it's in the patient's best interests?"

Fingal said nothing, even though the last sentence had been posed as a question. I'd question His Majesty himself were he a doctor and not giving his patients his best, he thought.

The admiral coughed. "I don't think Richard means that as a criticism, although perhaps he should have. I know that he does not run what we'd call a taut ship. I think he's suggesting to me that I should warn you that here we run this place along strict naval lines, and I can see what he means. You look a disgrace to the uniform."

"Sorry, sir."

"We'd appreciate it if in future you try to pay a great deal more attention to those matters."

Fingal was tempted to snap out a sarcastic salty, "Aye aye, sir," but simply nodded.

"Good. And he says I've to remind you to visit his wife at Fareham."

"Yes, sir." Fingal suddenly had an overwhelming need to escape this small, stuffy room. He started to rise, then realized he hadn't been dismissed. "W-will that be all, sir?"

"No, it will *not* be all," said the admiral. "And you have not been dismissed. Now we've dealt with the formalities, let me welcome you to Haslar. All newcomers get the lecture."

"Thank you, sir." This admiral was a bad-tempered bear, Fingal decided. One to be avoided as much as possible during Fingal's stay here. Maybe he could get the information he needed from a friendly surgeon captain and not bother this man.

The admiral rose, but said, "Don't get up," and walked to a picture hanging on a wall beside the window. "These are Haslar's first architectural plans. They were published in *The Gentleman's Magazine.* It's a venerable old building, you know. The foundations were laid in 1746 and the first patients admitted in 1753."

"I'm impressed, sir," Fingal said, and he was. He was fascinated by history.

"And the place has some pretty famous alumni. James Lind, who discovered that lime juice prevents scurvy; Sir John Richardson, who had been to the Arctic with Franklin looking for the northwest passage. T. H. Huxley was an assistant surgeon here. Do you know what they called him in his later years?"

"Yes, sir. 'Darwin's Bulldog,' because he defended Darwin's theory of natural selection."

"Well done."

Fingal lowered his head, but was warmed by the praise. Perhaps he was making some reparation for getting off on the wrong foot.

"Now, would you know who Edward Atkinson might be? He was once the vaccinator in the pathology department here."

Fingal debated. He did know the answer exactly, but didn't want to seem cocky. "I think, sir," he said, "Atkinson might have been on Scott of the Antarctic's last expedition?"

"Well done again." The admiral hitched his backside onto a corner of the desk, crossed his arms across his chest, leant back, and regarded Fingal before saying, "Good man. I've always thought us doctors tend to be too

specialised. You strike me as well rounded
—"

"Thank you, sir." Fingal instantly regretted
his interruption.

"— if a trifle impertinent to your seniors,
and remarkably scruffy. All right. Enough history. We have accommodation arranged for
you at the hospital in the medical officers'
mess. I would suggest you go there and get
yourself looking like an efficient naval officer."

"Sir."

"You might want to get a bit of rest too. It's
a bloody awful train journey from Liverpool
to here. I do know, and I go first class."

The words were spoken as a kindly uncle
might address a favourite nephew. Was the
admiral intimating that he understood why
Fingal looked like something pulled through
a hedge backward and wasn't quite as angry
as he had originally seemed?

"I imagine you might be a bit peckish, too.
The officers' mess steward will find you
something. By the way, we do dress for dinner. Just because there's a war on is no need
to let standards slip."

"My mess kit is being sent on, sir."

"Very well. We'll make allowances. The
working rig here is the same for everybody.
It's called 'Tiffies' rig. The officers, petty officers, and warrant officers have gold buttons,
and please understand we are a shore estab-

lishment, but run as a ship. Right is starboard, left port, and the lavatories are the heads. When we leave the premises we 'go ashore.' "

"I'll tr—" Fingal cut himself off from saying "try to" sarcastically and simply said, "I'll remember, sir."

"Good. Now, your course won't start until Monday, so I suggest you familiarise yourself with the setup here. The leader of your course is Surgeon Captain Angus Mahaddie. He's a highland Scot and eats Sassenachs for breakfast, but he might warm to a fellow Celt."

"I'll try to keep on his good side, sir."

"See that you do. And use your free days to attend to your non-naval duties. Letters home are a good idea. And each officer is permitted three phone calls through the switchboard during the week of their arrival."

Deirdre and Ma and Mrs. Marjorie Wilcoxson. The calls he'd promised on his last day on *Warspite* — to Tom Laverty's wife Carol to congratulate her on the birth of a son, Barry, and to Wilson Wallace's parents in Portstewart — would have to wait. Once "ashore" he'd find a pay phone and fulfil his obligations.

"Getting about in Portsmouth and Gosport can be a chore, so most young officers own a small motorcar, or at least buy shares in one. You can get a used one for about ten or fifteen pounds. Petrol is rationed, but a gallon of the lowest grade only costs ten pence."

"Thank you, sir. That's good to know."

"And don't forget, boy, you've to visit Mrs. Wilcoxson. Fareham's not that far. There's a train."

"Yes, sir." Another bloody train.

"And that's it, unless you have something to ask?"

Fingal blurted, "I want to get married, sir."

"Do you indeed? Do you have someone in mind, or is this just a sudden fancy since arriving in England?"

"Yes, sir. I mean, no, sir. I do have someone in mind. Very much, sir. We got engaged last July and would have been wed by now, but . . ."

"For the war. I understand." The admiral stroked his chin with the web of his hand. He muttered, "Uh-huh," nodded his head, glanced at his watch, picked up the phone, dialled, and said, "Leading Sick Berth Attendant Willis, come to my office, please," and replaced the receiver.

What the hell had that to do with Fingal's request? He fidgeted in his chair and waited.

"You're young to be thinking of marriage. It can inhibit a junior officer's prospects."

Fingal took a deep breath. He'd have to risk his superior's good opinion further. "With all due respect, sir, I'll be thirty-two in a few weeks, and although I am RNR, the navy's not my career. There's got to be some —" He almost stamped his foot.

"Young man." The admiral slipped off the desk and stood looking down on the seated Fingal. "Do not presume to tell the navy that there has 'got to be' anything."

Fingal clenched his teeth, tried to calm himself. This wasn't a boxing match to be won by battering his opponent into submission. Admirals did not submit to mere lieutenants. Ever. Diplomacy was required. "I'm sorry, sir. With your permission, may I rephrase that?"

The colour that had flushed the senior officer's cheeks seemed to be subsiding. "Very well, you may try."

There was knocking on the door.

"Wait outside, Willis."

A faint, "Aye aye, sir."

"I know the navy does nothing without a good reason, and I'm sure that for career officers, suggesting that they delay marriage until they reach a certain rank is probably wise."

"It is."

"But this is wartime and I'm not a career officer. Is there not some way round it?" Fingal held his breath and crossed his fingers.

"What was your rank when you were called up?"

"It had been sub-lieutenant when I did my year on HMS *Tiger* back in 1930, but in view of my time since qualification as a doctor, the Admiralty gave me a lieutenancy — with four years' seniority, sir."

"Did they? Interesting." The admiral raised his voice. "Come in, Willis."

The door opened and a man entered. "Willis, take Lieutenant O'Reilly's case and show him to the officers' mess."

Rank titles would be used in front of other ranks here. Nothing as informal as *Warspite*'s medical branch, Fingal thought.

"Aye aye, sir." The man moved to obey.

Fingal rose. "But sir —"

"You are dismissed, Lieutenant O'Reilly," the admiral said, "and I'm late for a meeting."

Fingal's shoulders sagged. He took a deep breath and began to follow the SBA when a voice from behind him, the same avuncular voice of moments ago, said, "I make no promises, Lieutenant O'Reilly, but I'll see what I can do. The navy has a drill for everything — and that includes promotion."

3
GENTLEMEN OF JAPAN

"Not far to the boozer now," said O'Reilly to Charlie, and lengthened his stride, forcing his friend to keep up as they left the Trinity College grounds and walked through the throng along Nassau Street. The two men had attended the Saturday morning lectures while Kitty and Pixie, Charlie's wife, enjoyed an exhibition organised by the Royal Hibernian Academy in the premises of the National College of Art on Thomas Street. The women were to meet their husbands in the pub.

Overhead, starlings whirled against the patches of blue that could be seen between the roofs of the eighteenth-century buildings. Pigeons strutted along the gutters. The stink of vehicle exhaust fumes filled O'Reilly's nose and, just as in the old days, the westerly wind bore the faint smell of roasting grain from the Guinness Brewery at Saint James's Gate.

"Shall we walk to the light and cross there?" Charlie said, eyeing the busy road.

"Och, come on, Charlie. We're not so old

that we can't get across Nassau Street without a light. I'll race you." O'Reilly led off, dodging between the bikes and motorcars. On the other side he said, "Just as busy as when we were students, and just as many bikes."

"Aye," said Charlie, puffing, "but I've only seen a couple of horse-drawn drays since we've been down here for the hooley. Guinness still use a few."

"Aye," said O'Reilly, wondering what might have happened to one of his old patients, Lorcan O'Lunney, who had made his living pulling a handcart. "And not a tugger in sight."

"Never mind tuggers, or the rag-and-bone men like Harry Sime they worked for in the Liberties and on the Northside. There's hardly a tenement left standing since our days, Fingal," Charlie said as they turned right into Duke Street. "The Dublin City Council have done quite a job of slum clearance."

"It was a great interest of my ma's, God bless her. She knew they were terrible sources of disease — TB, cholera, scabies, fleas," said O'Reilly, having to stop himself from reflexively scratching in memory of the times he'd picked up some of the little devils. "But I heard it broke the hearts of a lot of tenement dwellers when the old neighbourhoods were scattered to the new housing. People, friends for years, and even families lost touch." O'Reilly smiled. "I did enjoy working there, you know, way back when." And, he thought, they were good people, folks like one-armed Sergeant Paddy Keogh; John-Joe Finnegan, a cooper with a Pott's fracture; and a little boy with an infected foot, Dermot Finucane. He could picture each one, and wondered what had happened to them. Where were they today?

"Change does happen," Charlie said, holding open the door on the right side of the narrow front of Davy Byrnes Pub, "but this place? None of your 'All changed, changed utterly . . .' "

"Yeats," O'Reilly said, " 'Easter 1916.' "

Charlie guffawed. "Same old Fingal. Walking bloody encyclopaedia, but what I'm trying to say —" They went into the pub. "— nothing ever seems to be any different in here. I like that."

"Me too," said O'Reilly, taking in the atmosphere.

It was still the same long, narrow room of their student days, with tables to one side, mostly occupied. He could see Kitty at one near the back of the room, waving at him. He waved back. He and Charlie were approaching a marble-topped bar with a brass rail beneath, running the length of the dimly lit room with its familiar smell of beer and tobacco smoke. The muted hum of conversation filled the air. O'Reilly noticed that no longer were there any brass spittoons. Shortly after the war, all over Britain and Ireland, a massive public health campaign had helped control the spread of tuberculosis by, among other things, stopping people spitting in public. That had been a change for the better.

A middle-aged, rotund, double-chinned man in an apron was standing behind the bar. He stopped drying a straight glass as his eyes widened, and he said in a loud voice, a grin splitting his open face, "Holy Mary Mother of God and all the saints, stop the lights. Stop the feckin' lights and stall the ball there. Look what the cat's dragged in. Charlie Greer and Fingal Flahertie O'-feckin'-Reilly."

As the barman lifted the horizontal flap and came round the bar, hand outstretched, O'Reilly saw heads turning in their direction, sensed the unspoken questions.

"Jasus, lads, Jasus Murphy, lads, me oul' segotias, it's feckin' lovely to see youse both. Absolutely gameball."

"Terrific to see you too, Diarmud." O'Reilly shook the proffered hand and said, "It's been a while. How the hell are you?"

"I'm grand . . ." He shook Charlie's hand. "Grand altogether and all the better for seeing you two oul' bowsies."

A voice from behind O'Reilly said, "Can your estate sue if you die of thirst in a pub?"

"Arra be wheest, Kevin Haughey, you bollix. Isn't your pint on the pour behind the

63

bar? Christ, you've been coming in here for ten years. Do you not t'ink I know your feckin' habits by now?"

"Sorry, Diarmud." The voice sounded contrite.

Diarmud, who, as O'Reilly well remembered, was another member of the *always keep the upper hand* school, went on, "And aren't these two men that used to be students here t'irty odd years ago, now great learnèd medical men up in the Wee North, and haven't I not seen them since they were down here in '64 to see Ireland play Scotland at the rugby . . ."

"We lost six to three, remember?" O'Reilly said sotto voce to Charlie, who nodded.

"And haven't I the feckin' right to greet my old friends?"

"You have, Diarmud," Charlie said. "It's been a while and it's very good to see you. What have you been up to?"

"For starters, as you can see, I'm still on this side of the feckin' grass and I'm still bar manager here. Have been for the last ten years. Seems like a donkey's age since I started workin' here as a bar porter in 1930. I always remember because it was the year the R-101 airship crashed in France."

O'Reilly shook his head. It was as if he and Charlie had come in for a jar straight from Sir Patrick Dun's Hospital in 1936. There was a great feeling of coming home. The place, the cadence and expressions of the Dublin man's speech, and the familiarity of Diarmud, who had grown up with them. And O'Reilly liked it. He liked it very much.

"But if you'll excuse me, gentlemen, that Kevin Haughey's as thick as pig shite and he has a great lip for the stout," Diarmud said, not bothering to lower his voice.

"I heard that, Diarmud. I'm not feckin' deaf, you know."

"Nah, you're only a buck eejit, Kevin." The barman grinned like an impish child, and O'Reilly had heard the affection hidden in the apparent insult. "I'd better get him his pint. I'll maybe get a chance for a bit of *craic* with youse later, Docs."

"Away you go," said O'Reilly, "and when you've a minute . . ."

"Two pints," Diarmud said. "Kevin's not the only customer that I know what they drink . . . and the first two'll be on me. I'll bring menus when I bring your pints and —" Diarmud stopped. "Kitty O'Hallorhan. That's who it is sitting with that other nice lady at the back. I knew she looked familiar. I reckon Kitty's wit' you, Fingal? Just like she was the night you all came in here after you'd passed your final exams. And I tell you, she was a fine bit of stuff back then — and she hasn't changed a bit. Not one bit." And with that he winked and left.

"Regular rock of ages, our Diarmud,"

O'Reilly said. "You could never be offended by that man. He's got a heart of corn." He looked down the room and said, "Come on, let's join the girls."

As O'Reilly parked himself between Kitty and Pixie Greer, he said, "Afternoon, ladies. I see you have drinks."

"We're both having a nice white Bordeaux," Kitty said.

Charlie sat at the opposite side of the table and simply grinned.

"We've had a lovely time," Kitty said, "haven't we, Pixie?"

"We have indeed," said Pixie, a slight, fair-haired woman of medium height whose sharp retroussé nose and laughing green eyes had probably been the source of her nickname. "Kitty knows a great deal about painting and she was able to tell me all kinds of things. You really brought the exhibition alive."

Kitty smiled and lowered her head. "I'd glad you enjoyed it."

"The exhibition was to mark the fiftieth anniversary of the Easter Rising," Pixie said. "There were two paintings that I really liked, *Kilmainham Jail* by Maurice MacGonigal and *Go Lovely Rose* by John Keating. Kitty says his best painting is called *Men of the South* and is in a gallery in Cork."

"She knows her Irish artists," O'Reilly said, "and she's a dab hand with a brush and a palette knife too." O'Reilly was rewarded with a smile from Kitty. "She's exhibited at the RHA, but I'll bet she didn't tell you that." Kitty had always been one for hiding her light under a bushel, and while he wanted everyone to know what a talented woman she was, he also loved her modesty.

"I didn't know that," Pixie said, and there was admiration in her voice.

"Fingal," Kitty said, and shook her head. "You're embarrassing me."

A discreet cough announced Diarmud's arrival.

"Pints," he announced, "and menus." He set the glasses in front of the men and handed the menus around. "It's not changed much since you was here last, gents," he said.

"Lovely," O'Reilly said. "I'm so hungry I could . . . come on, Diarmud, tell us what a real Jackeen would say."

Diarmud hesitated and looked at Pixie and Kitty.

"It's all right, Diarmud, the ladies are broad-minded."

Diarmud shrugged and said, "Take your pick from 'I'm so hungry I could eat an oul' one's, ahem, derrière through a blackthorn bush,' or the same bit of the anatomy of a farmer through a tennis racquet."

Everyone laughed.

"I'll be back for your orders." Diarmud left.

"Sláinte," said O'Reilly, and took a drink from his pint.

"Cheers." Everyone else raised their glasses.

"Mother's milk," he said, wiping the white froth from his upper lip. "There's no Guinness in the world, not even ones poured up north, to compare with a well-pulled Dublin pint. Mind you, it only cost ten pence in 1931."

"Fingal," said Kitty, and he heard a serious tone to her voice. "May I ask you a favour?"

"Anything."

"You probably didn't notice when you came in, but Doctor Fitzpatrick's here. He's sitting all by himself and he looks forlorn. He's over there to your right, but don't look now."

"Serves the gobsh—" The way Kitty frowned and slitted her eyes cut O'Reilly off short.

"He was in your year. And he practises in the Kinnegar, very near us."

"And you think we should ask him to join us?"

"Welllllll . . ." She inclined her head.

When Kitty had that tone in her voice, O'Reilly would have handed her his heart on a silver platter — and asked if she'd like salt and pepper with it.

"All right," he said. "I'll go and invite him, if that's all right with everyone else . . . ?"

"Go ahead," said Pixie and Charlie together.

"But if Diarmud comes back I'd like steak and kidney and chips." O'Reilly rose, glanced right, and saw the man. He had a book in one hand, his pince-nez on the tip of his nose and a small sherry on his table for two.

O'Reilly walked over to the table. "Hello, Ronald," he said. He knew the man hated to be called by his second name, Hercules, which, considering his aesthenic build, was rather overstating the case.

"O'Reilly?" By the way he was frowning it seemed as if the man were perplexed.

"We saw you were all alone and wondered if you'd care to join us?" O'Reilly noticed that the book was a well-thumbed *How to Win Friends and Influence People* by Dale Carnegie.

"Gosh," said Fitzpatrick, picking up the book quickly and tucking it into the side pocket of his blazer. He whipped off his pince-nez and looked up at O'Reilly. "Golly. That would be quite lovely." His weak pale eyes looked down and then up again when he said in a whisper, "I was feeling a bit, well, a bit —"

O'Reilly sensed the next word was going to be "lonely" and that the man was having trouble spitting it out. So he forestalled him by saying, "Come on then, and bring your drink."

"That hit the spot," O'Reilly said, looking wistfully at his now empty plate, save for a few flakes of pastry and streaks of gravy. The

69

steak and kidney, which had been made with a pastry shell instead of a ceramic pie dish, was very nearly up to the standard of his housekeeper's. The cooking of Kinky Auchinleck, who had been Kinkaid, was the yardstick by which he measured every other chef.

"I think," said Kitty, "it's a good thing it wasn't a Willow pattern plate. You'd have scoffed the weeping willows and pagodas too."

Everyone laughed. And he knew it was because she and Fitzpatrick had been discussing matters Oriental that she had come up with that image. "Would anybody like tea? Coffee? Dessert?"

"Tea would be nice," Fitzpatrick said. "If that's all right?"

Charlie and the two women nodded.

"I'll go and ask for a pot and five cups," Charlie said, rose, and headed for the bar.

O'Reilly sat back contentedly and looked at the little company. Perhaps the book Ronald Hercules Fitzpatrick had been studying had influenced its reader. He had been quite reasonable company, and Kitty had played and was still playing a superb part in drawing the man out. When she'd asked, "And do you have any hobbies, Ronald?" — titles having been dispensed with very early in the meal — he had blushed and said, "I collect *netsuke.*"

O'Reilly had no idea what Fitzpatrick was talking about. He had a recollection of the P.

G. Wodehouse character Gussie Fink-Nottle, whose hobby was collecting newts. O'Reilly was choking back a laugh at the resemblance between Ronald and Gussie and wondering if *netsuke* was also some kind of amphibian, when Kitty said, "Which do you prefer, *katabori* or *men-netsuke*?"

"I have a collection of *anabori* and *obi-hasami, katabori.*" To which O'Reilly had to ask, "I had two — but the wheels fell off. Do you know what these two are blethering on about, Pixie?"

She shook her head.

"Please explain, Ronald," Kitty said.

Deftly done, O'Reilly thought.

The man had smiled. "I hope I'll not be boring, but in seventeeth-century Japan, men wore *kimonos* which had no pockets. Anything they wanted to carry was put into a container and suspended from their belt or *obi* by a cord. The little toggle at the end of the cord for fixing to the belt was carved from any of a number of materials like ivory or boxwood, boars' tusks."

O'Reilly was surprised that a dry old stick like Fitzpatrick could be interested in something so arcane.

"Fascinating," Pixie said. "I'd never heard of such a thing, but I suppose it's more than twenty years since the war and it's all right now to be interested in Japanese things again."

O'Reilly, who reckoned he had more reason than any at the table to resent the old enemies, said, "Why not. The war's in the past. Life is for living."

Kitty patted his hand and said, "Well said, Fingal." She smiled and continued, "Some of the *netsuke* are exquisitely beautiful. I learned about them in a course I took years ago. They're highly collectable and quite valuable — if you know what to look for. And clearly, Ronald, you do."

"I am very much an amateur," he said, and lowered his eyes before looking up and saying, "But I appreciate their beauty."

"What got you interested, Ronald?" Charlie had asked.

Fitzpatrick, who by now had opened up like a blooming rose, said, "My parents were missionaries to Japan, and I was schooled there. I left in May 1931 to come to Dublin so I could go to Trinity in September. My mother's sister Beatrice lived in Rathmines. She's getting on now, but I went to visit her yesterday, before the reception."

Kitty looked long and hard at Fitzpatrick before asking, "What happened to your parents? Do you mind me asking?"

The man's Adam's apple oscillated furiously, he shook his head, whipped off his pince-nez, put them back, then said, in a studiously steadied voice, "I don't mind. I had a letter from Mummy written in September of that year — 1931. Japan had invaded Manchuria. My parents thought war with the West was inevitable, and they were going to try to get out through Hong Kong . . ."

O'Reilly realised that they must not have made it. He put a hand on Ronald's shoulder and said quietly, "It must have been hard on you. You were very young."

The man nodded, pursed his lips. "It was. I never got another letter."

That struck a chord with O'Reilly. He saw the glint behind the pincenez and squeezed Ronald's shoulder, but said nothing. There were no words, he knew.

"Thank you, Fingal," Fitzpatrick said.

The conversation was less lively after that, and now here was Charlie with a tray carrying the teapot, silver jug of boiling water, milk, sugar, and cups. He set them on the table more or less at random, with the water jug near Fitzpatrick.

"I'll be mother," Pixie said. "Who takes what?"

O'Reilly demurred, but everyone else had a cup according to their taste. Fitzpatrick took his without milk or sugar, as the Japanese would.

It wasn't until Charlie asked for a second cup that O'Reilly had his second surprise of the afternoon.

"Pass the hot water jug, please, Fingal," Pixie said.

"Jasus. That's bloody hot." O'Reilly flapped his fingers then blew on the tips. The silver jug's heat seemed only a few degrees lower than the inside of a working blast furnace.

Despite that, Ronald lifted it as if it had been filled with ice water and slowly passed it across.

O'Reilly caught Charlie's eye and saw his friend raising an eyebrow before saying, "Did you not find it hot, Ronald?"

Fitzpatrick, who had by now collected himself, shook his head. "Temperature doesn't bother me."

O'Reilly saw blisters on the man's fingertips. Dear God. He couldn't feel that he was being burned. Loss of temperature appreciation and an inability to feel pain were symptoms of a number of nervous diseases, none of them trivial. He looked again at Charlie, who inclined his head and frowned. He must have noticed it too. And Charlie was a neurosurgeon.

Fitzpatrick was a doctor. He should recognise that he was sick, but perhaps, like many physicians, he refused to believe that illness could strike him and denied its existence. But those symptoms were serious. O'Reilly glanced again at Charlie, who made a rapid shaking of his head.

O'Reilly'd understood. Let matters pass — for now. But he and Charlie would discuss what to do as soon as they could. "Right,"

O'Reilly said. "I don't want to rush anybody. It's been a lovely lunch. Thanks for joining us, Ronald, and for the lesson in net . . . ?" He deliberately stumbled over the word.

"Netsuke," Ronald said, and smiled.

"Netsuke," O'Reilly said. "Now if you'll all excuse us . . ." He rose. "Kitty has an overwhelming desire to visit Clerys department store on O'Connell Street . . ." And I have a similar desire to get her alone back in our hotel room, he thought. "And then we'll all need to change into our formal gear again. We'll see you in the foyer about six thirty."

"See you then," Charlie said.

"Thank you," Fitzpatrick said.

Both men rose when Kitty stood.

"Come on, then," O'Reilly said to Kitty, and offered her his hand. "Next stop Clerys, so you can buy whatever you need to look beautiful tonight." He mock growled and said, "And, I'll have to look like a flaming naval officer — again."

4

ENGLAND'S GREEN AND PLEASANT LAND

Fingal lengthened his still-rolling stride and turned onto a privet-hedge-lined lane at the end of which was a cottage right out of the pages of *Country Life.* Behind the cottage, a sward swept down to the pollard willows along the edges of the Wallington River as it ran toward Fareham Lake. With metronomic regularity a man was casting a fly into the river's limpid waters. Farther downstream, a pair of swans looked haughtily at their own reflections.

Fingal stopped and took a deep breath. The warm September air was filled with the sweet smell of hay. A flock of sheep grazed nearby, woolly puff balls on a green carpet. In a distant field, a girl in what looked like the uniform of the Land Army was driving a horse-drawn reaper, making hay. The reaper's blades clattered in the distance and he could hear the song of a thrush rising above it.

A local call to Mrs. Wilcoxson last night had been greeted with pleasure and she'd

said she'd be delighted to see him today —
for lunch perhaps?

Fingal fiddled with the knot of his tie and
smoothed his uniform. From behind a church
with a squat Norman spire came the lowing
of cattle, the sound drifting in the still air. It
was a picture captured in a line from William
Blake's "Jerusalem." "England's green and
pleasant land." The contrast struck Fingal
with a force he hadn't been prepared for: the
pastoral beauty of the countryside and the
dismal shades of London's grey and black,
the stinking filth of the wanton destruction
he'd seen yesterday.

For a brief moment Fingal wondered where
his old *Warspite* colleagues were, could feel
the sway of the great ship beneath him, but
the lowing of the cattle brought his thoughts
back to the present. He was in Hampshire, a
few short miles from the English Channel.
He straightened his cap.

So, he thought, surveying the picture-
perfect cottage. This was the home of Surgeon
Commander Richard Wilcoxson and his wife,
Marjorie. Three first-floor latticed windows
jutted from beneath a thatched roof. A
varnished wooden door with a massive black
metal ring for a handle was offset to the right
side of the whitewashed front wall and was
flanked by three windows, one to its right,
the others to its left. The window frames were
all painted bright red. A yellow climbing rose

ran up a trellis on one side of the door. Its scent mingled with that of the newly mown hay. On the other side a wooden plaque read TWIDDY'S COTTAGE 1741.

England was a place of great antiquity, of deep roots, hallowed traditions. A place worth fighting for. How dare the bloody Nazis from their upstart Third Reich come and bomb Britain's ancient treasures, its stoic people? He surprised himself at the intensity of his emotion, shook his head, and rapped on a brass knocker.

"Coming," a voice called.

The door was opened by a middle-aged woman of medium height. She wore her silver hair in a chignon, instantly reminding Fingal of the housekeeper, Mrs. Kincaid, at Number One Main Street back in Ballybucklebo. Behind spectacles, blue eyes shone, and laugh lines spun webs at their corners. Mrs. Wilcoxson's voice was soft, cultured. "You must be Surgeon Lieutenant O'Reilly. Richard has told me a great deal about you. All very good." She chuckled. "Thank you for coming to see me."

"How do you do, Mrs. Wilcoxson?" Fingal said. "And please, call me Fingal. I'm very much off duty."

She wore a well-cut grey tweed suit and he noticed a small gold pin in the shape of a sheepdog on the shawl collar. A single string of pearls was round her neck. Peeking out of one of the side patch pockets of her jacket was what appeared to be a small baby bottle.

"Do come in, take off your cap and coat, and unsling that ridiculous gas mask."

"Thank you," he said, stooping under the door lintel — men had been shorter in the eighteenth century — and entered a hall floored by flagstones. Black beams supported the ceiling above and dark wood panelling covered the walls.

She hung up his things and ushered him into a long, bright room. The far end was arranged as the dining area, and to his left a large fireplace was filled with logs on black andirons. Above it hung a print of Turner's *The Fighting* Temeraire *tugged to her last berth to be broken up. 1838.*

An English sheepdog lying in front of the fire raised its shaggy head and peered at Fingal through its eye-obscuring fringe. It made a questioning "Arf?"

Marjorie Wilcoxson bent and stroked its head. "This is Lieutenant O'Reilly," she said. "Say hello, Admiral Benbow."

The dog sat up, raised one paw, threw back its head, and — Fingal could only describe the noise as yodelling.

"Thank you, Admiral," she said briskly. "That will do very well."

The dog flopped back into a woolly heap on the hearthrug.

"Richard has named all the dogs for admirals," she said. "We've a couple of foxhounds out in their kennels. They're Nelson and Drake. Mind you, we don't usually use their ranks. We don't want them getting ideas above their station."

Fingal had heard of how ditsy the English upper classes could become about animals, and several sardonic rejoinders came to his mind, but he decided to let the moment pass. "So I'm well and truly outranked," was all he said instead, and laughed.

"Only by the dogs. We've a Shetland pony mare called Boadicea — I named her. Tony has clearly outgrown her, but I can't bear to part with the little beast. And last week I found three baby hedgehogs whose mother was killed by a fox. I've named them Riddle, Mee, and Ree. They're living quite comfortably in a cardboard box by the kitchen range." She reached into her pocket, drew out the baby bottle, and looked at it. "Ah, I'd wondered where that had got to. I'm bottle-feeding them."

That explains the bottle, he thought, and smiled. "Animals are good company. It can be lonely when one's family is so far away."

"Quite so, Fingal," she said.

She led him to one of two comfortable rose-patterned chintz armchairs separated by a side table. They were arranged to face French windows looking out over a tiny formal English garden in front of an extensive vegetable plot. "One is supposed to 'Dig for victory,' " she said. "It was once all flowers out there — I do so love gardening — but needs must when the devil drives. My gardenias and dahlias are all gone . . ."

Fingal was hesitant to sit before she did.

". . . and for goodness' sake, do sit down. We were talking about families. Tell me about yours, please."

He obeyed. "My father was a professor of Classics and English at Trinity College Dublin. He died of leukaemia four years ago . . ."

"I *am* sorry. My condolences."

"Thank you. My elder brother Lars is a solicitor. He and my mother live in a small place called Portaferry about thirty miles outside Belfast. I spoke to Ma on the phone last night. She sounded well and says Lars is too."

"That will be a relief," she said.

"It was, and —"

"Forgive me for interrupting, but can I get you something before we eat? Richard taught me to like pink gin years ago, and don't look so worried. I know things are rationed, but the landlord of the Crown is kind to his special customers."

Fingal would have loved a decent pint of Guinness. He'd not had one for months, but said, preferring not to drink spirits so early in

81

the day, "I'll take a small sherry, if you have it?"

"I'll see to it," she said, "and please do carry on while I get the drinks."

"That's my immediate relatives," he said, "but I'm engaged to a wonderful girl, called Deirdre Mawhinney."

Glass chinked on glass as she said, "I certainly hope you've spoken to her."

Fingal shook his head. "She lives in the nurses' quarters of the Ulster Hospital for Women and Children in Belfast. Unless I know when she's off duty, there's no point calling."

"Mmm. Tricky, that." She handed him sherry in a small stemmed glass.

"Thank you."

Holding a cut glass with her pink gin she took the other chair, crossing her legs and, with her drink-free hand, smoothing her grey, pleated skirt. "Cheers, or as Richard might say on a Friday, 'A willing foe and sea room.' "

Fingal smiled. He'd not taken long to learn the traditional naval daily toasts. "Cheers."

They drank.

"You were telling me about your fiancée and it being tricky to phone her?"

"Ma worked out a way to deal with it," he said. "She phoned, spoke to an off-duty nurse, who then got Deirdre to phone Ma as soon as possible. She asked Deirdre to send me a telegram telling me the best time to phone. I'm going to this evening." He hugged the thought to himself and took another sip of the rich, dry sherry.

"Good for Mrs. O'Reilly. We mothers do rather come in handy sometimes. I'm delighted for you," she said. "I'm sure you can hardly wait." She lifted a photograph in a silver frame from the nearby coffee table.

Fingal saw a man in his late twenties wearing an open-necked white shirt and a naval officer's cap set askew, grinning at the photographer.

"Tony," she said, "our only offspring. We're very proud of him. He always tries to phone me when his ship's in, but it's not always easy. I'm afraid the bombs have cut a lot of lines."

"He looks like a sound man," Fingal said, but his mind was suddenly filled with the possibility that he wouldn't get through to Deirdre tonight.

"You Irishmen. Always adding new expressions to a perfectly good language. Tut." But she was smiling. "Sound?"

"I'm sorry. It means reliable, trustworthy, an all-round good type."

"I like that. Sound. He is." He could hear the fondness in her voice. "He has his own destroyer. Convoy work." And then the worry overlying the fondness.

"Mrs. Wilcoxson . . ."

"No," she said, "if I am to call you Fingal you must call me Marge if we're going to be friends." Her smile was wide. "Now," she said, "Richard tells me he has sent you to Haslar to study for three months."

"That's right and" — Fingal rummaged in his pocket — "he asked me to give you this." He held out a little parcel, which she took. "And I've to tell you he's fit and well, or was when I last saw him, and to tell you that he misses you and loves you very much."

"His last letter came two days ago. He's still fit and well."

"I'm very glad to hear it."

"And I think you are a very nice man, Fingal O'Reilly." Her smile was wry.

"I beg your pardon, but how so?"

"My reticent old curmudgeon of a husband would no more say such a personal thing in public as fly that old warship to the moon. Much too stiff an upper lip, but you knew I'd like to hear it, and little white lies, I'll bet, are part of your stock in trade to make your patients feel better."

Fingal blushed. This was a very perspicacious woman and one not to be fooled easily. He'd withdraw any reference to her being ditsy.

She patted his knee as his own mother might have done and said, "I think it was very sweet of you. Thank you. Now, I must see what's in here." She unwrapped the parcel, carefully folding the paper, opened the box, and took out a gold and amethyst necklace. "Why, it's lovely," she said, "and with an easy clasp." She removed her pearls, set them on the table, opened the new necklace, and reclasped it behind her neck.

"It looks charming," Fingal said.

"Thank you." She took a small card from the box, read it, and said nothing, but her eyes glistened. She sat very still, fingering the necklace and staring out the window, then cleared her throat and said, "Please forgive me."

Fingal became aware of a commotion near the fireplace. He turned in time to see Admiral Benbow struggling to his feet. A small rotund animal with a pointed nose and beady black eyes was scuttling across the carpet.

"Benbow. Leave it," she called, but it was too late. The dog had lumbered forward, lowered his muzzle, and was trying to sniff the creature which had instantly curled into a tight ball so that it presented nothing but spines sharp as needles to its would-be attacker. Benbow must have made the discovery, because he backed off, ululating, shaking his head, and repeatedly drawing his left forepaw over his nose while licking it at the same time.

"Silly boy," she remarked, leaping to her feet, crossing the room, and simultaneously comforting the dog while gingerly scooping up the hedgehog. "Never a dull moment with animals. This is Riddle. He has a much more highly developed sense of adventure than the others — Good Lord," she said as they both turned to the sound of a rapid knocking on the front door. "See who that is, will you, like a good chap?"

Fingal set his drink down, went and opened the front door.

"Tony, Tony, you're ho—" A petite, green-eyed girl hurled herself at Fingal, only managing to pull up short at the last minute. Her honey-blonde hair was barely restrained by a headscarf and she filled her Land Army uniform green sweater rather well. She had been flushed and panting for breath and now, clearly, she was blushing. "I-I-I'm most dreadfully sorry. I was mowing hay in the field there and I saw a young naval officer. I ran the whole way and I —"

"Thought I was Tony?"

"Well, yes, actually. I do apologise." Her blush, which Fingal found most attractive, was fading, replaced by a look of dread. He knew what she was thinking.

"I'm Fingal O'Reilly," he said quickly, "a friend of Richard's. I was visiting Mrs. Wilcoxson. Won't you come in."

"Oh. No," she said, "no thank you, I should be getting back to the horse," and with that she turned on her Wellington-booted heel and strode away.

She was, he reckoned, still confused, but at least she knew he wasn't here to deliver bad news. He admired the sway of her hips beneath her regulation corduroy jodhpurs. He closed the door and went back to find Benbow asleep and Marge standing waiting.

"I've got Riddle tucked up, poor little thing. He was all atremble," she said. "Now, who was at the door?"

"A blonde Land Girl who was a bit disappointed that I wasn't your son. She left."

Marge chuckled. "I think," she said, "you just met the Honourable Philippa Gore-Beresford. Her father, Lord Finisterre, is the local lord of the manor. Old naval family."

The title "honourable," Fingal knew, was given to daughters of barons or peers of the realm of even higher rank.

"Lovely girl, usually answers to 'Pip.' She's daft about my Tony and he's daft about her."

"Lucky Tony," Fingal said.

Marge nodded. "They've known each other for donkeys' years. I keep hoping he'll pop the question, but war and his destroyer are both stern mistresses." She began to turn. "Anyhow," she said, "I think it's time we ate."

She went to the dining end, he followed, and when she indicated his place he stepped behind her chair, pulled it out, and seated her before taking his own. "Looks wonderful," he said.

"Prawn cocktails," she said. "Fish, including shellfish, aren't rationed," she said, "and I know one of the Solent fishermen. The lettuce is from what used to be my flower garden. Now don't be shy, and eat up."

He tucked in. The Marie-Rose sauce was piquant and the prawns crisp. "Delicious," he said.

She acknowledged the compliment with an inclination of her head.

Conversation during the main course had been restricted to remarks like, "May I pass you the salt?" "A little more rabbit pie?" "This Chianti is excellent, thank you," and "I couldn't eat another bite, honestly."

After clearing the table she had served coffee in front of the French windows. "I'm afraid it's only Camp chicory essence, but . . ."

Fingal echoed her words as she quoted a popular slogan, "Blimey. Ain't you heard? There's a war on." They both laughed.

"Lord," said Fingal, "it's been lovely to forget about it for a while. Thank you so much. I'm staying in the medical officers' mess. Your cooking was perfection."

"It was my pleasure, and I hope I'll be seeing more of you, obviously making allowances for the requirements of the service."

"I'd like that," Fingal said, but thought about the requirements of the service and what they might mean to him and Deirdre. As he set his cup on the table he wondered when the Wilcoxsons had married. "Marge, may I ask you a personal question?"

"Of course."

"How easy was it for you and Richard to get married?"

"Not very," she said, "but then between the wars the navy was still pretty Victorian in its attitudes. We had to wait until Richard was promoted to lieutenant-commander."

This was not encouraging news. Fingal was a mere lieutenant.

"You're frowning," she said. "Now it's my turn to enquire if I might question you?"

"Please do."

"Are you considering marriage?"

"Yes. I want Deirdre to join me here, but if the navy are going to say we can't get —"

"She shall join you here regardless." Marge's voice was firm and she had squared her shoulders. She stood and put a maternal hand on Fingal's shoulder. "Just as quickly as you can get her here."

"But how?"

"She'll stay with me, of course. I and the menagerie would love the company. She'll be expected to get a job . . ."

"She's a trained nurse and midwife, but I'd rather she found something else." He grimaced. "If both of us are working on on-call rotas we might as well be living in separate countries."

"Yes, I can see the difficulty. You going off

duty just as she's going on," Marge said. "No, that won't do at all. But I can sort that. I'm an officer in the Land Army, and the work can be flexible. She and Pip will be of an age. I'm sure they'll be pals while you're working. Company for each other."

Fingal looked at this proper English matron in her proper grey worsted suit and threw convention out the nearest casement window. He stood up, hugged her, and spun her in a half-circle. "I love you, Marge Wilcoxson," he said as he released her. "Can you really put her up, get her a job?"

"Young man," Marge said stiffly, "now that you have allowed me to stop giving my impression of a whirling dervish . . ." She was trying to keep her voice stern but she soon began to giggle. "You *do* love her very much, don't you?"

And with everything in his soul Fingal said, "Yes. Yes, I do."

"So," she said, "it's settled then." She looked wistful. "I envy you your youth," she said, "but on a more practical note, have you taken any steps to see if you can get married?"

Fingal inhaled, blew out his breath. "I should have thought about it months ago, but I'm a civilian at heart. Simply never occurred to me to ask anybody. I spoke with Rear Admiral Creaser yesterday. He said he could see difficulties, but he'd see what he could do, but that'll take time and I am dying to see her."

"The admiral is a bit like one of my hedgehogs. Prickly on the outside, but what did you call my Tony?"

"Sound."

"The admiral is a very sound man. If it can be arranged, he'll arrange it."

That was music to Fingal's ears. He couldn't stop grinning. "She's expecting me to phone her tonight at six o'clock. I'll tell her, Marge, so please start getting things arranged. I don't know how to thank you enough, and if there's anything I can do for you in return —"

"I was going to have you help me wash the dishes," she said with a chuckle, "but if you've to be back at Haslar for six you'd better get going for the station. The next train will come in half an hour and then there's not another one until eight." She headed for the hall. He followed. She gave him his cap, coat, and gas mask. As soon as he was dressed she ushered him out, forestalled his thanks by saying, "Don't waste time thanking me, young man. Get on with you and let me know when to expect her," and with that she shut the door.

Fingal leapt up, clicked his heels, landed, and strode down the path. He began singing,

We'll meet again, don't know where don't

91

know when,
but I know we'll meet again . . .

The big hit of 1939 by Vera Lynn, the Forces'
Sweetheart. And what was better, he did
know where and when. On Portsmouth Station platform just as soon as Deirdre could
get here.

His reverie was interrupted by an eldritch
moaning, the rising and falling notes of air
raid sirens. He knew he was meant to take
shelter, but damn it, he couldn't afford to
miss the train. He broke into a run, his gas
mask bouncing on his hip.

Overhead he heard the thrumming noise of
unsynchronised aero engines, the hallmark of
German Heinkel 111 and Dornier 17 bombers. And the answering feral snarling of Rolls-
Royce Merlins that powered the RAF's Hurricane and Spitfire fighters as they climbed in
pursuit of their prey. The machine guns firing
sounded like tearing calico. He stopped for a
moment and, craning his neck, peered skyward. Four miles up, vapour trails were being
formed against the cerulean sky. From Portsmouth came the crack of shore- and ship-
mounted antiaircraft guns. They added their
black shell bursts like jet beads to the hairnet
tracery of the narrow clouds. And there, over
the sea, a flame dragged a smoky trail behind
it and a parachute, as seemingly tiny as a
dandelion seed, floated down.

But at six o'clock Fingal would place his call and tell Deirdre to pack and come to him, and — he took one last glance up before running again — not Adolf Hitler, not Reichsmarschall Herman Goering, nor the whole bloody Luftwaffe was going to keep them apart.

5

. . . My Poor Nerves

A muttering Arthur Guinness in the back of the Rover sniffed the air and thrashed his tail. "Settle down, sir," said O'Reilly, reaching behind him to chuck the dog under the chin. "You'll get your run later." He started to open his door, saying, "Thanks for coming with me, Barry. I think I need the moral support."

"Happy to, Fingal. I'm feeling at loose ends these days." He turned and gave Arthur an absent-minded pat, stroking one of the dog's long ears. "With Sue in Marseilles on this damn teacher exchange, I won't be seeing her until the Christmas holidays."

"And then wedding bells ringing in March for you two, is that right?"

Barry nodded. "Feels like a long time."

"Patience, my boy, patience." O'Reilly understood all about prenuptial patience. "Right. It's four thirty. Time to beard the lion —"

"In his den," Barry said, opening his door.

"If I remember correctly, that's exactly what you said the last time we were here, before Christmas '64. Is Doctor Ronald Hercules Fitzpatrick still a lion?" At the sound of the door opening, Arthur began his antics again, clearly hoping for a walk.

"You stay, lummox." Sighing like a barrage balloon deflating, Arthur stopped thrashing his tail and subsided on the seat as O'Reilly heaved himself out of the car.

Barry walked round to join him on the driver's side and O'Reilly inhaled the tang of the sea. Someone had scattered bread crumbs on the cement walk outside Number Nine, the Esplanade, and gulls pitched and wheeled, making crash landings, squabbling over the pickings.

"I thought perhaps he'd mellowed over the last few years, but his reaction to Charlie and me on Sunday was anything but mellow. There was Ronald, who ordinarily wouldn't say shite if his mouth was full of it, banging his fist on the table, gobbling like a turkey, and yelling, 'And there's not a blooming thing wrong with me. Nothing. Leave me alone. Go away.' And I quote." O'Reilly tightened his lips, blew out his breath.

"I'm no psychiatrist," Barry said, "but that's called denial." He looked down, then back up at O'Reilly. "It's going to be an uphill fight to get him to change his mind."

"I know, but something has to be done

95

about the man's refusal to seek help. He's not my favourite person in the world, but I'm still worried about him."

They walked side by side along the path as the gulls hopped and flapped out of their way. The nondescript three-storey grey stucco house, according to the signs outside, had solicitors' offices and a dentist on the first floor and a group of chartered accountants on the second.

"Since we worked out between us all the neurological conditions that might be at the root of Ronald's symptoms, I haven't been able to come up with any more causes. Have you thought of other possibilities?"

"Divil the one," Barry said. "What we think it could be is bad enough." His shudder was obvious, and O'Reilly understood why. "He must be stark-raving bonkers to refuse help from his friends — especially when one of them is an eminent neurosurgeon like Charlie Greer."

"Calling us friends might be pushing it. Ronald never really had friends at medical school. I think he's just scared silly and won't or can't face the facts." O'Reilly rang the bell under Fitzpatrick's brass plate, which was affixed to the wall beside a brown-painted front door.

The door was opened. "Fingal. Young Laverty. Do come in. We'll go through to my surgery." Fitzpatrick's smile was, like his chin, weak. He stood with his hands behind his back, leaning forward, looking like one of those African secretary birds. Fitzpatrick led the way along a hall still floored with faded brown linoleum. The same Landseer print, *Monarch of the Glen,* hung askew on one wall.

Nor had he changed the paisley-patterned wallpaper in his surgery. Perhaps, O'Reilly thought, Fitzpatrick feels about paisley the way I do about roses.

"Please sit, gentlemen," Fitzpatrick said, and indicated several kitchen chairs. He himself retired behind his desk, which was on a raised dais. "Now, Fingal," he said, "you were not at all clear on the phone this morning about why you wanted this meeting, but apart from the unfortunate incident when you and Greer tried to intrude on my private life —"

O'Reilly saw Barry flinch. This wasn't going to be easy.

"Apart from that, I must say your attitude and that of your lovely wife at the reunion was most collegial. Most. I enjoyed our lunch in Davy Byrnes enormously."

"Thank you," O'Reilly said.

"So what can I do for you?"

O'Reilly took a deep breath and made a tactical decision before saying, "Ronald, I came to say sorry. It was out of place for Charlie and me to try to interfere."

Fitzpatrick's sniff and Barry's raised eyebrows came as one. I know, O'Reilly thought, that young Laverty doesn't believe I've ever known how to apologise, but honey catches more flies than vinegar.

"Thank you, Fingal. I am a very private man. I'm sure your concern was well meant, but . . ." He held up his right hand and O'Reilly saw the bandages round the thumb and index finger. "I have always had a very high tolerance for pain. To this day I refuse local anaesthesia for dental fillings. As regards the blisters, I have everything under control. I always keep specially prepared dressings for burns. It's a County Leitrim cure. One part beeswax to four of mutton fat are melted, camomile flowers are added, and linen bandages soaked while the mixture is still liquid, then allowed to solidify. When applied, the body's heat melts the fats, the plaster adheres tightly, and keeps air and infection out. In ten days I shall be as right as rain. Never fear." His smile was condescending.

"I've heard of that before," said Barry, "and of camomile, butter, and goose dung for treating scalds."

"I'm a firm believer in country remedies, Laverty," Fitzpatrick said, "but even I might draw the line at goose dung." Back on his home territory, Fitzpatrick seemed to have reverted to the supercilious air that had neither won him friends nor influenced people when he was a student at Trinity College in Dublin. O'Reilly scanned the small shelf of books behind Fitzpatrick's desk but didn't find a copy of the classic he had been reading at Davy Byrnes.

O'Reilly thought fast. Regardless of what might ail Fitzpatrick, neurological disorders rarely had the urgency of acute conditions such as bleeding or fainting. Unless, of course, there had been bleeding into the skull. But that clearly wasn't the case here. A diagnosis didn't have to be made instantly, and when — not if, but when — Fitzpatrick did agree to see Charlie, the surgeon would not put Fitzpatrick on any waiting list. He'd be seen at once as a professional courtesy. O'Reilly had a little leeway. Today, when Fitzpatrick was so convinced of the rightness of his own treatment, any insistence on him going to see Charlie might close the doors forever to getting him looked after properly until it was too late.

Perhaps a more subtle method would be to feign all sweetness and light today and make another approach after some time had passed? "I'm delighted you're taking care of yourself," O'Reilly said. "Charlie and I only spoke to you because Kitty was really worried and persuaded us to. You know she's a neurosurgery nurse." He ignored Barry's wide-eyed stare. He'd have to remind the young pup to think twice before playing poker. He'd never be able to bluff.

"Your wife, Fingal, is a very handsome and caring woman, and you are a very lucky man."

O'Reilly was convinced Fitzpatrick had harboured an unrequited attraction to Kitty, perhaps even love, since their student days. "She even asked Barry and me to come round today to make sure you were all right and to ask — ask, mind you —" O'Reilly debated for a second and concluded it was worth going ahead. "— if you'd not reconsider seeing Charlie, let him give you the once-over? Just to be on the safe side. She says it would set her mind at rest."

"Shan't be necessary," Fitzpatrick said, "not one bit, I can assure you both, but I can understand her concern. Please thank her for me. I am touched."

All the flags were up in O'Reilly's assessment of Fitzpatrick's frame of mind. At this moment, trying to bully the man into doing what was the right thing for him would have about as much chance of success as a heifer on roller skates dancing *Swan Lake.* There was much to be said for letting time elapse, although eventually getting the right diagnosis was imperative. "Why not thank her yourself?" O'Reilly wondered why he had a mental image of a wet and wrinkled Archimedes leaping out of his bath yelling, "Eureka!" "She and I are going to Barcelona on Friday for a week to see an old friend." And to lay a ghost to rest from Kitty's past. "But when we

100

get back, why not come for tea?" And she and I can gang up on you.

There was a glint in the man's eyes when he said, "Thank you, Fingal. I'd like that very much."

O'Reilly rose and nodded to Barry, who joined him.

"Thank you for coming," Fitzpatrick said. "Bon voyage, Fingal. I'll look forward very much to seeing you and Kitty in a week or so." He smiled at Barry. "You are a very lucky young man to have Fingal as your principal."

"I know," Barry said, "even if sometimes I can't always follow his methods."

"Ah," said Fitzpatrick, "you'll learn, young man, that all doctors have their own little ways, but it has been my experience with your senior that when he sets his mind on something he seems always to get it."

"Och," said O'Reilly, "if we weren't all of the same stock I'd say it was only the luck of the Irish." He turned and began to walk away. "We'll see ourselves out, Ronald. Come on, Barry, and we'll give Arthur his run."

O'Reilly took a stick from Arthur's mouth and stepped aside as the big dog shook himself dry. "Begod," said O'Reilly, relishing the late-September sun's warmth on his face and the sparkly evening shimmer of the lough between the beach and the softening Antrim Hills on the far shore. In the distance, a V of geese cut diagonally across the sky and the two men stopped to watch them. "I've always had a soft spot for September. Start of rugby season, opening of wildfowling, gentle evenings like this."

"Soft spot? Soft in the head, more likely," Barry said, sotto voce.

"Huh," said O'Reilly, beginning to head for home. "Heel . . . and that applies to Arthur and impertinent young partners." But he was smiling. Now that he felt he'd done his best for Ronald Fitzpatrick, even if the outcome wasn't immediately satisfactory, O'Reilly's mood was much lighter. He was happy to be teased by young Barry Laverty, physician and surgeon, M.B., B.Ch., B.A.O. The boy made him as proud as if he'd been his own son.

"Away," said Barry with a grin, "off and chase yourself, revered senior partner," and fell into step at O'Reilly's shoulder.

They strode in the companionable silence of two men between whom a solid friendship, based not a little on mutual respect, was growing. Underfoot the sand was damp and firm where half an hour before the ebbing tide had been carrying bladder wrack and kelp fronds, flotsam and jetsam back out to sea.

"How's about ye, Doctors?" A perspiring, barefoot man in an open-necked collarless shirt with his corduroy trousers rolled up above his knees straightened up from bending to use a sand rake.

"Grand altogether, Leo," O'Reilly said. The man had been a patient for fifteen years, ever since first having to see Cromie for a case of *genu valgum* — knock-knees. Leo held up a burlap sack. "I've done very good, Doc, so I have," he said. "Would you like a few cockles for your tea, like?"

Boiled, the bivalve molluscs were delicious with salt and vinegar. "Pop some in here," O'Reilly said, and held out an oversized hanky, which Leo filled with the shellfish, each grooved with a fan-shaped pattern on its shell. "Thank you very much." O'Reilly knotted the hanky at the corners. "Don't let us hold you up, Leo. Good to see you."

"Enjoy your tea, sirs," Leo said, and bent back to his work singing to himself,

. . . sweet Molly Malone,
as she wheels her wheelbarrow
through streets broad and narrow
crying cockles and mussels alive, alive
   oh . . .

"I miss not having Kinky after five in her kitchen," O'Reilly said as he and Barry resumed their walk and Arthur bounded ahead, "but I've known how to cook these fellahs," he held up the bulging hanky, savouring its fresh, fishy smell, "since I was a wee lad in Holywood. You soak them for a few hours in cold salt water and they spit out any sand they may have ingested, then you boil them. If they don't open then, don't eat them. Those ones are dead already and may be toxic. We'll have the good ones tomorrow night."

"I'll be out," Barry said. "Having dinner with Dad and Mum in Bangor. But you and Kitty enjoy."

Tom Laverty, O'Reilly thought, navigating officer on *Warspite.* He glanced out to sea, and as if he needed a further reminder of the Royal Navy, saw the RNR coastal minesweeper HMS *Kilmorey* heading down the lough. As always, seeing the grey *Kilmorey,* tender to HMS *Caroline,* a veteran of Jutland and moored in Belfast as a training facility, brought back ghosts from his past. Kitty wasn't the only member of the family with one of those.

And as always he chased the phantasms back to their lairs by concentrating on the present. Another denizen of these familiar beaches was heading their way. Donal Donnelly, carroty hair sticking out from beneath his duncher, was walking on the sand dunes with his purebred racing greyhound Bluebird by his side. "Hello, Doctors," said Donal. "Out for a wee dander?" Somehow, O'Reilly thought, the tone of the man's voice did not have its usual cheerful innocence, and Donal was not smiling.

As Arthur and Bluebird, old friends, exchanged mutual bottom sniffs and a lot of tail wagging, Barry said, "Hello, Donal. How are Julie and Tori?"

Donal sighed. "They're grand, fit as fleas, and Tori never shuts up. I think her mammy, when she was carrying the wee dote, was scared by Cissie Sloan."

O'Reilly had to chuckle. It was an ancient Ulster superstition that exposure to external influences while still in the womb could produce lasting effects after a baby's birth. He could understand why Donal might think that proximity to the biggest chatterbox in the village and townland could lead to his daughter's loquaciousness. And yet there was still no smile and O'Reilly knew Donal was daft about his wife and daughter. "Something the matter, Donal?"

Donal sighed mightily, but said nothing.

"Donal?" O'Reilly said. "Is there something we can do for you?"

"It's Bluebird, Doc," Donal said. "I think she's pregnant. And I'm dead worried, so I am. I paid Dapper Frew a quare clatter of the oul' do-re-mi for his Athlone Racer — he's by Breckonhill Brave out of Loughbrickland Lass — for til stand at stud. That's quite a pedigree, you know."

"So why are you worried? The pups'll be worth a fortune, surely?" Barry said.

Another great inhalation. "I dunno. You see,

she come on heat eight weeks ago. I've had her in her dog run ever since. The local doggy Romeos have been round, but I didn't think they could get near her. I started putting Dapper's dog with her every other day from six days after she started, but she'd not accept him for another six days after that."

"But," Barry said, "I thought when a bitch was on heat she was receptive to dogs?"

Donal shook his head. "Nah. Early on it's just to signal she's getting ready til ovulate. If a dog goes near a bitch that's getting going, she'll simply plant her arse on the ground and snap at the fellah."

"Like 'Not tonight, dear, I have a headache'?" Barry said.

"You're dead on, sir," Donal said, "but once the bitch has ovulated she'll let a male serve her."

O'Reilly was impressed. Donal sounded like a professional canine reproductive specialist. "So how do you know when she's ready?"

"You don't, because heat can last anywhere from five til twenty-one days. What we do is put the sire in with her every other day after six days since she started showing signs. She'd no interest in the Racer until twelve days from when she started."

"Well, everything should be all right," Barry said with a smile.

"Aye. Mebbe," said Donal. "I dunno."

O'Reilly was distracted by the plaintive cry

106

of a curlew as the brown, curve-billed bird glided overhead. He always wondered if they were in permanent mourning.

"Why don't you know, Donal?" Barry asked.

Donal glanced all around as if fearing to be overheard and then lowered his voice so that Barry and O'Reilly had to crane forward to hear his next words. "See that there Mary Dunleavy? See her? No harm til her, but . . ."

From that line alone, O'Reilly knew the publican's daughter was about to come in for criticism.

"See thon Brian Boru of hers, that Mexican mariachi dog? She lets him wander. The wee bugger."

O'Reilly's mouth opened. He glanced at Barry. Both his eyebrows had shot up. "You don't mean — ?"

"I do. In soul I do. I caught the wee rodent wriggling out from under the wire of Blue-bird's pen the day before she stood for Dapper's Athlone Racer. I'd swear the randy wee bollix had a grin from one sticky-up ear til the other. And them innocent big brown eyes don't fool me."

"And you're worried —"

"I am that, so I am."

"But surely a wee Chihuahua couldn't — ?"

"Could he not? Could he not? He's a feisty wee weasel. I've seen how he used to browbeat poor ol' Arthur Guinness there, drinking his Smithwick's right out from under his nose . . ."

"Actually," said O'Reilly, "they're quite good friends now."

"Is that fact?" The intelligence didn't seem to interest Donal.

O'Reilly, picturing the coupling and the look, as described by Donal, on Brian Boru's face, had very great difficulty controlling his laughter.

Donal's features adopted the screwed-up set of contortions they always assumed when he was wrestling with a thorny intellectual problem. "And there's no way til tell until she's pupped, and that'll be about the week of October the sixteenth."

O'Reilly frowned. "I understand. If she has greyhound whelps —"

"I'm in like Flynn." Donal rubbed his hands and smiled. "Grues can have as many as twelve pups."

O'Reilly had never understood why Ulster-folk called greyhounds "grues."

"Dapper gets pick of the litter — that's always part of the stud fee, and wait til youse see what I'll get for Julie and Tori for Christmas when I've sold the others. There'll be grue-men queuing up from my house at Dun Bwee til Crawfordsburn Village making offers, so there will." He rubbed his hands together, much as O'Reilly pictured Ebenezer

Scrooge doing as he gloated over his pile of gold.

"But if thon wee bugger has got til her first." Donal's indrawing of breath was vast. "After paying Dapper, I'll not have two stivers to rub together. I'll have to do something, because who the hell's going to want to buy — I don't know what they'd be. Greyhuahuas? Chihuahounds? I don't suppose either one of youse would have any notions?"

Barry frowned before saying, "Not right off the top of my head, Donal. Canine fertility wasn't one of the subjects I studied in zoölogy in first year at Queens. Any ideas, Doctor O'Reilly?"

"Leave it with us, Donal. Maybe a notion will occur, but for now I think you're just going to have to be patient."

"Och, thanks for listening, Docs."

"Let's hope you've nothing to worry about and we'll soon hear that mother and children, of the right breed, are doing well," O'Reilly said. "You'll let us know, won't you?"

"Aye, I will," said Donal. "Come on, girl." And he and the *enceinte* Bluebird, who might well soon be the mother of the strangest-looking puppies ever seen in Ballybucklebo, headed off along the beach.

"Heel, Arthur," O'Reilly said. "Home, Barry." And started to walk.

"Have you any ideas what Donal could do

if he's stuck with a bunch of hybrids?" Barry asked.

"Not one iota of a notion," O'Reilly said, "but I don't think we need worry."

"Why not? Without the money from the sale of the pups, he's lost the cash he paid to Dapper."

O'Reilly shook his head and laughed out loud before saying, "I'll bet you a pound that if the worst does happen, Donal Donnelly, probably as good a con man as Ferdinand Demara, the Great Imposter, will come up with a solution himself, and probably have more money at the heels of the hunt than if Bluebird has purebred whelps."

Barry tilted his head, closed one eye, and scrutinised O'Reilly. "All right," he said at last, "you're on." He held out a hand to seal the bargain, but withheld a shake until he'd said, "But knowing Donal, I want odds of two to one."

6

MY FLESH ALSO
LONGETH AFTER THEE

In a private booth in the corridor of the medical officers' mess, Fingal O'Reilly stood a-tremble, ear glued to the telephone receiver. He'd been trying to get through since six, but his call had had to be rerouted through several telephone exchanges because the bombing had so disrupted service. Now Fingal was listening to a distant double ring, a voice that he was sure was Deirdre's saying "Hello," and a long-distance operator stating in a monotone, "I have a person-to-person call from Lieutenant O'Reilly to Nurse Deirdre Mawhinney."

"Speaking." It was her. It was her. The trembling worsened.

The operator's voice contained all the enthusiasm of a shopkeeper ordering rolls of toilet paper. "You are connected, Haslar."

"Thank you," the WREN on the Haslar switchboard said. "You may go ahead, sir."

Clicking and clacking and hissing on the line then, "Fingal? Fingal? Is it really you?"

"Darling. Deirdre. It is. I'm here in Gosport." The trembling had stopped. "I'm here. I've missed you. I love you."

"Fingal, my love . . ." the words poured in a torrent, "I thought you were never going to get there. It's been forever. I was over the moon when your mother spoke to me yesterday, thought six o'clock tonight would never come, but you've made it. I'm so, so happy. I do love you so much. When can I see you? How soon?"

He heard the catch in her voice and had to control the one that was damn near starting in his own. Deirdre. Deirdre. "Very soon, pet. Just as quickly as you can get here." And he'd hold her, kiss her, breathe her in. God bless Marge Wilcoxson and her offer of a place to stay for his dear girl. "Now listen, I've only got three minutes so I have to be quick. I'm asking you to take some risks when you come." He wanted her here, even if it was selfish, but he had to at least warn her, if only for the sake of his conscience. "The Germans have been bombing Portsmouth. It's lessening, but I don't think it's going to stop. Gosport's not been hit as hard —"

"I know. We've been listening to the BBC broadcast bulletins every day. Bombing?" She laughed and said, "I don't care. I want to be with you. Matron here's a pet. She's arranged for me to have leave until January."

That was when his orders instructed him to

travel back to *Warspite.*

"We can have three whole months together. It'll be wonderful." It would. He hardly dared imagine how wonderful, lest his heart should burst.

"And I'm not going to let any silly war or stupid German bombs interfere with that time. I'd come to you even if you begged me to stay here in Belfast. I'd come, Fingal. I'd come."

He loved her for her bravery. "I'll take care of you, darling." Which was an idiotic thing to say. How the hell could he?

"I know you will, sweetheart. Because you love me."

That stifled any more quibbling with himself, and their minutes were ticking by. "I hate to have to be so practical, but have you thought about how to get here?"

Lord, but he'd missed the throaty chuckle he now heard coming through the receiver. "I spent my last weekend off in Portaferry with Ma — that's what she wants me to call her now, seeing I'll soon be her daughter-in-law."

Fingal clenched his teeth. Perhaps. It all depended on the admiral. Even before Fingal had picked up the phone, he had decided to say nothing about a possible snag in their wedding plans. There was no point worrying her now, and all might be resolved by the time she arrived. Loving concern or moral cowardice? He shrugged. He'd cross that bridge when he came to it.

"We spent hours at the dining room table . . ."

Fingal could picture the room and the old bog-oak table with its high-backed chairs — and Ma. Practical, helpful. Already he'd seen some of Ma in Marge Wilcoxson.

". . . poring over maps, ferry sailings, railway timetables. I can get the Liverpool boat from Belfast, train to Southampton, and change there for Gosport."

Fingal wished that whoever had issued his travel warrant had been as thorough in his planning. Apparently there'd been no need for his hellish ride across the breadth of England, although in fairness ever since the start of the Blitz delays and rerouting trains past damaged tracks was becoming routine. "Terrific," he said, "so you'll not have to go to London."

He didn't want her anywhere near that bombers' magnet. The capital had suffered several massive daylight raids beginning on September 7, and the Luftwaffe had come back every night since. Citizens stoically went down into the tunnels of the London Underground, huddled in air raid shelters, cellars. Bombs rained down. Civilians, firemen, and those whose duties kept them out of shelters died or were maimed. The last place he wanted her was in that nightmare.

"And you'll not need to go as far as Gosport," he said. "I want you to get off at the stop before, in a place called Fareham. I'll meet you there. I'll explain where you'll be staying when I see you."

"Oh, Fingal, I do love you so much. Thank you," she said. "I'll book my tickets tomorrow and I'll wire you when to expect me. Wire me back to let me know everything's all right at your end."

"I will, darling." He'd get time off even if he had to go adrift, AWOL.

A woman's voice interrupted, "Your permitted three minutes will soon be up, sir."

"I love you, Deirdre." To hell with the Haslar operator overhearing if she was still on the line.

"I'll telegraph. I love you, Fingal. I'll see you soon, and I'll bring the black nightie I didn't get a chance to wear when we were in —" The line went dead.

O'Reilly chuckled. He thought, and damn the operator if she heard that too. His thoughts raced to their loving last night together in Belfast's Midland Hotel seven months ago, and the erotic longing to hold her, kiss her, breathe in her scent, caress her, almost gave Fingal O'Reilly apoplexy. And she'd be here soon. Soon, but God, the days were going to drag until she was.

He started to leave the phone booth, only to be pulled up short. In his reverie he'd quite forgotten to replace the receiver and was still grasping it in his right hand.

Fingal let himself into the well-furnished anteroom with several tables occupied by fellow officers wearing mess kit. The sweet music of Deirdre's voice was still in his ears, and he barely noticed the muted hum of conversation, the heavy aroma of pipe tobacco filling the air. None of the men were known to him. Two white-jacketed civilian stewards circulated, taking orders, serving drinks. He felt out of place in his everyday working rig, but, as he'd told the admiral, his formal dining gear was following him.

His eye was taken by a lithograph of a semicircle of uniformed, bewhiskered military men surrounding a bonneted, round-faced woman with an enormous bustle in the rear of her skirt. She was pinning something to the jacket of an officer in a wheelchair. The caption read, *Queen Victoria presents Commander Purvis with the Egypt Medal. Haslar Hospital; 1882.*

Not far from the picture was a small, redhaired, florid-faced man wearing the insignia of a captain, the four rings separated by the scarlet of the medical branch. Fingal took note of a miniature DSO along with some campaign medals adorning the senior man's mess jacket. It must have been awarded in the First World War for some deed of out-

116

standing gallantry. Fingal was curious, but it would be plain bad manners to enquire. The captain smiled and beckoned to Fingal.

Fingal frowned, pointed at his chest, and the little captain nodded. As Fingal approached their table, he took a quick look at the man's table companion, a young surgeon lieutenant-commander. Receding fair hair, pale blue eyes behind rimless spectacles, strong chin. A livid scar ran from the corner of his left eye to his lower lip, which had a permanent droop.

"Eh, you'd be O'Reilly, I'm thinking," the captain said. "Fingal, aye, 'the fair Gael' O'Reilly." His voice was soft, lilting.

"I am, sir."

"Aye. Just so."

The *J* of "just" was rendered as *ch,* "chust so," the mark of the Highlander's speech. Fingal guessed that this must be his course leader.

"Angus Mahaddie. Admiral Creaser told us to expect you and to forgive your undress until your kit arrives. I've been instructed to take you and five other officers under my wing. Teach you modern anaesthesia. This is David White, one of your classmates."

The young man with the scarred face rose and offered his hand, which Fingal shook. "Pleasure to meet you, O'Reilly," he said. Very definitely English public school, and his surgeon lieutenant-commander's rings were solid. He, like the surgeon captain, was regular navy.

"My pleasure," said Fingal.

"Aye, now, sit you down, my boy, and I'll get you a welcoming drink," said Mahaddie.

"Thank you, sir." O'Reilly sat facing his new colleagues.

"Aye. Just so, and remember there are no sirs in the mess. It's Angus, Fingal."

"I'm sorry, sir —" Fingal was relieved to see that his senior was laughing. "Angus."

"And what will it be?" He lifted an arm to attract the attention of a mess steward.

"Jameson's whiskey, neat please," Fingal said.

The older man shook his head. Sighed. "I wish I could say, 'Certainly.' We've plenty of beer, Plymouth gin, a cellar full of good claret from before the war, but when it comes to the *uisce beatha.*" He cocked his head at Fingal as if expecting a reply.

"The water of life, or *aqua vitae,* if you prefer the Latin."

The small man clapped his hands in apparent delight. "So a lot goes on in that head of yours, Fingal?"

"I hope so, sir, I mean, Angus."

"Good. You've both got a lot to learn. The usual anaesthetic course is four weeks, and I know you'll be staying longer with us, Fingal. I intend to work you hard."

"It's what we're here for," David said. "It

118

scares the living daylights out of me pouring ether on a mask and watching a patient turn blue. Naval colour, I'll admit, but it really doesn't suit people who should be — well, pinkish."

"Och," said Mahaddie. "Anaesthesia's the stiff discipline, right enough. Most of the time we're bored stiff with no one to talk to . . ." He took a long pause, then, "And every so often scared stiff when an anaesthetic goes wrong." He laughed at his own little joke, then continued. "Just so, but it's going to be my job to make sure you and others like you have as few scared stiff moments as is humanly possible."

Fingal nodded. He could still remember being terrified in Greenock last year when the ether he'd given had nearly suffocated a sailor who was having his appendix removed.

The steward appeared.

"Another pink gin, and two Johnnie Walkers please, Sutton."

The steward left.

"I'd sell me soul for a glass of the Dalmore. It's a single-malt whisky distilled not far from where I come from, Inverness, but . . . rationing." He shrugged. "Now," he said, "I have just met David and I'd like to learn a bit about my new juniors. Your turn, Fingal."

It took little time for him to outline his career from the Merchant Navy, then Trinity School of Physic, until the present when he expected to stay at Haslar for three months, the last two to learn more about trauma surgery or, if not enough cases presented, to further his anaesthetic studies. During this telling, the steward brought the drinks and Captain Mahaddie signed a mess chit. Fingal finished his potted autobiography.

"Aye aye." Mahaddie nodded, looked at Fingal from under bushy eyebrows, and said, "But you're not telling us that you were an Irish rugby player."

"I didn't think it had much to do with medicine."

"It doesn't, but when it comes to my officers I want to know about the man as well. The person."

Fingal nodded. He was beginning to think he could warm to this little Highlander.

"And you've seen all your service on *Warspite*?"

"Apart from a year on *Tiger* in, '30, '31 . . ." Fingal laughed. "And a short stint on HMS *Touareg* this year. I got there by breeches buoy. I can't recommend that."

"Just so. At least you kept yourself dry." The Scot's voice became serious. "David here was on *Glorious*. He got rather wet."

"Were you, by God?" Fingal whistled. The aircraft carrier had been sunk by the *Scharnhorst* and *Gneisenau* while trying to retrieve planes from the failed Norway campaign that had followed the second battle of Narvik. More than a thousand men had been lost.

The younger man's hand went unconsciously to his scar and he smiled. A clearly forced grin. "Bit chilly, the Sea of Norway, even in June," he said. Then changed the subject. "I hear our four classmates will all be arriving from the RNVR shore base HMS *King Alfred* at Hove."

Fingal could understand why David would not want to dwell on what must have been a hellish experience, when *Glorious* went down. He studied the man's face. A tiny nervous tic that Fingal hadn't noticed before caused the left lower eyelid to twitch.

"Aye," said Mahaddie. "Fresh from medical school and straight through ten weeks of navy training learning 'officer-like qualities,' and a smattering of seamanship, but in four weeks you — and they — will be as fine a group of anaesthetists as I can make you. You'll report for duty at eight o'clock on Monday in the number one operating theatre. It's in the cellars for protection against air raids."

Deirdre. He hoped to God he was doing the right thing bringing her here. He reached into his trousers pocket and touched the green silk scarf, the talisman, she'd given him the day he'd left to journey to *Warspite* for the first time.

"What is it, man? You look like you've seen

a ghost. Surely air raids are nothing new to you after being on a bloody great battleship?"

"No, no, it's not that, sir." He paused. His new senior seemed an approachable man, and perhaps here in the informal atmosphere of the anteroom, before matters became very professional on Monday, would be as good a time as any to get some questions answered. He sipped his whisky. "Angus, may I ask you a question?"

"Aye."

"I got engaged, more than a year ago." He rummaged in his inside pocket, produced a creased photo. "My fiancée, Deirdre." He handed it to Mahaddie.

The little man smiled. "Aye. She's one very bonnie lassie, Fingal. May I show her to David?"

Fingal smiled and nodded.

"Quite, quite lovely," David said, and returned the snap.

"I know it's early to be asking, but she's coming over from Ulster very soon and we hope to get married."

Mahaddie frowned. "Have you told the medical officer in charge?"

Fingal nodded. "He said there might be a snag, but he'd see what he could do."

Mahaddie nodded slowly and said in a soft voice, "Aye, just so, just so." He looked straight at Fingal. "Admiral Creaser is a very fair man. He'll keep his word, but —" He pursed his lips. "The navy is the navy. We'll have to see. In my day, och, but Morag Mac-Donald was worth waiting for." He really had an impish smile, Fingal decided.

"Hasn't been a problem for me," David White said, "but then I never was much good with girls. And now with this . . ." His hand went to his scar as he cleared his throat.

Being utterly at sea around members of the fair sex had been a common weakness among men of his generation who'd been to all-boys boarding schools and were innocents abroad by the time they left at eighteen. The practice produced many a "confirmed bachelor."

"I understand, sir — Angus."

"Sir Angus. Oh, aye, just so. I do like that. Sir Angus. But why stop there? How about a full peerage — Lord Strathtattiebogle of Deeside. Now there's a title with a ring." All three laughed. But then the little man's bantering ceased when he said, "As for you, David White, no need to be self-conscious about that scar. It's healed well and time will fade it. And women like their men a little battle-scarred. You earned it honourably and bravely."

"Thank you, sir." David White was looking intently at a spot on the floor.

"Now, Fingal, I don't mean to be pessimistic about your plans. If you can get permission, then I'll put on my kilt and sporran and dance at your wedding."

Fingal could see himself and Deirdre exchanging vows. It was so real.

"And if it does come to pass once the four-week course is over, I'll grant you leave."

For a honeymoon. Better and better. That black nightie she'd mentioned sprang to mind. Fingal finished his whisky. "Time for another?" He'd spoken to Deirdre; she was coming. Already encouraged by Angus, he felt he could start to plan.

"Aye," Mahaddie said. "I'll take a drink with you, laddie."

"Not for me, thanks, Fingal. Two's my limit," David said.

Fingal was about to try to attract the steward's attention when Mahaddie said, "I like fine to see young men happy, Fingal, but before you get carried away, remember what I said. The navy *is* the navy. Don't count your chickens before they're hatched."

But Fingal was busy ordering drinks, didn't want to believe what his superior, who after all was a career naval officer, was saying. Surely to God in 1940 a bunch of regulations formulated during Queen Victoria's reign couldn't stand between him and Deirdre. They couldn't — could they?

7

GREAT BALLS OF FIRE

Kitty had kicked off her shoes and was nursing a sherry after a long day at the hospital. She sat curled up in her favourite chair and started to chuckle — at what, O'Reilly hadn't the faintest idea. "Tell," he said. He was leaning against the mantel of the upstairs lounge. Barry sat in an armchair beside Kitty.

"I was thinking of what you told me a couple of minutes ago about Donal's Bluebird and Mary's Brian Boru," Kitty said. "I'm reading Hemingway — *For Whom the Bell Tolls* — because we're going to Spain soon, and I suddenly got a notion of wee Brian asking, 'But did thee feel the earth move?' It certainly must have for him."

O'Reilly guffawed and choked on his predinner Jameson. When he had wiped his chin with a hanky he said, "That paints a picture that would make a cat laugh."

Barry fondled Lady Macbeth's head. "Would it?" The little cat squirmed comfortably on his lap and stuck out her pink tongue.

"Apparently not," he said, "but it certainly gave us trouble keeping straight faces when Donal told us."

"I'm sure," O'Reilly said, "if Brian is going to be a daddy of little mongrels, Donal will work out some way to salvage matters."

"If he doesn't, you're going to be two pounds out of pocket," Barry said. "We shook on it."

"Least of my worries," O'Reilly said, and frowned.

Kitty's smile faded. "It's Ronald Fitz-patrick, isn't it? I'm guessing you weren't able to persuade him to see sense," she said.

"That man wouldn't know wisdom if it bit his backside," O'Reilly said. "He can be thick as two short planks. I invited him round for tea when we get back from Spain. I can only hope you'll be able to persuade him to — never mind seeing sense. We have to get him to see Charlie, Kitty."

Kitty smiled at him and said, "I'll try."

Lord, he thought, if Kitty had flashed her smile at Pharaoh, his hard heart would have melted and the children of Israel would have been given picnic lunches to help them on their way to the Promised Land.

"I'll be happy to have him round and I will do my best," she said, "but knowing you, Fin-gal, I'm sure that between now and then you'll have come up with a Plan B —"

A phone on the coffee table shrilled its

double ring and all three stared at the device. "Good God," said O'Reilly. "I keep forgetting that thing is there." Recently, at Kitty's urging, and not without bitter complaints about the cost, O'Reilly had had the General Post Office install phone extensions so calls could be taken here and in the doctors' bedrooms.

He picked up the receiver. "O'Reilly." He paused, listening intently. "I see, Mister Beggs. Any bleeding? Labour pains? Right. Keep her in bed. Nothing to eat or drink and someone'll be right out. What? Not at all. You just sit tight." He replaced the receiver and sighed. "That was Davy Beggs. Irene suddenly complained of a violent pain in her belly and she's thrown up twice. No bleeding and labour pains, but someone's got to get out there. She's your midder patient, but I'm on call tonight," said O'Reilly.

"I'll go," Barry said, decanting Lady Macbeth, who looked indignant even before she hit the ground, then stalked off and leapt onto Kitty's lap.

"Fingal, don't forget we still have to finish getting our packing organized for Barcelona on Friday," she said.

"We will, love. Well before Friday, but I've seen Irene several times, and I'm the one on call," O'Reilly said. He and Kitty weren't exactly seeing eye to eye on how much and what they should take.

"I don't think you realise how hot it can get even in September," she said. "You should bring lighter stuff."

He laughed. "I'll be grand," he said, "and now's not the time to start quibbling over what to take."

"Go on, then," she said, "go and see your patient."

"I'm fine seeing her by myself, Fingal, really," Barry said. "I'd like to. I've got the details in my head. Pap test normal at twelve weeks. Everything pretty well normal at her last antenatal visit. Fibroid I found in her last pregnancy was bigger, but asymptomatic. Let's see. Last period, February the twenty-first, due November the twenty-eighth, so she'd be about thirty-two weeks now. And why it should be important I don't know, but I also recall she collects butterflies and moths, and has a brother in Canada in a place called Medicine Hat."

O'Reilly laughed and nodded. "And I remember your first months here and you being baffled because I could remember my patients without needing to look at their records. It just takes practice. You're growing into the job, Barry. I'm proud of you."

"Thank you, Fingal." Barry's smile was broad, but O'Reilly also knew he was getting a look that said: "I'm a full partner now. I don't need you to supervise me."

"I still think I should come," he said, giving

Kitty a furtive glance. "You don't mind, do you, love?"

" 'Course not," she said, smiling. "The packing can wait. And there's a good police programme on TV. Off you trot."

He dropped a quick kiss on her head as he walked past.

"My guess is that she probably has red-degeneration of her fibroid," said Barry, following behind. "But you know as well as I do it could be anything from something wrong with the pregnancy, including the fibroid, to any of the ills of the flesh that can afflict non-pregnant patients and be purely coincidental. But that's what we're here for," Barry said as they reached the hall. "Puzzling things out."

"Aye," said O'Reilly, turning toward the kitchen. "And seeing I'm going to be away for a week it's a good thing you'll know all about her. Now," he said, crossing the room and opening the back door, "they live out near Maggie Houston's old cottage by the seafront on the way to Bangor . . . Back into your kennel, sir."

Arthur Guinness, who had come bounding down the garden, stopped wagging his tail and retreated into his doghouse. By the look in his brown eyes and the way his head drooped O'Reilly knew the big dog was woe-struck, but it couldn't be helped. "You've had your walk today and it's still only September, lummox. We'll start bringing you into the kitchen for the night when the weather turns."

Barry smiled and said, "From what I've seen since I've been here, once you do start, he spends more time in front of the fire upstairs than in the kitchen."

"Och," said O'Reilly, opening the back gate. "He's family." After all, O'Reilly was only talking to Barry, who had never lifted a shotgun. If the real shooting fraternity knew that O'Reilly treated his gundog like a person they'd think the good doctor had gone astray in the head. Country dogs were working animals, not pampered pets.

"Shall we take Brunhilde?" said Barry, heading for his little green Volkswagen beetle.

"In cases of severe pain," O'Reilly said, "I always want to get there as quickly as possible, so we'll take my Rover." He wondered why Barry's eyes suddenly uplifted to the heavens. Now the boy was grimacing and seemed to be crossing his fingers. Silly lad. No one knew the roads of County Down like Fingal Flahertie O'Reilly and, cyclists notwithstanding, nobody could navigate the winding narrow ways more skilfully.

"Out." O'Reilly didn't even wait for the big Rover to stop shuddering on its springs after slamming to a halt. He grabbed his bag and walked the last few paces across a gravel path to the Beggses' bungalow.

Past the building and across Belfast Lough,

the sun's burnished disk was starting to slide behind the blue Antrim Hills and pinks, yellows, and scarlet dyed the undersides of low clouds. Beneath them the lough was at peace and yet, as often happened near the sea even on a night as tranquil as this, O'Reilly found himself imagining his old *Warspite* in the fury of an Atlantic gale.

As Barry came and stood at his shoulder, O'Reilly banished the image, pushed a ceramic doorbell, heard a distant *ding-dong,* and waited until the door was opened by Davy Beggs, a short man in a grey V-necked pullover, collarless shirt, moleskin trousers, and tartan carpet slippers.

"Thanks for coming out," he said, then noticing Barry, "is it bad enough that it's going to take two of youse?"

She was Barry's patient. O'Reilly waited.

"Not at all, Mister Beggs," Barry said. "I've been looking after Irene's pregnancy and you know I delivered your last, wee Vera. Doctor O'Reilly came out to keep me company, that's all."

"And," Barry really didn't need any moral support, but the next statement wouldn't hurt, O'Reilly thought, "Doctor Laverty has had an extra year of training in midwifery at the Waveney Hospital."

"Right enough? So I hear."

O'Reilly nodded. "Now perhaps we might see the patient?"

"Aye, certainly. Come on, on in. She's on the bed, so she is." He stepped aside to let them in, closed the door, and led them along a hall. In what must be a lounge to the right, a TV blared. O'Reilly recognised the Ulster tones of a character, Bert Lynch, played by James Ellis from Belfast in a popular series, *Z-Cars*, the police programme Kitty was probably watching back at Number One.

"In thonder, Doctors," Mister Beggs said, opening a door and standing aside.

The room was well lit, had the inevitable female perfumes of powder and face cream, but over them hung the acrid smell of vomit. Beside a ceramic baking bowl on the bedside table stood a brilliant blue butterfly mounted and behind glass in a glossy black frame.

"Here's your doctors, love," Mister Beggs said. "I'll leave youse all in peace."

O'Reilly hung back and let Barry approach the bed.

"Hello, Irene," he said. "Not feeling so hot?"

The fair-haired young woman lying on the bed shook her head and moaned softly.

O'Reilly could see a faint sheen on her forehead, her eyes were listless, and her lips were caked. A tear track was drying on her left cheek.

Barry hitched himself onto the side of the bed. He took her pulse while saying, "Tell me what happened."

"We'd just finished our tea — Davy got us a nice bit of haddock from your man Hall Campbell . . ."

O'Reilly well remembered Irene Beggs. She could be as loquacious as Cissie Sloan. He crossed his arms and waited to see how Barry might handle the torrent of words.

". . . him that runs the boat with Jimmy Scott, and —" She screwed up her face and took a series of deep breaths before saying, "Then I took this pain right here." She pointed to the front of her distended belly and clutched it with both hands. "Next thing I knew I'd to run til the jakes, for I'd to boke in the toilet bowl. Twice. That's when Davy phoned youse."

So far the symptoms fitted with their original suspicions, although sudden bleeding behind the placenta, called *abruptio placentae* or accidental haemorrhage, a condition potentially lethal to mother and child, could present that way. Barry would have to make sure it wasn't the case.

"And did the pain move anywhere else?" Barry said. "Or does it come in regular waves like labour pains?"

"I'm not in labour," she said. "I know what that's like . . . at least them pains give you a rest."

Although something going wrong with a fibroid could precipitate the premature onset

133

of contractions, it didn't seem to have done so here.

"And since it come on it's not moved an inch, so it's not. I wish it would go away."

Just about any other non-pregnancy-related condition would hurt elsewhere. Appendicitis in the right lower belly, twisting or rupture of an ovarian cyst in one side or the other, kidney troubles high under the ribs at the back, serious illnesses of the bowel all over the abdomen and usually crampy.

"It's dead chronic, so it is." She whimpered. "Could youse maybe give me something for the pain, like?"

"Perhaps when I've finished examining you," Barry said. "Now, have you felt cold? Taken the shivers?"

"No," she said, "but I feel hot and sweaty."

Barry looked at O'Reilly. "She has a temperature and her pulse is up. Have you a sphygmo in your bag?"

"Aye." O'Reilly fished out the blood pressure measuring device.

Barry asked, "Have you noticed any bleeding down below?"

"Not a drop. Just this God-awful pain." She looked at Barry and touched his sleeve. "Do you think my baby's all right, Doctor?"

"Pretty sure. I'll know for sure when I've finished." Barry started to take Irene's blood pressure. "Let's see how your blood pressure is."

No bleeding. Labour was often preceded by some loss of blood, the so-called show, and often some blood was lost in cases of *abruptio,* but in them the real damage was caused by the blood trapped behind the placenta, and the blood didn't always escape to the outside world. *Abruptio* couldn't be excluded yet.

In moments Barry was able to remove his stethoscope and say, "One twenty over eighty. Perfectly normal. Same as it was at your last antenatal visit."

That made *abruptio placenta* much more unlikely. It was almost always accompanied by signs of shock, which included a rapid pulse and low blood pressure.

"That's a good sign, then, Doctor?"

"It is," said Barry. "Now, let's have a look." As she undid her skirt's waistband, Barry was rapidly looking under one of her eyelids to get a rough appreciation of her haemoglobin level, sniffing her breath. "Put out your tongue." He nodded and said, "Bit dirty."

O'Reilly saw her stiffen and frown.

Barry smiled at Irene. "And I'm not calling you dirty, Irene. What I think ails you makes your tongue look furry."

"Oh," she said, and visibly relaxed.

Good lad, O'Reilly thought. Don't neglect the patient's feelings.

"Can you pull up your blouse, please?"

Barry stood up and faced her.

O'Reilly couldn't quite see what was going on, but he knew that Barry would first feel the abdominal muscles. In cases of *abruptio,* they would be rigid.

"Tummy's nice and soft," Barry said, and O'Reilly relaxed. It wasn't what he had been worried about. He rummaged in his bag and produced a foetal stethoscope. "You'll need this." He handed it to Barry and waited. Eventually Barry finished, turned to O'Reilly, grinned, and winked. "No sign of abruption," he said, and by his wink, O'Reilly knew Barry was relieved too. "And the pain is localised to the fibroid." He turned back to Irene and said, "All finished, and now I know for certain your wee one's fine."

Good lad. It was the first and foremost worry of every unwell pregnant woman.

"Right size, right place, and the wee heart's rattling away."

"That's a quare relief," she said.

"You're not quite well, but it's not something to worry about, and I'm going to explain what's wrong. Do you want us to get Davy in to listen?"

"Not at all," she said. "Men only know how til make babies." For a moment a smile broke through her constant grimace. "My Davy's dead on at that, so he is."

O'Reilly smiled.

"There's only one problem, and it's sore I know, but probably not serious. There's a bump on the front of your womb. It's called a fibroid."

"A fireball? That's ferocious. My cousin Biddy, her what lives in Clougher, had fireballs, and she needed one of them 'ectomies, you know. I'm not sure what kind. Will I need one?"

"No. I promise. And in case you're worried, it's not cancer."

"That's all right then."

"You've had the fibroid for some time. Your womb is a big muscle, you see, and sometimes a part of it starts growing into a big bump."

"Like an oak apple on an oak tree?"

"Exactly, although oak galls are caused by a kind of wasp. No one knows what causes fibroids, but sometimes, particularly when a woman is pregnant, the fibroid outgrows its blood supply and dies. We call that condition red degeneration. But it's only the bump that's dying. Unfortunately, in doing so it causes pain."

"Pain? You can say that again, sir." She clutched her tummy.

"Can I have a quarter of morphine, please, Doctor O'Reilly?"

"Aye." O'Reilly prepared the injection.

"Usually with good nursing, a light diet, and regular painkillers, women get better in no more than ten days, but I'm afraid we're going to have to admit you to the Royal Maternity."

"But can't I stay —"

Barry shook his head. "We simply don't have the nurses available for round-the-clock care at home, Irene."

"If you say so, sir. And I want that injection now. Will youse explain til Davy? He'll have for til get my other cousin who lives in the Kinnegar til take care of wee Bert and Vera."

The Kinnegar. O'Reilly thought of Ronald, picturing him changing the dressings on his burnt hands, then gave Barry a prepared hypodermic and a cotton wool ball soaked in methylated spirits. The fumes stung his nose.

"All right, Irene. I'll give you your jag now, then we'll explain to Davy and arrange for you to go to hospital."

She yelped once as the needle went home.

"Right, Doctor O'Reilly," Barry said as they left the bedroom to make the arrangements, "I think we're just about done here and then we'll head for home, and please remember we are not going to be rushing to a fire, nor are we likely to be pursued by wolves. No need to break the sound barrier."

"Huh," said O'Reilly. "I have to compliment you, Barry, on the way you handled the case."

"Thank you."

"But I must say to you that my driving is a thing of beauty, and we *are* in a rush. I haven't finished my preprandial Jameson yet."

He wondered why Barry's shoulders sagged.

138

■ ■ ■ ■

From where he stood at the sideboard O'Reilly could see that the lad looked pale. Yet as far as O'Reilly was concerned the Rover hadn't come within a beagle's gowl of that cyclist they'd encountered on the Bangor to Belfast Road, and they'd got back from the Beggses' in jig time.

"Jameson," Barry said.

"Welcome home," Kitty said. "Now shush. I'm listening. It'll be over in a minute."

The big room was filled with the splendour of the fourth movement of Beethoven's Fifth Symphony in C minor. When O'Reilly looked at a seated Kitty and inclined his head to the drinks decanters, she shook hers. He busied himself pouring Barry's whiskey.

The symphony ended in a series of chords and a final enormous *Pom pom.* Kitty rose and switched off the radio. "BBC Third Programme," she said. "They do some wonderful music shows."

O'Reilly handed Barry his glass. "I'll bet you didn't know the fellah who invented radio transmission and the whiskey you are holding had a close connection."

"I did not," said Barry, taking what looked like a restorative gulp.

"Guglielmo Marconi's da married an Irish girl," O'Reilly said, and smiled at Kitty.

"Sensible chap. She was Annie Jameson, granddaughter of John Jameson, who owned this distillery." He raised his own glass. "And by way of an encore, old Guglielmo's granny was Margaret Haig of the Scotch whisky—making family."

"Good Lord. I suppose that would have made him a spirited kind of man?" Barry said. "Whisky was in his blood, so to speak."

Kitty laughed and said, "That was terrible, young Laverty." She looked at O'Reilly. "More to the point, how's Irene?"

"On her way to the Royal," O'Reilly said. "Barry did a great job, making a spot-on diagnosis, and allaying her concerns." He inclined his head to Barry, who took up the story.

"We knew she had a fibroid. It's degenerating, but with any luck will resolve by itself. She should be fine, but she'll need hospital care for a few days."

"I'll pop in and see her if you'd like," Kitty said. "Royal Maternity's no distance from my ward."

"The very place where that pig-headed bollix Fitzpatrick should be getting his neuropathy sorted out."

"If I can't persuade him," Kitty said, "I may have stumbled on another way to try to get him to see sense."

"Oh?" said Barry.

"It was on *Z-Cars*. The police were trying

to get a villain to confess. Bert Lynch and Inspector Barlow cooked up a scheme."

"Go on," said O'Reilly.

"Bert went at the criminal like a Gestapo interrogator, but then Barlow took over and was all sweetness and light — and it worked. The hard man broke down and confessed."

"Probably won't need to go as far as that," he said as he wandered over to the window and looked out at the steeple of the church opposite, limned dark against the soft velvet of an Ulster sky. "I'm sure," he said as he closed the curtains and again pictured Ronald's bandaged hands, "everything will all turn out fine."

8

JOURNEYS END
IN LOVERS MEETING

The telegram had come yesterday. ARRIVING
FAREHAM MONDAY 12:17. Deirdre was on
her way, and Angus Mahaddie, bless him, had
agreed to let Fingal leave early this afternoon.
David White had even offered the loan of his
1933 Austin Seven "Ruby" motorcar, England's answer to Henry Ford's Model T,
provided Fingal had petrol ration coupons.
He'd made damn sure he did.

Deirdre was coming. Today. He still had
the telegram in his pocket, and he touched it
now to assure himself that it was true.

"Good morning, gentlemen," Surgeon
Captain Angus Mahaddie said from where he
sat on a brass operating stool. He glanced at
his watch. "One minute to eight. You are all
on time, I am pleased to say, even you,
Lieutenant O'Reilly."

David was grinning at him and giving him
a discreet thumbs-up. Fingal could feel the
colour rise in his face. Mahaddie knew better
than anyone how difficult it was going to be

to put thoughts of Deirdre aside and pay attention to this morning's introductory session.

Fingal, David, and four new RNVR surgeon sub-lieutenants stood at attention in a semicircle around their chief in one of Haslar's underground operating theatres.

"Please, all stand easy."

Feet clattered on the tiled floor and the noise echoed from the walls and ceiling of a large, white-painted, barrel-vaulted room. Fingal had vaguely noticed the operating tables and instrument trolleys. What registered most sharply was the oppressive feeling of the place, despite the bright lighting and the smells of disinfectant and anaesthetic vapours.

"Welcome to the bowels of Haslar," Mahaddie said. "We operate down here in the cellars so we are protected during air raids."

Just like the way the medical staff was protected deep in the heart of *Warspite* when the ship was at action stations.

"The wards, many named for famous admirals, are on the ground floor above us, as you will discover when you are doing your rounds. There are two hundred and fifty surgical beds and two hundred and fifty medical beds served by twenty-four permanent medical staff, plus, of course, trainees. As you can see, the staff here has been busy getting ready for today's patients."

Young women whom Fingal recognised from their uniforms as either members of the Volunteer Aid Detachment (VAD) or the Queen Alexandra's Royal Naval Nursing Service sisters (QARNNS) went quietly about their duties.

"We leave the medical patients who don't need operations to the physicians. Our job — surgically — is to deal with both those conditions that have nothing to do with war injuries, just like a peacetime hospital, and with casualties." He sighed. "And we're getting a lot more of those since the air raids started. Originally we were only for navy personnel, but, eh, since Dunkirk we now take soldiers, airmen, civilians, and we treat Germans. It is rumoured that some less-than-charitable sick berth attendants had been telling POWs that we'd not be wasting anaesthetics on them." There was steel in his voice. "Eh, I put a stop to that. A full stop."

Despite the man's apparent affability, Fingal realized Angus Mahaddie was not one to be crossed.

"You six have been selected to become better-trained anaesthetists, and I am your chief teacher. Your four-week course will be intense and a simplified form of the one offered in the Nuffield Department of Anaesthesia at Oxford University. It was established in 1937 as the first of its kind in the United Kingdom and was where I was trained by

144

Professor Robert Macintosh.

"Today I will be briefing you about what to expect, then you will be detailed for individual apprenticeships to one of the surgeon commanders and lieutenant-commanders on the permanent anaesthetic staff. The list is on that notice board." He pointed to one wall. "You, O'Reilly, because you'll be staying on for another two months of training, will work with me."

"Aye aye, sir." Fingal grinned. He reckoned he'd got the plum assignment.

Mahaddie smiled, swung his legs back and forth, and then pointed between them. "This stool was here in 1910 when King George V visited the place, but today I'm not going to weary you with Haslar's history. I'm here to tell you what to expect.

"You will learn, in short order, the medications we use to prepare patients for anaesthesia, 'premedication,' how to start the anaesthetic or 'induce anaesthesia,' with intravenous sodium pentothal, a barbiturate first introduced in 1935 . . ." He pulled a contraption on wheels round in front of him. ". . . and the use of the Boyle's apparatus."

Fingal saw the cylinders, each colour-coded for the gas it contained, flow meters, knurled wheels, corrugated rubber tubes. He remembered a patient the ether anaesthetic had nearly suffocated on *Warspite* and how Leading Sick Berth Attendant Ronnie Barker had used oxygen from a Boyle's machine to revive the man.

"You'll learn how to use it, what gasses work best, and how to put a tube into the patient's trachea — 'intubation' — and how to connect it to the machine. I imagine most of you are reasonably happy with the open Schimmelbusch mask" — he reached behind him and lifted one from a trolley — "and ether or chloroform. Still tried and true, but we'll hone your skills."

Fingal nodded. It was the only technique with which he was reasonably comfortable.

He slipped off the stool and stretched. "So," he said, "if there aren't any questions?" He paused but no one spoke. "Right. That's enough of a lecture today. O'Reilly?"

"Sir."

"Come with me. The rest of you, your duties are on the list." He began to walk away and Fingal hurried to follow after. "This morning," Mahaddie said, "we'll be working with Surgeon Commander Fraser. It's a routine list; couple of gallbladders, sailors are forever rupturing themselves so we've a hernia to do, and a set of varicose veins."

They left the operating room, walked along a corridor, and began to climb a staircase. "I want to see the patients and arrange for their premedications. Any ideas about what I might be using?"

"I read your article in the *Journal of the*

Royal Naval Medical Service, sir," Fingal said. "You prefer to give one-third of a grain of omnopon and one-seventy-fifth of a grain of atropine three quarters of an hour before anaesthesia."

"Just so, and do you understand about how the drugs of the premed work?"

"The omnopon's an opium derivative. It calms the patient, and the atropine dries up their normal secretions so they are unlikely to inhale saliva and mucus."

"I see you've done your homework, laddie. Don't suppose you'd be looking for some time off for good behaviour?" Mahaddie said. There was mischief in his deep-set eyes. "And I'll do my best to get you some. You're going early today."

Fingal grinned, but his grin faded when Mahaddie said, "But we also have to remember the requirements of the service. I may not be able to get you free again until the weekend."

"I understand, sir." Fingal knew he must look crestfallen and tried to compose his features.

Mahaddie smiled as they emerged into the open air. "Dinnae fash yourself —"

"I'm sorry, sir?"

The little Highland man chuckled. "I mean, don't worry. I'll let you go in good enough time to collect your Deirdre. Any word from the admiral yet about your wedding prospects? I don't have any influence with him, you know."

Fingal shook his head. "I understand, sir."

"Aye, just so." Mahaddie smiled. "But we can hope, can't we?" He held open a door. "Here we are," he said. "This is the Admiral Collingwood Ward. Let's go and see the victims."

"The Gosport train will be delayed for half an hour due to repair work on the tracks."

"Blue, blistering, blasted, blazes." Fingal had barely been able to make out the distorted words through the loudspeaker system. He didn't want to think about what was being repaired and why. Deirdre was not going anywhere near London on her trip from Liverpool, but he knew that bomb damage on a line was always a possibility.

He'd tried to be philosophical. He'd been waiting for months to see her, had parked David's car outside the railway station a good fifteen minutes before the train was due in the hope that if he was early the train might be too. What difference did another thirty minutes really make? He looked at his watch again, knowing full well that he would not relax until Deirdre was safe in his arms.

The early-autumn sun was shining, although there was no heat in it today, and the smell of fresh hay was blowing in on a stiff wind from a newly mown meadow. And

148

somewhere in a hedge bordering the railway line, a songbird was making sweet music. Yet the extra wait on the deserted platform seemed like an eternity.

At last a powerful locomotive appeared round a bend. The smoke from its funnel and the steam from its screeching whistle announced the train's arrival. Both were blown away by a fresh wind off the Solent. Wheezing, clanking, and shuddering, the engine passed where Fingal stood. Sparks flew from the brake shoes and finally the long train stopped. He knew that most of the carriages would be empty on their way to pick up more recovering patients from Haslar for transfer to other hospitals inland, away from potential air raids.

Only one door opened and closed and he started to trot. The guard was waving his green flag and blowing his whistle, and with a toot, a *chuff-chuff* of steam, and a clanking of the driving rods, the locomotive began to draw away on to Gosport, the end of the line. As it did, he saw a female figure, suitcase in one hand, the other clasping a hat to her head.

He bounded forward. It was her. He roared, "Deirdre. Darling."

"Fingal. Fingal." The wind whipped away her hat as he enfolded her, lifting her off her feet as he crushed her to him, covered her mouth with his own, and tasted the warmth of her, the sweetness of her, of Deirdre. Of his girl.

Tears ran down her smiling face as finally she laughed and said, "Fingal, you idiot. Put me down."

"Sorry," he said, "but I can't believe you're here," and before she could protest he said, "I love you," and kissed her again. He heard her drop her suitcase. The kiss broke, he lowered her gently to the ground, then bent to pick up her suitcase. "Your hat," he said.

"Never mind the silly thing, darling," she said. "It's in Wiltshire by now, and you're here." She stood on tiptoes, flung her arms around his neck, kissed him, and then said, "Fingal, I've missed you so much. And I do love you, so." She kissed him again. "It's taken a while to get here —"

"And you must be starving," he said, grabbing her hand. "Come on." He had her to himself and he wasn't going to share her with Marjorie Wilcoxson. Not yet. Besides, he thought, she'll need a little time before she meets Marge, who, for all her kindness, could be a formidable woman. He'd been told of just the place for lunch. A pub with private booths was less than a five-minute drive away.

He hurried her into the station where the stationmaster, resplendent in a sleeved waistcoat with gilt buttons and a peaked cap, took her ticket. "Welcome to Fareham, Madam. I hope you have a pleasant —"

"Thank you," Fingal said, then hustled Deirdre out to David's car, chucked her suitcase in the back, helped her in, and rushed round to the driver's side. He'd barely closed the door behind him when he'd leant over and kissed her again. "Darling. Darling. Darling."

She smiled at him, that "Slow down, you great Labrador puppy" smile, and said, "I do love you so much, Fingal, but —"

"But you've been on ferries and railway trains forever and would kill for a decent cup of tea?"

"You're a mind reader, and a considerate one at that," she said. "And it's one of the reasons I love you." She patted his thigh, sending electric shocks everywhere. If she'd let him, he'd take her now in this cramped little car.

He looked at her and saw his beautiful girl. But she did look as if she could use a fortifying cup of tea, not a quick tumble in the back of an Austin Seven, and he berated himself for being a randy fool. "Right," he said. "Right. I'll have you to a pub in no time." He started the car and drove off, narrowly missing a cyclist.

"I can't believe I'm here with you." Deirdre stared at him. "You've lost weight." He heard her concern. "You've not been sick, have you?"

"Only lovesick," he said, "and the grub on

the troopship left a certain amount to be desired." Desired. He managed a glance at her. He knew what he wanted more than life itself.

"We're here," he said, driving across a wide courtyard and braking beside a clematis-covered wall, a few late-season flowers the size of tea plates dotting its thicket of vines. He trotted round, opened her door, helped her down, and took her hand.

A few paces brought Fingal into a low-ceilinged bar room redolent of tobacco smoke and beer. He led her down two carpeted steps toward a long bar where two men who must have been locals, one wearing a farm-labourer's smock, sat nursing dimpled pint glasses and playing dominoes. They were keeping score on a cribbage board. A dart-board was studded with darts on a far wall and he tried to remember which ancient English king had decreed that men should play darts on Sundays in lieu of archery practice. The longbowmen had been England's battle winners, at Crecy and Agincourt.

"Afternoon, Lieutenant." The barman who, Fingal guessed, just like Mister Dunleavy back in Ballybucklebo, was probably mine host too, stood behind his counter polishing a glass. The man had a face pocked with acne scars and sported an Old Bill moustache.

"We wondered if we could get a cup of tea

for the lady, and perhaps lunch?"

The man turned and shouted through a hatch behind him, "Pot of tea, please, Mabel." He grinned at Fingal then said, "Only be a tick." He pointed at a chalk-lettered blackboard. " 'Fraid the menu's a bit restricted, sir, but it's on the board. You're only allowed to spend five bob each on each meal." He sighed then said, "Blooming rationing."

"Darling?" Fingal said.

"Let's order later," she said. "I'm not very hungry." She squeezed his hand. "I'm too excited, and a bit . . ." She covered her mouth with one kid-gloved hand.

"Are those real Melton Mowbray pies? From Leicestershire?" Fingal asked.

"That they are, sir." There was pride in the man's voice.

"Pint of bitter for now," Fingal said, and remembered a promise made in *Warspite*'s anteroom, to "have a pie" for Richard Wilcoxson.

"Would you like to have a seat in a booth, sir, and I'll see to it?" The barman took hold of a beer pump handle and started pulling Fingal's pint. "We're a tied house, sir."

Fingal understood the expression. Tied houses were controlled by breweries and had to sell that brewery's beer. Free houses could sell what they liked.

"I hope you like watered Worthington's. The government makes the breweries dilute the beer because of the war, and I have to close the bar from three to six thirty."

"Fine," Fingal said. As long as the beer was wet and bitter he didn't care. His Deirdre was here and that was what mattered. Still holding her hand, he led her to a booth. It was not as ornate as the ones he remembered in Belfast's Crown Liquor Saloon, but it was in a private nook and overlooked the court-yard.

She sighed. "Thank you, Fingal. You don't know how lovely it is to sit on something that's not moving. I'm afraid I didn't get much sleep last night. The bunk was damp and lumpy, and the cabin pitched and tossed all night and stank of fuel oil. But I'm here."

He'd made Channel crossings from Larne to Stranraer and was familiar with British wartime rail travel too, in crowded compartments or standing in the corridor, but he said, "No. But I do know how lovely it is to sit down," he took a seat opposite, "and stare at the most beautiful girl in all the world." The wind on the platform had tossed her hair, she had dark circles under her eyes, and she wore virtually no makeup, but she *was* the most beautiful girl. *His* most beautiful girl.

She smiled at him. "You're sweet." She held up a hand to forestall any more protestations of love and said, "Now, before I forget, Ma sends her love. She asked me to tell you that she and Bridgit are both very well and that Ma's busy as a bee raising money for a second Spitfire. Apparently the RAF bent the last one."

Fingal laughed in spite of himself, feeling for the fighter pilots, the Brylcreem Boys, who had "bent" a large number of their aircraft — and themselves — defending the home island after the fall of France in June.

"And Lars is collecting scrap aluminium. He came and saw me off in Belfast." She opened her raincoat and pointed at a wilted purple flower in the buttonhole of her suit jacket. "He gave me this orchid." She took a deep breath. "They're both sorry, but travel restrictions —" She clearly was yawning now behind her hand. "— won't let them come to our wedding. I don't even know what day —"

"Your tea, madam." A heavyset woman wearing a floral pinafore over her dress set a tray on the table. "And your pint, sir."

"Thank you," Fingal said, and his gratitude wasn't only for the drinks. Deirdre had been stopped from asking about their wedding date. He would tell her about the uncertainty, but not yet. He became aware of a commotion outside and looked through the window. "Look at that," he said, thankful for yet another distraction.

Three columns of older men in civilian dress, each with a weapon sloped over his left shoulder, were marching in step into the courtyard. The weapons ranged from double-barrelled shotguns to pitchforks to scythes, and Fingal was certain he saw one flintlock, and, good God, a blunderbuss. A man in First World War uniform, his trousered calves wrapped in puttees, not modern gaiters, marched to one side. The three stripes of a sergeant were sewn on the upper sleeves of his khaki tunic and good conduct stripes adorned the lower. He gripped his pace stick under his arm.

"Lef' right, lef' right. Companeeeeeee . . . Wait for it. On my order, company will halt — Halt."

"Golly," Fingal said without looking at Deirdre, "the Home Guard out training."

The men halted, not with the precision of a Guards regiment, but pretty much together. Their sergeant marched to halfway down one side of the column. "Company will turn to the right. Riiiiight. Turn."

To a man they turned to face him.

"Company will dismiss. Diiiiis — miss."

Fingal shook his head and smiled. He knew he shouldn't laugh. Out there were brave old men, many probably survivors of the trenches, who had volunteered to be their country's last line of defence if the Germans did invade. By the way that, to a man, they were heading to the pub's door, he reckoned they had other things on their minds right now, and if he and Deirdre wanted to eat they'd better order. He looked at her, and bless her, she was leaning against the side of the booth, eyes closed, mouth open, breathing in small gasps and making a whiffling noise.

He shook his head. Typical of both of them. He'd been so sure he knew what she wanted, what was best for her — a stop at a pub for a restorative cup of tea before she met Marjorie. Rubbish. In reality, he'd just wanted her to himself for a while. And Deirdre had been too much of a lady to disagree, always willing to put her needs after his. He loved her willingness, her selflessness — and at this moment despised his own selfishness. He should have known what someone who'd travelled here for thirty-six hours from Belfast needed. A bath and a few hours of sleep.

He polished off his pint in two gulps, stood, bent, and kissed her forehead.

She stirred. Her eyes opened. She blinked then said, "I'm sorry. I must have nodded off." She sat up straighter. He knew her smile was forced and that she was probably worrying he hadn't had his lunch. "We really must order."

"No," he said. "You must finish your tea. I'll settle up and then I'm taking you to Marge's for a bath and a sleep. And we're invited for dinner tonight."

She yawned and this time made no effort to cover her mouth. "You are a pet, Fingal," she said. "So thoughtful. It's why I love you so much."

And inside him his heart swelled and nearly burst out in a flood of happy tears. He cleared his throat and said as he headed for the bar, "I'll be back in a jiffy, darling. Don't go away." Don't ever go away.

9
To Remember What Is Past

"I think," said O'Reilly, craning to look to the top of an ornate Corinthian column, "your man Christopher Columbus there is facing the Americas, all right." Pointing west, with his raised right arm extended toward the Mediterranean, stood the statue of a determined-looking fellow in fifteenth-century robes.

Kitty was already consulting the guidebook and had shown only a passing interest in the popular Barcelona landmark. "It's less than a mile to the Picasso Museum from here. We head along here, the Passeig de Colom," she said, beginning to walk. "We'll turn left onto the Via Laietana, right at the Carrer de la Princesa, and right onto the Carrer de Montcada." She took his hand and squeezed it. "I'm really looking forward to seeing the paintings. I've always wanted to."

Her pronunciation sounded flawless to his ear. He wasn't surprised. She'd worked at a small orphanage in Tenerife just before and in the early part of the war with only a fellow nurse her sole English-speaking colleague. But he could also hear nervousness in Kitty's voice that hadn't been there yesterday.

"I remember seeing a print of Picasso's *Guernica* before the war. Powerful, very powerful." He was eager to keep her chatting. She'd been her usual self since they'd arrived, and for the first two days it had been a second honeymoon for them. But since rising this morning there'd been this brittleness to her. Still, they'd enjoyed stopping at a small tapas bar for a late lunch on La Rambla, Barcelona's wide, pedestrian-only street.

This excursion to the museum would be a good diversion before they met this woman, this Consuela Rivera y Navarro, née Garcia y Rivera, who was the closest thing Kitty had ever had to a child. "I will go wherever you lead me, love," he said, taking off his sports jacket and tie, and opening the neck of his shirt. The midafternoon sun here in Barcelona was a damn sight hotter than it would be, if it were shining at all, in Ballybucklebo.

This was what they had come to Barcelona to do — to meet the daughter of the man Kitty had loved and lost when she'd had to return to Ireland in 1941.

"The original's in the Museo Reina Sofia in Madrid," she said, taking a deep breath and frowning.

Damn it, the mere mention of Madrid,

where Mañuel Garcia y Rivera had been born and had died four months ago, must have jogged a train of memories that she probably didn't want to face just yet. There would be time enough for that when she met Consuela. Perhaps he could distract Kitty by asking her a question about the artist.

"Pablo Picasso rolls off the tongue easily enough, but do you know his full name?"

"As a matter of fact," she said, "I do. It's Pablo Diego José Francisco de Paula —"

"Whoa," he said, laughing. "Enough."

"But there's more, I just can't remember them," she said, her smile turning into laughter. "I think his parents were really hedging their bets naming him after all those relatives and saints."

He was relieved to see that his laughter had brought on hers. "And I thought Fingal Flahertie O'Reilly was a mouthful."

"Eeejit," she said, "but thank you." She squeezed his hand and her eyes smiled at him as if to say, I know what you're trying to do, Fingal, and I'm grateful. "We'll get through this — together."

He squeezed her hand in return and they made their first left turn, and although they were now walking away from the harbour, gulls wheeled overhead, mewing and screeching, relatives of the same birds that would have flown in the wakes of Columbus's *Niña, Pinta,* and *Santa Maria.* The same species had been the feathered forebears of the scavengers that followed fishing boats off Ireland, and in the war, battleships off Alexandria on this same Mediterranean Sea. The last thought brought up his own string of memories, and he paused to look out to sea before putting a protective arm around Kitty's shoulders and continuing along the Via Laietana.

Three hours later they had made their way from the museum along a maze of narrow, cobbled lanes to a small waterside café, El Crajeco Loco, The Crazy Crab. The restaurant was on the ground floor in a row of four- and five-storey buildings with stucco fronts in pastel shades of blue and orange. Pink-framed bay windows alternated with wrought-iron-railinged balconies. Two women called to each other across a gap between first-floor balconies. O'Reilly wondered if they were speaking Catalan, but their high-pitched tones reminded him more of the bickering gulls.

He found a table on the terrace under an awning, immediately behind a low railing with a view over a broad, palm-tree-lined path where people strolled. The promenade separated the restaurant from a marina. The shiny white yachts of the wealthy were crammed side by side, masts jostling for space and reaching skyward. Columbus's Pillar was visible in the middle distance.

A white-aproned waiter, black hair oiled and neatly parted, white towel over one arm, stood patiently beside their table.

"Beer, Fingal?" Kitty asked.

"Please." Although the museum had been cool, the walk here had been in dappled sunlight through airless alleys and he was hot and not a little sweaty.

"Una cerveza grande, una copa de vino blanco, y tres menús, por favor."

"Sí, señora." The waiter left.

"Once she gets here, I'll let Consuela handle the Spanish," said Kitty, "but for now mine's good enough to get by." She smiled at him. "I'm afraid I didn't know how to say on your behalf, 'My tongue's hanging out for a jar, so it is,' but I guessed by the look on your face it was how you were feeling."

"And you were right," he said, and laughed.

Kitty was sitting so she could watch pedestrians approach the café, and her eyes were intent on the passing parade.

"Did you enjoy the exhibition?" He wanted to keep her talking, in part to ease his own discomfort. How was he going to feel meeting the daughter of a man Kitty had once loved so deeply?

"Marvellous," she said. "We've all got so captivated by his modern works we've forgotten what a superb traditional craftsman Picasso was in his early years."

"I really like his *Man with Beret,*" O'Reilly

said, "and *Ciència i Caritat* with the doctor taking the sick woman's pulse is exactly how I have imagined my nineteenth-century predecessors at work. But the *Portrait of James Sabartés with Hat and Ruff*?" He shrugged and held out his hands, palms up. "I'm no connoisseur but it looked to me like a picture of James Joyce after a very long night at Davy Byrnes pub."

"Philistine," she said, but her smile was warm. "I think what Picasso was trying to capture —"

The waiter appeared, setting a large, frosted glass of pale beer in front of O'Reilly and a glass of white wine for Kitty. *"Los menús."* He handed O'Reilly three cardboard folders.

"Muy agradecido. Muchas gracias," Kitty said.

"De nada." He smiled and left.

"Cheers," O'Reilly said, raising his glass and drinking. The beer was chilled and pleasantly bitter. He set the menus on the table and opened one. "I'll need help with these," he said.

But Kitty was rising and he automatically followed suit. A young woman stood outside the railings, smiling broadly and saying, *"Buenos tardes, Tia Kitty. Bienvenidos a Barcelona."*

"Tia Kitty." Aunt Kitty. When she'd first told him what Consuela had called her as a little girl, O'Reilly had felt insecure and jealous. But now it seemed natural.

"Consuela," Kitty said, leaning over the balustrade and holding the young woman by both shoulders. "Consuela. Let me look at you."

O'Reilly looked too. She seemed younger than her thirty-two years. Long dark hair hung to the small of her back. Her face was tanned and her ebony eyes were slightly slanted above high cheekbones, full lips. A short-sleeved white blouse was tucked inside a narrow leather belt supporting a mid-thigh denim skirt. Very chic, he thought.

"You're beautiful," Kitty said, "and you still have your father's eyes . . ."

He listened but heard no trace of regret in Kitty's voice.

"But then you always were a pretty child."

Consuela lowered her head then said, "Thank you, and you haven't changed either from what I remember." Her English, though accented, seemed fluent.

"Rubbish," Kitty said, and laughed. "Now come around and meet Fingal, my husband."

As Consuela walked to a gate in the railing, Kitty said to him, "Oh, Fingal, she is quite, quite lovely." Now there was the slightest catch. "She was seven the last time I saw her, all spindly arms and legs. Hair in bunches. I used to brush it for her and sing to her."

And the longing he heard, was it for lost love, lost youth, or for the children of her own Kitty had never borne and never would?

"Here," Kitty said as O'Reilly pulled out a wicker chair. "Please have a seat."

All three sat.

"This is Fingal. I told you about him in my letter," Kitty said. "We've been married for more than a year, but we first knew each other not long before you were born."

"I'm very pleased to meet you, sir."

Consuela offered a hand, which O'Reilly took and turned, lowering his lips to within an inch of its back, in the European fashion. "Can we offer you a drink?" he asked.

"Please. A glass of red wine."

O'Reilly gestured to the waiter and said, *"Una copa de vino tinto, por favor."*

Kitty's eyes widened.

Consuela's left eyebrow rose. "You speak Spanish, Doctor O'Reilly?"

He shook his head. "Divil the bit, but I memorised a few critical phrases like that, and like, *'Dos cervezas grandes y dos más,'* in case of great thirst. And it's Fingal, by the way."

"Fingal," Kitty said, "you really are incorrigible."

Consuela laughed and said, "I think, Tia Kitty, I'm going to like your Fingal."

"I hope so," said Kitty. "I'm really quite fond of him."

All three laughed.

The ice certainly has been broken, and so

far painlessly, O'Reilly thought.

Then Kitty said, "Your letter back in July came as quite a shock. I was so sorry to hear about Mañ— your father."

Was she being sensitive to my or Consuela's feelings by not using the man's Christian name? he wondered.

"Poor Papá. I miss him very much," Consuela said. "It was hard, so hard, to watch. He was in hospital, on oxygen, his remaining lung couldn't cope. There was nothing the doctors could do."

O'Reilly shivered despite the heat. He'd seen enough patients die of oxygen lack, slowly suffocating, gasping for breath, knowing they were dying. He remembered a young man called Kevin Doherty with congestive heart failure in Sir Patrick Dun's Hospital in Dublin and glanced at Kitty. As a nurse she knew too. He watched her stretch out her hand, cover Consuela's. It needed to be their moment.

"I was his only blood family apart from a brother and some nephews and nieces in Argentina. My husband José was at home with our daughter Josélita."

"I remember your grandparents in Tenerife. They were kind to me," Kitty said.

"They're both gone," Consuela said. "I was with him at the end." Her lustrous dark eyes fixed on Kitty's grey ones. "Shall I tell you?"

Kitty glanced at O'Reilly.

He nodded at Consuela. Go ahead, but thank you for asking my permission, considering my feelings, guessing how I might feel if Kitty bursts into tears. He gripped his chair with one hand, and the other reached out briefly to touch Kitty's waist, to let her know that he was there.

"He was struggling to breathe. He managed to squeeze my hand, whisper that he loved me." She stared at the table. "He said, 'Please write to Tia Kitty.' " She glanced at O'Reilly. " 'Tell her . . .' "

She looked into his eyes and he nodded. " 'Tell her I still love her. I always have,' and then he drifted off to sleep. He died in his sleep that night. I think his last moments were comfortable, he was glad to go." Tears glistened on her cheeks.

Kitty, whose own eyes were damp, leant across and hugged the young woman, stroked her hair and murmured, "It's all right. It's all right."

And O'Reilly leant forward in his chair, elbows on the tabletop now, fingers steepled, chin on fingers. He felt himself withdraw slightly, to leave space for the two women who, both in their own way, had loved a man. One had lost a father so recently and had a daughter's grief. The other had lost the man she loved thirty years before and, because of a recent letter, had been forced to lose him for a second time. Yes, losing him again was

168

the correct way to think of it, O'Reilly knew, because he was certain Kitty still held a corner of her heart for this man, and that there it would beat "Mañuel" forever, just as a corner of his still held the deep imprint of Deirdre. Was he jealous? Did he feel hurt, wounded? How could he? He knew Kitty loved him, but she had needed to hear what she had just been told. Did he hurt for Kitty and Consuela's loss? How could he not?

As the two women held each other, he waved the red-wine-bearing waiter away and gave them the personal privacy they needed to share the moment. And inside himself, deep inside, he hoped, no damn it, he knew that Lars had been right to advise this meeting and that Kitty, Tia Kitty, at last had laid her ghost to rest beside a gentle sea beneath a warm Catalonian sky.

10
WHAT IS THE ANSWER?

"Nearly finished. Closing," Surgeon Commander Fraser said as he started suturing the skin. "Ugly green brutes, gallbladders," he muttered to no one in particular. "That one's better out than in."

Fingal let his attention stray from the patient and his surgeon for a moment to look at the time. With only one more case to do, the list would certainly be finished early enough for him to keep his appointment with Surgeon Rear Admiral Creaser.

"Right," said Angus Mahaddie, who was sitting beside Fingal. "I held your hand all day yesterday and for today's first two cases. I've shown you how to give intravenous pentothal, insert an endotracheal tube, and connect it to the Boyle's machine. I've pointed out the valves to operate, gasses to use, and how to tell if the anaesthetic is too shallow or too deep. I've hung back, not said a word to you about how you've been managing this case. Let me see you wake him up without my help, and if you manage that smoothly you'll, in RAF parlance, have 'gone solo,' and be well on your way to becoming a useful anaesthetist."

Fingal swallowed, but admitted to himself that with the Scotsman's careful guidance he was feeling more comfortable and more confident when he administered an anaesthetic. He was proud of his achievement. He looked at his gear. Clamped to the sides of a trolley were cylinders for oxygen and the anaesthetic gases, all of which he could now identify and turn on and off and regulate their rate of delivery to the patient. Pipes from the cylinders led through flow meters and through a device for vaporising and mixing the gasses. Next a mechanical bellows delivered the nitrous oxide, oxygen, and ether mixture through one of a pair of black corrugated rubber hoses connected to a Magill tube in the patient's trachea. The other hose removed carbon dioxide and the gasses as the patient exhaled.

He reduced the flow of nitrous oxide and ether and gradually opened more widely the one supplying oxygen so the level of anaesthesia would be less deep before he actually woke the patient up. In very short order the man began to move as he should — much to Fingal's relief.

"Christ," said the surgeon, "keep him still. I haven't finished suturing yet, O'Reilly, and when you do bring him round, I don't want him coughing and ripping out my stitches because of your ham-fisted anaesthetic."

Fingal inhaled through his nose but, saying nothing, reopened the gas valves. The patient lay still. There was no thank you. Already Fingal had decided that the acerbic surgeon commander was the antithesis of the helpful and good-humoured Angus Mahaddie.

A few minutes later, "Now I'm finished," the surgeon commander said. "Do try to get him awake quickly, O'Reilly. We don't have all day before the next patient." Fraser turned from the table and ripped off his rubber gloves. "Come on, Sister," he yelled at the circulating nurse. "Stop daydreaming. Get my gown off." He started dictating his operative notes to a clearly nervous young VAD clerk. ". . . external oblique fascia. Are you sure you can spell that, girl?"

The masked QARNNS sister who had been handling the instruments caught Fingal's eye and raised her own to the heavens as if to say, bloody prima donna surgeons. In 1937 in the Rotunda Hospital the look of two shining eyes above a surgical mask had led him to ask a certain midwife, Deirdre Mawhinney, for a date. He smiled at the memory of those eyes.

Angus said quietly, "You're doing fine, laddie. Now what should you do?"

"Shut off the gasses and ventilate lungs with

carbon dioxide and oxygen." Fingal spun the knurled wheels. "And give 5cc of coramine intravenously, sir, and get him extubated." Fingal gave the injection.

As the patient's eyelids fluttered, Fingal withdrew the endotracheal tube and held a rubber mask over the man's nose and mouth.

"Well done, and now —"

Outside, the air raid sirens howled into rising and falling life, giving advance warning of incoming bombers somewhere in their vicinity. The police sounded the sirens for one minute when a red alert was given, meaning the planes were twelve minutes away. Thank God for radar and the system of plotting the tracks of enemy aircraft. It gave the defending air force and the potential victims of the bombing enough time to react. The racket did not mean Gosport would be the target, but precautions would already be under way, because the hospital would have been informed by telephone on the yellow alert — planes twenty-two minutes away. That would be eighty-eight miles for a squadron cruising at 240 miles per hour.

Down here in the cellar operating theatre, the orderlies began moving the patient onto a trolley. He'd not be going upstairs to the Admiral Collingwood Ward, but to a bed in the cellar air raid shelters. Even in the theatre, Fingal was aware of tramping feet in the corridors outside, and the cries of patients who'd be frightened or in pain as they were moved.

Every moveable patient was being brought down by the nursing and sick berth staff, helped by ambulatory patients, all under the watchful command of the ward master, a commissioned sick berth attendant. God help the poor bastards in traction who had to be left to their fate upstairs on the wards. Fingal felt for them as he had felt for the unprotected upper-deck crew on *Warspite* when she was being bombed or shelled. Perhaps the large painted red cross in the quadrangle might dissuade the German airmen from aiming at the hospital if Gosport was indeed the target. They'd not know until the raid was over and the unwavering note of the "All Clear" had been sounded. Then the patients would be taken back upstairs. There was bustle in the theatre.

"It's going to be crowded in here if it's a big raid," Angus said. "They'll be bringing in two more tables so three surgical teams can operate here, and the same in the other underground operating theatre."

"Will it be crazy in here?" Fingal said, but even before he saw Angus shake his head, he knew it wouldn't. Not really. More a form of orchestrated chaos. He'd seen how it worked on *Warspite* at Narvik.

"We have our moments. But we're pretty well drilled," the little captain said with a smile. "You'll see. We've a highly developed system, just like the one afloat. The wounded are taken to a clearing centre and divided into those who can wait, those who need surgery at once, and those, God help them, who are beyond any help but hot sweet tea, morphine injections, and a visit from one of the chaplains."

The sirens had long ceased their howling, replaced by the asynchronous beat of German aero engines. The buggers were coming in low. Staccato pounding of Portsmouth's AA guns was punctuated by the far-distant crumps of exploding bombs. Fingal was pretty sure the dockyard several miles away was getting it again. Selfish as he knew it was, his immediate thought was, Rather Portsmouth than Fareham — where Deirdre would be settling in with Marge. He wondered what she'd be doing. If the sirens had gone off there, he hoped she'd be taking shelter as a precaution too.

"Here we go again," said Angus Mahaddie. "There'll be casualties arriving soon." He glanced over at the surgeon, who was now complaining about something else to the VAD. Leave the poor child alone, Fingal thought.

"Aye," Angus said, nodding to himself. "Just so. Sometimes I think some surgeons have what we in the Highlands would call 'a very good conceit of themselves.' " He winked at Fingal. "You did very well, laddie. Pay him no heed." He stretched. "We'll not be doing the routine case for a while. That patient'll have to wait until we've looked after the injured. Could you manage to drink a cuppa cha? It'll be at least an hour before the first victims start arriving, and I'm parched."

"I would like that," Fingal said. It probably meant he'd be kept here well past five thirty by the inflow of casualties. Damn it. He shrugged. Couldn't be helped. He'd known for years that when it came to patients they always came first.

"Aye," said Angus, "and don't worry. You're a trainee. I'm sure we'll be able to do without you for an hour. Come five o'clock I'll manage on my own for a wee while. We can't have you late for seeing the admiral, now, can we?"

The man was a mind reader.

It was a long walk to the admiral's office from Fingal's quarters in the medical officers' mess. He'd headed there as soon as Angus Mahaddie had released him from the theatre so he could ensure his appearance was now all ship-shape and Bristol fashion, as the navy quaintly put it. Admiral Creaser had been clearly insistent upon proper dress, and there was no need to antagonise the man. Fingal strode along the cloisters under the ward blocks. A shortcut led up the centre of the quadrangle from the entrance to the hospital and along to the church, but it wasn't called the Admiral's Walk for nothing. A lieutenant would no more think of treading on those hallowed flagstones than flying to the moon in a submarine.

As Fingal walked, one thought kept step with his footfalls. What if he said no? What if Surgeon Rear Admiral Thomas Creaser RN flat-out said, "No." Were there any arguments Fingal could advance, any appeal process? He shook his head. He'd no idea. He pursed his lips and, barely recognising what he was doing, crossed his fingers.

Memories of yesterday and getting Deirdre settled into Twiddy's Cottage flooded back. Marge had welcomed her into the house like a long-lost daughter and Benbow, the sheep-dog, had stirred from his shaggy heap by the fire to lick her hand and cover her with his long, wiry fur. He and Marge had watched as Deirdre handled the baby hedgehogs Riddle, Mee, and Ree with a childlike mixture of awe and gentleness. The two women had hit it off at once. "I think that you and I are going to get along famously," Marge had said as she ordered Deirdre upstairs for a bath and a sleep before dinner while Fingal and Marge planted leeks in the Wilcoxsons' tidy vegetable garden.

Deirdre coming downstairs after her rest had looked gorgeous. How much he'd wanted her.

And just when he thought he should have

devised some way for them to be alone, Marge had made her astonishing pronouncement: "I've some *utterly* boring Parish Council meeting and I won't be back until ten."

And he of the huge appetite had barely noticed the pheasant and bottle of Pol Roger they'd had for dinner, but Deirdre's kisses, her caresses, the violent urgency of their lovemaking, the languorous afterglow, and the reaffirmation of their love would be with him in every detail forever.

He left the cloisters and went along a corridor. If the interview went well they would have nearly three whole wonderful months to be together before he must go back to sea. But if it didn't?

He halted in front of the door to the admiral's office, straightened his tie, dusted off his coat, and as regulations demanded, tucked his cap under his arm. Before he knocked, Fingal remembered the conversation with Marjorie after she'd arrived home at five past ten last night. "I do hope you two have had a lovely evening." She'd beamed and said, "I'm sure you have. I am married to a sailor, you know. It's wonderful when he comes home."

Fingal had swallowed, trying to think of a tactful reply, but she'd continued, "I was very happy to make myself scarce this evening, of course," she said, "but we can't be making a habit of it, can we? So do be a good boy and hurry up and get married."

His knock was answered by a terse, "Come."

He opened the door and stepped into the office. A fire burned in the central fireplace surmounted by the massive coat of arms.

"O'Reilly. Have a seat." Surgeon Rear Admiral Creaser was seated behind his desk behind a stack of files and indicated the chair in front of it with an absent wave of his hand, the same chair Fingal had occupied last Thursday. "Glad to see you've taken my advice and are in the correct rig of the day. Good."

Fingal took the chair and the small compliment as a good omen and a reminder of the admiral's final words to him on Thursday: "I'll see what I can do."

"We'll make this brief. I'm informed that the raid on Portsmouth is keeping us busy, and you'll want to get back on duty, I'm sure."

"Yes, sir."

"I know why you've sought this interview." The senior officer took a deep breath. "As I promised, I have spoken to the Admiralty." His gaze fixed on Fingal. "I must explain this to you in some detail. I'm sorry, O'Reilly."

He didn't need to say one word more. How often had Fingal himself used "I'm sorry" as a prelude to bad news? But it would be impolitic to interrupt. He held his breath.

"Even in wartime, they expect you to wait until you are a lieutenant-commander."

Fingal exhaled. Damn it. Damn it all to hell. It had been wonderful seeing her, but if they couldn't live together, what was the point in Deirdre being here? He had brought his darling girl here for nothing, and subjected her to risk and danger along the way. His shoulders sagged and he stared at the desktop.

"It's not all gloom and despondency," the admiral said. "With your four years seniority as a lieutenant, I can ensure that you will be promoted at the earliest opportunity."

A flicker of hope. Fingal raised his head and asked, "And when will that be, sir?"

"Promotions are granted twice a year. June and December."

"December?" He heard his own voice rise in pitch. December? He was going back to sea in January. He felt an emotional thump as powerful as a hit by one of *Warspite*'s fifteen-inch shells.

"And become effective six months later." The admiral steepled his fingers and looked at Fingal who, despite his disappointment, heard compassion in the senior officer's voice, saw it in his eyes.

Fingal gritted his teeth, wanted to yell, demand that the rules be bent. He took a deep breath, struggled to control his temper, and asked, "And that's final, sir? Nothing can be done?"

The admiral shook his head. "I am dreadfully sorry."

For a moment Fingal simply stared at the desktop, then he said, "Thank you, sir." What else could he say? Damn you, damn your regulations, and damn the whole bloody war? To what purpose? He merely rose. "I'd better be getting back, sir."

"Carry on, O'Reilly, and try to bear up."

Fingal didn't reply. As was fitting, according to regulations, damn them, he stood at attention, replaced his cap, about turned, and marched to the door. As he let himself out his only thought was simply, How the hell am I going to tell Deirdre?

11
Never Look Long upon a Monkey

"I want advice from the pair of you," said O'Reilly. Slouched in the swivel chair in the surgery, he eyed the two youngsters and adjusted his half-moon spectacles. He and Kitty had arrived home on Saturday night after their most satisfying week in Barcelona and it was his turn to take the surgery this Monday morning. He'd asked his juniors to come into the office before he started seeing patients.

"I reckon," he said, "you, Barry, should know how to screen for Rhesus isoimmunisation, and you, Jenny, fresh out of working with Doctor Graham Harley, will be au fait with what's being done for it at Royal Maternity." He spun around to the rolltop desk, picked up an antenatal record, and swung back to his colleagues. "Kinky met Lorna Kearney last Thursday in the butcher's. Lorna's expecting and Kinky told her to get in here today to start her antenatal visits." He pointed with the folder at the door. "She's out there now." He looked from one to the other. "I need your help on her case."

"Fire away," Barry said, and Jenny nodded.

"Obstetrics has moved along since I spent a year as a junior in Dublin's Rotunda Maternity Hospital in the late '30s," O'Reilly said.

"I don't imagine," said Jenny, "there'd have been much call for midwifery skills on your battleship either."

Barry laughed. "Sounds like a sketch from TV's *That Was the Week that Was.* Naval medical officer says, 'Push please, Wren Petty Officer Joan Jenkins.' Then another, very cultured English voice says, 'Number two and three batteries. Fire.' "

"Eejit." O'Reilly shook his head. "It might have happened in Nelson's navy. Some wives were permitted to go to sea. But modern WRENs didn't in my day, although some did fly aircraft. And the order to the guns is 'shoot,' not 'fire.' Goes back to wooden ships too. Yelling 'Fire' on one tended to upset people." He smiled at the two, each perched on one of the patients' chairs. "Now stop acting the lig, Barry. I really do need your advice."

"Aye aye, Commander."

"Thank you. Now, I've read about potential Rhesus blood group incompatibility between mother and baby. But I've never seen a case since I came to practice here. We didn't know what the devil it was back in the '30s. Just that, tragically, some babies died in the uterus and were swollen and oedematous when they were stillborn. That was called *hydrops foetalis,* and it was rare, but if it did occur it happened in pregnancy after pregnancy in the same woman. The Catholic church forbade contraception and the poor craytures conceived again and again with no hope of ever having a live baby."

"That's ghastly," Jenny said. "Sometimes I think religions, all run by men by the way, have a lot to answer for when it comes to what they do to women."

O'Reilly decided to avoid that discussion for the moment and continued. "Some other babies turned yellow after birth, *icterus gravis neonatorum,* and some of those did survive, but many showed signs of cerebral irritation. We called it *kernicterus.* They died about a week after they were born. We'd no idea what caused any of it. It was damned frustrating, I can tell you."

"We do still see the same cases now," said Barry. "But we are getting better at managing them, because we understand the condition now."

"But Fingal, you could hardly have been expected to know about it," Jenny said. "The Rhesus factor wasn't discovered until 1940, and I imagine that you'd have been too pre-

184

occupied with the results of the Battle of Britain and trying to win the war to be paying attention to current civilian medical research into blood groups."

"You'd be right," O'Reilly said. "Although patient-to-patient blood transfusion was being done, it was discouraged in ships at sea. A blood transfusion service was eventually set up at a hospital called Haslar near Portsmouth. I worked there in 1940, but the transfusion service came in after I'd left."

Jenny said, "It was way before our time; I was only one."

"And I was born that year," Barry said.

"But I know about Lansteiner and Stetson," said Jenny, glancing at Barry. "In 1940, they discovered that 83 percent of the human race shared proteins on their red blood cells with the Rhesus monkey, but that 17 percent did not. The first ones were said to be Rhesus positive and the others Rhesus negative. Now we know that a baby's blood cells can get into the mother's circulation, usually in a first pregnancy. Then in 1941 — is that right, Barry? Was it just a year later . . ."

O'Reilly watched the two young people comparing notes and thought about 1941 and how even now, twenty-five years later, the memory of that year still clutched at his heart.

"Another doctor, Doctor Levine, found out that if a mother was Rhesus negative and the baby was Rhesus positive, there could be trouble," Jenny continued. "The mother's immune system would recognise the proteins on the baby's red cells as foreign — just like a virus or bacteria — and set about producing antibodies that could cross back into the baby and attack its red cells."

"But usually not in a first pregnancy," Barry said. "It's the later ones you have to worry about. The antibodies raised in the first are at a low level. It's not until the mother is exposed to more foetal red cells in a subsequent pregnancy that she starts cranking out high levels of antibodies. Effectively, the mother is trying to kill the baby's red blood cells as if they were a dangerous invader. That causes what is now called haemolytic disease of the newborn, in all of its manifestations that you knew by highfalutin' names like *hydrops* and *kernicterus.* Fifteen of every hundred affected babies are stillborn."

O'Reilly frowned and said, "So that's 15 percent, if they do have the incompatibility, right? But the condition itself is still pretty rare, isn't it?"

"It is," said Barry. "They taught me that immunological differences between a mother's blood group and the baby's only occur in six of every one thousand babies born. Not surprising you've not seen a case here. It would be rare as hen's teeth in a wee place like Ballybucklebo. But in all of Ulster at least today, when it's discovered, things can be done."

"Doctor Charley Whitfield has a major research project running at Royal Maternity," Jenny said. "If Lorna Kearney needs to be seen there, Fingal, I can have a word with Doctor Harley, my old boss. Speed things up."

"Grand," said O'Reilly. "I knew I'd come to the right folks for advice." He picked up an antenatal history form. "It's Lorna's second baby. The first, Reggie Jr., was perfectly normal a year ago, but it does say here her blood group is O Rhesus negative. She's been a bit naughty. Didn't come in for a first visit before the third month as pregnant women are supposed to. Typical busy farmer's wife. Sees her sow farrow, cows drop calves, cats have litters, and reckons there's nothing to pregnancy."

"How far on is she?" Barry asked.

"She told Kinky she was about four and a half months."

"Not the end of the world," Barry said. "You'll have all her baseline information from her last pregnancy."

O'Reilly consulted the chart. "Everything was pretty much normal. She's a young woman. Only twenty-four. Had her appendix out ten years ago. Nothing else to worry about."

"So at this visit, Fingal, you should arrange

to have Rhesus antibody levels checked, although they don't usually develop until after the end of the fifth month. That's why seeing her a bit late's not critical. The husband's blood group and details about it are important and —" Barry hesitated. "Would you like me to see her? It might be simpler."

O'Reilly thought how turning Lorna's care over to Barry would be simpler. But damn it all, O'Reilly, you might be getting a bit older, but you're not senile yet. He sat up in his chair and looked at Barry. Some old dogs still could learn new tricks. "I'd like you to see her with me today if you've time, but no, I'd like to manage the case. I need to learn about it."

"And," said Jenny, "as I don't think I can offer much help now and I've a stack of paperwork to do, will you excuse me? If you need me to pull any strings, Fingal, just let me know. I'll be in the upstairs lounge." She rose and left.

"Nothing urgent about my home visits," Barry said.

"So be a good la—"

"And nip along to the waiting room and get her?" Barry laughed. "You said that to me the very first day I started working here." He shook his head. "I seem to remember something about leopards and spots."

"And Ethiopians and skin," said O'Reilly. "Jeremiah 13:23. And isn't there a comfort to the tried and true?" His smile was beatific. "Now do please nip along — like a good lad."

"You can get dressed, Lorna," O'Reilly said. "So far everything looks great. You said your last period started on April the third. Today's October the tenth so you're twenty-six weeks and five days now, and due on January the tenth. Your blood pressure's good, uterus is the right size for the length of the pregnancy, and there's no ankle swelling."

"And the urine sample Kinky asked you to bring's clear," Barry said, from where he had been testing it at the sink.

"Grand," said O'Reilly. He'd not needed to explain Barry's presence. Lorna had said she'd known all about the young man's extra training.

Lorna Kearney was a thickset young woman with close-cropped fair hair and the same kind of farmers' arms' suntan as a man might have. She had biceps to match, and O'Reilly could picture her, sleeves rolled up, swinging bales of hay with a pitchfork up into a hayloft. She sat up on the examining couch and started to tuck her shirt into the waist of her trousers. She'd taken off her Wellington boots before climbing up on the couch. There was a hole in her right knitted sock near the great toe. "Aye," she said, fixing her unusual pale blue eyes on Fingal with an intensity that unnerved him. "And didn't I tell Kinky, Lord knows I know she means well, but didn't I tell Kinky she was making a fuss about nothing? I've work to do on the farm and Reggie Jr. to see to. I could've waited for another couple of weeks before I come here, so I could." She slipped down off the couch.

O'Reilly glanced at Barry before saying, "Sure, all us doctors are nothing but fusspots, but it's always better to be safe than sorry. And your case is a wee bit different, Lorna."

She finished pulling on her second boot before straightening up and saying, "Different? What way?"

O'Reilly pursed his lips. The trick was to get her to understand the potential severity of her condition without scaring the living bejasus out of her. She could be one of the ones at risk of losing her baby. "We need to make sure that you —" He had been going to say "won't hurt your baby," but stopped short. Not smart. What expectant mother would? And the offence taken at the suggestion would be vast. He remembered Barry describing thyroid hormones to Cissie Sloan as "little thingys in the blood." Something like that might work. "Take a pew, Lorna," he said, indicating one of the chairs as he dropped into the swivel one. "The last time you had a baby, we noticed a thingy in your blood."

"A thingy?" She leant forward and frowned. "What kind of a thingy?"

O'Reilly hesitated. "It's a bit tricky to explain," he said, "but did you ever go to the zoo at Bellevue in Belfast?"

"Aye," she said.

"And did you ever notice how alike the monkeys are to us?"

"Aye," she said.

The taciturnity of some Ulster patients was legend.

"Well, about four out of five humans share something with monkeys . . ."

"Aye?" There was an upward inflection.

"And one in five, don't."

"Aye," she said, brightening, "and that's me and my big Reggie, so it is. We're good Christians. None of this evolution, Darwin rubbish. We don't believe in that there clap-trap that we come down from the apes." She chuckled. "Except maybe thon Donal Donnelly. His hair's about the right shade for an orang-ootang."

O'Reilly let that pass, but his mind was whirling. He'd not meant to open that particular debate, and if he persisted he might suddenly find his patient had gone to the Kinnegar to see Ronald Fitzpatrick for medical advice. The more fundamental Protestants took their book of Genesis very literally. "Quite," he said, and reflexively fumbled in his jacket pocket for his pipe so he could play for time as he sought a better explanation . . .

Barry said, "May I, Doctor O'Reilly?"

O'Reilly nodded. He was making a right bollix of this and Barry had more experience in explaining the condition.

"Do you remember getting your vaccination for smallpox, Lorna?" It had been compulsory since 1883 for every child in Ulster.

"Aye." Her hand rubbed her left shoulder where the vaccination would have been given.

"That was so your body's defences would recognise the germ that causes smallpox and have been prepared to attack the germ and destroy it if it ever tried to infect you again."

Her eyes widened. "Honest to God? I never thought of it that way."

"Sometimes," Barry said, "the body's defences can get muddled. We know that if you are one kind of blood group and your baby is another, your defences, they're called antibodies, could mistake the baby's blood for something like a germ and attack the baby's blood cells."

She drew back. "I never would. My wean?"

"It wouldn't be your fault, Lorna," said O'Reilly. "You'd have no control over it."

"That's what Doctor O'Reilly was talking about. We know your blood group is negative . . ."

"Negative what?" Her eyebrows knitted.

Barry smiled. "I'm sure you know that guinea pigs are used in research, and white mice."

"Aye," she said, "I've heard tell."

"The doctors who specialise in this use serum from a kind of monkey called Rhesus to help identify blood groups. People are either positive or negative."

"Boys-a-dear, isn't modern science a wonderful thing?"

"According to your records, you are Rhesus negative, but if your husband Reggie is positive, the baby might be too and —"

She pointed a finger at Barry and said, "And them antibody thingys you were talking about could make my baby sick?"

Not all country folks, O'Reilly thought, to maintain the country idiom, were as green as they were cabbage-looking. Barry's explanation had been lucid, and certainly Lorna had been very quick on the uptake.

"That's right," Barry said, "but we'll not know for sure. We need to do some blood tests for you."

"Sure, that's wee buns."

"And it would help to get your husband's blood group established."

"I'll see til that, so I will."

"So," Barry said, "I'll save Doctor O'Reilly the trouble and fill in the forms, and you and Reggie can get the samples taken in Bangor Hospital."

Good man, O'Reilly thought, because I'm not entirely sure what tests to ask for.

"You get the tests done tomorrow, and I

believe Doctor O'Reilly would like to see you back here in two weeks for your next checkup and to get the results. Now hang on a jiff while I fill these things in." Barry worked fast, ticking boxes and writing in the patient's name and age. "Here," he said, handing them over, "your forms."

She tucked them into her handbag.

O'Reilly said, "So you trot on home, Lorna, do as Doctor Laverty has told you, and come back . . ." He consulted a calendar. ". . . on the twenty-fourth to get the results."

"We will, Doctor, and thank you." She shook her head at O'Reilly. "You near put my heart in my mouth, sir, saying them things about monkeys. But young Doctor Laverty explained it all right lovely, so he did. I'll be running along and I'll see you in two weeks." She hesitated on her way to the door and said, "With all that talk about monkeys and yokes in my blood, I near forgot. Reggie telt me til tell you, Doctor O'Reilly, that you know that bit of bottom wet land with all the rushes?"

"I do."

"The snipe's in something lovely this year and there might be a few pheasants too. Off the marquis's estate, like, so if you'd like for to bring Arthur and your gun? I know you don't shoot, Doctor Laverty."

Barry laughed and said, "I used to be a sailor. Still am when I can get a bit of time off." He looked straight at O'Reilly.

"Thank you, Lorna," said O'Reilly. "That's very kind." He peered over his half-moons at Barry. Two can play the innuendo game. "If I can get away, I certainly will." Not only would he enjoy the sport, but if Lorna was willing to let him shoot on their land, he could be assured that no offence had been taken today. Nor would have Barry, who enjoyed a bit of mutual teasing as much as his senior partner.

Barry rose and held the door for her.

"Thank you, Barry," O'Reilly said after the door had been closed. "That was nice about the snipe shooting. I'll look forward to that, but what a silly girl. Leaving it so late for her first antenatal visit. Still, there's no point yelling at her. What's done is done and it looks like it's so far so good except for the Rhesus business. You saved my bacon on explaining that one."

Barry laughed. "In darkest County Antrim, the folks of Ballymena are just as much creationists as the County Down people. You soon learn how to skate round it when you have to talk about Rhesus monkeys. More to the point, we have to figure out what to do when her results come back."

"Go on," said O'Reilly. "I'm listening."

"It's all going to depend on her husband's blood group. If he's Rhesus negative then there's nothing to worry about. The baby will be too. But if Reggie's positive then I'll have to work out the likelihood that the baby might be Rhesus positive and affected. It's a bit complicated, so in your own immortal words, 'We'll cross that bridge when we come to it.' I also asked for an antibody level. It's called a titre. It's unlikely to be up so early. We start looking for them again at about thirty-two weeks if the hubby's group seems to pose a risk. Where we go next, if we have to, will depend on those results."

O'Reilly nodded. He had a lot to learn about this condition. "Will you sit in with me next time she comes?"

"I'd be delighted," Barry said.

"Good," said O'Reilly. "I'm going to need your help."

"That's generous of you to say so, Fingal."

"Och," said O'Reilly, "you don't keep a dog and bark yourself." Having saved a little face, he continued, "Now, when you went to get Lorna, was the waiting room busy?"

"It was filling up."

O'Reilly took a three count before grinning and saying, "Then be a good lad and nip along there and yell, 'Next.' "

12
THE PITY OF WAR

"I," said Angus Mahaddie, "am knackered." The little man had managed to shave during the long night, but there were dark bags under his eyes. "But it's our turn to see the postops and arrange premeds, so we'd better get at it."

"I've been brighter myself." Fingal was yawning, and no wonder. Tuesday's bombing raid on the dockyard had been a big one and none of the surgical staff had had much sleep until about three on Thursday morning, when the last of the wounded had been treated.

Things were now returning to their normal routine, but managing to snatch only about six hours' sleep in the last forty-eight had hardly been conducive to feeling full of vim and vigour.

The Germans had come over in waves of about sixty to a hundred Heinkel 111 and Junkers 88 bombers, heavily escorted by Messerschmitt Bf 109 fighters. They'd pressed home attacks until late afternoon.

Those fighter pilots of the RAF's 11 Group who had survived the dogfights must be even more exhausted than Fingal. He thought about the airmen, some of them barely out of school when they joined up. Poor boys.

Angus led the way onto Admiral Collingwood Ward, a Florence Nightingale type that had been created years ago by knocking out the wall between two smaller rooms to make one large, better-ventilated space. A bow arch was all that remained of the previously intervening wall. If he closed his eyes, Fingal could have thought himself back in Sir Patrick Dun's Hospital in Dublin. The same unmistakable hospital sounds and smells filled the air.

Looking through the archway to an identical room, he saw rows of cast-iron-framed beds on each side — nearly all occupied. Large windows in the whitewashed walls let in the pale autumn light. He and Angus had been working nonstop since he'd left the admiral at five thirty on Tuesday afternoon. When he'd had a spare moment to think about anything other than administering anaesthetics and making postoperative rounds to ensure that the patients were indeed recovering from the effects of his efforts, he'd struggled with his conscience, knowing he should let Deirdre know the truth about their wedding plans. But even if he'd had the time to call, which he hadn't, the telephone exchange had been hit by a bomb and the General Post Office engineers were still making repairs.

"Morning, Sister Blenkinsop," Angus said.

"Morning, sir. Morning, Lieutenant O'Reilly." The QARNNS senior sister in charge of the ward's nurses was a tall, angular, iron-grey-haired woman who Fingal already knew was the absolute mistress of her trade. She was tidy in her starched headdress called a veil, short cape called a tippet, and white apron over a dark blue dress. "Ready when you are." She was accompanied by a junior sister and a young VAD.

"We're getting back to normal now, sir," Sister said. "We've got all the ones from downstairs back up to the wards and a number of the recovering ones taken by train to inland hospitals away from the bombing. Some of the less badly injured go to convalescent homes in the Meon Valley."

Which, Fingal thought, would account for the empty beds.

"Thank God the Jerries haven't been back, but we're quite ready if there is another raid."

"Thank you, Sister," Angus said. "Perhaps we're going to get a bit of a reprieve down south here. The BBC said this morning on the eight o'clock bulletin that the Luftwaffe hit the City of London and the docks again last night." He shook his head. "Again."

"Poor devils," Sister said.

"Twenty-six consecutive night attacks on London since September the seventh. The bastards — sorry, ladies — the Huns can't be everywhere at once, so poor old London's loss, at night anyway, seems to be our gain." He coughed, and said, "And as we can't stop the air raids, we can at least do our part in fixing up the damage. Now, Lieutenant O'Reilly's the one being trained, so he'll do the work. I'll only give advice if I'm asked." Although Angus managed to smile, it was a tired one.

"I'll do my best, sir." Fingal stifled a yawn, feeling the stubble on his chin, which hadn't seen a razor for two days. Since "flying solo" on Tuesday afternoon he, with gradually increasing confidence, had given ten anaesthetics by himself, although with three tables in service in the theatre Angus had always been nearby working on another patient. David White had manned the other table and another trainee the third. As yet Fingal was unsure of just how many procedures they'd done, but with two operating theatres going all out it must have been close to sixty major cases and Lord knew how many walking wounded.

Between shifts in theatre, shifts on the wards, and snatched meals and naps, there'd been no time for social chitchat, and Fingal had only been able to give Angus a curt "not good" after his interview with the admiral.

That felt like a hundred years ago. "Let's get started, please, Sister." It was always politic to keep on the good side of senior nurses.

The little entourage moved to the first bed, where a patient was trying to lie at attention, as regulations prescribed. Bloody regulations. Fingal clenched his teeth. A cylindrical cage under the blue-and-white blanket held the bedclothes over where his legs had once been. Crushed under a toppled dockyard crane. The cage kept the weight of the bedclothes off the stumps.

Sister handed Fingal a clipboard where the man's temperature, blood pressure, pulse, and number of bowel motions had been recorded. He scanned the numbers quickly and said, "Good morning, Benson. You seem to be doing well." All the man's vital signs had been normal, but doing well? Fingal grimaced at his own banality and deep in his guts could feel the hurt of what he saw. Twenty-three and no legs. What a bloody waste.

He looked into the eyes of the drowsy man, whose pupils were constricted, the results of morphine given for pain relief. The man mumbled something. Patients heavily dosed with the opiate often did and it was nothing to worry about, but Fingal still struggled to understand what the man was trying to say, alas to no avail.

"We'll keep him on a quarter of a grain of

morphine every six hours please, Sister." Fingal handed her back the clipboard, which she immediately passed over to the VAD to write the order.

The next patient, like several others, was sitting beside his bed stiffly, with arms folded. They all wore the hospital uniform, serge trousers and blue shirts. Fingal took a deep breath. Above a distinct smell of disinfectant hung the stink of Sinclair's glue, the adhesive used to attach traction devices to the skin of broken limbs. He could see two patients farther along the ward in Balkan beam beds with gantrys, ropes, pulleys, and weights keeping traction on the splinted limbs.

Those poor divils would have been left alone up here during the raid on Portsmouth with the racket of exploding bombs and antiaircraft fire, the ward lit by garish red and yellow flashes as the bombs went off some miles away. Even today, there lingered a whiff of brick dust and smoke mingling with the usual hospital smells. The smoke was not only from fires. Portsmouth Dockyard was ringed with generators called "Smokey Joes" that were lit up to try to generate a smoke screen.

Many of the German planes would have passed directly overhead, because the raiders often used the hospital's distinctive water tower as a navigation point. Waiting for a bomb to hit the hospital must have been terrifying for those men — alone, vulnerable, unable to move a muscle to save themselves.

"Here you are, sir." The sister handed Fingal a chart. "Chief Petty Officer McIlroy. He's an instructor at the gunnery school on Whale Island. If we've no emergencies, he's booked for a —" She lowered her voice to a whisper as a sop to the man's privacy. "— haemorrhoidectomy. He's been examined by the admitting doctor and is fit for anaesthesia."

"Fine," said Fingal, "and no previous illnesses?"

"No, sir," she said.

"Usual omnopon and scopolamine premed then, please. Usual timing."

"Excuse me, sir," the man said in a thick Ulster accent, "begging your pardon, but you're one of my lot, aren't you?"

"From Ballybucklebo." Fingal was surprised to find how homesick he felt hearing the man's harsh tones.

The patient's grin was vast. "Away off and chase yourself — sir. You never are. I'll be damned, and me from Helen's Bay, just down the road, so I am. And my old oppo, fellah called Thompson, he's just been posted til . . ." he lowered his voice, "*Warspite.* He's a Ballybucklebo man."

"I don't think I knew him back in Ireland," Fingal said. "I was on *Warspite.* I'll be going back to her so maybe I'll meet him there." He ignored Sister impatiently clearing her

throat. "One of our gunnery leading seamen . . ."

"Alf Henson. He's on my course. Sharp as
a tack, thon one, sir. He'll go far, so he will."

Sister cleared her throat once more. "I'm
sure that's very interesting, Chief Petty Officer," Sister Blenkinsop said, "but we must be
getting on." She fixed Fingal with a glare and
then glanced over to Angus, as if asking the
senior to pull rank. But the Highlander was
clearly being true to his word and had no
intention of interfering. Instead he took a
sudden interest in his fingernails.

"Good luck," O'Reilly said.

"Thanks a million, sir. You've made my
feckin' day, so you have. Up till now it's been
a right pain in the arse."

Fingal stifled a smile and saw Sister Blenkinsop raise her hand to her mouth to hide
her own grin.

And so the round went until Fingal and
Angus had completed their duties and had
retired to Sister's office for a cup of tea and a
piece of her homemade shortbread. The office was at the end of the ward and had a
small bow window looking onto the ward so
she could keep an eye on her staff and her
patients. They met David White coming off
duty.

"Eh," said Angus, leaning back in his chair.
"This is the first chance we've had to talk
about anything other than what gasses to use.

I'm guessing your remark, that the interview was 'not good,' means you can't get permission?"

Fingal nodded. "I've to wait until I'm a lieutenant-commander."

Angus shook his head. "I know when promotions are made, laddie. Too late for you. I'm very sorry."

"That's pretty rotten," David said. He helped himself to a sugary wedge of shortbread, bit into it, and said, "Sister, this shortbread is jolly good."

Sister Blenkinsop was stirring her tea with one hand and writing up progress notes with the other. "I got the recipe from my mother and she used to win prizes at village fairs with it."

"It really is top hole," David said.

Fingal glanced over at David. Pretty rotten. Top hole. These bloody English public school boys all sounded like something out of the fictitious Greyfriars School created by Frank Richards, or Kipling's *Stalky and Co.*

He must have seen Fingal's scowl, realised the enormity of his waxing lyrical over shortbread when his friend had received bad news. "Dreadfully sorry, Fingal," he said. "I really am."

"Can't be helped," Fingal said. He shrugged. "I appreciate the sympathy and I know in the grand scheme of things, there're worse things happening —" He gestured out the door to the ward. "But the damnable thing is, I — well, I haven't told Deirdre yet. I feel like a bloody fool. I was so sure it would be all right. I've had no time since the raid, and now the phones are out."

"So the admiral didn't say anything about —"

Fingal leaned forward in his seat. He knew he must look like a cat ready to pounce. "Yes?"

"Eh, I'm sorry, lad. I shouldn't be getting your hopes up," Angus said, and frowned. "It's just that I'm surprised the boss didn't think of it, but running this place since the Blitz started has been a hell of a job —"

"Didn't think of what?" Fingal remembered the towering stack of files on the man's desk.

"And he never loses control, but he must be constantly preoccupied. He's being relieved next month by Admiral Bradbury. The old man'll need a rest."

"But what didn't he think of?" Fingal was close to shouting.

"There may just be a way to speed up your promotion."

"What?"

"May be, and I don't want to get your hopes up, but if I can get hold of a friend of mine in London."

"Come on, Angus, tell me," Fingal said. "What way?"

Angus shook his head. "Just bide for a wee

while until the phones come back on. Sister tried about ten minutes ago, but our switchboard can't get through." He looked at his watch. "Nine thirty. I tell you what, seeing as how you can't phone your lassie, would it help if I let you go out for a couple of hours? Things are slow again now." He looked at David. "You'll not mind filling in for Fingal?"

"My pleasure," David rushed to say, clearly trying to make amends for his earlier lack of sensitivity. "And if you want the car . . ." He offered the keys.

Fingal jumped up and had to restrain himself from grabbing them out of David's hand.

"Be back for twelve thirty," Angus said. "The phones may be working by then, and when they are I'll start making enquiries. But, laddie?"

"Yes."

"I'll not be saying anything until I have the answer cut and dried."

13
FRIENDLY PERSUASION

Kinky's sniff was of such force that O'Reilly was sure the kitchen walls would move inward. "It does be a very charitable thing you and Kitty are doing, sir, having that man Fitzpatrick for dinner this evening." She gave the bread dough she was kneading a punch. O'Reilly reckoned it could have flattened the current world heavyweight champion, Muhammad Ali. Kinky sighed mightily. "I do understand that you are very concerned about his health, but I cannot warm to that man at all, so."

O'Reilly remembered back to the day in December 1964 when Fitzpatrick had called Kinky "my good woman." O'Reilly had had a nasty chest cold and had told Kinky "no visitors." But Fitzpatrick had always had a peremptory air about him, and he had been determined to see O'Reilly. He had ordered Kinky to step aside as if she were a mere skivvie. And her response had been sub-Arctic, her defiance like that of Horatius at the bridge.

"I've had no time for him since we were students together," O'Reilly said, "but Kitty and I learned some things about him when we were in Dublin last month. I think they can explain to a degree why he is the man he is today." He pulled up a stool to the counter and sat down. "He was born and brought up as an only child in Japan, sent back to Dublin in 1931 for his medical education, and never ever saw his missionary parents again. Now add to that that he's not a well man."

"If you say so, sir, and that would all be very sad. The poor little spalpeen. And I'm sure you'll help him over his illness, so." She tutted as she packed the dough into several small compartments in two baking tins. "I'll leave this to rise for a second time and have it in the oven later so you and your guest can have fresh rolls with your mushroom soup."

"Thank you, Kinky." Clearly the Cork-woman was not overly interested in what O'Reilly had learned in Dublin about Fitz-patrick, but then Kinky was not one who'd listen to any kind of gossip. He'd not been surprised that her expression of sympathy had been tinged with a lingering disrespect. "Little spalpeen" was not a term of affection.

She set the dough-filled tins aside, dusted off her hands on her apron, and turned her attention to three ramekins, each containing a base of her own rich custard flavoured with

209

orange zest. "Seeing both young doctors will be out tonight I've only made three desserts. Kitty tells me they call this *crema Catalana* in Barcelona."

"The French call it *crème brûlée.*"

"And when I was taught to make it, we just called it burnt cream, so." She chuckled. "I'd like to have seen the look on my own face when my teacher caramelised the sugar —" She indicted a bowl of nearby brown sugar. "— with a shmall-little blowtorch. I thought she'd taken leave of her senses. She'd worked in a posh London place, the Café de Paris, before the war."

O'Reilly pursed his lips. "Aye, the war. If I recall correctly, that place was hit by a bomb in 1941. A band leader called 'Snakehips' Johnson was among those killed."

" 'Snakehips'? He'd not get a name like that in Ireland. Saint Patrick drove those creatures out."

O'Reilly chuckled.

Kinky said, "By 1941, thank the Lord, my friend Emer was working at Ballybucklebo House for the marquis's father, God rest them both," Kinky said. "Now, tonight I'll be home with Archie," her smile was beatific, "so Kitty'll have to finish off the desserts before serving. And the little torch and matches are there, sir," she pointed. "I'm sure Kitty will manage fine, so."

"I'm sure she will," O'Reilly said, thinking

how well things had turned out since Kinky's marriage and feeling rather satisfied with his lot. Then he was struck by an idea. If, by the end of the meal, he and Kitty had been forced to use the tactic she'd seen on *Z-Cars* and he had taken Fitzpatrick severely to task, then coming down here to do the caramelizing would give Kitty a chance to try to work her gentle wiles on the previously softened-up victim. He liked the notion. "Kinky?"

"Yes, sir?"

"Show me how to put on the sugar and use the torch, please."

Her eyes widened, her jaw dropped.

He laughed. "Now come on, Kinky," he said. "It's not as if I've not done a bit of cooking."

"No, it is not, sir." She smiled. "Your curried canned corned beef that you learned in the war is a thing to behold, and cooking does be a thing more men should do. I'm teaching Archie simple recipes. He's a dab hand now with a boiled egg, and his cheese and scallion omelette could be fluffier, but he's getting the hang of it, so." She lifted the sugar bowl and began. "You only need to make a thin little crust, so."

O'Reilly poured himself a Jameson. It was five thirty and Barry had given Kinky a lift home on his way to Belfast for a night out with his pal Jack Mills, the budding general

211

surgeon. Kitty would be home any time now.

"Hello, Fingal." Doctor Jenny Bradley came into the upstairs lounge. "I'm just heading out. I'm having dinner with Terry in the Causerie." Her voice seemed to hide a chuckle, like a stream bubbling over its bed on a summer day.

"Jenny," he said, "you look lovely." And she did. Her shining blonde hair was nearly covered by a pillbox fur hat and her double-breasted grey wool suit had a shawl collar of the same fur. The skirt was mid-thigh — Mary Quant's miniskirt had taken the world of fashion by storm and Jenny's shapely legs in sheer dark tights suited the length well.

"Thank you, Fingal," she said. "I want to look my best tonight."

"And you do." What was it about her, he wondered, that was so special tonight? She certainly was wearing more makeup than she would at work. False eyelashes were all the rage and her lipstick was bright. But it was something about the lightness of her voice, her tread, her great beaming smile. Something was making Jenny Bradley very happy. "Would you like a drink?"

"Mmm. Small sherry, please," and she sat in one of the armchairs as he poured. Immediately Lady Macbeth leapt up on Jenny's lap.

"Here you are." He handed her the glass and took the other chair. *Sláinte.*

212

"Cheers." She sipped and said, "Fingal, there's something I want to tell you."

"Fire away."

"Terry has asked me to marry him," she said in a rush. "And I've said yes, and he's giving me the ring tonight."

O'Reilly let a roar out of him like a wounded banshee. "He what? Oh lovely, bloody lovely. Well done, girl."

Lady Macbeth screeched, flew off Jenny's lap, and, as she always did in times of great stress, went straight up the curtain to crouch on the pelmet and hurl feline vituperation at the world.

O'Reilly leapt to his feet, hauled Jenny to hers, and gave her an enormous hug. "I'm absolutely, bloody well delighted."

"About what, pray tell? I heard the bellows of you, Fingal O'Reilly, when I was still outside in the street," Kitty said as she came in. "And as I recollect about a year ago, you promised something about forsaking all others."

O'Reilly looked over Jenny's shoulder at Kitty's scowl and knew she was teasing him. Releasing Jenny, he grabbed his wife in an equally ferocious hug that lifted her off the ground, kissed her, and roared, "Terry and Jenny are getting married."

"Put me down, Fingal," Kitty said with a laugh. "And Jenny, pay no attention to your senior. He has no sense of decorum."

"Decorum? Decorum? Are you deaf, woman? Jenny's getting married. We need to celebrate. What would you like?" He nodded at the sideboard.

"I'd like," Kitty said, turning to Jenny and giving her a gentle hug, "to wish Terry and Jenny every happiness."

"Thank you, Kitty."

"A small sherry, I think, Fingal."

"Which you shall have." O'Reilly went to pour.

"I'd also like to remind you that our guest will be here in fifteen minutes. I'm afraid one of the night shift nurses didn't show up and it took a while for me to get a replacement. I have time for a quick drink and then I must change. I'm sure Kinky has things well in hand in the kitchen."

"Blast," said O'Reilly. "I'd forgotten about Fitzpatrick." He sighed, then grinned. "Even so, there's time enough to lift our glasses to the happy couple."

"To you and Terry. We wish you much joy and contentment in your marriage, Doctor Jenny Bradley," Kitty said, and drank.

"Hear hear," O'Reilly said, and finished his Jameson in one swallow.

"You've both been very good to me," Jenny said, returning to her armchair.

"Nonsense," O'Reilly said. "You're a terrific asset to the practice." He wondered, Does this mean she'll leave? He hoped not.

"And your well-woman clinic is working a treat."

Jenny frowned. "I have to be honest," she said, "I'm not sure if I'll be able to stay on once we're married. Terry has just been given a partnership in his law firm in Belfast."

"Good for him," Kitty said. "You must be proud of him."

"I am," Jenny said, "very, but you can see how difficult it would be for him to leave and move here, and my job is really only part-time." She looked straight at O'Reilly. "I know that it makes life a lot easier for you and Barry when I share call. I think at least at the start, if I could still have the attic, I could drive down at night, give you both extra time off."

O'Reilly took his drink, wandered over to the mantel, and said, "Jenny, you are on your way to see the man you love, take his ring, and have a wonderful night out. Why don't we worry about the details of the practice in a couple of days?"

"Fingal's right," Kitty said. "Off you trot and enjoy your evening. I'm sure it will all work out."

Jenny finished her sherry. "Thank you both." She stood. "I really don't want to leave the practice."

O'Reilly put an avuncular hand on her shoulder and said, "I thank you for telling us so we can be prepared if you have to leave, but as I am very fond of saying —"

Kitty made her voice deep and gruff, "We'll cross that bridge when we come to it."

He and Kitty were both laughing as Jenny said, "Thank you both," and left.

"Now," said O'Reilly, striding over to the curtains and looking up, "I'll get this blasted cat down and you go and attend to your toilette before our guest arrives."

Once the greeting pleasantries with Kitty were finished and O'Reilly had ushered the man into the upstairs lounge, Doctor Fitzpatrick moved to stand in front of the fireplace. His gold-rimmed pince-nez shone in the setting sun's rays and his Adam's apple bobbed. He proffered a small, neatly wrapped parcel to Kitty, who sat in one armchair, Lady Macbeth, now returned to her usual composed self, curled up in her lap. "I've brought you a small gift, Mrs. O'Reilly," he said.

"Why thank you, Ronald," Kitty said, accepting the parcel, "and please, it's Kitty."

"And while Kitty's opening it and you're taking a pew," O'Reilly indicated the other armchair, "what can I get you to drink, Ronald?"

"Um. I'm not one for a lot of alcohol, but seeing it's a special occasion could I possibly have a small shandy?" He sat perched on the edge of a chair.

O'Reilly had to open the sideboard to find

a bottle of Bass beer and one of Cantrell & Cochrane's white lemonade. He busied himself pouring a half-and-half mixture into a glass tumbler. "Here you are," he said, handing it to Fitzpatrick. "Cheers."

"Cheers," said Fitzpatrick, and sipped, "and thank you for inviting me to your lovely house."

"Should have done it months ago," O'Reilly said, parking his ample backside on a pouffe and turning when he heard Kitty's cry of pleasure.

"Ronald, he's quite beautiful," Kitty said. She offered a tiny carved figure to O'Reilly. "Look, Fingal. Isn't he exquisite?"

O'Reilly took from her a three-inch figurine. It was a small man with a bald pate, infectious grin, exaggerated ear lobes, breasts, and a pot-belly hanging over a loin cloth. He wore an open robe and carried a sack. The facial features were Oriental. The material looked like discoloured ivory. This must be an example of the *netsuke* that Kitty and Fitzpatrick had discussed so knowledgeably at the lunch in Davy Byrnes back in September. Somehow "exquisite" wasn't quite the word O'Reilly might have used, but then he was no art aficionado. He'd been at sea with a lot of the more modern works in the Picasso Museum in Barcelona. "Delightful," he said, and handed it back.

"I believe he's *Hotei*," Kitty said.

"Well done." Fitzpatrick nodded rapidly. "*Hotei* in Japanese, or *Budai* in Chinese. He represents contentment. The Japanese call it *wa,* a sort of inner peace and tranquillity." The man stared at the floor, then looked up at Kitty and said softly, "Which I wish always for this house."

O'Reilly heard the sincerity in the man's voice and was touched.

Fitzpatrick took another drink. "I hope you don't mind my wishing that?"

Kitty reached out, touched Fitzpatrick's hand, smiled, and said, "I think it's the most charming gift and the loveliest sentiment. Thank you, Ronald. Thank you very much."

Fitzpatrick blushed beet-red.

O'Reilly had been forced to stand and walk to the window so neither Kitty nor, more importantly, Fitzpatrick could see the shine on O'Reilly's eyes. With his back still turned, he said, "Thank you, Ronald. It was most gracious of you." Damn it, this awkward, infuriating man had revealed such a thoughtful side they must be friendlier to him in the future, and for now it was even more important that he and Kitty find a way to get him to see Charlie Greer. They'd agreed to let that hare sit until the break between the main course and dessert.

For a moment no one spoke. Then Kitty rose. She walked to the mantel and placed the figurine upright in the centre. "What do you think of him there, Fingal?" she said.

He turned. "The wee fellah looks right at home, Kitty." He smiled.

"And every time we see him there, he'll remind us of your wish, Ronald."

"Well I — that is —"

"I think," said Kitty, and it was clear to O'Reilly that she was covering the man's shy embarrassment, "that if you gentlemen will bring your drinks, the mushroom soup and hot rolls will be just about ready."

O'Reilly surreptitiously undid his waistband. The soup had been delicious, Kinky's roast beef, Yorkshire puddings, seasonal vegetables, and roast potatoes things of beauty. Kitty had selected a rich red Burgundy and Fitzpatrick had been persuaded to take a glass, in part because O'Reilly felt it a shame not to complement a great meal with wine, but also in the hope that it might help Fitzpatrick be less inhibited and be more amenable to suggestion. Certainly, the man's conversation had been animated and interesting. Now, between the main and dessert courses, was the time to get down to the real business of the evening — once the right opportunity arose.

Kitty was saying, "I'd missed that. The Allies released Albert Speer from Spandau Prison late last month?"

"And Baldur von Schirach," Fitzpatrick

said. "Both on the thirtieth."

Throughout the meal O'Reilly had been surprised by the wide range of Fitzpatrick's interests. Apart from collecting *netsuke* and being expert on aspects of ancient Japanese culture, he could converse fluently about Irish politics, orchids — an interest he shared with O'Reilly's elder brother, Lars — folk remedies, and the operettas of Gilbert and Sullivan. It also transpired that he took a very serious interest in current affairs.

Now O'Reilly was looking for an entrée to a discussion of Fitzpatrick's health. He might have found it in the last remark about Spandau, the prison for Nazi war criminals. "That only leaves Rudolf Hess," O'Reilly said. "I remember when he flew to Scotland in May of '41. Apparently the man is a pathological hypochondriac." He stole a glance at Kitty, who nodded once. She'd picked up the cue. "He's always going on about vague stomach complaints," O'Reilly said, and waited.

Fitzpatrick nodded, pulled off, polished, and replaced his pince-nez. "Yet," he said, "even with malingerers, we cannot afford to ignore our patients' symptoms. Remember, Fingal, when we were students." He glanced fondly at Kitty. "Doctor Micks told us about the senior consultant coming back from a weekend off and asking the houseman, 'How are my patients?' 'All very well, sir, except the neurotic hypochondriac with nothing wrong.'

'Yes. What about him?' 'He died, sir.' " Fitzpatrick's titter was like dry pages being crumpled.

Kitty, clearly caught unaware by Fitzpatrick's willingness to tell an ironic story with a moral, chuckled loudly, but O'Reilly had seen his opening. "I agree. It is our responsibility to take people's complaints seriously." He made his voice as soft as possible. "That's why, Ronald, I wish you'd go and see Charlie."

Fitzpatrick jolted upright in his chair. His Adam's apple went up and down like a yo-yo. "I beg your pardon?"

"I said," and O'Reilly put steel into his voice, "go and see Charlie."

"I believe, Doctor O'Reilly," the sudden formality was not lost on O'Reilly, "I believe we had considered that matter closed."

"Maybe you had, but I can't see a fellow human being —" O'Reilly hoped his next sentence might be the edge of the lever that would allow Kitty to get Fitzpatrick to see sense. "— one who could become a friend, a friend, behaving like a rank *omadahn.*"

"I'm sorry, I don't speak Irish."

"Idiot. Moron. Imbecile. Are those plain enough for you? You're a sick man. For God's sake, get expert advice." O'Reilly rose, and without waiting for Fitzpatrick's reply, said, "See if you can talk sense into him, Kitty. I'll get the dessert." As he strode through the

221

dining room door he heard Fitzpatrick gobbling like a turkey.

Caramelizing the sugar was as simple as Kinky had said and took just enough time to give Kitty her opportunity. O'Reilly loaded the three ramekins onto a tray and headed back, but as he walked past the waiting room, he saw Fitzpatrick's coated back, head under a trilby hat, leaving through the front door. It didn't look as if Kitty had had much success.

She shook her head when he entered.

"No luck?"

"I told him, Fingal's only trying to be your friend."

O'Reilly nodded.

"And that we both care a great deal about him."

"And?"

"He was on the verge of tears, Fingal. All he said was, 'Thank you for a lovely evening,' and you saw him go."

O'Reilly blew out his breath in exasperation. "Eejit," he said.

"Come and sit down, Fingal," she said. "I don't think we could have done any more."

"I know. And I don't think his gift is working."

She frowned.

"He said his wee Buddha . . ."

"*Budai*. They're not one and the same."

"I didn't know. Anyroad, he said his wee fat man was meant to bring inner peace and tranquillity." He looked at her and saw understanding in those grey eyes. "I'm not feeling one bit peaceful. I'm not even sure I want my pudding. Damn it all, Kitty, I just don't know where to go for corn. I'm stuck. And meanwhile, Ronald is getting sicker by the minute. Did you notice how his right hand has developed a tremor?" O'Reilly took a deep breath. "I suppose all we can do now is wait and see."

"I did notice his shake," she said, and then like a mother to a child who has lost at marbles, "and you're right, we can do no more and it's not your fault. Now please sit down."

He did, and before he could protest, she set a ramekin in front of him and took one herself. "I know it won't make Ronald any better, but I think it would be a shame to let all your culinary work go to waste. Eat up."

He shook his head and smiled. Kitty O'Reilly, née O'Hallorhan, might not have been able to persuade Ronald Fitzpatrick, but once more she had worked her wiles on Fingal Flahertie O'Reilly and, by God, the *crema Catalana* was as delicious as the ones they'd had in the Crajeco Loco in Barcelona with Consuela. And, O'Reilly thought, always able to find comfort in his grub, there was the extra one that Ronald Hercules Fitzpatrick, the *omadahn,* had so ungraciously not bothered to eat.

14

EMPTY WORDS OF A DREAM

Fingal was sorry that he'd cut it close and left a cyclist in the ditch, but he didn't want to waste a minute getting to Twiddy's. He wasn't going to prevaricate any longer. Deirdre was entitled to know what was happening, and he knew no matter what, she'd be brave. Deirdre. Sensible, calm, and very beautiful. He pictured her coming downstairs after her nap and her bath on Monday. She'd rearranged her hair and used just enough makeup to highlight her eyes and lips. Her sleeveless, knee-length, cherry-red dress had a neckline verging on the reckless, and together with dark silk stockings and black patent leather court shoes, the effect was stunning. "You look gorgeous," he'd said.

"Thank you, sir," she'd said. She'd glided across the room. To Fingal, she'd seemed to be fine as a bee's wing, light as ocean spray. The rest was a blur until Marge had had to go out, leaving them alone, and he'd been holding her, wanting her, loving her.

"Woof." Admiral Benbow's sharp bark brought him back to the present. It seemed the big shaggy sheepdog was on watch.

"Coming." It was Marge's voice, not Deirdre's, and Fingal stifled his disappointment.

The door opened. "Fingal. How lovely."

The new necklace her husband had given her had replaced the — for an Englishwoman of her class — statutory string of pearls. "Is Deirdre here?" he asked, and tried to peer past Marge. "I've got to talk to her. It's important."

Benbow demanded attention by thrusting his cold nose against Fingal's hand, so he absently patted the dog's head.

"It must be," Marge said. "Not bad news I hope?"

Fingal pursed his lips. He meant to tell Deirdre before anyone else, but Marge had been so kind, so understanding. The words tumbled out. "I can't get permission to marry."

"You can't? Oh, Fingal, I'm most dreadfully sorry," Marge said. "You'll have to break the news to her at once. And Fingal?"

"Yes?"

"Deirdre can stay with me for as long as she likes."

"Thank you, Marge."

"Now you must go and see her. You remember we'd talked about me getting her a job as a Land Girl?"

He nodded.

"Your Deirdre isn't one to let the grass grow under her feet. She rested on Tuesday and yesterday, but it was up Guards and at 'em today. It's the end of haymaking season. She's over at Hutchinson's with Pip and some other girls."

"Oh." He had to get there. "Can you — ?"

"Of course I'll give you directions," she said — and did.

He shuddered to think what bouncing over the ruts was doing to the springs of David's little car, but according to what Marge had said, Fingal's quickest way of getting to the hayfield was to park at the end of this lane, clamber over a five-bar gate beneath an old oak tree, cross a pasture, and the Land Girls would be working on the far side of a hedge.

There was the gate and the massive oak, laden with acorns. In moments he'd parked, climbed over the gate, and was running, dodging steaming cow claps, across the pasture so fast a herd of brown-and-white Herefords didn't have time to wander over in the way of their kind to investigate the stranger.

Even in early October, the sun was warm and he was sweating when he found the gate in the far hedge.

He let himself through into a field where the grass had been mown in swaths and was losing its greenness. The scent of recently cut hay filled his nostrils. Nearby, up a shallow hill where they'd have been hidden from his view as he crossed the pasture, he saw several young women grouped round a wagon being pulled by a great Clydesdale horse. He heard a sweet soprano singing, "Little sir Echo, how do you do."

And the girls singing, "Hello (hello). Hello (hello)."

With every repeated hello, they swung their pitchfork loads in unison onto the wagon. He'd never heard a popular song used like a sea shanty before, but it seemed to be effective. He recognised Pip standing up there holding the reins and Deirdre, her hair done up in a scarf knotted over the middle of her forehead, working away with a will. She looked strong, her movements sure and capable, and he realized that the girl he'd always tried to treat like Dresden china was a lot tougher than he'd imagined. "Deirdre," he called. "Deirdre." He saw her hesitate, wave, start toward him, then turn back and speak to Pip. Deirdre must be asking permission to stop work. She was in an army of sorts, after all. Then she was running to him.

She came into his arms, kissed him, and stepped back. "Gosh," she said, "but you're a bristly man."

"I've been too busy to shave," he said gently, pulling a strand of hay from her hair, and then gathered her into his arms again and kissed her back.

"Lord, I do love you." She was smiling. "What brings you here today? I thought you'd be working."

"I love you too," he said.

"Do you have a day off? Can you stay for a while? Pip says I've got to be back in five minutes, but we'll get half an hour for elevenses. Fingal, I was so worried about you when the bombs started to fall, but Marge told me they were too far away to be hitting Gosport." She paused for breath.

"Hello (hello). Hello (hello)." Her fellows were back at work, it seemed.

"I was quite safe," he said. "Please don't worry."

"I'll not," she said, taking his hand.

He took off his cap with the other and wiped the sweat off his brow. "Darling," he said, "there's something I want to talk to you about."

"Oh?" she said. She was still smiling.

"I didn't want to worry you —"

"Fingal, you're not sick?" She frowned. "You've not been posted away?"

"Nothing like that," he said.

"Good," she said in a very matter-of-fact voice. "Then it can't be too serious."

"I've not told you anything about our wedding," and before she could reply said, "I thought I'd have it all sorted out by Tuesday so I didn't want to worry you, and I didn't tell you anything."

She frowned. "Anything about what?"

"It seems we need the navy's permission. I didn't find that out until last week and was so sure it would be granted I didn't say anything to you when we made arrangements for you to come here. I should have. I'm sorry."

She didn't scold him or say anything silly like, "They couldn't refuse you," but turned her head to one side, tilted it, and said softly, "And they've refused?"

He hung his head, nodded, heard her sudden intake of breath, and looked straight at her while saying, "Yes." He waited. He knew of girls who would have burst into tears, thrown a hysterical fit, suspected they were being jilted at the last minute on some fabricated excuse.

"Won't you come over and play (and play)."

And the big horse whinnied and made a rubbery noise with its lips.

Deirdre straightened her shoulders. "Thank you for telling me, darling." She leant forward and touched his hand. "And there's no need to apologise. I'd still have come to you. I love you so much."

In all of Ulster, all of Ireland, he couldn't have found such a sensible, loving girl. And his heart swelled. He took her other hand and lifted them both to his lips. "I don't want to get our hopes up, but —"

"But?"

"My boss, Surgeon Captain Mahaddie, thinks there may be a way round. It seems I need a promotion before I can marry. It's the way they do things in the navy. But he's going to look into it once the telephones are working again."

"But they are," she said. "Marge was talking to Pip at eight this morning, telling her that Tony Wilcoxson's ship will be in and he'll be coming up next weekend."

"Fareham must be on a different exchange," Fingal said. "Nothing was going in and out of Haslar at nine thirty this morning, I'm afraid. We'll have to be patient."

"Darling," she said, "I can't pretend I'm not disappointed. I am, bitterly —"

"I'm so sorry, Deirdre."

"No, don't be, truly. It's not your fault."

How often had he, the professional, said that to a grieving patient?

"Thank you." His words were soft.

"We have to wait until we see what your captain finds out. If we can get married, it will be wonderful."

"But if we can't?"

She put her arms round his neck. He inhaled her faint perfume.

"If we can't, we can't have a ceremony, that's all." She glanced behind to make sure she was standing in such a way that no one could see, then put his hand on her left breast, and said, "Can you feel my heart?"

He swallowed and said, "Yes."

"In there I don't need a piece of paper. In there and," she put her hand on his left chest, "and in there, dearest Fingal O'Reilly, we're as married as any man and woman can be. And always will be." And then she kissed him.

He nodded, not wanting to speak.

"We'll have to wait for your captain's answer, but if it is no, I know Marge will let me stay on at her house . . ."

"She will," he said. "She's already said so."

"Good old Marge. She likes having me there. It helps her, what with her husband and Tony being away. You and I can see each other as often as your duty allows. I am not going back to Ulster until your time here is finished."

"Hello (hello). Hello (hello)."

The girls' voices were accompanied by the creaking of harness and the squealing of what sounded to Fingal like an axle badly in need of oil as the cart moved forward.

"Thank you," he said, marvelling at her composure, her willingness to make the most of a bad job if it came to that. "Thank you, darling." His pulse was slowing but still fast. "If it does come to that, I'm sure we'll have chances to be alone."

"Sure?" she said, and laughed. "I'm bloody well certain."

And in the background the soprano finished

her song, "But you're always so far away. (away)."

"I think," Deirdre said, "my five minutes are up."

"And I'm not so far away," said Fingal. "I'll let you know the minute I hear anything and I'm not on duty next weekend so I'll see you then." He kissed her and stood for a long moment watching her as she rejoined her work party and took up her pitchfork before he set off to trudge back across this field.

He was in no hurry as he strode through the pastures, letting the sun warm him and the sweet smell of the hay seep past his nostrils. By the time he'd reached the five-bar gate, he was surrounded by the herd of inquisitive Herefords, lowing and swishing their tails, and for a moment, Fingal O'Reilly felt as if he was back home, crossing such a field in the quiet of the Ballybucklebo Hills. He sighed, wishing he was there — with Deirdre, but he knew that it was early days, Britain was all alone against Hitler and Mussolini, and it seemed as if the war would never end.

15
LET EVERY PUPPY DRINK

"Them nice doctors at the Royal Maternity kept me in for near a week, so they did," said Irene Beggs from where she lay on the examination couch in O'Reilly's surgery. "That lovely Doctor Holland, him what his friends call 'Buster,' was looking after me. He's called the 'senior tutor.' I dunno why. He never taught me nothing. Maybe I'm not senior enough?"

O'Reilly laughed. Irene was in for her scheduled antenatal visit. And while she was Barry's patient, Barry had been called out for a home visit to a child with what sounded like croup. "It's a title given to the most senior of the young doctors at RMH. Doctor Holland has finished all his training and passed all his exams and he's waiting for a vacant senior post. Part of his job is to teach the more junior doctors." O'Reilly continued with the routine examination, paying particular attention to the uterus, while Irene prattled on, seemingly unconcerned that he might not be listening.

"I see," she said, clearly losing interest in the subject. "Anyroad, they kept me in bed for six days then said everything was lovely, the wean was fine, and I could go home and for til see my own doctor. So I seen Doctor Laverty while you and Mrs. O'Reilly was in Spain. I hear it's dead lovely at this time of the year. My friend Jeannie Jingles and her man went to Tossa del Mar on one of them package tours. Said it was wheeker, so she did. Maybe me and Davy'll get to go one day, but not likely, is it? With two at home and this one on the way?"

"And this one's doing fine. Wee heart's going away like the clappers. Today's October the fourteenth so you're thirty-three weeks and four days. Your fibroid's behaving itself, I can hardly feel it." Which was often the case. Benign tumours tended to soften and flatten as the pregnancy progressed and the uterus enlarged. "Your blood pressure's fine and there's nothing in your urine. Will you come in in two weeks and see Doctor Laverty, please?"

"Aye, certainly." She started to get dressed. "And do I really have til have the baby in hospital?"

O'Reilly paused. The art of midwifery that he'd practiced as a young man in Dublin, had, since the war, become much more conservative — and much safer — with the introduction of antibiotics and blood transfusion to treat the two great killers of pregnant women, infection and haemorrhage. If there was any chance of complications, the home was no place to manage them. He didn't want to frighten Irene. The fibroid did still represent a risk factor for several of those complications, so he simply said, "If that's what the specialists advised."

"Och, dear," she said, "but I suppose it'll be for the best."

"We'll do one more antenatal visit here. That'll save you the trouble of travelling to Belfast, and then when you're thirty-six weeks, they'll want to see you at RMH once a week after that."

He heard the phone ringing in the hall, and although the ensuing words were muffled, he knew Kinky would be saying in her soft Cork voice, "Hello. Doctor O'Reilly and Doctor Laverty's practice."

"Boys-a-dear," Irene said, now fully dressed, "all them bus and train trips back and forth to the city." She pursed her lips, but then smiled. "Och well, it's all for the good of the wean, isn't it, sir?"

"It is that, Irene." He took off his half-moon spectacles. She was the last patient of the day. "Off you go and we'll see you in a couple of weeks, and you can call us anytime if you're worried." As she left, he pulled out his briar and lit up.

Immediately the door opened and Kinky came in.

Oh-oh, he thought, an emergency. "Yes, Kinky."

"Can you come to the telephone, sir? It does be that buck eejit Donal. He won't tell me what the trouble is, and he wants to speak only to yourself, so."

What the divil was Donal was up to now? O'Reilly rose. "Thanks, Kinky. I'll look after it." He made his way to the hall, Kinky following. As O'Reilly picked up the receiver, Barry came in through the front door. "Hello, Donal?" O'Reilly said. "What's up?"

At the mention of Donal's name, Barry stopped and looked at O'Reilly.

"You've a surprise for me at Dun Bwee? What kind of surprise? Is anybody sick? . . . That's a relief. All right, well, no time like the present. I've just finished surgery for the day. I'll be out soon. Right. Good-bye." O'Reilly chuckled and said to Barry and Kinky, "Donal has a surprise for me, but he wants to keep it hush-hush." He winked. "Of course he didn't say a thing about not discussing it with a professional colleague. Maybe, Barry, you should come to give a second opinion?"

"I always enjoy a visit to Ballybucklebo's arch schemer, but I'm on call," Barry said.

"I'll know where to find you, sir," Kinky said. "Off you trot."

"Come on then," said O'Reilly. "And we'll take Arthur. He and Donal's Bluebird are great pals. How was your patient? It sounded like croup."

"Young Dermot O'Malley? It was croup," Barry said. "Acute laryngitis. Nothing serious. I gave his mum a prescription for penicillin and sulphadimidine, told her to keep a kettle steaming in his room, and that one of us would visit tomorrow."

O'Reilly clapped Barry on the shoulder. "Couldn't have done better myself. Early retirement looms ever closer now with you to take over, Barry."

Barry held the kitchen door open, guffawed, and said, "Retirement? You? Doctor Fingal O'Reilly, away off and feel your bumps. They'll have to shoot you in harness — and you know it."

And laughing together they walked through the sun-dappled back garden, collected a grateful Arthur, and headed to the Rover.

"I agree," Barry said as O'Reilly put the big car into the hairpin bend. Donal's lane ran from its crown. "Irene's fibroid is on the front of the uterus and doesn't seem to involve the cavity, so the risks of it causing *abruptio placentae* or interfering with the way the baby lies are pretty remote. It could cause premature labour, but the baby should be all right if Irene can carry for another three or four weeks. She'll be safe enough staying at home with us keeping an eye on her."

"Hang on," said O'Reilly, indicating for a turn and changing down. He made a sharp left and the car jounced along the lane.

In the backseat Arthur started his usual throaty mutterings with which he greeted every ride over rough ground. He knew he'd be let out soon.

"I still think the consultants are right," Barry said, "about having her give birth in hospital. Fibroids can slow the progress of labour . . ."

"And cause problems once the baby's born, but the afterbirth still has not been expelled and the uterus can't contract fully to control the big blood vessels that supply the placenta," O'Reilly said. "Before the war I had to watch a woman bleed to death. She'd given birth at home in the Liberties. Her doctor couldn't stop the bleeding, of course. There was nothing he could do in that situation back then. She was rushed to the Rotunda. We'd no blood transfusions in those days. All we could offer was a hysterectomy. But it was too late." He braked outside Donal's cottage and stared at the sturdy white-stuccoed structure, as if seeking reassurance from its permanence. Because for a moment he'd been back in the maternity hospital in Dublin, the smell of blood and disinfectant thick in his nostrils, the dying woman pale on the operating table clutching his, a young trainee's, hand and begging, "Please, Doctor," before she passed out from loss of blood.

"I think that experience tipped the scale for me," he said softly. "That was when I decided obstetrics wasn't for me and that I preferred GP." He opened his door. "Come on, let's see what Donal has for us." He opened the car's back door. "Heel, Arthur." The big dog bounded out and tucked in at O'Reilly's heel. I don't believe I've ever told Kitty about that case, he thought as he waited for Barry to walk round the car, and my decision to pack up obstetrics. He smiled as Barry neared. "Do you know, young Laverty, I do enjoy having you as a partner." And ignoring Barry's pleased but puzzled look and the young man's beginning of a frown, he started to walk round the cottage with its yellow straw thatch and scarlet doors and window frames.

Donal had come out through the back door even before O'Reilly knocked. He'd clearly been watching for the Rover. What was he up to? "I see you brung Doctor Laverty. Well, that's all right, for he knows about it, but I don't want the word getting out just yet. Thanks for coming, sir. I promised I'd let you know when Bluebird whelped."

So that's was this was all about. O'Reilly remembered the conversation in the sand dunes last month.

Donal shook his head and inhaled. "Two days ago."

"I take it that they are not purebred."

"Divil the bit," said Donal. "They're like no greyhound pup I've ever seen, sir. Neither me nor Julie have a baldy notion about what til do with them, and I don't want no one to know about them."

"Why not? Don't you want to find homes for them?" O'Reilly asked.

"I do. But I want til think on what to do to see if I can sell them for money. Nobody's going to pay for a mongrel pup. Can you and Doctor Laverty keep this under your hats for a while, just until I puzzle out what to do?"

O'Reilly glanced at Barry, who nodded, a trace of a smile on his face. "We can, but I'm not sure there's much else we can help you with. Who else knows that Bluebird was pregnant?" O'Reilly said.

"Ever since I caught Brian Boru, the merry Mexican marauder, coming out of Bluebird's pen, I've been worried something like this might happen. So I've hardly told a soul. We're off the beaten track out here and we don't have many visitors. If I'd been wrong and she'd had purebred pups, everything would have been grand, but now? Only us knows, and you'll not have told anybody." Donal sounded anxious.

"You can trust us," O'Reilly said, and Kitty, he thought. She was a very experienced nurse and knew not to gossip about any of the practice's patients.

"And I've had a wee word with Dapper on the QT. He'll keep mum too." Donal shook his head. "Honest til God, they're funny-looking wee craytures."

"Can we see them, Donal?" Barry asked.

"Aye, certainly. They're with their ma in her run. This way and, Doctor O'Reilly, would you mind putting Arthur back in your motor? Bitches can be very protective of their litters round other dogs."

"Of course," said O'Reilly. "I should have thought of that." He spoke to Arthur. "Come on, lummox. Back in the car for you, and don't worry. I'll give you a good run once I've taken Barry home."

By the time he'd got Arthur settled and had returned, Barry and Donal were already in the chain-link-fenced run where, close to her kennel, Bluebird lay on her side on the grass. In the concavity of her body a mass of grey and brown dappled puppies, all with their eyes shut, formed a squirming heap. He guessed there must be ten or twelve. Some were latched onto her nipples, some were fast asleep. One, who somehow had become separated and must be feeling the cold, was mewling loudly, and Bluebird twisted her body so she could reach the little creature. She picked it up in her mouth, returned it to the company of its brothers and sisters, and began to wash it.

O'Reilly unlatched the gate and let himself in.

Barry said, "I'm no great judge of dog flesh, but as best as I can tell they're going to have their mother's long legs, skinny tail, and arched back."

"Aye," said Donal, "and with my luck they'll probably have their wee git of a daddy's funny nose, pointy ears, and big, brown sticky-out eyes. They'll be about as much use as chocolate teapots, so they will." He shrugged. "Och well, I suppose somebody maybe up in Belfast might want one or two for pets, like. The folks down here won't. I can't see these wee buggers being much use to anyone, and a country dog has til work for his keep." He pursed his lips. "If anything, it's going to be the other way round."

"I'm sorry," Barry said. "I don't understand."

"Four weeks from now they'll start wanting solid food. Someone has til buy it and that someone's me. And the bigger they get, the more expensive it'll be."

"I see," Barry said. "That is a bit awkward. It looks like there may be as many as a dozen of the little mites."

O'Reilly nodded, scratched his head. "I don't suppose there'd be any point asking Cahal Cullen, the marquis's shepherd, if they could be trained as sheepdogs. If they have their mother's legs they should be good runners."

O'Reilly had a moment of déjà vu when Donal said, "No harm til you, sir, but away off and feel your bumps." The same suggestion that O'Reilly should examine his cranium had been made by Barry half an hour ago. "Cahal wouldn't have the time and I'd not have a clue how til train them myself." He bent and patted Bluebird's head. "You poor wee thing," he said. "You'll have your work cut out for you for the next while looking after that lot, and God knows how I'm going til find homes for your pups." He squatted on his hunkers beside her and the gaze from those big liquid eyes never left his face. "Anyroad. Never you worry. That's my job." He rose. "Doctors, I think we should leave them be now." He opened the gate and waited until Barry and O'Reilly were outside before coming through himself and snibbing it shut.

"Have you decided what to call the, um, breed?" Barry asked.

"I suppose Greyhuahua'll have to do," Donal said, "and if I can't come up with something, I'll give them away, so I will. Maybe young Colin would like another wee dog."

"You'll keep us posted, Donal?" O'Reilly said.

"Aye, certainly, sir," Donal said. "Now, Julie's inside with wee Tori. She asked me til

243

ask you if you'd like a wee cup of tea in your hand?"

"That's very kind, Donal," O'Reilly said, "but we have to be running along. Doctor Laverty's on call so we've no time for tea. We'll just pop in to say hello and then be on our way."

And when O'Reilly and Barry had spent a little time with Julie and the chattering little Tori, they took their leave. As the car jolted along the lane, O'Reilly contentedly singing, "You ain't nothing but a hound dog," he heard Barry say, "I am truly sorry for Donal, but that two pounds you're going to owe me when Donal doesn't figure out a way to sell the pups is getting closer and closer."

To which O'Reilly could only answer, in song, " 'You ain't never caught a rabbit and you ain't no friend of mine,' and my boy, we'll just have to see about the bet, won't we. Time will tell. Time will tell."

16

A DREAM COME TRUE

"And how are we this bright and breezy morning, Surgeon Lieutenant-Commander O'Reilly?"

There had been a knock on Fingal's door on Saturday morning and there had stood Surgeon Captain Angus Mahaddie, grinning like the Cheshire cat and offering a handshake.

"Who?" Fingal shook the man's hand but then took a step backward, not sure he'd heard correctly. "Lieutenant-commander? You're serious?"

"Of course I'm serious. Now, are you going to leave me standing out here in the hall, or are you going to invite me into your palatial accommodation?" Angus looked around at the iron-framed single bed, free-standing wardrobe, and plain table with two wooden chairs. "Aye, I'd forgotten how small these rooms are. The sooner you're out of here and into married quarters, the better."

"Good God, Angus, I don't know how to

thank you enough. Come in. Come in." Fingal motioned his senior into the cramped room and closed the door. "But how did you do it?"

Angus took a chair, but Fingal remained standing. He knew he'd not be able to keep still. He wanted to rush to the nearest telephone.

"A department head — that's me — can apply, in an emergency, for promotion of a lieutenant to acting lieutenant-commander in his unit if the best interests of the service demand it. And the rank, once approved, becomes effective immediately."

"You mean . . . you mean . . ."

"Just so." The little Scot's eyes twinkled. "I've set the wheels in motion to have it confirmed. And given our recent workload, I honestly believe the service does demand it. I've had a word with Admiral Creaser, who says he's delighted with the idea and he is sorry he didn't think of it himself. He's approved so it'll go up through channels like a rocket. It might take a week or two before you can put up your extra half ring but," the Scot winked and said, "the admiral says Nelson's not the only one with a blind eye. We'll not quibble over the exact date of your promotion. He reckons our chaplain, John Wilfred Evans, could probably do the deed in Saint Luke's Church on Friday, November

246

the first. Eh, that's just over three weeks away."

Fingal paced to the far wall. He stared out the window to see the side of the chapel in the foreground and the administrative block in the distance. They looked utilitarian and drab in the greyness of the October day. Barely trusting himself to speak, he then turned and said, "Bless you, Angus."

"Now I imagine you'd like to pass the word to your fiancée." Fingal heard the naval "pass the word," and was reminded of how Haslar really was run as a ship at sea, even here in this great redbrick hospital complex on its peninsula between Haslar Creek and the Solent. Angus glanced at his watch. "It's nine thirty. There'll be a transfer train taking recovering patients from Gosport Station, leaving in —"

Fingal was already grabbing for his cap and gas mask.

"— half an hour. If you ask the driver, he'll make a stop for you in Fareham. They're pretty accommodating with Haslar staff."

Angus's words were already growing faint as Fingal tore through the door yelling, "Thank you," over his shoulder.

"My goodness, Fingal, you're out of breath," Marge said, "and we weren't expecting you until lunchtime, but do come in. Deirdre and I were having coffee. I'm afraid it's only that

247

awful chicory Camp stuff, but if you'd like a cup?"

"Please," Fingal said, trying to control his panting. He'd run all the way from Fareham station. And admit it, he told himself, you're not as fit as you were when you were playing rugby football. He followed her into the now-familiar room where Admiral Benbow, lying by the fire, barely deigned to glance through his fringe and blow out his breath as if to say, Huh. Him again.

But Deirdre gave a yelp of delight when she saw him, leapt up from her seat, and rushed to him. "You're early, Fingal. Terrific."

He took her in his arms, kissed her, and said, "Darling. I've got some wonderful news."

"Pay no attention to me," Marge said as she poured him a cup of coffee. "But do sit, Fingal, and tell the girl. By the way, do you take sugar? I've forgotten."

"Please." Fingal, holding on to Deirdre's hand, was happy to be led to one of the armchairs. As they walked he said, and loudly enough for Marge to hear, "If it would suit you, we can tie the knot on November the first."

She stopped dead, forcing him to do the same. Deirdre had, since they'd confessed love for each other, put an unshakeable trust in him that was humbling. "Darling, that is wonderful news," she said, "isn't it, Marge?"

"I am overjoyed," Marge said, "if only because I'll get my spare bedroom back." Her words sounded uncaring, but Fingal had rapidly become accustomed to the English upper class's refusal to show emotion in public, and anyway, her grin belied the coldness of her words. "Here you are," she said. "Coffee . . . of a kind."

Fingal accepted the cup and sat beside Deirdre. "Thank you." He drank in the coffee and the bright sparkle in her eyes. Bless you again, Angus Mahaddie. "We'll have to make arrangements," he said.

"In a minute or two, Fingal," Deirdre said. "I just want to get used to the idea that in no time I'll be Mrs. O'Reilly. At last. It's wonderful. I'm so happy."

Fingal looked more deeply into her eyes. "Me too," he said, and in his head he could hear the lyrics he'd known since he was a boy.

Oh no, 'twas the truth in her eyes ever
    shining
That made me love Mary, the Rose of
    Tralee.

"I'm very happy for you both," Marge said. "Is there anything at all I can do?"

"Yes." She said the word in a happy sigh, but the words that followed were practical, down to earth. "None of our families will be able to come over from Ulster."

Fingal nodded. Bloody war.

"I'd be deeply honoured if you'd be my matron of honour, Marge, and do you think Pip would be my bridesmaid?"

Marge leaned over and lightly kissed Deirdre's cheek. "It would give me enormous pleasure, my dear. But I can't speak for the Honourable Philippa Gore-Beresford. You can ask her yourself. I'm sure she'll say yes."

"I will, Marge. I will. We've become such friends since I came. She's been so kind," Deirdre said.

"That's our Pip," Marge said. "Now, you shall need somewhere to live. Have you thought about that, Fingal?"

"Yes, as a matter of fact. The Crescent in Alverstoke has quarters for married naval officers. WREN officers who work at HMS *Hornet,* the Motor Torpedo Boat base, live there too. It's only about a mile's walk to the hospital."

"I'd suggest you pay them a visit this afternoon. Try to get a spot," Marge said, "and you'll be able to get, within wartime constraints, a decent supper in the Anglesey Hotel. It's part of the terrace."

Deirdre said, "Let's do it, darling. Let's go and see if we can find our first home together."

And that prospect so filled Fingal with delight that, if it would not have been impolite, he'd have forgone lunch and headed to Alverstoke at once.

"Looks pretty Georgian to me, all those Doric pillars holding up a first-floor balcony and those chimneys on the roof," Fingal said. "I've been to Bath and the old Roman Aquae Sulis. There are more curved terraces like this there."

As he and Deirdre stood looking at the grubby white three-storey crescent of terrace houses, three WREN officers, talking animatedly, left through what must be the entrance — a narrow set of six columns in the middle of the terrace that ran almost to the roof and supported a small roof of their own. The women were headed in Fingal and Deirdre's direction.

He pointed to his right at the four-storey Anglesey Arms. "That's the hotel," he said. "The staff at Haslar uses it quite a lot as their local, they tell me."

"Looks like somewhere that should have serious-looking mutton-chopped admirals coming in and going out, making sure Britannia still rules the waves."

He laughed, but had to come to attention and return the compliment as the WRENs passed and saluted. When they'd gone he took Deirdre's hand and led her toward the entrance. "I'm told," he said, "that a couple of current admirals live in houses at the far end of the Crescent."

The buildings were separated from the road by a low redbrick wall, and even if there was a war on someone had found time to trim a privet hedge that stood behind the wall. He wondered if the red bricks had been left over from the time of Haslar's construction. The clay for making them had been taken from the very grounds where the hospital was built. "Marge said we should ask at the hall porter's. I think it'll be in there."

He led her into an echoing foyer with a tiled marble floor, very high ceilings, and staircases to either side. Two potted aspidistras, looking limp and dejected, sat in one corner, and a chief petty officer, looking marginally more lively, sat in a glass-fronted cubicle in the other. He was a man of about sixty, probably ex–Royal Navy called back for noncombatant work by the "requirements of the service," and Fingal blessed them. The man rose, but as he was uncovered, did not salute. Nor did Fingal.

"Can oi be of assistance, zur?" His accent placed him at once as a Westcountryman. Probably from Somerset.

"Please. I'm Surgeon Lieutenant O'Reilly, temporarily attached to Haslar. My fiancée, Nurse Mawhinney," he nodded to Deirdre, "and I will be married in three weeks. We've been advised to enquire about getting a furnished flat here."

"You've come to the right place, sir. We do have a number of vacancies. If you'd like to inspect one?"

"Very much." Fingal felt Deirdre give his arm an almighty squeeze.

"Here's the keys to number 2B. It's the best of the lot," the man said. "Up that left-hand staircase, then turn to your left, and it's the fourth door on the right. It's a front-facing one so you'll have a bit of a view over the Solent. You can watch the Fishbourne-Portsmouth Ferry go by."

"Thank you," Fingal said, accepting the keys and thinking that while the ferry must be a delightful sight to see, in moments he was going to have Deirdre all to himself in private, with the door closed.

As soon as it was shut, he enfolded her in a massive hug and kissed her with all the longing deep in him. She kissed him back, lips on lips, tongue on tongue, a long, yearning kiss that made him shudder, but then she moved back.

"I want you so much, darling," she said, "but not here. Not yet."

He couldn't speak, simply stood holding her hand, waiting for his breathing to come under control, his heart to stop pounding.

"I do love you so, Fingal," she said. "Later."

And he wondered how much later?

"Can we have a look around?" she said, and began to lead him along a narrow hall.

He was less interested in the physical surroundings. The place was clean with no musty smell, and a small hall led to a combined sitting room and dining room. Doors led to bedrooms, one on either side of the hall.

"Look, Fingal. A double bed," she said.

"Splendid." Vivid images of lovemaking filled his mind.

"And a coal fire. We can roast chestnuts at Christmas." And make love in front of the fire. He pictured that too.

She disappeared through a door at the side of the dining area. He heard drawers being opened and shut, the clanking of pots and dishes. When she reappeared she said, "I'm sure it's a lovely kitchen, but I'm not much of a cook. I'll have to buy a cookbook."

Images of home-cooked meals fled and he laughed. "Well, if we're stuck, I'm sure we'll be able to get a bite next door in the hotel."

"The hotel," she said, and he was surprised by the huskiness of her voice. She came back into the main room, composed again, her voice matter-of-fact. "Have you any idea what you have to do to get a flat here?"

He laughed again. "Well, that CPO didn't look like someone who'd take a bribe. He did say there were vacancies. I'm sure people are always coming and going. I reckon if we go through the proper channels, Mrs. O'Reilly-very-soon-to-be, and we're good little boys and girls, the navy will let us stay here." He hugged her again and kissed her, but gently.

"Not too good, I hope. Do please try to get it for us, Fingal." She stared out the window over the street, a few low houses, a green space, and out to the grey, choppy Solent and the Isle of Wight beyond. "And I love the view," she said. "It's not quite the same as looking across Belfast Lough to the Antrim Hills, but it does remind me of home. I can hardly wait until November the first. Shall we have a honeymoon?"

"Angus has promised me a short bit of leave."

"Wonderful," she said. "We must ask Marge's advice about where to go."

"All right," he said.

"Now, did someone suggest a meal at the Anglesey?"

"Marge said they do a decent supper," he said.

"And she told me that Queen Victoria used to sleep there on the way to her house on the Isle of Wight." She began a slow, inviting smile as she rummaged in her handbag. "It must be nice to sleep there, in the Anglesey," she said, and that husky tone was back.

What was she hinting? Fingal wondered. Even in wartime, English hotels, at least the reputable ones, would demand evidence that a couple was married. His eyes widened. Good Lord.

Deirdre had produced a shiny, narrow, gold-coloured ring and slipped it on the ring finger of her left hand. "I believe," she said, "you're not on duty again until Monday, and I'm perfectly sure the man at reception will never have seen either of us." She ran the tip of her tongue over her lips.

Fingal shuddered, took a very deep breath, and, trying to control a slight tremble in his voice, said, "But we've no luggage. They'll still not believe us." Amazing how the war had brought so many social conventions tumbling down. The desk staff were still duty-bound to go through the motions of insisting that a couple be married before they could get a room, but young people, driven by the very real fear that the man might never come back, were determined to seize life — and love.

"Oh, Fingal," she said, moved against him and kissed him long and hard. "I'm sure you have a suitcase in your quarters and it's only two miles there and back." Her next kiss was harder, her tongue on his, her firm breasts against his chest. "I'm certain a walk would do us good, and I'm sure it'll help us work up quite an appetite." Her wink was slow.

So that's what "later" had meant. And Fingal O'Reilly laughed as if he'd never stop, then held her and said, "I love you, Deirdre Mawhinney. And I'll love you to the grave and beyond." He tugged her toward the door. "Come on," he said, "let's go for a walk."

17
THE BIRD IS ON THE WING

"There you are, John." O'Reilly handed the Marquis of Ballybucklebo a prescription for hydrochlorothiazide. "One tablet twice a day'll keep the old blood pressure under control for another six months."

"Thanks, Fingal," the marquis said, "and I appreciate your coming out to the house to examine me, particularly on such a miserable day." There was a tired note to his voice.

The October drizzle had started after Kitty and O'Reilly had finished their lunch, just before she'd headed off to her third-Saturday-of-the-month painting group in Belfast and he'd collected Arthur and driven out here. Jenny, who still hadn't made up her mind about leaving, was on call, and Barry had gone with Helen Hewitt to watch Jack Mills play rugby.

Raindrops coursed down the mullioned windows of his lordship's study.

"A bit of rain never hurt anybody," O'Reilly said, and laughed. "And we can't expect the lord of the manor to sit in my waiting room with the peasantry. I was passing anyway. I'm going snipe shooting at the Kearney farm."

"Are you, by Jove?" The marquis looked wistful. "I envy you."

"With all your pheasant on the estate and grouse up on your moors above the Glens of Antrim?"

The marquis frowned and sighed. "Your rough shooting doesn't cost you a penny. I spent all day yesterday with the estate manager, going over my expenses for the last quarter."

O'Reilly waited but was not surprised when the marquis left the matter hanging in midair. He was not the kind of man to wash his dirty linen in public, even if that public was his friend and trusted physician. That notwithstanding, O'Reilly inferred that John Mac-Neill was worried about money — again. Since the institution by the Asquith government in 1914 of heavy death duties on big estates, running one had become a burden for many titled landowners. O'Reilly knew his friend was still paying off the duties occasioned by the death of his father. "Got you worried?" he asked.

The marquis pursed his lips. "I'll have to start cutting back somewhere. Didn't sleep too much last night trying to decide where."

O'Reilly hesitated. His formal medical training told him to ask a leading question, try to get the man to talk more about his concerns. His knowledge of John MacNeill suggested a different approach. "Would an afternoon out with me and Arthur in the bog cheer you up? I'm sure the Kearneys won't mind if I bring you along."

The marquis smiled, then sobered. "You're quite sure I wouldn't be intruding on your privacy?"

"Not at all. Arthur and I would enjoy your company."

"Do you know," he said, rising, "I think it would work wonders. I really do. Blow away the cobwebs. Give me a minute, Fingal. I'll get myself organised. And thank you."

He tugged a cord that would make a bell ring in the servants' quarters. "Will we need another dog? I can bring Sophie."

"No need. It's not a big piece of cover and with two dogs we'd be finished in no time. I want Arthur to earn his keep today. It's his idea of doggy heaven pushing up and retrieving game."

"Fair enough."

Thompson, the valet/butler appeared. "My lord?"

"Thompson, I'm going snipe shooting with Doctor O'Reilly."

"Yes, sir, and good morning, Commander O'Reilly."

"Morning, Thompson." The man had been a CPO gunner on *Warspite* in the Med. He always used O'Reilly's naval title.

"The twenty bore with number eight cartridges and your game bag, sir?" Thompson said.

"Precisely," the marquis said, "and if you'll excuse me, Fingal, I'll just be a minute changing into my shooting gear, then we'll be off."

And the lift in his voice, the grin on his face were all that it took to convince O'Reilly that he had indeed prescribed the right medicine for his old friend.

O'Reilly knocked on the door to the Kearneys' farmhouse. Blue smoke straggled up from a chimney and the air was redolent of burning turf. He turned up the collar of his Barbour waterproof jacket. The rain wasn't heavy, but was, as the locals said, the kind that wets you. And the temperature was down. If it sank a couple more degrees, O'Reilly reckoned the drizzle would turn to snow.

Arthur, seemingly uncaring of the cold, sat and stared up at his master. His otter tail made lazy trips back and forth across the flagstones of the path.

Lorna opened the door. She stood with one hand supporting the small of her back. Her thirty-week pregnancy was obvious now. "Doctor O'Reilly." She smiled and glanced at the game bag slung over O'Reilly's shoulder,

261

the open double-barrelled twelve-bore shot-gun cradled in the crook of his arm. "Come for a shot at the snipe?"

"If that's still all right with you and Reggie and —"

Her eyes widened and she dropped a curt-sey as the marquis walked from the car, bent to give Arthur a quick pat, and stood at O'Reilly's side. "My lord," she said.

"I hope you and Reggie won't mind if his lordship keeps me company," O'Reilly said.

She stood and spoke to the marquis. "It would be a great honour, sir," she said.

"It would be very gracious of you and your husband," the marquis said, "and I shall be most grateful."

"You tear away, sirs . . ." She frowned, pursed her lips, inhaled.

Clearly, O'Reilly thought, she's trying to work out the correct thing to do. By her smile, she'd arrived at a decision.

"And if you're cold when you're done, call in for a cup of tea in your hand," she smiled, "or maybe you'll be ready for a wee hot half-un?"

"It would be a very great pleasure," the marquis said, "and please do not go to any trouble. I know I should be delighted to have a whiskey."

"Ah," said O'Reilly, "mother's milk. I'll take you up on that too." Clever of the marquis, he thought, asking for whiskey. If there'd been any suggestion of a cup of tea, she might have spent the rest of the afternoon baking, getting out the best china, probably washing and ironing her best tablecloth.

"We'll head on," O'Reilly said.

"Rather you nor me," she said, and shivered. "You'd think as a good Ulsterwoman I'd be used til the rain, but, och." She hunched her head down into her shoulders. "I'd rather curl up in front of the fire with a good book. I've just started on *Some Experiences of an Irish RM.* Them two what wrote it were quare gags, so they were."

She's got over her shock at seeing the marquis, O'Reilly thought. John MacNeill had a knack for putting folks at their ease.

"Sommerville and Ross," the marquis said. "As I recall they were cousins, two women actually. And weren't they funny indeed. Very funny. I believe my father met them several times, fox hunting."

"Honest to God, your lordship?"

"Mmm."

"Sometimes," said O'Reilly, "I think one of their characters, the ever-scheming Flurry Knox, was a model for our Donal." O'Reilly wondered how Bluebird's pups were doing.

"Donal? One of a kind, but with a heart of corn." She moved a step back. "Anyroad, I'd keep you colloguing all day, sirs, so away you on and enjoy your sport. Just walk in when you get back. I've for til go til my sister's, but

263

Reggie'll be here and he'll see til youse."

O'Reilly blinked raindrops from his eye-lashes, pulled the brim of his Paddy hat down, said, "Thank you, Lorna. Come on, John," and began to walk. "Heel, Arthur."

The marquis walked at O'Reilly's shoulder and the big dog tucked in.

As they walked in silence, O'Reilly pictured Lorna going round like a liltie getting the living room redd up and prepared for a visit from a peer of the realm. She'd boast about it to her friends for months. He reckoned she'd been too overawed by meeting the marquis to enquire about the blood tests. Which was probably all to the good. The results were back and her husband Reggie was Rhesus positive, and nothing more could be done until about thirty-four weeks, when further testing would be needed to see if the baby was affected.

They climbed over a stile in a low drystone wall and into a field that sloped gently down to marshy, low-lying land. Ahead in the distance, the battleship grey of the waters of Belfast Lough fused with the darker Antrim Hills whose tops seemed to have been welded to the pewter-coloured sky.

In this pasture, whin bushes were scattered here and there, their yellow flowers in sharp contrast to their dark green spikes. He stopped in front of the largest clump, took two cartridges from his pocket, slipped them into the chambers, and snapped the gun shut. "Might get a rabbit here, John."

The marquis chuckled. "Or one of my pheasants. If a hen breaks cover, please let her go, Fingal, but feel free to take a cock."

"Thank you," O'Reilly said.

The marquis walked about twenty yards from O'Reilly, who bent to Arthur and said, "Hey on out."

Arthur, who had sat at his master's feet the moment O'Reilly stopped walking, put his nose to the grounds and charged into the clump with a great crashing of shrubbery and thrashing of branches. The sounds and motion soon stopped and were replaced by a more subtle rustling. As O'Reilly watched, a hare, great hind legs pumping, big ears flying, brown fur and white scut damp in the drizzle, broke cover. In a fluid motion, O'Reilly threw the shotgun forward, releasing the safety catch as he did, brought the butt into his right shoulder, sighted, and swung the muzzles through the running animal to lead it by the length of its body. He was just about to squeeze the trigger when the hare jinked ninety degrees to its left and headed straight for a small herd of black Dexter cattle that was wandering over to investigate the men and their dog. He laughed, put his gun up, and set the safety catch. Two things struck him. Mrs. Hannah Glasse's Georgian recipe for jugged hare, which began, "First, catch your hare," and memories of a pasture outside Fareham, Hampshire, in 1940, when a herd of Herefords had brought to him a sweeping feeling of homesickness and a longing to be back here in Ulster.

Arthur reappeared from the gorse patch. A dog couldn't shake his head with a look of contempt and say, with a curled lip, "I did *my* job, you bollix." But by the big Lab's bearing, he managed to convey those sentiments.

"Sorry, Arthur," O'Reilly said. "I'll try to do better with the birds." He tucked the gun under his right arm, started walking toward the cows, waved his left hand at the herd, and yelled, "Away on to hell out of it. Go on. Hoosh. Hoosh." They were so close he could smell their bovine breath. He kept on walking, pursued by Arthur.

One cow gave an almighty bellow, kicked up her heels, and charged down the hill, hotly pursued by the rest. The herd then stopped as if on command, turned, and stared at the intruders.

"Daft bloody animals," he said when he caught up with the marquis, then flinched as a raindrop found its way under his collar. "That rain is cold. Still, as Ma used to say to my brother Lars and me when we were little, 'You're not made of sugar. You won't melt.' Then she'd shoo us out to play on a rainy day so we'd get some fresh air and she could paint in peace."

The marquis laughed. "Nanny used to say the same thing to Myrna and me, then sit by the nursery fire, drink a pot of tea, and read *The Strand Magazine.*"

O'Reilly smiled at this glimpse into John MacNeil's childhood, then hunched his shoulders and shivered. He wasn't worried about melting. Quite the contrary. His fingertips and, he was sure, his lips, were turning blue. It was more likely he'd freeze solid. He lengthened his stride and glanced at his friend. The marquis, born and raised into Ulster aristocracy, would have been trained from childhood to seem impervious to physical discomfort like the cold.

A blackthorn hedge marked the boundary between the pasture and the wasteland, and he had to push hard to get a rusty iron gate to open. "After you, John."

No farmer would want his beasts straying into the marsh. Immersion in the water, it was believed, would lead to the highly contagious foot rot.

Once through it and the gate securely closed, O'Reilly and the marquis walked along a path that skirted the swampy field and led to the far end.

"You know," the marquis said, "my family used to own this farm." There was wistfulness in his voice. "When Father died, the only way we could raise the estate taxes was to part with a fair bit of property."

"The MacNeills owned the Mucky Duck too, didn't they? I remember you telling me that when you helped us stop Bertie Bishop's attempted takeover," O'Reilly said. "It must have been difficult for you, having to break up the estate?"

Overhead a flock of green plover flapped lazily across a leaden sky. Their cries of "Pee-wit, pee-wit" gave them their local name.

The marquis sighed. "I know why you invited me today, Fingal. We've known each other for far too long. I can practically hear you thinking. You're concerned because I'm worried about money. So you decided it was for my own good that I should have a bit of fun today."

"And isn't that my job? You're a patient as well as a friend."

"You and I, Doctor Fingal Flahertie O'Reilly," said the marquis, "are two of a kind."

O'Reilly laughed. "I'm not worrying about money."

"And I'm very glad of it. But you *are* worrying about me and every other soul in the village."

"Well —"

"Well nothing. You are, aren't you? Who helped Sonny Houston get a roof on his house? Who got me to help him stop Bertie's plans to buy the Duck? Who helped Donal

Donnelly and his pals when they made a bad investment in a racehorse?"

O'Reilly shrugged. "Touché."

"It's not really the money itself that bothers me. My family has for centuries been the biggest employer in the village and townland. It's been passed on down for generations that the current marquis, and that's me, has unavoidable responsibilities to fulfill to the villagers. Just like you have as a physician."

"But John, you do fulfill them. How many committees and boards do you serve on at no charge? You never miss the annual fete, the gymkhana, the rugby club Christmas party for the kiddies. Shall I go on? You fund a scholarship to the university. How many people — house servants, grooms, jockeys, gamekeepers, shepherds — do you employ, aye, and keep in decent and affordable housing?"

The marquis's smile was rueful. "It's going to be a lot fewer when I go. If my wife Laura were still alive, the estate would pass directly to her, without any taxes being due. That's the law. But with Laura gone —" He hesitated and O'Reilly did not intrude on his friend's thoughts until he said, "Sean will inherit, and he'll have to pay. Even now, for me to continue employing any of my staff, I'm going to have to let others go and sell the things they worked on. Perhaps my horses, my grouse moor." He scowled. "I'll miss the things, but

I feel terrible about hurting the people. It's the people that are important."

"And you feel helpless?"

The marquis shook his head and looked down.

"I know that feeling. Right now, I have a colleague who is seriously ill and is refusing my help. I can't do a damn thing for him." He hunched his shoulders as they passed a gap in the hedge and a rain-bearing gust ripped over the rusty barbed wire fencing that blocked the hole.

"Two of a kind, all right. I still don't know what to do, but I feel better knowing I'm not alone. Thank you, Fingal." He stopped because they had come to the field's end. "I think your tactic of getting me to relax is working. Let's start the first beat and forget about our worries at least until the shoot is over."

"Fair enough," O'Reilly said. "Seeing as we've only the one dog, I suggest we both follow Arthur and take the shots turn about."

"Fine, if you go first."

O'Reilly nodded and said, "Hey on out, Arthur."

Arthur ran ahead, his paws plashing through the puddles, his tail up like a flag waving, appearing and disappearing between the thigh-high rushes of the kind that for centuries had been used to thatch roofs in Ireland. O'Reilly and the marquis followed.

Snipe hunting was simply a matter of walking from one end of the field to the other with a dog out in front quartering the ground, driving out the birds. The little wading creatures, which when startled would leap into the air, flew away with an erratic jinking pattern that made shooting them more a matter of luck than good aim. Then guns and dog moved twenty yards to one side and walked back, repeating the process until the entire area had been covered.

O'Reilly's Wellington-booted feet crunched into ice rime at the edges of puddles and squelched through the mud. The reeds swished with his passage, the stink of marsh gas assailed his nostrils, and the drizzle falling competed with a mist rising from the groundwater to make the air palpable.

A harsh, craking noise up ahead came from a snipe flying away low over the reeds, juking from side to side like a slalom skier. O'Reilly had the gun to his shoulder, covered his bird, and fired. Its wings folded and the snipe tumbled to earth. "Hi lost." O'Reilly smiled. He'd not lost his touch.

"Good shot, Fingal," the marquis said.

Arthur came splashing back, sat soggily at O'Reilly's feet, and offered the bird.

"Good boy," he said, patting Arthur on the head and taking the limp bird from the big dog's soft mouth. The Labrador's tail thrashed so hard it flattened the reeds.

271

O'Reilly looked at the snipe. Its velvet brown eye was misting in death, although its light brown body, though damp, was still warm. The head with its long straight bill drooped on a flaccid neck. O'Reilly frowned. He felt sorry for the little bird. More and more lately, he'd begun to wonder about his wildfowling. As a youngster, he and Lars had taken to it as their birthright, but Lars had put away his guns and volunteered with the Royal Society for the Protection of Birds as a conservationist.

The light was beginning to fade when they completed the final beat and had added a few more birds to the bag. "Time for that whiskey, John," O'Reilly said. "I don't know about you, but I'm foundered."

"This'll hit the spot," said O'Reilly. He savoured the aroma of his hot half-un: Bushmills Irish Whiskey, cloves, sugar, and lemon juice all topped up with boiling water. In his hurry to drink, he scalded his lip. "Holy thundering Mother of —" He remembered that the Kearneys were devout Christians and bit off the rest.

"You all right, sir?" said Reggie Kearney from where the three men sat in front of the hearth in a sitting room smelling of lemon furniture polish and burning turf from the fire.

He had obviously been briefed by his wife

and had not been overawed by the marquis when he and O'Reilly had shown up ten minutes ago.

Reggie Kearney paused from his knitting. It had surprised O'Reilly the first time he'd seen Reggie, who stood more than six feet and had shoulders like an ox, working the wool and needles, but Reggie had explained that he enjoyed making things and that his mother had taught him how when he'd been a wee lad.

"Just teaching myself to take my hurry in my hand," O'Reilly said. "No real harm done. But it was nippy out and I wanted to get the whiskey into me." He smiled at Reggie. "We've had a great afternoon. Thanks for letting us have a shot on your land."

"Sure you're welcome any time, Doctor. And I know your family used til own it, my lord, so it's right and proper you should be here, so it is. And you're both country men. You know to ask permission, not to let my beasts out, not to trample my crops. Last week some buck eejits from Belfast with not a by-your-leave went onto Dermot Kennedy's place and put lead pellets into one of his pigs. Dermot was raging, fit til be tied, so he was, but Mister Porter, the vet in Conlig, got them out and the pig'll be fine."

The marquis tutted and said, "It's appalling. Some city folks have no manners, and less sense."

O'Reilly remembered Dermot, with the ferocious squint, and his daughter Jeannie, who'd had to have her appendix out and had a pet pig called Gertrude. "I hope it wasn't Gertrude on the receiving end of those lead pellets. Jeannie's barmy about that pig."

The two other men, as one, turned to regard Fingal.

"Well, she is," he said defensively, and they all laughed. He hitched his chair closer to the heat. Life was returning to his numb fingers. The raw damp had penetrated more deeply into his marrow. Arthur, who had been dried off with an old towel, was in the back of the car with the guns, the game bags, a blanket, and a couple of Bonio dog biscuits, his usual reward after a good day's sport. He'd be warm and dry in there.

"Lorna said she was going to her sister's," O'Reilly said. "I thought she was looking well."

"She is. She has Reggie Jr. over for til see his cousins," Reggie said. "It was a promise she couldn't break." He smiled at the marquis. "She was main disappointed she'd not be here when you came back, sir. It's an honour."

"No," the marquis said. "It's I who am honoured to be here."

Reggie cocked his head. "Hang on a wee minute. I need til cast off." He frowned and wiggled his fingers. "Got it," he said with a smile. "Excuse me, sir," he said, "seeing as how he's here, I thought I'd ask the doctor a question or two about my missus. She's in the family way."

The marquis began to rise. "I'll wait in the car."

"Och," said Reggie, "it would skin you out there. I don't mind if you listen in, sir. Honest." He looked at O'Reilly. "Will that be all right, Doctor?"

"It's up to you, Reggie. I'm sure you can trust his lordship to keep it to himself."

"Fair enough, Doctor," he said. "So, can you tell me what's going on with the missus? I think I understand that if the wean's one blood group and Lorna's another, she could make things to attack its wee blood cells and make it very sick."

O'Reilly sighed. "That's right, Reggie, and I think it might happen, because we got the results of your blood work back and you are positive. According to Doctor Laverty, who studied all the new stuff last year, there's a fifty-fifty chance the baby will be too." He took a sip of his now cooler whiskey. There was no point hiding the truth.

"And if it is, what can youse doctors do?" His gaze was set on O'Reilly's eyes. "It'll break Lorna's heart if the baby dies."

"It won't come to that." O'Reilly managed a reassuring smile and said, "But we can do nothing for a while. We have to let the baby

275

grow more. I'll not pretend it'll not be a worry, but things have come on in leaps and bounds since I was a young man in Dublin getting my training. There'll be more tests, then the experts at RMH — and they are experts — will decide what to do." He put a hand on Reggie's arm. "It really is difficult to explain because there's a lot of, 'If it's A we'll have to do B, or if it's not A we'll wait, and if it's C we'll do D.' " He met Reggie's gaze. "Can you understand what I'm trying to say?"

The farmer frowned. "Aye. I think so. It's like when the soil experts come down from the agricultural school and take samples. There's no point asking them what to do until they have the samples analysed. I think that's what you're trying til say, sir."

O'Reilly nodded. "We'll be doing the next tests in about three weeks and we'll have a much better idea then. Can you trust us until then, Reggie?"

O'Reilly was shaken when Reggie Kearney stopped his needles' clacking, held out a big callused hand, and said, "We'd trust you with our lives, Doctor O'Reilly."

O'Reilly seized the hand. He swallowed and said very quietly, "Thank you, Reggie. Thank you very much."

"Aye," said Reggie, "and I believe when you first explained to Lorna about them Rhesus monkeys, she told you we followed the Good

Book?" He let go of O'Reilly's hand.

"She did."

"So, no harm til you, Doctor, of course we trust you, but, well, we'll also put our faith in the Lord." The words were said with a sincerity that moved O'Reilly, himself not a religious man.

He pondered for a while, seeking the right reply, then said, "You do that, Reggie. You do that, and here on earth us doctors, who are not gods, will be grateful for all the help we can get."

"It's really none of my business, Mister Kearney," the marquis said, "but I feel sure your faith, both in the Almighty and in your doctors, will not be misplaced, and I wish you and your wife and your new baby when it arrives the very best of everything."

"That's very decent of you, sir."

"And with your permission, if Doctor O'Reilly will notify me of the birth, I'd like to give the child a christening present as a small token of my thanks for an excellent afternoon's sport and for letting me into your confidence."

It seemed the offer had rendered Reggie Kearney speechless.

And that, O'Reilly thought, is typical of John MacNeill, twenty-seventh Marquis of Ballybucklebo. A gentleman of the old school. Considerate to a fault of other people's feelings. No wonder the poor man was in knots about which of his staff and possessions to let go.

18

So Much Been Owed
By So Many to So Few

"This is Pilot Officer Dennison. DFC, Hurricane pilot, 229 Squadron," Sister Blenkinsop said. Her voice cracked. "He's nineteen and a half."

No wonder they were called "fighter boys," Fingal thought. The poor lad was little more than a child and, with a Distinguished Flying Cross, already decorated for gallantry.

"He's had a quarter grain of morphine and hot sweet tea about two hours ago and, as you can see, we've got him under a shock cage."

Fingal looked at the face on the pillow. It was unrecognisable as that of a brave young man. More like a piece of raw beef punctuated by two staring blue eyes with constricted pupils. The rest of the bed was humped up with the blankets covering a wire half-cylinder inside which were lit rows of incandescent bulbs. The shock cage. The heat from the bulbs was believed to be therapeutic. His arms lay on either side of the cage and Fingal could see that the airman's hands were not burned. That was something to be grateful for.

"The triage officer who has examined him says that apart from the patient's face and a couple of minor cuts and bruises, he's okay. No broken bones."

"What happened?" Fingal asked. "I didn't think there'd been any raids today."

"He was sent up to find a lone German reconnaissance plane, got shot down over Bognor Regis, bailed out, and was brought here," Sister said. "We've been told that one petrol tank in the Hurricane fighter is in the nose of the aircraft, immediately in front of the cockpit. And I'm afraid," said Sister quietly, "there's no fire wall between the tank and the pilot."

Fingal shuddered and bit back a curse. Perpetually burdened with a vivid imagination, he could picture the pilot frantically trying to get out of his blazing aircraft. It wasn't a great leap to picture *Warspite* sustaining a torpedo hit or heavy bomb damage, and fire spreading down to the medical distribution station where Fingal would be working again in four or five months. He realised that while he could face the possibility of death, he was mortally terrified of being burned.

Sister, perhaps more inured to such cases, continued quite placidly. "His pulse is very rapid at one hundred and twenty, and his blood pressure is only one hundred over sixty."

The man was in shock, no wonder, and he could die from it. "We have plasma available?"

"I've sent for some."

"First thing," Fingal said, "is to give him some intravenously, then we'll have to take him to theatre, get his face cleaned up and treated. Have we sent for Surgeon Commander Fraser?"

"We have."

"Right," said Fingal. "I'll set up the infusion as soon as the plasma arrives. Meantime, we'll premed him with atropine one-hundredth of a grain. It's too soon after the morphine to give him any more narcotic." He wondered what the best anaesthetic would be. One thing was for sure — there was no question of trying to put a mask over that ruined face.

"Good for you for getting plasma into the boy," Angus said as two SBAs lifted the burned pilot from a stretcher onto the table in the underground theatre and hung a glass bottle one-third full of the straw-coloured blood plasma, whole blood from which the red cells had been removed, on a pole attached to the table. "And now I'm going to teach you to use a thing called a Flagg's can."

"All right."

"Just so. Come over here and I'll tell you about it before the surgeon arrives." Angus led Fingal to the head of the table where a strange-looking device lay on a towel on a trolley top. It was simply a small cylindrical metal can. Its screwed-on lid was perforated in several places and a single red rubber tube came out through a larger hole in the lid's centre. The tube was joined to a narrower one. Fingal frowned. It looked pretty primitive, and he said as much to Angus.

"Eh, I agree. No one," said Angus, "in their right mind would use this thing if he had a Boyle's machine handy and a supply of endotracheal tubes. But, in wartime, who knows what will be available where?"

"True."

"And of course, with the situation our young flyer is in, this is the perfect application." Angus glanced over to where Phillip Dennison lay beneath the shock cage and exchanged a concerned glance with Fingal. "An American called P. J. Flagg invented the can and tube device and he showed it to Professor Macintosh, who taught me in Oxford.

"Professor Macintosh found he couldn't get his hands on any endotracheal tubes when he was helping with an international brigade during the Spanish Civil War and dealing with some pretty bad facial injuries. So he rigged up a can using a Tate and Lyle syrup tin just like Doctor Flagg had shown him how and, hey presto, it worked."

Fingal said nothing, his attention suddenly pulled away several hundred miles and several years — to Dublin in 1936 and Kitty O'Hallorhan, who'd left him to go and work in an orphanage in Tenerife during the Spanish Civil War. He needn't deny it to himself. He'd been in love with her then. The past didn't disappear just because now his Deirdre filled his heart.

"Fingal?"

"Right. Sorry, sir. I was paying attention. Your mention of Spain just got me thinking of something, well someone, actually. But I heard you. How exactly does the thing work?"

"There's a sponge inside the can. You drop ether through the holes in the lid and introduce the narrow tube into one nostril and on down into the trachea. The patient's own breathing draws room air and ether into his lungs, and that's it. You're going to use it on this case."

"All right."

"Don't sound so dubious," he said sternly. "One day you and your patients may bless P. J. Flagg, laddie."

"Are you ready for me?" Surgeon Commander Fraser called, striding into the room. "I haven't got all day."

"Eh, not altogether," Angus said, "but if you'll go and wash your hands like a good wee surgeon man."

Fingal had to struggle to hide a grin. No one was going to ride roughshod over the little Scotsman.

Fraser did not try to hide his scowl, but he said nothing and, turning on his heel, strode out of the room.

"Here." Angus handed Fingal a loaded hypodermic syringe. "Sodium pentothal. Give it intravenously for induction, and stick the needle into the intravenous line. It'll save you looking for another vein to puncture."

Fingal did.

"Ordinarily," Angus said, "the drooping and closing of his eyelids would give us a pretty good idea that he was going under, but the poor bastard hasn't got any. Christ."

Fingal was surprised, because never before had he heard Angus Mahaddie swear or blaspheme.

"I hate burns. Hate them."

Fingal nodded and thought, So do I, and I fear them. "Can't we do anything?"

"Not much here, but there's a New Zealander, chap called Archibald McIndoe, working at the Queen Victoria Hospital in East Grinstead, who's doing wonders for burn cases. He calls his technique 'plastic surgery.' You'll see what we can do here when — " He lowered his voice. " — the monarch of the glen goes into action. Our job is to keep the patient asleep." He looked at the man's pupils, squeezed the skin of his forearm. No response.

"Right," he said, handing Fingal the can. "There's ether on the sponge. Start feeding the tube up his right nostril."

Fingal did as he was instructed. "It's stuck."

"Just so," said Angus. "It can be awkward finding the entrance to the trachea, but there's a trick. I'm going to tell you what to do, but you're going to do it. You learn by doing, not being lectured at." Angus moved forward. "Let me hold the can. An SBA can do that for you if you're on your own. Now be gentle, but use your hand to tip his head back. Now pull his mouth open."

Fingal stared into the open mouth and saw the tube at the back.

"Use this laryngoscope."

Fingal accepted the instrument, which allowed him to pull the tongue forward and directly observe the vocal cords.

"Take a pair of Magill's forceps." Fingal did. "Now grab the tube and manoeuvre it where you want it to go."

To Fingal's delight, the thing slipped easily into the trachea.

"Now, advance it, and Bob's your uncle."

"And," said Fingal, completing the lines, "Fanny's your aunt. Thanks, Angus." He straightened up.

"About time," said the gowned and gloved surgeon. "Now, out of my way, you two."

Fingal moved to his place at the head of the table.

"Right," said Fraser. "Cleansing. I'll need ether-soap and saline, Sister."

As Fingal attended to his patient's anaesthetic needs by periodically adding more ether, he admired the gentleness with which the surgeon cleaned the charred tissue away.

"In sequence, Sister, give me swabs soaked in first one percent aqueous gentian violet, next ten percent silver nitrate, and then fifteen percent tannic acid."

Fingal watched as the surgeon successively applied the solutions with the care of a master painting a portrait. Once the tannic acid had been applied, a black coagulum began to form.

"Saline-soaked patches for the eyes," Commander Fraser said, beginning to strip off his gloves, leaving the task to his minions. "We'll keep him on Collingwood Ward for three days, they know the postoperative routine in these cases, then ship him to the nearest receiving hospital."

Fingal remembered what Angus had said about plastic surgery. "Excuse me, sir."

The Surgeon Commander stopped with his left glove still half on. "What?"

"Could we perhaps arrange for him to go to East Grinstead? It's an RAF unit and Captain Mahaddie says Mister McIndoe —"

"I believe I said the nearest hospital."

"But —"

"Lieutenant. When I want your advice, I'll tell you what it is." And with that, Commander Fraser swept from the theatre.

Fingal, cheeks scarlet, breath stuck in his throat, managed to make a growling noise. But he wasn't angry because he'd been insulted. His ire was on behalf of a nineteen-year-old patient who, because of a senior's arrogance, was going to be deprived of the opportunity of a chance of having his missing eyelids replaced. "Angus, I —"

The captain put his hand on Fingal's arm. "Bide a wee, laddie. Take a deep breath and see about waking your patient up. Dinna fash yourself about where this young man's going." His gaze bored into Fingal's eyes. "But we'll not discuss that here." He smiled at the nursing sister, the VAD, and the SBAs.

Fingal understood. As usual, Angus had something up his sleeve but did not wish to discuss it in front of the staff. Nor had he used his superior rank to challenge the commander in front of them. That was entirely ethical — and prudent, given Fraser's short temper, to which Fingal had already been exposed. Fingal nodded and started to remove the tube of the Flagg's apparatus. He cocked his head and looked at his senior. This man's a superb teacher, Fingal thought, and not only of technical skills. I could do a lot worse than try to emulate his apparent willingness to do whatever was necessary to achieve better care for his patients. Fingal grinned. "Fair enough," he said. "I'll not get . . ." He couldn't bring himself to say "fashed" in case Angus thought Fingal was imitating him. "I'll not get too worried."

The patient made a groaning noise, stirred on the table, but his pulse was regular, his breathing deep and slow. "He's ready to take back to the ward, I think, Angus."

"I agree. SBAs."

The attendants grabbed the stretcher, gently loaded the patient, and carried him away.

"I thought you did very well, Lieutenant O'Reilly."

"Thank you, Sister," Fingal said, and he glowed.

"And," she said, "I don't mean just with the anaesthetic. Not many juniors would challenge a commander's decisions." She lowered her voice and leant her head next to his ear. "But be careful," she said. "Commander Fraser can bear a grudge."

19
ON THE EVE OF ALL HALLOWS

Kitty O'Reilly pulled her long, black tail onto her lap and crossed her legs, elegant in slim black pants and ankle-length black leather boots. "It doesn't seem like a year since the whole village was done up in fancy dress for Halloween," she said. She was Puss to O'Reilly's Dick Whittington, seemingly escapees from a production of the pantomime *Puss in Boot*s.

"Aye," said O'Reilly. "I find it comforting the way the year rolls around here, season following season. Mind you, last Halloween nearly lived up to its old Celtic name, the Festival of the Dead." He pretended to leer at Kitty's legs then clutched the left side of his chest. Lowering his voice so it was just audible over a recording of "Wild Thing" by the Troggs, he said, "And looking at you dressed like that, my love, isn't doing my old ticker any good either."

Kitty laughed and said, "You're hopeless, Fingal O'Reilly. Go and get me another G and T, please."

"Right," he said, clutching his stick and bundle like the one with which, it was said, the impoverished Dick Whittington had set out for London. There, aided by his trusty cat, he had four times become lord mayor. "Barry, keep an eye on the Kitty-cat, but beware the ides of March."

"Will do," said Barry, who was wrapped in a purple-edged toga, had a laurel wreath encircling his head, and was holding a half-finished pint. "Yond Fingal has a lean and thirsty look."

"I don't know about lean, but definitely thirsty," said Fingal with a laugh. "I always liked the rest of that speech. 'He thinks too much,' your man Caesar says of Cassius. 'Such men are dangerous.' Sometimes I wonder if Doctor Ronald Fitzpatrick thinks too much. He's definitely becoming a danger to himself."

"Can't believe he just walked out on you like that, and before one of Kinky's crème brûlées? The man is definitely astray in the head. He's got no wit."

"Divil the bit. And it had actually been a pleasant evening up until then." O'Reilly shook his head. "Anyway, I can do nothing about it tonight. I'm talking shop and this is a party. It was game of you to come out by yourself."

"I thought about staying at home," said

Barry, taking a sip of his pint. "I miss Sue and I knew this bash wouldn't be the same without her. But I think the village expects their physicians to attend these functions — with or without a partner. And besides, I want to be here."

"Not just noblesse oblige then?" said O'Reilly. "I'm proud of you, Barry. It shows how well cut out you are for rural GP work." O'Reilly glanced at the others at the table at one end of the Ballybucklebo Bonnaughts Sporting Club clubhouse. "Anybody else need a refill?" he asked. Jack Mills, Barry's friend from boarding school and medical school, was a shaggy Robinson Crusoe for the evening, and his partner, Helen Hewitt, well into her second year of medical studies, was a stunningly seductive Cleopatra, complete with rubber asp.

"No thanks, Fingal. We're fine. But I'm keeping an eye on old Barry this evening. Didn't Julius Caesar have an affair with Cleopatra at some point?"

"Eejit." Helen hit Jack over the head with the asp and the whole table laughed.

"I'll see to the drinks, Kitty. Won't be long," O'Reilly said, and started to head toward the bar, but returned to prop his stick and bundle against the table. "Bloody thing gets in the way," he said, and set off again to skirt the dancers and get Kitty her gin and tonic.

The hall was decorated with cobwebs,

cutout skeletons, cardboard ghosts, and jack-o'-lanterns carved from turnips. The Troggs had been replaced by the Rolling Stones, belting out "Paint it Black." A steady hum of conversation was punctuated by a descant of children's laughter and screams coming from a haunted tunnel made of bamboo hoops covered in sacking. The noise was underpinned by the shuffle and thump of feet on the dance floor. Smoke drifted up to the rafters.

O'Reilly felt something poking into his back and heard a voice say, "Stick 'em up, Doc." Colin Brown, in a white cowboy suit and a black mask, held a toy revolver with its barrel pressed against O'Reilly's spine. He raised his hands above his head. "I surrender," he said.

"There ain't no runnin' from the Lone Ranger, pardner," Colin said in a remarkably accurate imitation of Clayton Moore, who played the character on TV and had once appeared on stage at Belfast's Grand Opera House.

"How are you, Kemo Sabe?" O'Reilly said. "And how's Murphy tonight?" Colin was daft about the pup he'd been given by Sonny and Maggie Houston.

"I had to leave him back at the corral with Tonto," Colin said.

"Good for you," O'Reilly said, "but now, pardner, it's time for me to head to the saloon." He began to lower his hands slowly.

Colin laughed and, reverting to his normal tones, said, "You're great *craic,* Doctor O'Reilly, so you are."

"Och sure, I used to play cowboys and Indians too, but a long time ago. When I was at school."

The boy's eyes widened as if he couldn't believe that such a thing could ever have happened.

"And speaking of school, Colin, what was your exam like?" Colin had sat the Eleven Plus, and if he passed would be able to go to grammar school for an education that might lead on to university.

"I think I done pretty good, you know. They'd all kinds of daft questions like, 'Spot the odd man out. Apple, pear, golf ball, banana, pineapple.' " He laughed. "You'd have to be soft in the head not til get the answer. Anyroad we'll be getting the results on the fifth of November."

"Good luck to you," O'Reilly said, but Colin wasn't paying attention. He was firing his revolver, the caps making sharp cracks and smelling of burnt gunpowder. "Dar. Dar. You're dead, Art Callaghan."

O'Reilly chuckled and made for the bar.

"Evening, Doc." Willie Dunleavy, mine host of the Mucky Duck, was serving drink here tonight. "What'll it be?"

"Gin and tonic, and another pint, please."

Willie at once put a pint of Guinness on the pour, tipped a measure of Gilbey's gin into a tumbler, and snapped open a small bottle of Schweppes tonic water. "Here you are, sir. That'll be three shillings." Willie handed over the gin, bottle of tonic, and pint; Fingal paid and began making his way carefully back to his table.

He passed Donal Donnelly, a ragged-looking, carrotty-haired Robin Hood, and Julie, her long blonde tresses shining and setting off her Maid Marion outfit. They were deep in conversation with Dapper Frew, the estate agent, and his wife Audrey, who O'Reilly guessed were John Steed and Emma Peel from TV's *The Avengers*. "Evening all," O'Reilly said, and was greeted by the company.

Donal looked up and grinned, showing his buck teeth. "How's about ye, Doc?"

"Grand, thanks, Sir Robin," O'Reilly said. "Getting ready to take from the rich and give to the poor?"

Donal's grin fled. "How the blazes did you know that, Doctor?"

O'Reilly frowned. "Know what?" His throwaway remark had clearly hit an unsuspected mark.

"C'mere here, Doc," Donal said, his tones conspiratorial as he rose. "I'll be back in a wee minute, so I will," he said to the others, and headed toward a corner of the room.

Intrigued, O'Reilly followed.

Just then Popeye the sailor man hove into view.

"Ahoy, matey," O'Reilly said, and beckoned.

Gerry Shanks, clutching a can labelled SPINACH in one hand and a beer in the other, came over.

"Do me a favour?" O'Reilly said.

"Aye, certainly, Doctor."

"Do you think you can take this gin and tonic to Mrs. O'Reilly, Puss in Boots tonight, and tell her I'll be along soon, but I'm having a word with Donal?"

"I'm your man, Doc." Gerry stuck the can of spinach in the pocket of his trousers and, juggling his own beer, took the bottle and glass from O'Reilly. "Never you worry," he said and, still juggling, headed off into the fray.

"He's a good head, Gerry," O'Reilly said.

"But not too swift," Donal said. "When it comes to using the loaf, your man would be out of his depth in a playground puddle."

O'Reilly thought this was rather rich coming from Donal, but he said nothing, just lifted his pint. "*Sláinte.* Now, Donal," he said. "What's up?"

Donal lowered his voice. "It's about them puppies."

"The greyhuahuas?"

"Aye, them. I think between Dapper and me —"

"I thought you were keeping them hush-hush?"

"I was trying til, aye, but there could have been one wee flea in the ointment."

"Fly, Donal." O'Reilly hid his smile at another Donalpropism.

"Aye. Right. Fly. Dapper owns the sire. He can do sums as quick as me and he knew when Bluebird was going til pup. You remember I explained I had til tell him, so I had. He thought on it for a wee while. He's such a sound man he offered to refund half the stud fee, but a deal is a deal." Donal stuck out his jaw.

You're a sound man yourself, Donal Donnelly, O'Reilly thought.

"He knows I have til sell the pups and he had this wee notion. In his business, selling houses, he says you can get a brave wheen more money for one if you can persuade buyers who are really warm —"

"Warm, Donal?"

"You know, those with lots of the ould do-re-mi."

"Right, rich."

"Aye. If you can persuade them that some feature is dead unusual — something like a sunk bathtub or a gazebo in the garden. Them things is rare as hens' teeth in Ireland, so nobody else will have one, and do you know what else?"

O'Reilly chuckled, wondering what was coming next. "No," he said.

"Dapper says not very long after, he's getting enquiries from their rich friends about how can they get one too?"

"Aha," said O'Reilly. "That's called 'keeping up with the Joneses.' "

"Is it?" said Donal. "It's more like 'A fool and his money's soon parted,' if you ask me."

Something at which Donal was skilled. "So you're going to try to persuade folks that your mongrels are a rare breed?"

Donal managed to look offended. "Well, they are," he said. "Damn right they are, sir. They're the only ten Woolamarroo herding dogs between here and Australia."

O'Reilly, who had just taken a mouthful, laughed so hard that Guinness came down his nose. "Where?"

"Woolamarroo," said Donal. "We looked up an atlas of Australia. There's no such place, but it sounds like Wooloomooloo, and that's in Sydney near King's Cross and Pott's Point."

"Donal, you absolutely amaze me," O'Reilly said. "And what do they herd?"

"Quokkas." Donal face was deadpan.

"What in the name of the wee man is a quokka?"

The 1920s strains of vo-dodie-oh-doh music filled the room as the New Vaudeville

Band began to sing "Winchester Cathedral."

"We looked that up too. It's a marsupial about the size of a cat. Only lives on a few islands off Western Australia."

"Quokkas? Never heard of them," said O'Reilly.

"And you're one of the learnèd men here, Doctor O'Reilly, so if you haven't heard of them who else might have, do you think?"

O'Reilly shook his head. "Damned if I know."

"You're dead on. Nobody, that's who. And that's another thing. People who think they're no goat's toe don't like to show their ignorance. Tell them the dogs herd quokkas and they'll just nod, look as if they understand, smile, and say, 'Right enough? Good for them.' "

He's right, O'Reilly thought. "Damn it all, it might just work. But will people expect pedigrees?"

"Aye, mebbee," said Donal. "Dapper an me's still working out the wrinkles, but we reckon the first step is for til start a rumour that I'm bringing in a clatter of these rare dogs. And anyroad, the pups can't leave their ma until somewhere after December the fifth, so we've loads of time yet to get all our plans in order."

"Starting a rumour shouldn't be difficult here," O'Reilly said.

"If you know the Psalms, sir, you'll know

the one 'Out of the mouths of babes and sucklings.' Do you mind how the stewards at a greyhound race trusted wee Colin Brown?"

"I remember it well."

"I'm going to tell wee Colin I'm bringing in these rare dogs and ask him til spread the word."

"Donal, it's just daft enough that it might work."

"And you'll keep it til yourself, sir?"

"Mum's the word," and he pictured a wartime poster encouraging people not to indulge in loose talk: "Be like dad. Keep mum."

From the speakers came "You stood and you watched as my baby walked by . . ."

"I'll not say anything, except to Doctor Laverty," said O'Reilly, "but I'm going to be watching you, Donal. Woolamarroo quokka herding hounds, by all that's holy." He clapped Donal on the shoulder. "What the hell will you be getting up to next?"

Donal grinned and started to answer when O'Reilly glanced at the dance floor. "Got to go, Donal." Puss in Boots was dancing with Robinson Crusoe — a little too close for O'Reilly's comfort.

20

. . . Would Meet in Every Place

Collingwood Ward was quiet. Only half the beds were full. Angus had been right. While London continued to receive a nightly pounding, Portsmouth and the surrounding area had been left in peace for nine days — except, of course, for the lone snooper that had shot down Pilot Officer Dennison four days ago. Gunnery Chief Petty Officer McIlroy, the Ulsterman who instructed at Whale Island, had had his operation and been discharged. He'd promised to remember Fingal to Henson.

The patients, now an officer was on deck, all sat or lay at attention. Two men, who were sitting at the table in the middle of the ward, stopped playing uckers, a board game using dice and round playing pieces that was an obsessive pastime with the lower deck. Even the SBA pushing the beer trolley came to a halt. Beer rounds, when each man was given a bottle of Brickwoods Ale as a tonic, was the high spot of the day. The bottles were called

300

"Little Brickies."

Fingal spoke to a leading SBA, the senior rating on duty. "Tell them to stand easy and carry on."

"Aye aye, sir."

The order was given. Conversations began again. Cigarettes and pipes were lit and the bottles on the beer trolley made a cheerful clinking as it was moved from bed to bed. The mid-October afternoon sun poured in through the big northwest-facing windows.

The rattle of the uckers dice was drowned by one player calling, "That's an eight-piecer. I win."

Fingal was off duty and on his way to his quarters to change into civilian clothes before meeting Deirdre at the Portsmouth Guildhall. Marge was picking up her son Tony there and would give Deirdre a lift. Fingal had come to say good-bye to the burned pilot, who was being transferred to East Grinstead later today. Angus, without bothering to inform Surgeon Commander Fraser, had simply made a couple of phone calls, spoken to Mister McIndoe himself, and arranged for an ambulance to make the ninety-mile run. Fraser was none the wiser. Yesterday morning he'd had to go up to London on naval business. It was true — what the eye doesn't see, the heart doesn't grieve over. If George Fraser had a heart.

Now that the shock cage had been removed,

the young pilot lay under only his bedclothes. The top blanket, blue and white with a fouled anchor crest, matched every other top blanket on the ward. To Fingal, the man's face, covered by the black tannic acid coagulum and white eye patches, looked like the reverse of a panda bear's visage. "How are you feeling today, Flip? It's me. O'Reilly." The man's Christian name was Phillip, but as was practically de rigueur in the RAF, he went by a nickname.

"Lieutenant O'Reilly?" He turned his head to face where Fingal had taken a seat and spoke, slurring his words because his lips were swollen, although not badly burned. They must have been protected by his oxygen mask. "A bit better, thanks, but to quote Gracie Fields," his Oxbridge accent faded and he said in thick Lancashire tones, " 'I'm one of the ruins that Cromwell knocked about a bit.' "

"You're a brave lad, Flip, to joke about it."

"It's been a funny few days," he said quietly now, "but I've hardly noticed them pass. With all the morphine, I've done nothing but sleep when they'd let me. But this morning I was feeling a bit more like myself, I suppose. Wanted to know what's been happening while I've been out of it. So I asked Sister Blenkinsop. She said the nurses had been painting my face every two hours. Now it's every three. Sister says they use camel hair brushes to put on the same stuff they put on during the operation."

"It's tannic acid," Fingal said.

Flip nodded slowly. "The stuff that's in tea. So I understand. They'll cut it down to once a day soon, and by day seven the crust should start to peel off."

"I hear the tannic acid really does help the burns to heal," said Fingal.

"But it won't give me back my moustache or my eyelids." There was no hint of bitterness. "I have to wear these eyepads. They get changed during the day." Fingal heard the catch in the airman's voice. "When they took them off this morning, I could see. It was blurry, but Sister tells me my sight will keep getting better, thank Christ. I was terrified I was blind. I don't think I could have taken that."

Fingal reached out and took the man's hand and squeezed. "And you'll be pleased to know your mitts are perfectly well." The flames in a plane's cockpit often destroyed the pilot's bare hands too.

"Thank you. I'd kept my gauntlets on, but like a silly clot I'd pushed up my goggles so I could see better." He wriggled in the bed. "I say, would you do something for me, old boy?"

"If I can."

"I'm gasping for a fag. They're in the locker."

Fingal found a packet of Player's Navy Cut, took out a cigarette, and tapped its end on the packet to tamp in the tobacco. He put it between his own lips, took out Swan Vesta matches, and lit up. "Here," he said.

Flip inhaled deeply and blew out a cloud of smoke. "Lord," he said, "but that's better."

"Excuse me, sir?"

Fingal turned to see a young VAD standing at the foot of the bed.

"Yes, nurse?"

"Sister says can you leave in five minutes, please? We need to get Pilot Officer Dennison ready to go."

"Thank you. Of course." He rose. "I'll just help him finish his smoke." Fingal took the cigarette and tapped the ash into an ashtray. "Here." He replaced it between Flip's lips. "You're a lucky man," he said. "You're going to the best plastic surgeon in Britain. He'll rebuild your eyelids and if you want, you'll be back in a Hurricane in no time."

Flip took a deep drag and said, "Not me. I'm fond of the old Hurri; I'm going to ask for a Spitfire. It's an absolutely marvellous kite." He handed the half-smoked cigarette to Fingal. "Would you put that out, please."

Fingal did. "I'll be off then," he said. "Good luck, Flip."

The pilot managed a weak laugh. "It was a few days ago I needed luck. Flaming great Dornier 17. Had him dead to rights. Should have been a wizard prang, but their rear gunner got his squirt in first. Thank God my brolly worked."

The Brylcreem Boys really did speak a foreign language, Fingal thought.

Flip offered his hand. "Thanks for everything, Lieutenant-Commander O'Reilly, especially coming every day to chat."

Fingal shook the hand. "If you get a chance, drop me a note. Let me know how you're getting on." He'd become fond of the disfigured young man and his courage.

"I will and —"

"Lieutenant O'Reilly." The voice behind him was curt, officious.

Fingal spun and saw an irate-looking Surgeon Commander Fraser.

"What is this man doing here? I left instructions to get him moved yesterday."

Fingal came to attention. "I'm sorry, sir. Unavoidable delay. He's going in a few minutes." Fingal's mind raced. It would be so easy to hide behind the fact that Angus, senior in rank to Fingal, had made the arrangements in the best interests of the patient, but, not wanting to prolong the discussion in front of the patient, he held his peace.

"See that he is, and Lieutenant? I'll expect all my orders to be obeyed in future. Is that clear?"

"Yes, sir."

With that, the commander turned on his

heel and stamped off.

"I think," Flip said, "you just got what us RAF types call 'torn off a strip.' "

"The navy calls it a bottle, but yes, you're right." And the theatre sister had said that Surgeon Commander Fraser was a man who bore grudges. He sighed. Och well, what can't be cured must be endured. "Good-bye again, Flip. Take care."

"You too, Doc, and I will write. I promise."

"Excuse me, sir," Fingal said to a young lieutenant-commander standing smoking a pipe outside the neoclassical Portsmouth Guildhall. The building, with its Roman temple columns, pediment, and frieze, reminded Fingal of Ulster's parliament buildings at Stormont. He knew the bell tower housed five bells called the Pompey Chimes. Their familiar tones were as much a part of Portsmouth as its busy dockyards. "You're not by any chance Tony Wilcoxson?"

"As a matter of fact I am, actually. How did you know?"

"I'm Surgeon Lieutenant Fingal O'Reilly. Your father was my boss on *Warspite* and I've seen your photo at Twiddy's." At least, Fingal thought, I've seen your younger self. This man's face was weatherbeaten and the bags beneath his eyes were puffy. The North Atlantic in winter on a small ship was gruelling. "My fiancée's staying with your mother, who should be here any minute to collect you."

Tony Wilcoxson took Fingal's proffered hand and shook it. "How do you do, Fingal? And how is Dad?"

"He was in fine fettle the last time I saw him, but that was months ago."

"He's a tough old boy and the navy's his life." Tony took his pipe from his mouth. "He told me in a letter he was sending you to Haslar. Enjoying it?"

Fingal thought for a moment of his encounter with Commander Fraser, decided to forget it, and said, "Enormously. I'm learning a great deal, sir. Have you just arrived?"

"Mmm." He stifled a yawn. "Came in to Liverpool from Halifax, Nova Scotia, last night. Bloody awful convoy. We lost one of the escorts, she was torpedoed off Iceland, then sweet bugger all but gales the rest of the way. And please, Fingal, it's Tony, not sir when we're off duty."

Fingal did not have a chance to reply. A black Ford Prefect slammed to a stop at the kerb near them, and three of the four doors flew open. Pip hurled herself at Tony, who swept her quite literally off her feet. Deirdre gave Fingal a chaste kiss and said, "Hello, darling," and Marge, standing between the two couples, said, "Nice to see you, Fingal, and, Tony, when you've quite finished ravishing Pip, do give your mother a kiss."

Tony, still clutching Pip's hand, kissed his mother's cheek. "Hello, Mother, it's good to be home."

Fingal wondered when he'd get a chance to see his own mother, and berated himself because her last letter was a week unanswered. But at least she knew he was relatively safe in England. And Deirdre, who was a better letter writer than he would ever be, had dropped her a note a couple of days ago.

"And it's good to have you home, dear boy," Marge said, and Fingal saw how her eyes glistened. Marge cleared her throat and said, "I'm very cross with Deirdre — this is my son, Tony, by the way."

"How do you do?" he said to Deirdre.

Fingal, who always wanted to ask an Englishman who posed that question "How do I do what precisely?" was proud of her good Ulster reply.

"I'm pleased to meet you, Tony."

"As I was saying," Marge said, "I'm cross with Deirdre because she positively refuses to bring Fingal for dinner tonight. It's going to be a treat, a Land Army special, deep-filled homity pie, but she insists it's a family reunion."

"It is, Marge, and that's final."

Fingal smiled. That's my girl. Beneath her gentleness, willingness to accommodate other people, lurks a steel backbone when her mind is made up.

Marge rummaged in a voluminous handbag, produced a torch, handed it to Deirdre, and said, "The last train's at eight from Gosport. This thing's shaded, but you'll need it to find your way home in the blackout. I'll leave the door unlocked."

"Thank you," Deirdre said. "Now come along, Fingal. Marge says the best places are on Commercial Road just round the corner, and it runs up to Edinburgh Road where there are more shops." She winked at him. "I know how you love to shop."

"There's also a good pub restaurant, the Trafalgar, very close by," said Marge. "So don't despair, Fingal. Now I'd better get my lot home."

Fingal and Deirdre stood and waved as the little Ford lurched away.

Clearly it hadn't been necessary to say it, but the prospect of a pub dinner held out more interest for Fingal than shopping. Still, if it was what Deirdre wanted to do, then he was ready to do it.

"You look smart in a blazer and flannels," Deirdre said as they walked hand in hand toward Commercial Road in the heart of Old Portsmouth. The great naval dockyard was a stone's throw away up ahead beneath a flotilla of silvery barrage balloons. The fire brigades had put out all the fires after the last air raid nine days ago, but the smoky smell lingered.

"It saves an awful lot of saluting," he said

as they passed another knot of uniformed sailors. "They'd all have to salute me, and me them, and seeing I'm going shopping with my girl, I'd really like to pretend that I'm not a salty sailor man — at least for a few hours and —"

His words were smothered by a snarling roar, rising to an ear-splitting crescendo. He felt Deirdre clutching his arm, saw her eyes widen, her mouth form a speechless O. Everyone looked up to see a flight of planes in finger-four formation racing over the town and on past the dockyard. The sight of the RAF roundels on their wings, not the black crosses seen on Luftwaffe machines, was reassuring. "Spitfires. Ours," he said to Deirdre, who smiled and nodded, clearly reassured. The sound of Rolls-Royce Merlin engines faded as the planes moved away. God speed you, he thought, remembering young Flip, and keep their pilots safe from fire.

"Those planes are so graceful," Deirdre said. "What a shame they have to be used to kill."

"If they can stop the German planes killing our civilians, if they and others like them can shorten this war, I'm all for it," Fingal said. "You must have seen some of the bomb damage on your way here. I still wonder if I did the right thing bringing you to England."

"Fingal O'Reilly," she said, "there is nowhere on God's green earth I'd rather be.

I'm with you and in nineteen days we'll be married. I feel safe with you, Fingal. I know you can't stop the bombs falling if the Germans come back to Portsmouth, but everyone here's so brave, I must be brave too. We're together, that's what's important. So don't ever feel that you did the wrong thing."

"Thank you," he said, loving her calm, no-nonsense courage. She squeezed his arm and smiled and they continued down Commercial Road arm in arm.

Fingal pushed his empty plate away — he'd had that Melton Mowbray pie Richard Wilcoxson had asked him to have for him on that last day on *Warspite*. "If we finish up our cups of tea in about twenty minutes, it's only a short walk from here back to Guildhall Walk. *Stagecoach* with John Wayne and Claire Trevor is on at the New Theatre Royal there. We'd have time to see it and catch the ferry back to Gosport and get you to the station."

"That would be lovely," Deirdre said, and smiled at him across their table in the crowded Trafalgar pub restaurant. Conversations were muted and tobacco smoke filled the air. Her purchases, mostly of "women's things" for her trousseau, were in a number of paper bags with sisal carrying loops. She'd set the bags on one of the two extra chairs at their table. "You were very good about me dragging you round all those shops. Wartime shortages don't make finding things you want easy. And I do like Claire Trevor."

He shook his head and laughed. He understood exactly what she was saying, but not out loud. You've paid your dues this afternoon, Fingal darling, and were quite bored to death, I know. I'm not very fond of Westerns, but if it's what you want, pet, I'm happy to oblige.

"Good," he said. "That's settled then." And like a schoolboy on a first date, he hoped the back stalls were very dimly lit.

There was the loud creak of a spring hinge and a draft as the pub door opened. Fingal reflexively glanced over to see who had come in, not expecting it to be anyone he knew. He was wrong. In walked Leading Seaman Alf Henson with a petite blonde on his arm. She wore a red suit with padded shoulders and a pale blue beret tilted to one side of her head. The headgear had a large satin bow on its front. There was a slightly sallow tinge to her complexion. The rating was smartly turned out in his best shoregoing square rig: circular hat set at a slight tilt, tally ribbon round it and bearing the letters HMS knotted over his right eye, flat collar with its edge of alternating blue and three white stripes hanging behind the neck of his regulation jumper. The stripes were, erroneously, believed to celebrate Nelson's three victories. The bellbottoms of his trousers had five razor-sharp horizontal creases. If Henson had been taller there would have been seven. He carried a standard-issue Burberry raincoat over his arm.

Henson looked round and was clearly disappointed that he could not find a place. Fingal knew Deirdre would not mind company, and although the navy frowned on fraternisation between officers and men, Fingal was not in uniform. It would be the decent thing to do to offer to share the table. He rose. "Henson. Henson."

The Yorkshire man looked round, saw Fingal, and immediately came to attention. "Sir."

"Belay that 'sir,' " Fingal said. "Stand easy, bring your young lady over here and have a pew. We'll be leaving in a few minutes." He stood up.

A battle raged across the man's open face as he clearly struggled with a great desire to get his girlfriend seated and his awe of an officer, even a mere lieutenant.

Meanwhile Deirdre had set her shopping bags on the floor.

Henson approached. "If you're sure it's all right, sir."

Fingal grinned and said, "I'd like you to meet my fiancée, Nurse Deirdre Mawhinney. Deirdre, this is Leading Seaman Henson. He was the first man to welcome me aboard *Warspite* in the Clyde last year."

Deirdre smiled her generous, welcoming

313

smile and said, "So you and Lieutenant O'Reilly are shipmates?"

"Yes, miss."

"And who's your charming friend?"

"Elsie Gorman," Henson said, the pride in his voice obvious. "She's a right bobby-dazzler, isn't she?"

Fingal thought it impolite on such short acquaintance to agree that she was indeed very lovely. Instead he said, "Well, Elsie, if you don't sit down soon, my tea's going to get cold." He held a chair for her.

"Ta ever so much," she said, and sat. "Come on, Alf. The nice officer won't bite."

Henson sat at attention.

"Having a run ashore, Henson?" Fingal asked, remembering that all of the navy's shore establishments, "stone frigates," were organised as if they were ships at sea.

"I am that, sir," Henson said.

"Good for you. So am I." Fingal noticed that Deirdre had already drawn Elsie into conversation by showing the girl one of the afternoon's purchases.

"And begging your pardon, sir, it was kind of you sending your regards with CPO McIl-roy." Henson sat less stiffly. "He's a right good bloke, for an Irishma —" Henson must have recognised the enormity of what he had just said. Wasn't his lieutenant one? He blushed beetroot red, muttering, "Sorry —"

"He is," Fingal said with a grin, fully

understanding that the huge regional mix in *Warspite*'s crew brought inevitable rivalries. He followed up in kind. "And you're not a bad lad — for a Yorkshire tyke." His voice became more serious. "And I took no offence, Henson. So don't worry."

"That's right decent of you, sir, and I do apologise."

"Accepted." The poor man was trembling. "So tell me, because I'm certainly having fun learning new things," move the conversation along, "how's your course going?"

Henson's smile was the vast gap-toothed one Fingal remembered from *Warspite*. "I couldn't be happier, sir. All the instructors want us to learn. I told you that I'm career navy. The chief reckons I'm going to come out top of my class."

"Excuse me, sir?" a waitress in frilly apron and starched white cap said to Henson. "Would sir like to order?"

"Yes, please. Two cream teas."

"And could I have our bill?" Fingal finished his tea.

"Certainly, sir."

Henson explained to Fingal as the waitress left, "Elsie and me made up our minds before we came in that's what we wanted. We come here quite a lot. Anyway, he reckons if I go on like I am, I can expect to be a petty officer soon. And I'll be going back to *Warspite*."

"Me too," Fingal said.

Lord knew what the two women had found so funny, but peals of laughter rang out.

"If you don't mind me saying, sir, your fiancée is very lovely."

"I don't mind one bit. So's your Elsie."

Henson lowered his voice. "She's a bomb girl."

That explained her sallow complexion. Girls were now doing men's jobs, and young Elsie Gorman would be spending her days, and perhaps nights, filling shells with highly explosive cordite and sulphur in a munitions factory in some hush-hush location. The chemicals in the explosives turned hair and skin permanently yellow.

"I worry about her all the time." He looked down at the tabletop. "There was an accident at her factory last week. Two girls killed. They have to be so careful, one spark and . . ." He looked fondly yet with concern at her. "I'm daft about her. I've not bought the ring yet, but she says she'll wait and once I am a petty officer and can afford it and the war is over . . ."

And Fingal's heart went out to the ambitious, lovesick young man. "I'm sure everything will work out perfectly," he said. "They're a bloody brave lot, those girls. Miss Mawhinney's doing her bit in the Land Army . . ."

"Your bill, sir," the waitress said.

Fingal looked at it, produced a ten-shilling

316

note, and said, "Keep the change."

"Thank you, sir." She turned to Henson. "And your teas will be here in a minute, luv."

Fingal rose. "I wish you the best of luck, Henson, on your course. Keep on working hard because I know you're going to succeed." And that wasn't a platitude. Fingal was cheering for the man to do well. "I'll look forward to seeing you back on our ship, and your getting a petty officer's two fouled anchors and a crown on your sleeve, and, for goodness' sake, man, don't get up."

As Henson retook his place, Fingal said, "Deirdre, time we were off." He helped her to pick up her purchases.

Now a lady was standing, Henson did rise. "Thank you very much, sir, for sharing your table and for the encouragement. I know I'm going to do well. I just know it." His enthusiasm shone.

"So do I." Fingal smiled at Elsie and said, "Nice to have met you, briefly. Enjoy your tea."

She bobbed and said, "Thank you."

"Good-bye, sir," Henson said. "Safe home."

Fingal held the door for Deirdre and they walked together along blacked-out Edinburgh Street.

She held his hand, made him stop, and kissed him. "Fingal O'Reilly," she said, "I think that was the sweetest thing inviting a rating and his girlfriend to join us. I don't think many officers would have."

Fingal frowned and said, "He's a nice, hard-working, ambitious young man; we had spare seats. It seemed natural. I discovered he's in love."

"Elsie told me. Elsie's really funny, I was perfectly happy to have them, but you are a lieutenant and there is naval protocol."

"Bugger protocol," he said. "And I'll not be a lieutenant for long," he said, and kissed her. "And when I'm a lieutenant-commander, I'm going to marry the most beautiful girl in the world." He started to walk and tugged her hand. "Now," he said, "let's go and see John Wayne shoot the bad guys — and for just a bit longer forget there's a war on."

21
I WILL MAKE THEE
A TERROR TO THYSELF

O'Reilly ignored the ringing of the telephone and, putting down his newspaper, said to Barry, "I see they're forecasting there might be floods in Florence and Venice by tomorrow."

"Worrying," Barry said. "But, of course, as Robert Benchley telegraphed to David Niven about Venice: 'Streets full of water. Advise.' So it shouldn't change much there at least."

O'Reilly's chuckle was cut short by a "Doctor O'Reilly" from the hall.

There was something different in Kinky's voice.

"I think you'd better come to the phone, sir. Now."

This wasn't the amused tolerance of a couple of weeks ago when she'd asked him to speak to Donal Donnelly. She was disturbing him in the middle of lunch to speak directly to a patient. Something serious was going on. He left Barry to finish his meal and galloped to the hall where the usually unflappable

Kinky stood, hand over the mouthpiece, eyes wide, and saying sotto voce, "It's that Doctor Fitzpatrick, sir. Something's very wrong and he won't tell me what. I do not like the man at all, but he sounded mortal petrified, so." She offered O'Reilly the receiver.

"Ronald? Fingal here. What's wrong?"

The man's voice came over the line. "Fingal, can you come to my surgery at once, please? Please?" The tones were quavering. The man did sound terrified.

"Do you want to tell me what's up?" O'Reilly said. He lifted his shoulders at Kinky and widened his eyes in question.

"Please just come. I'm — I'm frightened."

"Leave the front door open. I'm coming," O'Reilly said and, not waiting for an answer, put the phone down. "Doctor Fitzpatrick's in some kind of trouble." O'Reilly called through the dining room door, "Barry, will you make my home visits this afternoon? I have to rush round to Fitzpatrick's. I've no time to explain."

"Sure," came back the answer. "Never worry."

Blessing Barry's good-natured willingness, O'Reilly grabbed his bag from the surgery and charged through the house and back garden yelling a quick "stay" at Arthur.

He piled into the big Rover, started the engine, slammed the car into gear, let out the clutch — and promptly stalled. "Jasus Murphy," he said aloud to himself. *"Festina lente."*

Once on Ballybucklebo's Main Street he had no choice but to make haste slowly. Thursday was market day, and even in early November it was a busy time. Cars and carts were parked higgledy-piggledy at the sides of the road, reducing traffic flow to one lane, which was creeping along behind a farmer on a rusty bicycle, and his border collie driving a small herd of Jersey cows up the middle of the road. Attar of cow clap mingled with car exhaust in the sea-misty air. O'Reilly sat pounding his fist on the steering wheel and yelling, "Come on. Come on." Fortunately, the cattle were going his way and were no respecters of traffic lights. They meandered on through the green, amber, and red, which gave him the chance to turn right onto Station Road and, thirty-mile-an-hour speed limit be damned, roar on to the Kinnegar.

He only wished his Rover had a siren and flashing lights like the police cars driven by TV's Sergeant Joe Friday of *Dragnet.* Whatever neurological disorder ailed the man, it must have worsened.

He parked by the seawall on the Kinnegar's Esplanade, grabbed his bag, piled out, and tore through Fitzpatrick's hall and on into his surgery.

Ronald Hercules Fitzpatrick sat behind his desk on the raised dais with his elbows on the desktop, his forehead resting on the palms of his hands. He looked up and Fingal saw that beneath the gold pince-nez were tear tracks down the man's hollow cheeks.

"Fingal," he said, "thank God you've come." He sniffed, swallowed, and his Adam's apple bobbed. "It's my legs," he said. "My legs." His voice quavered. "I can hardly move them." He stared into O'Reilly's eyes. "Help me. Please."

"Of course." Fingal stepped up on the dais and, very sure of the importance of human touch to a man in distress, laid a companionable hand on Fitzpatrick's shoulder, handed him a hanky, and said, "Here. Blow your nose. You'll feel better."

"Thank you." Fitzpatrick sniffed and honked.

O'Reilly's mind was racing like one of those newfangled IBM computers. Add weakness of the legs to lack of pain and heat sensation in the hands and almost certainly something ominous was happening in the spinal cord. Probably at the place where it left the brain to run down the spinal column and provide the body with its controlling nervous system that conveyed messages to and from the brain. The range of potential causes was large, and the investigation, diagnosis, and correct treatment — if the causative condition were to be treatable — were far beyond the capabilities of a rural GP.

"Ronald," O'Reilly said, "I hope you'll

agree, but I don't think there's much point in me trying to make a diagnosis. I think it's time we took you to see Charlie Greer." He waited.

"Whatever you say, Fingal."

"Where's your phone?"

"In the hall."

"I'll just be a minute." O'Reilly left, and after the usual and seemingly interminable delays at the hospital switchboard, he was put through to Ward 21, where the ward clerk who answered the phone soon had the ward sister, Kitty, on the line. "Fingal? What's the matter?"

Her abrupt question did not surprise him. He rarely phoned her at work. "It's Ronald. He's taken a turn for the worse. He's going to have to be admitted, but he's agreed to see Charlie. Have you a bed?"

"I'll find one and I'll find Mister Greer." She'd not refer to him as Charlie in front of her staff and junior doctors, who would be on the ward. "He has a clinic this afternoon. I'll let him know to expect the patient."

"Grand," said O'Reilly. "I'll drive him up myself." He hung up then realized he'd done so without telling Kitty he loved her. He'd been distracted wondering, with Fitzpatrick having difficulty standing, whether he'd be able to get him into the car. There was only one way to find out. He tried to oxtercog the man, but Ronald's legs dragging helplessly

323

slowed their progress. "Be damned," said O'Reilly, and simply picked Fitzpatrick up bodily, surprised at how light such a tall man could be, and carted him out to the backseat of the Rover. Throughout the entire undignified exercise, the man remained as quiet as a scolded child. The car smelled strongly of damp dog, but O'Reilly didn't care and his passenger didn't comment. The first priority was to get this sick man up to the Royal.

"Ronald is not a well man," Charlie said to Fingal and Kitty as they sat together in his office on Ward 21, the neurosurgery unit in Quinn House, a recent addition to the Royal Victoria Hospital. "My initial physical examination confirms what we anticipated back in Dublin. Loss of pain and heat sensation in his right hand." Charlie was every inch the senior surgeon in his long white coat with the tools of his trade — a tuning fork and a patella hammer like a small tomahawk with a rubber head — sticking out of one pocket. Kitty looked coolly official in her red senior sister's uniform dress, white apron, and white triangular headdress called a fall.

"There's more, now I've had a chance to examine him properly. He's retained the ability to sense light touch, feel the vibrations of the tuning fork, and he can sense position. There's some wasting of the small muscles of his right hand and his tendon reflexes are gone. And now he's had this sudden loss of power, some spasticity of his legs, and his Babinski reflex is extensor."

O'Reilly remembered being taught how to scrape a key along a patient's sole. All was well if the great toe curled down, but if it went up in extension as it had with Fitz-patrick? He clenched his teeth.

"Taken all together, that says to me in a loud voice, 'high spinal lesion,' " Charlie said.

"I'm afraid diseases of the nervous system were never my strong suit," O'Reilly said. "Have you made a differential diagnosis?"

"Aye." Charlie nodded. "I never really seri-ously considered *Tabes dorsalis.*"

O'Reilly understood why Kitty was trying to hide a smile. Despite the gravity of the situation for poor Fitzpatrick, the thought that he, of all people, might be suffering from late-stage syphilis was incongruous enough to be risible.

"And because it causes upset of all sensa-tions and Ronald can feel light touch and vibrations, I'm pretty confident that *Tabes* is a nonstarter."

"Good," said Kitty. "I just can't picture dear old lugubrious Ronald as a roué."

"Nor me," said Charlie. "Those signs are pretty typical of either local compression of the spinal cord or some degenerative nervous disease in an early stage."

"Degenerative diseases like multiple sclerosis or the one you get with vitamin B12 deficiency?" O'Reilly asked.

"It's called subacute combined degeneration of the spinal cord," Charlie said. "Quite a mouthful. I'm tending to think it's not degenerative, because those conditions are more likely to be more generalised. So I'm thinking either syringomyelia or a space-occupying lesion."

O'Reilly saw Kitty flinch and knew why. Syringomyelia was an ill-understood condition where there was degeneration of the grey matter, the actual nerve cells of the spinal cord, the cells that relayed messages like pain and feelings of heat and cold to where they were interpreted by the brain and experienced by the conscious mind. The degeneration led to the formation of a cystic structure filled with cerebrospinal fluid, the so-called syrinx, which as cells died could expand up and down the spinal cord. It was incurable, although it was believed that radiation might slow down its progress. "Space-occupying lesion" was a euphemism for "tumour," and O'Reilly knew that there was quite a list to pick from. Some were benign. Most were not.

"So," said O'Reilly, "what happens next? Tests?"

"Aye," Charlie said. "I'll tell you both what they are and, Kitty, will you please make the arrangements?"

"I will," she said.

"He'll need some blood work, most important a haemoglobin assessment and, if it's low, an examination of a smear of the cells to exclude or identify B12-deficiency anaemia that could be associated with subacute degeneration. And even if he is a friend, I'd be remiss not to ask for a Wasserman to exclude syphilis."

Kitty ticked off the boxes on a lab requisition form.

"From my perspective, I have to establish if there is indeed cord compression, so he'll need a spinal X-ray. And a chest X-ray. If there is a space-occupying lesion, it may be a secondary from a lung cancer."

O'Reilly flinched. That would be a death sentence. "Ronald never smoked cigarettes as far as I know," he said. The link between smoking and lung cancer had been recognised in 1929 by German physician Fritz Lickint.

"Two years ago, the American surgeon general recommended that cigarette smokers quit," Kitty said. "The news was all over the BBC. I don't think anyone here paid a blind bit of attention."

"Lung cancer can affect nonsmokers too," Charlie said, "but I'm not unduly concerned about Ronald. Just being thorough. It's more a question of determining if there is such a lesion, and if so, is it inside or outside the cord? That means a myelogram, I'm afraid."

O'Reilly shuddered. He vividly recalled how

his last patient who had required the test had received an injection of a radio opaque dye into the spinal canal so X-rays could follow its progress along the canal as the patient was tilted on a special table. John Cowan, a local labourer, had described it as having green fire poured along his back. Poor Ronald.

"I'll speak to the radiologist myself," Kitty said. "Make sure it's done by a consultant, not a trainee." Her gaze met O'Reilly's and she pursed her lips and rapidly shook her head.

He could tell she too was cringing at the thought of what the poor man must endure. But that was Sister Kitty O'Reilly. Skilful, efficient, and with a heart like a duck-down pillow when it came to her patients.

"I'll try to get them organised for tomorrow, before the weekend. Doctor McIlrath in that department owes me a favour."

"Thank you, Kitty. Do your best," Charlie said, and rose. "Now if you'll excuse me, I'll go and try to explain to Fitzpatrick. It won't take long, then I'll have to get back to outpatients. I'll pop in before I go home, Kitty. See what you've got organised."

"Thanks, Charlie," O'Reilly said. "Thanks a lot." He hesitated. "Can I come with you?"

"Sure."

Together they went to a one-bed ward where Ronald Fitzpatrick lay propped up on pillows, reading.

"Fingal's come with me, Ronald," Charlie said, stating the obvious. "He's concerned for you and he wants to understand as much as possible so he can try to help you."

Fitzpatrick looked over his gold pince-nez at Fingal. "I appreciate it, Fingal, I truly do."

O'Reilly smiled and lowered his head.

"I'm not going to wrap it up, Doctor Fitzpatrick," Charlie said. "I've examined you, made a differential diagnosis, and ordered some tests. Sister O'Reilly is arranging those now. You'll need some blood work and some X-rays."

"I see," Fitzpatrick said. "If you remember from Sir Patrick Dun's, I was quite good at internal medicine."

O'Reilly did remember. The man should have won the gold medal in that subject but for a careless error. In fact, he'd never understand why Fitzpatrick had gone into general practice. He had seemed destined for some kind of specialization.

"I know that you are the expert, Mister Greer, but if I may hazard a guess? I suppose very few doctors would fall ill without trying to make the diagnosis themselves."

Charlie smiled and said, "True. Go ahead."

"You're trying to decide between syringomyelia . . ." There was a catch in his voice. "I've been terrified that's what it might be ever since I picked up that hot teapot in Davy Byrnes. Or it might be a tumour."

"I'm afraid so," Charlie said.

Fitzpatrick smiled. Clearly his satisfaction with making the correct diagnosis had momentarily overridden his fear. "I suppose I'll need a myelogram?"

Charlie nodded.

Fitzpatrick swallowed and his Adam's apple bobbed. "I shall try to be brave," he said.

"Good for you, Ronald," O'Reilly said, marvelling at how well the man seemed to be taking the news of what must be done, what might be found. "I'll make you a promise. Kitty'll let me know when the test results are in and I'll pop up and see you." Let you cry your heart out with another human being if the news is bad and you need to, he thought.

"Thank you, Fingal. I'd appreciate that. I shall try to stay positive." He forced a tiny smile. "I've been reading this. It was in my pocket." He handed a slim volume to O'Reilly. *The Power of Positive Thinking.* "I'm trying to practice what Doctor Peale preaches."

O'Reilly opened the book at random, his eyes drawn to a passage the gist of which was not to imagine obstacles, but despise them, shrink them. "Difficulties . . . must be seen for only what they are and not inflated by fear." Probably good advice for a man in Ronald Fitzpatrick's situation.

"I have a favour to ask, Fingal."

"Fire away."

"Could you and your young friends look after my practice — just for a while? Until I'm back on my feet?"

Not having a clue exactly how running the man's practice was going to be done, O'Reilly nevertheless said, "Of course. You'll not need to worry about it."

"Then," said Fitzpatrick, "that's settled. It is a great weight off my mind. Thank you, Mister Greer. Thank you, Fingal. May I have my book? Thank you." He began to read then said, "I'm sure you are both very busy men." Obviously, they were being dismissed and the man must want to be alone to grapple with his thoughts.

"I'll be seeing you tomorrow," Charlie said. "I've left you a sleeping pill, Ronald. Try to get a good night's sleep." He led O'Reilly out of the room. "He's an odd fish," Charlie said, clasping his hands behind his back and heading down the corridor toward the outpatient department, O'Reilly in step beside him. "For weeks, maybe even months, he's been so terrified he's been denying the truth to himself. Now that's no longer an option, he seems to be quite reconciled. He's an odd fish all right, but you have to admire his pluck."

"I know you'll do your best for him, old friend," O'Reilly said.

Charlie shrugged. "It's what they pay me for, you know. Doing my job."

His friend was a highly skilled technician in

a field where many of his patients, despite his best efforts, were incurable. O'Reilly knew from long experience with the breed *Homo surgicus* that Mister Charlie Greer had been forced to develop what looked to be a cynical carapace. Inside, though, he knew, Charlie was concerned that he'd had to order a horrible test for his patient and even more concerned because of his deep understanding of how devastating the results might be.

22
LET'S HAVE A WEDDING

The Reverend John Wilfred Evans, B.A., stood in front of the altar and beneath the ornate baldacchino in Haslar hospital's Church of Saint Luke, built in 1762. Behind him hung a painting of the *Restoration of Sight to Bartimaeus*. The healer was Jesus Christ. "All ye that are married or intend to take the holy estate of matrimony upon you . . ."

Fingal tried to listen, but it was a particularly dry and lengthy part of the service and his mind kept wandering to how he had come to be standing here, neat and starched in his dress uniform complete with his brand-new lieutenant-commander's insignia and sword. That which had seemed impossible a month ago, his wedding to Deirdre Mawhinney, was now almost complete. Fingal tried once again to concentrate on the chaplain's instructions about the duties of husband and wife, the final act of the Anglican service before the benediction and dismissal. He stole a sidelong glance at his bride. She stood to his left, the veil of her white headdress, now that the vows had been exchanged, thrown back. She was gazing intently at Reverend Evans, but soon sensing his eyes on her, she turned slowly and smiled.

Twice in his life Fingal had come close to experiencing feelings of ecstasy; the day he'd passed his finals and had become Doctor O'Reilly, and the day he'd put on the green shirt with shamrocks on the left breast to play rugby football for his country. But the sensation in his chest when he saw Deirdre's smile reduced those events to the humdrum.

The blue eyes sparkled and her blonde hair, which she usually wore shoulder-length, was done up in a fashionable reverse roll. A simple narrow band of gold now encircled her ring finger beside the little solitaire diamond engagement ring he'd given her fourteen months ago. He glanced behind her and caught Marge surreptitiously wiping away yet another tear. As matron of honour, the woman had taken the wedding on as if Deirdre had been her own daughter.

". . . you shall have a white wedding," Marge had said with a measure of authority when Fingal had been visiting Twiddy's two weeks ago. "I presume you can use a sewing machine, Deirdre, because I'm going to need your help."

Marge and Deirdre had been making plans

for the big day, the three of them drinking Camp coffee in the armchairs round the log fire with Admiral Benbow serving the function of a canine hearth rug. A vague aroma of singed hair was in the air, the result of a stray piece of smouldering wood that had fallen onto his long coat.

"Of course," Deirdre had said, "but with rationing I don't know where on earth I'd be able to get the material."

"I'll be back in a minute," Marge said, then rose and left.

Fingal took the opportunity to lean over and kiss Deirdre. "Love you," he said.

She laughed. "Behave yourself, Fingal. Marge'll be back in a minute," but she took his hand and squeezed it, then planted a warm kiss on the back of his right wrist. "I wonder what kind of a rabbit she's going to pull out of the hat this time?"

"More likely to be a hedgehog." A much larger Riddle than the bundle Fingal had met on his first visit trundled across the carpet toward the kitchen.

They both laughed.

Marge returned bearing a long cardboard box smelling of camphor mothballs. She opened it and pulled out a floor-length dress of white satin. "Take the train," she said to Fingal, who rose and pulled the material out to its full eight feet.

"Marge, I couldn't possibly —" Deirdre

started to say.

"And I'm not meant to see the bride-to-be in her nuptial finery before she walks up the aisle," Fingal said.

"Fiddlesticks to you both," Marge said. "You're spouting superstitious Celtic Twilight stuff and nonsense, Fingal Flahertie O'Reilly, and nothing would bring back happier memories of my own wedding than to see you in it on your big day, my dear Miss Mawhinney, so stand up please."

Deirdre did as she was told and Marge held the dress against her. "Mmm. I'll need to get a tape measure. It's not bad for height, but I think I outscored you in the *enbonpoint* department even when I was a gel." She pointed at her considerable bustline and rear. "Certainly in the flying bridge and quarterdeck."

Fingal had found himself helplessly laughing. Marge Wilcoxson really was one of a kind.

The Reverend Evans's voice brought him back to the present as the chaplain droned on, "Likewise the same Saint Paul, writing to the Colossians, speaketh thus to all men that are married: Husbands love your wives and be not bitter against them . . ."

Fingal looked at Deirdre, who gave him another brilliant smile that melted him. How could anyone, never mind her new husband who loved her to distraction, be bitter about anything she did? She had charmed Marge and Pip, making strangers into lifelong friends in a matter of days. Both women looked teary but smart in neat tailored suits and hats with half veils. Marge had scoured the neighbourhood and managed to find six late-blooming roses for Deirdre's bouquet, filled out with some feathery ferns and branches of lavender from Pip's mother's knot garden.

Between them, Marge and Deirdre had done a magnificent job of altering the Edwardian dress with its fitted bodice and lace-edged three-quarter-length sleeves. The train had been carefully removed and the necessary nips and tucks taken so it fitted Deirdre perfectly. It would be returned to Marge after the ceremony in case — as Marge had said wistfully — ". . . my sailor man son ever gets round to proposing to the honourable Philippa Gore-Beresford."

Tony had not got around to it on his most recent visit, but he had brought peace offerings: six pairs each of the new nylon stockings for his mother and Pip. The much-sought-after hose were unavailable in Britain, but he'd managed to buy these in Halifax, Nova Scotia, when his destroyer had been docked there after sustaining damage to her steering in a violent gale. Pip and Marge had each given Deirdre a pair for her trousseau.

"And in his epistle to the Colossians, Saint

Paul giveth you this short lesson: wives submit yourselves unto your own husbands . . ."

Fingal hid a smile. Saint Paul was backing a loser with that one today. Deirdre, while considerate and accommodating to other people's needs, would no more submit to anybody than Winston Churchill would bow down to Adolf Hitler when she knew what she wanted and had the right to ask for it.

He could picture her last Monday, neatly turned out in her Land Army uniform, standing by his side in front of Admiral Creaser, who sat at his desk surrounded by piles of paper. How she'd managed to arrange the appointment, Fingal wasn't sure. He suspected Angus had been involved.

After a few social preliminaries, and the admiral's congratulations to Fingal on his imminent promotion, she'd looked the senior man in the eye. Deirdre never played eyelash-fluttering maiden-in-distress games when she wanted something. She simply said, "Admiral Creaser, we have a very great favour to ask of you."

He smiled. "Miss Mawhinney, if it is within my power . . ." He looked at Fingal. "I believe I owe it to you, O'Reilly. It was my forgetfulness that almost prevented you two from getting married."

Fingal lowered his head in acknowledgement. It was the closest an admiral could come to apologising to a junior officer.

Deirdre continued, "None of my family nor Fingal's can come over for the wedding, and I don't know anybody here who can help."

The admiral leaned forward. "Help with what?"

"I need someone to stand in for my dad and give me away on Friday."

"Friday?" The admiral's face broke into a broad smile. "Why, it just so happens I'll be hauling down my flag the day before. Turning over command — and all of this" — he pointed to the papers on his desk — "to Admiral A. B. Bradbury. He's a countryman of yours from Maze, County Antrim. Friday will be my first day of freedom and I can't think of a more delightful way to spend it. It would give me the greatest pleasure, Miss Mawhinney."

She bent over the desk and kissed his cheek. "Thank you, sir. Thank you very much."

And the admiral had blushed like a schoolboy and grinned from ear to ear.

The Reverend Evans continued, "Saint Peter doth instruct you very well, thus saying . . ."

"Your chief is a great teddy bear of an admiral," Deirdre had said to him after the appointment. It was a side of the commanding officer that Fingal had yet to observe, but then Deirdre could bring out the teddy bear in any man. He'd been so proud of her minutes ago, walking up the aisle on Admiral Creaser's arm.

". . . whose daughters ye are as long as ye do well, and are not afraid with any amazement." The chaplain beamed at the happy couple and Fingal realised that the instructions were over and that by a slight wave downward of his hand the chaplain was indicating that Fingal and Deirdre should kneel.

They did so, and once the final prayer blessing the marriage was done, the priest held up his first two fingers and intoned, "The peace of the Lord be always with you." And from behind them, the little wedding party, consisting of a few of the medical staff Fingal had befriended during his month here and their wives; Admiral Creaser; the Matron, Miss M. Goodrich; and Angus's wife, Morag, replied: "And also with you." Damn it, but he wished Ma and Lars and Deirdre's father, mother, and younger sister Daphne from Antrim could have been here. Once this blasted war was over and they were all back in Ireland, they'd have one hell of a ta-ta-ta-ra. One that would be talked about for years.

Fingal helped Deirdre to her feet as the smiling priest came toward them and said, "Let me be the first to congratulate you, Lieutenant-Commander and Mrs. O'Reilly."

"Thank you," Deirdre said.

And Fingal O'Reilly, happier than a pig in

the proverbial, just stood and grinned and grinned as the choir of uniformed QARNNSs, VADs, SBAs, medical officers, and eight boy trebles who'd been let out of school early to perform for the ceremony gave a spirited and harmonious rendition of "Jerusalem," William Blake's poem set to music. It suited the occasion, rousing and patriotic. He would have liked something Irish, but the rousing Celtic songs were all about rebellions. And although Fingal regarded himself and Deirdre as Irish as any Dubliners, his allegiance until cessation of hostilities was to Britain and her titanic struggle.

Conversations rising and falling and punctuated by gusts of laughter came from the guests at the reception in the Medical Officers' Mess behind and to the left of Saint Luke's Church. At Fingal's request there was no head table. Instead, the round tables and chairs were unassigned so guests could sit with their friends. The bridal party and the Reverend Evans had dined together.

As always happens at parties, as if on some telepathic signal, everyone stopped talking at once and a single voice could be heard clearly. ". . . thought he'd show a bit of swank, brought his destroyer in at fifteen knots . . ." pause for effect then, "nearly swamped the admiral's barge, and shortened

341

the pier by twenty feet . . ." Not only the naval officers and their wives at the speaker's table, but those sitting nearby roared with laughter at some poor wretch's misfortune. "Admiral gave poor old Willoughby no end of a bottle."

Fingal took a pull on his beer and smiled. He had no difficulty picturing the scene, and as long as no one had been injured, it had a certain slapstick appeal, at least to those with naval backgrounds. Certainly Marge, Pip, Angus and his wife, the minister, and Admiral Creaser were chuckling. Only Deirdre looked puzzled and said to Fingal, "Poor chap. He must have got into awful trouble."

"I think it's the 'pride comes before a fall' aspect that everyone finds amusing. Nobody likes show-offs. And he did deserve a telling off."

"Oh. I see." And Deirdre's smile seemed to light up the whole reception, where the noise level had risen again.

"Fingal's right," Marge said. "Don't waste your sympathy on the young clot. My Tony'd not do a silly thing like that. Much too sensible." She sighed and said, "He's back at sea again."

"Destroyers, isn't it, Mrs. Wilcoxson?" Admiral Creaser asked.

"He's skipper of one of the Hunt-class boats. HMS *Swaledale.*"

"Lucky man," the admiral said. "I hear

they're great sea boats, not like the old L-class torpedo-boat destroyer *Lawford* that I was on in the first war. She took on so much water with a sea running that the crew said she was a prototype submarine."

Everybody at the table laughed. Of course they did, Fingal thought. The man's an admiral.

Deirdre was on her feet. She held a Kodak Brownie camera that Marge had brought in her handbag and given to Deirdre after the ceremony. "I wonder, could the gentlemen stand behind the ladies? I'd like to get a couple of snaps of the wedding party and I'm sure there's enough light in here. I'm using a very fast film and a slow shutter speed."

Fingal and the men rose and went round the table and waited until the ladies had moved to sit close to each other.

This interest in photography was something Fingal had learned about only last year when she'd confessed to him — and no one else — that she'd taken first prize at a major photography competition in Belfast. Deirdre thought that her taking candid snaps would be much less intrusive than hiring a professional.

"Now," she said, sighting through the viewfinder, "nobody move but everyone say 'Cheese.'"

Click went the shutter.

"And again."

Click.

Angus moved over to her. "Give me the camera, Mrs. O'Reilly, and go and stand with your husband. I'm sure you'd like one of the two of you together." He'd also taken snaps of the bride and groom leaving the church.

From the waist up, Angus was properly attired in his formal uniform jacket, white shirt, and black tie. Below his cummerbund, though, he sported a kilt in his clan's tartan, a whiskery sporran, and woollen knee socks, down one of which was stuffed a *skean dhu,* a black knife with a bone handle. How it fitted naval regulations, Fingal did not know.

Deirdre stood at Fingal's side and he put his arm around her waist. Angus had no need to ask for a smile. Fingal was grinning like a Cheshire cat, and dear love her, Deirdre, it seemed, nearly always had a smile on her face.

"Right," said Angus, handing back the camera. "Back to your places, everyone."

When he was seated, he said, "Looks like everybody's well fed by now."

Fingal glanced at a long table at one end of the room. A cold buffet now lay in ruins with little left but a couple of curled-up cucumber sandwiches and a few slices of bread covered in fish paste, shreds of smoked trout from the nearby River Test, and one lonely Robertson's jelly.

Angus said quietly to Fingal, "I'm sure you're busting to get away with your bride."

Fingal nodded.

"So I'm going to get the formalities over and done with."

"Remember, no speeches," Fingal said.

"Agreed," Angus said. "Leave it to me." He stood and called out, "May I have your attention?" He rattled a spoon on a glass. Gradually the hum of conversation began to subside. The mess servants circulated. Lord knows where the caterers had managed to find it, but every one of the folks was being offered a glass of champagne to drink the health of the bride and groom.

"Aye, just so. Settle down now, settle down. Ladies and gentlemen, as best man it falls to me to be master of ceremonies at this reception to celebrate the wedding of Lieutenant-Commander Fingal O'Reilly and his lovely bride . . ." He had to wait until a respectful round of applause had died away. "Thank you. His lovely bride Deirdre, now Mrs. O'Reilly." Angus lifted his glass. "As is naval custom there is no need to rise for the loyal toast. Admiral Creaser, ladies and gentlemen, I give you his Majesty King George the Sixth. The king, God bless him."

Fingal's voice boomed out with the rest.

Angus said, "You may now smoke."

Matches scraped, lighters clicked, and flames flared as cigarettes and pipes, including Fingal's, were lit. Smoke twisted up in lazy blue spirals to the high ceiling.

"Now," said Angus with a bow to Reverend

Evans, "let me give you the order of service. At the request of the groom, there will be no speeches."

Cheers rang out and somebody started singing, "For he's a jolly good fellow," and the assembly joined in.

"Aye, just so," Angus said. "As I was saying, all that will be done is as follows. I've here" — he held up a sheaf of paper — "some telegrams from friends and family who cannot be with us today. They will be read. After that, I will propose the toast to the bride and groom, and finally, although it is Surgeon Lieutenant-Commander and Mrs. O'Reilly's big day, I have their permission . . ."

Fingal nodded.

"Also to propose a toast to the health of Admiral Creaser, who is leaving Haslar after three years of unremitting work and service." He set all but one telegram on the tabletop. "If you feel like applauding, I'd ask you to wait until every one of these has been read." He began, " 'Every happiness for your big day and forever. Stop. Welcome new O'Reilly. Stop. Much love. Stop. Mother, Lars, Bridgit.' "

Fingal nodded.

" 'All our love to you both. Stop. May your future burn brightly. Stop. Father, Mother, Dolores.' "

Fingal glanced at Deirdre and saw how her eyes glistened. She'd be missing her family today, he knew.

" 'It's about time you made an honest man of him, Deirdre. Stop. I'd love to give you a big kiss, but duty calls. Stop. Your hotel will be paid for, my gift to you. Send me the bill. Stop. All my love to you both. Stop. Bob Beresford.' "

Typical Bob, Fingal thought, no expense spared — none of the abbreviated sentences usually used because telegrams were charged per word, and a most generous gift. He'd write to Bob first thing tomorrow.

"One from your friends at the Ulster Hospital in Belfast, Mrs. O'Reilly, 'Our love to you on this happy day. Stop. Party for you when you get back. Stop. All your midwife friends.' "

"That's sweet," Deirdre said.

"And finally, one from Cromie and Charlie, two more old friends and classmates of the groom. 'Brandy makes you randy and whiskey makes you frisky but . . .' " Angus's cheeks reddened. "And I think I'll leave it at that." As the guests applauded, he handed the telegrams to Fingal. "You may want to keep these as souvenirs."

"Thank you," Fingal said, and as Angus got on with toasting the bride and groom, he glanced at his friends' message. Cheeky buggers, he thought, shoving the flimsies into his inner pocket as the crowd shouted, "To the bride and groom," and someone who may have celebrated rather too much added the wish, mostly heard at ship launches, "May God bless them and all who sail in them."

The admiral was duly toasted, hugs and kisses exchanged, and Deirdre fled to Fingal's room to change into her going-away outfit. Then it would be Fingal's turn, and then they'd be off in the little Austin that David White, who was now on his way to join HMS *Illustrious,* a new carrier, had sold to Fingal for seven pounds ten. They'd be driving in it to an inn in the New Forest for their one-week honeymoon.

Fingal admired the cut of Deirdre's best suit and the ridiculous product of the milliner's art that perched on the side of her head, adorned with a pheasant's single tail feather. He took her gloved hand and helped her climb into the passenger seat of his recently acquired car. As she climbed in, her skirt rode up and he was granted a glimpse of creamy thigh above a dark nylon stocking top. He made a guttural noise in his throat and hoped that there'd be an enormous four-poster bed in their hotel room.

He closed his eyes and exhaled, shut the door, gave a last wave to the little throng who'd come to see them off, and drove away to a tinny clattering. Someone had tied a string of cans to the back bumper. "Well, Mrs. O'Reilly," he said, "alone at last," and he leant over and kissed her cheek. "I have to say I did enjoy our reception," he said. "I thought Angus did a superb job."

"It was nice of our friends to send telegrams, and very generous of Bob," Deirdre said. "I remember him from Dublin days. He's sweet even if he does have an eye for the ladies."

"He's a very sound man," Fingal said, "and I'm glad you got a chance to meet Cromie and Charlie before I was called up."

"They're both lovely men too," Deirdre said, "but not as lovely as you." She squeezed his thigh. "How far is it to the hotel?"

"About thirty-five miles. I've made dinner reservations for seven so we've lots of time." He thrilled to her touch, and in his hurry to get to the inn trod down on the accelerator.

"Perhaps," she said, "a little more slowly? It's getting dark and the shades over our headlights and no street lights don't help."

He eased off, saw a lay-by ahead, and pulled over. "Won't be long," he said as he got out. "I'm getting rid of those cans." He cut the string and with a surreptitious glance round, chucked the tins over the hedge. The "Just Married" sign went next.

He climbed back in. "Now," he said, "we're just an old married couple having a little break." He leant across the car and took her in an enormous hug and kissed her long and hard. "And that's the way it's always going to be, even when we are long married. I love you, Deirdre, and I'll never stop." He put the car in gear. "Now to paraphrase Queen Victoria, it's to the inn, James, and don't spare the horses." And her throaty chuckle was music to his ears.

"Tell me what the rest of the last telegram said, Fingal." And she started to stroke his thigh.

Deirdre was no prude, and given the effects of her stroking, the punch line was entirely appropriate. "All right," he said. " 'Brandy makes you randy and whiskey makes you frisky, but a stiff Johnnie Walker makes you pregnant.' "

And her peals of laughter rang so loudly as the car passed a village duck pond, that a couple of startled mallard took off in fright.

23
AS THE SMART SHIP GREW

O'Reilly inhaled the mouth-watering vapours rising from a casserole simmering on the stovetop.

Kinky was standing with her back to him, untying her apron. It was well past her going home time, but Kinky Kincaid had never been a clock-watcher. She was talking to Arthur Guinness and Lady Macbeth, who lay stretched out in front of the stove. The white cat, presumably having decided to call a truce, was curled up in a ball against Arthur's tummy, which naturally was on the side closest to the warmth. "This is *my* kitchen, so," Kinky said, "not Bellevue Zoo in Belfast. It does be very kind of himself to bring you in, Arthur Guinness, out of the November cold and damp, but he's been known to call you a great lummox and by all that's holy, that's what you are. A great big lump that's always getting under my feet, so. Now I do be very fond of you, but I need to look in that casserole and you're coming between me and my stove . . . again."

O'Reilly had to clap a hand over his mouth to muffle his laughter. Hikers in Canada, he'd been told, were cautioned never to come between a mother bear and her cubs. Doing so to Kinky and her stove could produce much the same response.

Arthur, who presumably knew nothing of the ursine world, opened one eye, regarded Kinky, twitched his eyebrows — and went straight back to sleep.

Apron clutched in one hand, both hands on her hips, Kinky drew in a very deep breath. A storm was about to break.

"Kinky," O'Reilly said, "Kinky, that smells wonderful."

"What?" She flinched, turned, pursed her lips, and said, "Doctor O'Reilly, you do be very light on your feet for a big man, but you should not creep up on a body, so. You threw the fear of God into me."

"I'm sorry," he said. "I came to see Barry. I thought you'd have gone home by now. I didn't mean to give you a shock."

"I'd be very much obliged, sir, if you'd ask your dog to move."

"Arthur. Here."

Arthur didn't so much get up as uncoil. He ambled over to sit, tail sweeping the floor, at O'Reilly's feet. Lady Macbeth moved closer to the stove with a look that seemed to say, Mine now. As it normally is and rightly should be.

"Thank you," Kinky said, leaned over, lifted the lid of the casserole, and sniffed. She gave its contents a good stir with a wooden spoon. She then pointed at a plate nearby as she turned down the heat under the stew pot. "Please have Kitty turn up the heat a bit and pop these suet dumplings in twenty minutes before you'd like to have your beef stew." She replaced the lid, patted Arthur's head, and said to the big Labrador, "And I did leave a good bit of the scrag end of the stewing steak for your tea . . ." She gave O'Reilly a dazzling smile, but said to Arthur, "Lummox." Yet O'Reilly heard the deep affection that Kinky Kincaid had for all members of what, despite the fact that she was married now and living with her husband Archie, she regarded as her household. "Now, sir," she said, "it's not my place to be nosy, but is there news about Doctor Fitzpatrick?"

He nodded. "He's in the Royal. My friend Mister Greer's taking care of him. The man'll need a clatter of tests before we know exactly what ails him."

"I hope," said Kinky, "it all turns out for the best, poor man."

"Generous of you," O'Reilly said. "We all want him to get better."

She shrugged. Clearly for Kinky, the matter was closed.

"Get on home now with you, Kinky,"

O'Reilly said. "We'll see you tomorrow."

"You will, sir, and enjoy your dinner. There's leftover sticky toffee pudding in the fridge for dessert." And with that she hung up her apron, put on her hat and, carrying her coat and handbag, headed for the hall and the front door.

As O'Reilly crossed the kitchen, Arthur meandered back to the stove, where he stood and looked at Lady Macbeth, who spat once. He clearly decided that discretion was the better part of valour and subsided where he was, big head on outstretched front legs.

O'Reilly knocked on what had for thirty years been Kinky Kincaid's door. Her quarters off the kitchen were now Barry's, and O'Reilly knew the young man was enjoying the extra space.

"Come in."

O'Reilly stuck his head round the door. "Got a minute?"

Barry had his back to O'Reilly. "Just give me a tick. I'm at a tricky bit. Have a pew."

"Don't mind me. Take your time." O'Reilly closed the door behind him. The curtains were drawn, but he could hear the rain of an early November gale pelting against the windows. Better old Arthur was in the house. He spared a thought for Kinky walking home in the downpour, but of course the natives, himself included, were pretty much inured to the Irish climate.

The overhead light made the room bright, a coal fire burned in the grate, and regardless of the weather outside, the room was cosy. Kinky's sampler of the mediaeval Irish poem about a monk's cat named Pangur Bán that she'd started in 1939 and worked on for a year hung above the mantel. She'd left it behind as a parting gift when she'd moved to her own place in April.

Barry was sitting at the table in a pool of light cast by an Anglepoise lamp.

O'Reilly went to an armchair beside the fire and perched on the arm so he could watch the young man at work. His face was screwed up, his eyes narrow. Clearly Barry was focussing all his energies on the task in hand. In front of him a modeller's vise was clamped to the table's edge. It had a flat base and two long, parallel jaws that firmly held the keel of a model boat. Barry had started working on it when he'd come back in January to assume his position as partner in the practice.

"Didn't know you were a modeller," O'Reilly had said when he'd visited Barry here some months ago and seen the vise holding the keel and a half-finished under hull made of individually applied pine planks.

"I started on balsa wood and paper aeroplanes," Barry said. "My first was a de Havilland Chipmunk trainer. It flew very well, powered by a twisted elastic band. My last was a Spitfire. Much trickier to build."

"Ah, the Spitfire. My mother and the marquis's wife raised money to buy them during the war. Marvellous aeroplane," O'Reilly said, remembering the snarl of Merlin engines when the nearby squadron flew low over Haslar hospital, the grace of their elliptical wings.

"That's what Dad says too. But he knew I was keen on sailing, so when I was fourteen, he suggested I move up from planes to shipbuilding, so he and I built HMS *Bounty* to scale. She's back at Dad and Mum's place in Bangor. I didn't get much chance when I was a student or houseman, but I'm enjoying getting back to it now."

"Good for you," O'Reilly had said. "It's very important that you don't become one track and let medicine rule your life. You've got to have outside interests too."

"I have had," said Barry, with an edge of sadness in his voice. "One married a surgeon. One found a more interesting bloke in Cambridge."

Back then, O'Reilly had hoped the schoolmistress, Sue Nolan, might begin to fill that kind of interest for his young friend, and the hopes had borne fruit.

The rattle of a lump of coal falling more deeply into the grate distracted O'Reilly, who glanced at the fire then back to Barry and his work. The eighteenth-century, twenty-gun, three-masted frigate that Barry had told him was a replica of the real HMS *Rattlesnake* had come on apace since that conversation. Barry was spending even more time working on it since Sue had gone to Marseilles as part of a teacher exchange. The under hull was now covered in mahogany planks, each held in place by tiny brass nails. The upper strakes had been sanded and varnished and the lower hull and keel painted white. The upper works, fo'c'sle, gangways, main deck, and quarter-deck too were completed. The muzzles of ten black cannons on each side poked through the open gun ports.

O'Reilly watched as Barry manipulated two sets of surgical forceps using the same technique he would have to tie a knot when suturing. He finished lashing down the tiny longboat he had built plank by plank. It now sat firmly on chocks in the centre of the main deck.

"Got it," Barry said, and straightened up. "Sorry to keep you waiting, Fingal, but I've just spent ten minutes working on that lashing."

"Your patience amazes me, Barry," O'Reilly said. "And such finicky work."

"It's fun," Barry said, picking up a miniature oar in his forceps and manoeuvring it into the longboat. "And with Sue in France it keeps me away from bad company . . ."

O'Reilly could understand that a young man, full of vim and vigour, could be tempted when his fiancée was away for six months, particularly when he had a friend like Jack Mills, whose genetic makeup must have DNA strands from Don Juan, Casanova, and a Grecian satyr.

"And yes, I do mean Jack," Barry said, and laughed.

"I didn't say a word." Fingal raised his hands, cocked his head.

"Jack jokes about how it's the perfect time to play the field a bit, before Sue and I get married. That what the eye doesn't see —"

"The heart doesn't grieve over. I know." Yet O'Reilly also knew that nothing would distract Barry. In all his time here, he had consistently shown he was a young man who believed that a promise was a promise.

"Anyhow, you have my attention now," Barry said. "What's up with Fitzpatrick?"

"I'm just back from running him up to the Royal. He's in there now with an as-yet-undiagnosed neurological disorder. Probably high spinal. Fair play to the man; not only was he terrified about what his medical future would hold, he also had the worry about what would happen to his patients in his absence. Medically there's nothing us GPs can do. That's up to Charlie Greer and his staff."

"And does your friend Mister Greer have any notion, Fingal?"

O'Reilly nodded. "He reckons something's going on between the base of the skull and the fourth or fifth cervical vertebrae. They'll be running tests tomorrow. Should have a better idea by the afternoon. I intend to go up to see Fitzpatrick later in the day. The poor divil has no family and I don't think he's got many friends."

Barry shook his head. "He's not the friendly type."

"That's partly why I'm going to go," O'Reilly said. "And I'm curious to learn what's wrong. Then, regardless of the diagnosis, hopeful or hopeless, we have to do our bit for him in the short term. He has patients out there who need care. I've promised Fitzpatrick that we'd cover his practice."

"Least we can do," Barry said at once. "And I'm sure we can count on Jenny."

"Good for you." Barry's immediate response pleased O'Reilly. He'd known doctors who, when faced with an increased caseload, would complain and try to avoid the work. Barry Laverty didn't merely work as a doctor, he was one from head to toe. "I'll ask her first thing tomorrow. I'm sure we can work out the details and cope for a while anyway."

"Anything you say, Fingal. I know you'll organize things fair and square." Barry lifted a miniature capstan, inspected it, and unscrewed the lid of a tube of glue. He held the capstan in his forceps and put a tiny drop of glue on its bottom, then placed the capstan gently down in the centre line of the foredeck.

"One thing occurs to me about Fitzpatrick's patients, though."

"Let's hear it."

"What about getting their medical records?"

O'Reilly frowned. "I hadn't thought of that. I'll talk to Ronald about it tomorrow. I'm sure there'll be a way."

"I'll leave it with you, but it would help to have them." Barry made a fine adjustment to the capstan's positioning.

"I think you've got that spot-on," O'Reilly said.

Barry cocked his head to one side and inspected the now-installed capstan. "Pretty much." He set down the forceps. "The extra work. It'll put a bit of a crimp in my boat-building, but I'm not on any deadline to finish it." He recapped the glue tube. He sighed. "I'll be honest though, Fingal. If Sue was here and not in France, I'd not be so keen to do more medicine. I'd do it, but —"

"You're missing her, aren't you?"

Barry nodded. "A lot. Sue's fun to be with and we love spending time together, but she also seems to understand that I have a demanding mistress — medicine — and doesn't mind. She has interests of her own. But she also doesn't let me make it all-consuming."

Like it was for a certain rural GP until Kitty O'Hallorhan came back into his life, O'Reilly thought.

"What you said earlier this year about doctors needing other interests? I'd given up my sailing all the years I was at medical school. I've just been able to start again in the summers with Sue as part of the crew. It's been wonderful. And I'm back to doing this." He pointed at the ship. "I read, do crosswords, take Arthur out for walks, but they're all pretty solitary pursuits. Sue makes me do new things, and with her they're all exciting. You'd be amazed how interesting archaeology is, and how much Neolithic stuff there is all over Ireland. Just before she left, Sue and I visited the Norman motte at Holywood and Carrickfergus Castle over on the Antrim shore. It was built in 1177."

O'Reilly laughed. "You'd be amazed how much I've learned about wines, oil painting, even a bit of cooking since Kitty and I got married. Before that, listening to my records, reading, and wildfowling . . . and you're right, they are solitary." *Which is all I wanted after Deirdre.* But, close as he and Barry were becoming, and even though he had explained a bit about his first marriage to Barry, O'Reilly did not want to dwell on that today.

"Three more months before she's home," Barry said. "It'll seem like an eternity."

"It'll pass. And the practice will keep you busy," O'Reilly said.

Barry smiled. "At least," he said, "I may be able to finish old *Rattlesnake* here."

"How long before you start on the rigging? It must be a pretty fiddly job."

Barry got off his chair. He went to a small desk, came back, and unfolded a large sheet of paper, which he laid on the tabletop. "Come and have a look at this. It's the rigging plan."

O'Reilly crossed the floor. The page showed the hull cut off at deck level. The masts, bowsprit, and the assorted yards, the horizontal poles from which the square sails would be set, were drawn in. From them and to them ran a veritable spider's web of lines, blocks, and tackles. He laughed and said, "The rigging's a lot more complicated than on my old *Warspite,* but it's not as jumbled up as it looks, because, like everything else in the Royal Navy, they had a system. The fore and main masts each had three sections. The lowest that was set on the keel and came out through the deck was the mast. The next was the topmast, and the highest the t'gallant mast. Some supporting ropes ran fore and aft. The main stay went to the main mast, the main topmast stay to the second of the vertical poles, and the main t'gallant stay to the t'gallant mast."

"I'm impressed," Barry said. "Did you have to learn about square riggers in the war?"

"No." O'Reilly shook his head. "No, we'd no time for learning useless arcana. I've loved C. S. Forester's 'Hornblower' books about

Nelson's navy since I was a lad."

"My dad has them too. They're terrific," Barry said. He glanced back at the plans. "It's going to be a lot of work, rigging her, but there's a shortcut." He winked at O'Reilly. "All the standing rigging, the ropes that held the masts up, as opposed to the running rigging used to control the sails, is meant to be dyed black. It takes forever, but I have a source of great black thread of exactly the right size."

"Oh?"

"Yep. Jack Mills pinches surgical silk sutures for me."

"Does he, by God?"

Barry nodded.

"Young Laverty," O'Reilly said, "I think you've been in too close contact with Donal Donnelly."

The two men laughed, then O'Reilly said, "I just heard Kitty come in. Why don't you finish up whatever you need to do to your ship then join us for a predinner drink? We can tell her how we're going to help Fitzpatrick and his patients so she can brief him tomorrow when she goes to work. That'll maybe take a bit of a load off the poor man's mind before he goes for all the delights," O'Reilly shuddered, "of lumbar punctures and myelograms."

24
BY THE OAK TREES' MOSSY MOOT

"Penny for the Guy, guv?" Two scruffy kids, both in short flannel pants, grey shirts, and raggedy V-neck pullovers, were dragging a two-wheeled handcart containing a straw-stuffed effigy of a man with a thin moustache, vandyke beard on his painted face, and a pointed black hat. The boys stopped Fingal and Deirdre as they strolled hand in hand along the single-lane High Street of Lynd-hurst in the centre of the New Forest. The houses on each side were of different heights, most with second storeys fronted with white stucco and black half-timbering in the Tudor style. Fingal could picture a gunpowder plotter feeling quite at home here if the cars were replaced by horses.

"Where are you two from?" Fingal asked. "Guv," short for governor, was London slang.

"Me and my brother Fred's from Wapping near London Docks. We're wot's called 'vacuees.' Been here since September."

Thousands of children had been evacuated

from the bigger cities to the countryside to protect them from air raids, and given the pasting the London Docks had taken, a bloody good thing, too.

"We always had a big party on Guy Fawkes Night back home . . ." the bigger boy sounded sad, "and I didn't want Fred to miss it too like he's missing Mum and Dad, so penny for the guy, guv."

"You'll have to sing for it," O'Reilly said with a grin, "and tell us who Guy Fawkes was."

"Ready, Fred?" They chanted rather than sang, their high voices in unison,

Remember, remember the fifth of
    November, gunpowder treason and plot
We see no reason why gunpowder treason
    should ever be forgot.

Deirdre laughed and clapped her hands. "Well done, boys. Now, do what you've been asked, tell us who Guy Fawkes was. We're from Ireland and we don't have Guy Fawkes Night there."

The taller said, "Righty-o, missus. In 1605, a bunch of men plotted to kill King James the First. One was called Guido Fawkes. They hid gunpowder under the House of Lords in London to blow the king up. But their plot got found out and . . ." He bared his clenched teeth, widened his eyes, and scrunched his shoulders, before saying in a quavery voice, "The plotters was hung, drawn, and quartered." The boy stopped to draw in a breath, clearly relishing the grisly fate of the men. "Ever since, us English have celebrated the saving of King James by having bonfires and letting off fireworks on Guy Fawkes Night, the fifth of November."

"But we can't let off any fireworks or have any bonfires," said his brother, " 'cos of the bleeding blackout. Bloody Hitler . . ."

"But me and my brother reckoned we could still try to collect a few bob today just like before the war to help remember, like, and remember Wapping —" He broke into a wide grin. "And we've got some sweetie coupons."

"Good for you," Fingal said. "Here. Here's sixpence." He handed Fred, the smaller boy, the little silver coin.

"Oooh. Thanks, guv," the taller one said, and tugged his forelock. "Come on, Fred." And off they trotted down the street, dragging their cart behind them.

Fingal and Deirdre continued at their leisurely pace toward their hotel, the New Forest Inn on Emery Down. After a simple lunch at the White Rabbit on Romsey Road, they'd strolled along the High Street, passing the imposing, redbrick Saint Michael and All Angels Church, high on a mound overlooking the village, its towering spire of silvery slate glinting in the sun.

"Kids," Deirdre said, and laughed. "Shall we have lots, Fingal?"

He chuckled. "Many as you like," he said. "I've always fancied being a daddy, Mrs. O'Reilly." He lowered his head to be nearer her ear and added, "And it's lots of fun trying. Shall we try again when we get back to our room? It's only about half a mile to go." And he wrapped himself in the glow of their honeymoon, now five days old. Fingal O'Reilly had never been more content, more happy, more hopelessly in love in all his thirty-two years.

Deirdre looked up into his eyes and said sternly, "You, Surgeon Lieutenant-Commander O'Reilly, are a typical sailor man if all reports about them are true. You're turning into a satyr, or if you prefer Ulsterese, a randy old goat. What you need is a bit of exercise to work down your lunch."

"Aaaaaw," he said, turning his lips down to twenty to four. Could the girl who had blinded him with her responsiveness, her sometimes furious, sometimes languorous, always loving, lovemaking be tiring? Or was she teasing him?

"And calm your ardour too. Do you remember the day in September last year when you proposed to me?"

"At Strickland's Glen, and we met a man with a dog called O'Reilly."

"And I raced you to the beach and you gave

me this ring." She pointed at the little solitaire.

Where was this leading? "Yes."

"I'll race you to our hotel. If you win . . ." her voice became husky, "I'm sure we'll both need to go and lie down." She ran the tip of her tongue over her lips, raised one eyebrow, and squeezed his hand. "But if I win, I want you to take me for a walk into the forest proper." With that, she let go of his hand and took off along the Bournemouth Road, her pleated skirt flying, one hand clutching her hat.

Fingal was so startled he'd let her get a good ten yards' lead before he put his head down, imagined he had a rugby ball under his arm and that the New Forest Inn was the opponent's goal line, and made for it at top speed.

To no avail. She was waiting for him, legs apart, arms akimbo, face aglow, barely panting.

He stopped beside her, unable to speak, gasping for breath. The air was burning in his chest, sweat running down his brow. It might be November, but it was one of those bright, crisp days under an English heaven where there was still lingering warmth in the sun and the sky was eggshell blue. The inn sat behind a low redbrick wall, and a signpost stood on the corner of two country lanes running beside the building. Or it would have been a signpost if all direction pointers hadn't been removed so as to stymie an invading army. Even here, deep in a peaceful forest, the bloody war kept trying to intrude. But he was damned if he was going to let it.

"All right," he managed to gasp, "you win. Where to?"

"I love you, Fingal," she said softly. "I'm sure a lot of men who were worked up the way you were a couple of minutes ago would have taken the strunts if their wives said no and would have hustled her inside right now to work their wicked will."

He shook his head and laughed at her solemnity. "Not my way of doing things," he said.

"I know. You didn't get cross. All you did was say, 'You win. Where to?' Thank you for that, darling. Do you know," she said, "for tuppence I'd drag you upstairs myself, you big, gentle gentleman."

Fingal, momentarily tempted to offer her the two pennies, simply kissed her and said, "I couldn't be anything else with you, my darling girl. And it's because there's so much about you to love. 'How do I love thee? Let me count the ways. I love thee to the depth and breadth and height my soul can reach.' Elizabeth Barrett Browning wrote that, and I can't say it any better. Now," he took her hand, "you wanted to go for a walk in the forest, so come with me." And he made for the footpath at the corner of the inn.

They lay side by side on the grassy bank of a shallow stream that flowed tinkling and murmuring from a stand of leafless oak trees to their right. Their branches almost reached the far bank. The brook continued across a sizable clearing before disappearing into another coppice of recently planted fir trees. What little breeze there was whispered through the trees on the far bank of the stream. Deirdre lay on her back, her head propped on Fingal's jacket. He lay on his side, his head supported by his bent arm.

A small drift of black pigs with a broad white stripe at the shoulder wandered in and out of the oak grove to the right, probing with their snouts and noisily crunching acorns.

"Golly, look at them, Fingal. Look at those great floppy ears. Do you think they've escaped from a farm?"

"Don't think so. Apparently," Fingal said, pointing at the animals, "local people have what are called 'commoners' rights,' at least so mine host at the inn told me. They're allowed to let their pigs out into the forest from September to November to forage for beech mast and acorns."

"The same way the locals're allowed to graze their ponies," said Deirdre, watching the swine closely.

Fingal had been forced to stop the Austin

Ruby several times so Deirdre could take pictures of the shaggy little New Forest ponies, for which the area was famous. "The rights were granted hundreds of years ago."

"It's a pretty ancient place, isn't it?" Deirdre said.

"I had a quick look at a guidebook Marge lent me when she suggested coming here. Apparently there are about two hundred and fifty round barrows, Neolithic burial mounds, all over the place, so it's been inhabited for three thousand years or so. William the Conqueror made it a royal deer preserve back in 1079 so he and his court could hunt, and it appears in the Domesday Book as *Nova Foresta.* The only other thing I remember is that there was a great storm in 1703 and four thousand oak trees were destroyed."

"Imagine all these beautiful oaks crashing down. Dreadful." She shuddered. "Did they ever teach you at school about the Major Oak in Sherwood Forest? They reckon it's eight hundred to a thousand years old. Makes you feel a bit impermanent, doesn't it?" Deirdre said. "I mean what's a life span of seventy years or so compared to that?"

"True," said Fingal, and kissed her gently, "but I don't think an oak tree's ever been kissed."

She laughed. "Hold on. I'm trying to say something important here. Be serious for just a minute, can't you?"

"Lying beside the most beautiful woman in the New Forest it'll be difficult, but I'll try. You really do want to say something, don't you, pet?"

She nodded. "We are so . . . so transient," she said, "and when we go there's nothing left behind. I asked you back in Lyndhurst 'Shall we have kids?' I was half joking then, but I'm not now. Well? Shall we? You and I've never discussed having children." She paused.

"True," he said, banishing any suggestion of levity from his voice. "I assumed it was one of the reasons two people got married, to have a family, but you're right, we've never actually talked about it."

"I'd really like to have your children," she said. "Our children, but is it fair?"

"Fair?"

"In the middle of a war with all the horrid bombings? You've heard the BBC with me every morning since we came here. London's still being hit night after night as if it'll never stop, although the bombers didn't come on the third. But it was only a brief pause. Those two little lads and their Guy. Missing home. Missing their mummy and daddy."

For a moment Fingal paused. He stared into her eyes. If it were peacetime, he'd not have hesitated for one second before answering her question about starting a family with an instant, "Of course." But she did have a point. "Darling, we are living in dangerous

372

times. I'll not beat about the bush. You'll be going back to Ulster in January. I'll be going back to my ship." He hesitated before saying, "It is possible that I might not come back."

She sat up, wrapping her arms round her knees and staring across the stream. "That's what I'm afraid of," she said.

He sat up beside her, putting his arm round her. She leant her head on his shoulder. "Please come back to me, Fingal," she said. "Please."

What to say? "Of course" would be trite and clearly a promise over which he had no control. Death was an occupational hazard of a sailor on active service. And Deirdre was far too clever to be fobbed off with platitudes. "I'll do my best," he said. "I'll do my very best. I promise."

"Thank you," she said, and kissed him as might a sister.

He held her tightly until the shaking that was a part of her silent crying had stopped and she'd sat up straight again to continue gazing out over the stream.

"I'm sorry to be so silly," she said.

"You're not silly," he said, and stared at his knees. "You're worried and rightly so. And you asked a very sensible question. Would it be fair to have kids just now?"

"Shhhhh." She said, "Look, Fingal, and move very slowly. Look over there. Straight ahead."

He slowly raised his head. Coming through the oaks and down to the stream, presumably to drink, were two deer. The rutting season had ended in October. He and Deirdre were downwind of the animals, which seemed unaware of the presence of the two humans. The buck, his dark brown coat in contrast to that of his lighter, brown-spotted doe, was about three feet at the shoulder and sported a fine set of antlers, the blades of which were flat. "Fallow deer," Fingal whispered. "The doe's probably pregnant."

Deirdre neither spoke nor moved.

The buck, constantly turning his head from side to side, nostrils flaring to detect the slightest scent, walked a little ahead of his doe. She trod level with his shoulder until together they stood at the stream's edge. The buck waited on guard until the doe had lowered her head, only raising it when she had drunk her fill, then he drank. Together they turned and in a moment were swallowed up by the trees as if the deer had never truly existed.

Deirdre sat very still for several moments then turned to him. "Fingal," she said, eyes glistening, "they were so beautiful," and she was saying it not with her lips but with her soul.

And Fingal O'Reilly, still conscious of how protective the buck had been of his mate, was overwhelmed by the need to shelter his gentle, doe-like Deirdre. He held her head to his chest, smoothing her hair, and finally said, "I love you, Deirdre O'Reilly. I'll do anything in my power to protect you, and while it might not be fair to the child, yes, I do believe we should try to start a family before I go back to sea."

"Let's," she said. "I agree. Let's try, my love."

"If we succeed," he said, "you'll have a little Fingal or a little Deirdre to look after while I'm away." And, he left the thought unspoken, a little of me if, heaven help us, I don't come back.

25
THE DOCTOR'S DILEMMA

". . . and the floods forecast yesterday for Florence have become a reality," said the BBC announcer on O'Reilly's car radio. "The River Arno has burst its banks, causing what is believed to be the worst inundation since 1557. Many people are reported to have been killed and many ancient masterpieces and millions of rare books destroyed. The city itself has been cut in two. We will bring you a further report at six o'clock."

"Poor buggers," he muttered as he parked the Rover in the car park at the back of the Royal Victoria Hospital. Barry's amusing reference to Robert Benchley's famous telegram now seemed insensitive in the face of the death and destruction.

A different radio announcer's voice said in jocular tones: "Aaaaall rightee, and to kick off this afternoon's programme, here's 'Feelin' Groovy,' or if you prefer, 'The 59th Street Bridge Song' by Simon and Garfunkel." Ordinarily O'Reilly, who liked their music, would have waited to listen for a few moments, but he found the instant switching from a calamity affecting thousands of Italians to lighthearted fluff incongruous, and switched off.

He hurried through driving sheets of rain. Leafless trees were being thrashed by the relentless downpour, and even the chain-link fencing that surrounded the tennis courts by the morgue was rocking on its posts. He soon reached the hospital's main corridor and strode past twenty wards on his way to 21.

The corridor was its usual bustling self. Nurses, both staff and student, identifiable by their different headdresses, rubbed shoulders with porters, floor cleaners and their electric polishers, visitors, medical students in their short white "bum-freezer" coats, and junior doctors in long ones. A volunteer heading for the wards pushed a book trolley from the hospital's lending library. For a moment, O'Reilly recalled an SBA shoving the clinking trolley for beer rounds on the wards of Haslar hospital back in 1940.

The corridor smells today were no different than they had been back then: floor polish, disinfectant, tobacco smoke, damp overcoats. At least here in 1966 there were no lingering stinks of a recent air raid, although he well knew that Belfast and Bangor had been attacked during the war. He put that thought away.

"Fingal," a familiar voice said. "What brings you here?"

He stopped. "Cromie," he said to his old friend. "Good to see you. I'm going to see Charlie. Ronald Fitzpatrick has developed some nasty neurological disease. He's on 21. The tests should be finished by now and Charlie should have a diagnosis established. I'm hoping a decision has been taken about what treatment's going to be needed."

"Fitzpatrick? Poor divil. Wish I could help, but it doesn't sound like he needs an orthopaedic surgeon," Cromie said, starting to walk down the hall. "I never could warm to the man, but please do give him my best wishes for a speedy recovery."

"Of course." O'Reilly kept up.

"I'd pop in now with you and wish him well myself but young Mills — he's turning out very well, by the way — has started on a Pott's fracture. Open reduction can be tricky, so I want to scrub with him."

"Off you go. Any chance of you and Button coming down for a bite? I know Kitty'd love to see you both."

"I'll give you a call." And Sir Donald Cromie disappeared through a door leading to the operating theatres.

How different, O'Reilly thought, the non-stop, all-go business of the great teaching hospital that never slept, from the comparative amble through the medical day and occasional night of rural general practice. They had busy days at Number One Main, of course, but nothing like this. And he had no doubt which one he preferred.

He arrived on 21 and went straight to Kitty's office, where she was sitting alone behind her desk, writing on a chart. She looked up and smiled. "Hello, love," she said. "Come to find out about Ronald?"

"Uh-huh. Is Charlie about the place? I'd like to know what the form is before I go and see Ronald."

"Charlie should be back in a couple of ticks." She lowered her voice. "He's just gone to shed a tear for the old country." Her voice regained its usual level. "I'll let him explain what the tests have shown." She stood up and stretched. "Would you like a cup of tea?"

He shook his head. "No thanks. Listen," he said, "I just ran into Cromie. Asked him and his missus if they'd like to come down. He's going to ring. All right by you?"

She sat again. "I'd love to see them," she said. "Just tell me when."

"Hello, Fingal," Charlie said as he walked in. "Come for the results?"

O'Reilly nodded.

Charlie smiled. "They could be better, but they could be a damn sight worse. A damn sight."

That sounded promising.

"First off," Charlie said, "he's not anaemic,

so that excludes vitamin B12 deficiency degeneration of the spinal cord, and his Wasserman's negative, so we can forget about syphilis."

"I don't think we ever really considered it," O'Reilly said.

"Right," said Charlie, "and his chest X-ray's clear, so no lung cancer. I did the lumbar puncture for the myelogram myself."

O'Reilly flinched at the thought of the wide-bore needle being inserted between the fourth and fifth lumbar vertebrae until it had entered the fluid-filled space between the membranes that surrounded the spinal cord and the cord itself. He remembered that Americans called a lumbar puncture a spinal tap.

"Then I attached the needle to a manometer and did a Queckenstedt test."

Kitty nodded. This would all be old hat to her as a specialist nurse, but to O'Reilly it was unfamiliar. "I didn't learn that one at Sir Patrick Dun's."

"It hinges on detecting rises and falls of the fluid in the manometer when pressure is exerted on the jugular vein and abdomen. I'm afraid that pressure on the vein did nothing, but pressure on the belly did move the fluid. We know that confirms that something is pressing on the subarachnoid space between the membranes and the cord, causing a blockage to cerebrospinal fluid flow."

"And that something could be?" O'Reilly asked.

"Pretty much what I said yesterday, syringomyelia or a space-occupying lesion either inside or outside the cord."

O'Reilly pursed his lips. "Not good. Sounds to me that we're between the divil and the deep blue sea."

"Not quite, you old sailor man," Charlie said. "We did the myelogram and I am pleased to be able to tell you that Ronald does not have syringomyelia, nor a tumour inside the cord. They tend to be gliomas and haemangioblastomas, both of which are not good."

A polite euphemism for usually lethal. O'Reilly knew that much.

"Whatever's causing the compression is extramedullary," Charlie said.

"So there's a chance you can do something, Charlie?"

Charlie nodded. "Depends on what it is. The ordinary X-ray wasn't much help. We're stuck with his having either a primary or secondary tumour, an abscess, some blood and bone marrow disorders, or some degenerative bone diseases, but my and Teddy McIlrath's best reading of the myelogram is that there is a tumour."

O'Reilly sucked in his breath.

"And," Charlie said, "I'll not know for certain until we've done a few more blood tests, so we're sure there aren't any blood or marrow diseases, to be on the safe side. But I'm convinced that there is a growth and it's operable."

"That's a step forward," O'Reilly said, "isn't it?"

Charlie nodded. "The best bet if it is a tumour is that it's either a neurofibroma, and those are benign, or a meningioma, and it's pretty rare for those to be malignant."

O'Reilly realised he was crossing his fingers so tightly his hands were cramping. He took a deep breath and relaxed them.

"But we'll not know until I've got the thing out and off to the pathology department."

Kitty said, "When will you operate, sir?" A student nurse had come into the office and formality was demanded in front of juniors. "Yes, nurse?"

"Mister Gupta needs a chart, Sister. May I?" She gestured to the chart trolley.

O'Reilly remembered the young Indian trainee who had saved Donal Donnelly's life after a head injury.

"Of course. Sorry, Mister Greer?"

"We'll have the rest of the blood work back on Monday. I'll look at it then, and if it's all right, please put him first on my Wednesday list. And don't look so worried, Doctor O'Reilly. They are both very slow-growing types of lesions. He'll not be at any risk by waiting for a few days, and I have some patients with much more urgent conditions."

"It sounds promising," said O'Reilly. "Now, if it's all right, I'd like to visit him. May I tell him what you've told me," — the student nurse, chart in hand, was leaving — "Charlie?"

"Fire away, but I've already had a blether with him. I think he understands." Charlie glanced at his watch. "I've got to dash. Bloody management committee."

"I'll take you to the patient," Kitty said, and rose. "Charlie's done everything he can to reduce the risk of post–lumbar puncture headache, but it can affect one in three patients so we nurse them in dimly lit, quiet rooms and keep them lying flat."

It was a whole new field to him.

She led O'Reilly to a single-bed room. The curtains of the windows looking out to the corridor were closed. Quinn House, where Ward 21 was situated, was an octagonal structure. On its inside were a number of single rooms separated by a corridor from a series of peripheral, four-bed units. Each looked out over the hospital grounds to the redbrick Royal Maternity Hospital and past a static water tank that had been put in for fire-fighting during the war and in summer served as a swimming pool. Today the pool was empty, drained for the winter and littered with dead leaves. The red bricks of the maternity hospital were darkened by the rain.

She held a finger to her lips and opened the door. In the half-light he could see Ronald lying on his back. His eyes, weak-looking without his pince-nez, stared up at the ceiling. "Fingal's come to see you," Kitty said.

"Thank you, Fingal." Fitzpatrick's voice was low and quavery. "It's very kind of you."

"How are you?" O'Reilly asked.

"I'll live," Ronald said, "at least in the short term. Everybody's been very kind, but I did not like that myelogram."

"I hear it can be pretty tough," O'Reilly said, "but Charlie seems pleased with the results."

"He came and told me," Ronald said. "Most considerate of him. He's probably going to have to operate. I don't mind telling you, as my friend, I'm scared."

O'Reilly heard the pleading in the man's voice. "I reckon I'd be pretty frightened myself," O'Reilly said. "It's the waiting, the not knowing, that really gets to you."

"Charlie has been most honest. I appreciate that. He says the chances are very good that once the tumour has been removed, I stand an excellent chance of making a good recovery."

O'Reilly sat on a chair at the bedside, debating with himself for a moment. Men in Ulster typically shrank from physical contact other than handshakes. He reached out and took Ronald's hand. "You couldn't be in better hands," he said, instantly recognising the double entendre. "Charlie Greer is one of the top brain surgeons in Ulster, probably the world."

Ronald did not, as could easily have happened, pull his hand away. Perhaps, as O'Reilly hoped, he was deriving some comfort from the personal contact.

"I know, but he is also a very honest man. He didn't beat about the bush, and anyway, I am a doctor so I do know that people can die from operations on their spinal cords, or end up paralysed." He rolled and looked at O'Reilly's face. "I think I'd rather die than have that happen."

"I know there's a risk," O'Reilly said, "but I'm convinced you'll pull through." Then, to get Ronald's mind off that honest but morbid line of thought, he said, "And you'll not need to worry about your patients. I promised I'd make arrangements, and we have. Young Barry and Jennifer and I will share the load. I'll not bore you with the details, but there is one thing . . ."

"Oh?"

"Can we get your records?" O'Reilly waited to see how Ronald would respond. He fully expected resistance. Many doctors regarded medical records as belonging to them alone. They were part of the way a physician could maintain the loyalty of his patients, who were, after all, his bread and butter. Very few country folk could pluck up the courage to demand their files and transfer to another physician's care.

"In my locker there is a key to my surgery. There's a green filing cabinet beside my desk. I think you and young Laverty could manage to carry it to your Rover. Please take it."

"Thank you, Ronald," O'Reilly said. "Thank you for trusting us." He was deeply moved, and more deeply yet when Ronald said, "You know I lost my parents to the Japanese before the war? I'd had very few friends all my life in Japan. And ever since, I've thought my parents had let me down by not joining me in Dublin in 1931. That's how it felt, even though it was nonsense. It wasn't their fault, I know, but I've found it very hard to befriend anyone, trust anyone. But Fingal, I'd trust you and Kitty with my life. Thank you."

O'Reilly could not speak.

"There's a letter in the locker too that I'd like you to read. Please get it and the keys now."

O'Reilly stood, let go of Ronald's hand, opened the locker and removed the keys and letter. He pocketed both.

"I'm very tired," Ronald said. "I think I'd like to sleep now."

"Of course," O'Reilly said, "I'll go. Kitty'll be here for you nearly every day, Ronald. She'll keep me posted on your progress, and if you need to see me about anything, let her know and I'll be straight up."

"Thank you."

He headed for the door and, looking back at the man in the hospital bed, searched for something to say that might let him leave on a lighter note. "And when you're all better we'll have you down for dinner again. I think you'll really enjoy Kinky's créme brûlées." He opened the door and didn't wait for a reply but made his way back to Kitty's office. Only then did he realise he'd forgotten to give Cromie's regards to Ronald. Next time. "I'll be off," he said, popping into the office. "I'll see you back home, but before I go, Ronald left me a letter. I'd like to read it."

"Go right ahead."

He tore it open, read, and, unable to speak, handed it to Kitty.

She scanned the letter. "Good God. If he doesn't get better he wants us to have his *netsuke* collection?" There was a catch in her voice, a gleam in her eyes. "Oh, but look. It's dated the twelfth of October. He must have written it after he stormed out that night when we were trying to help him. The poor man must have been scared out of his wits by what was happening to him, had a pretty good idea where it was leading, and was embarrassed at refusing our help as well."

And Doctor Fingal O'Reilly, gruff and hard as nails, yet shaken to his core, could only say to hide how touched he was by Ronald's offer, "When you see Charlie again, Kitty, you tell him from me that I expect him to send Ronald Fitzpatrick home in one piece and in good working order."

26

THE SHOT OF ACCIDENT

"You're late, O'Reilly." Surgeon Commander Fraser stood beside Sister Blenkinsop at the entrance to Admiral Collingwood Ward. "I suppose it was difficult dragging yourself away from wedded bliss and your glamorous little Irish colleen." These last words were uttered in an execrable stage Irish accent that made Fingal cringe.

He stifled an urge to thump the stroppy bastard, not that Fingal objected to being berated for tardiness — that was fair game. But a slur made by any man on Deirdre was risking retribution. "I'm sorry, sir." He would give no explanation, and there was some truth to what the commander had said. Their wonderful honeymoon in the New Forest had ended four days ago, and it was hard leaving the flat in the Crescent in the mornings. Deirdre went to her Land Army work, he to Haslar.

"I don't want to be late for the service of

remembrance," said Fraser. "So let's get going."

Neville Chamberlain had died yesterday and today was November the eleventh, and except for staff performing critical duties, everyone was expected to attend the service in the Garden of Remembrance near the Paddock, a vast burial ground behind the hospital and its outbuildings.

Fingal followed the surgeon, Sister, and a VAD note-taker pushing a chart trolley onto the ward. As usual, the patients lay at attention in their navy-grey-painted iron beds, or sat rigidly with arms folded. The first man was on a chair, his left arm in a sling. Fingal took the chart Sister proffered. "Leading Seaman Jackson, Colles wrist fracture reduced and set yesterday, sir."

"Feeling well today, Jackson?" the senior surgeon asked.

"Yes, sir." The man stared fixedly ahead, his face expressionless.

"Discharge today back to — ?"

Fingal got the information from the chart. "HMS *Vernon,* sir." Rather him than me, Fingal thought. The stone frigate carried out the work of defusing German mines, many of which were booby-trapped. It was also where Scott of the Antarctic had trained as a torpedo specialist.

"Excused duties today and tomorrow. Light duties after that. Back here in six weeks to have the cast off, and return to full duty."

"Aye aye, sir." The man sounded disappointed. No wonder. In civvy life, he'd have been off work for six weeks, but in wartime, it was a physician's duty to get men back to work as quickly as possible.

"Just wait until the rounds are over, Jackson," Sister said, "and we'll get you seen by the medical officer in charge so he can complete your discharge papers, and then you can go."

"Come on," said Commander Fraser. "We haven't got all day."

"Chief Petty Officer Brandon," Fingal said at the next bed, where an ashen-faced man lay. "Perforated duodenal ulcer repaired two days ago." A red rubber tube was taped to the side of his face. Its far end was in the patient's stomach so the gastric contents could be removed to give the repaired bowel a better chance to heal. Fluid from a bottle of saline was dripping into an arm vein. Fingal read from the chart: "Temperature, blood pressure, pulse, and respirations all normal. Blood electrolyte values all in the normal range. Output-input —" He scanned the chart, where the amount of saline administered was compared to the man's fluid loss through the naso-gastric tube as well as through urine, sweating, breathing, and through the skin. "— balanced, sir."

Fraser grunted then said, "Let's see his belly."

Sister drew back the bedclothes, took a pair of scissors from her apron pocket, and deftly snipped the adhesive tape that held a bulky dressing in place over the man's upper abdomen. The incision, closed with black silk sutures that ran from the top of the V between the ribs to the umbilicus, was now a dark red scab. Commander Fraser bent his head and sniffed. "Good. No infection." He palpated the upper abdomen. "That hurt?"

"Not much, sir."

Of course it bloody well hurt, Fingal thought. Fraser was palpating around a recent incision. It was necessary — one of the first signs of peritonitis was severe tenderness — but the examiner could choose to be gentle. Fraser did not.

The surgeon manoeuvred his stethoscope in his ears and moved the bell over the abdomen, listening intently. "No bowel sounds. Early yet, of course. Keep on the fluid and analgesics as before." Without a word to the patient, he moved on to the next bed. The VAD left for a moment to get a sister to redress the wound and tuck the patient in.

Fingal bent, touched the man's shoulder, and said, "You're doing very well. We'll have you back to HMS *Victory* in no time." It was the Portsmouth Dockyard headquarters, where the man would spend the rest of the war — or another shore establishment like it. The navy did not want anyone on seagoing duty with an ulcer that might burst again.

The CPO smiled. "Thank you, sir."

"Lieutenant O'Reilly." The commander's voice was hard. Imperative.

Fingal trotted to the next bed. Words from his old senior Phelim Corrigan in Dublin rang in his head. "Never let the patients get the upper hand." He was sure Phelim would extend his motto to imperious senior surgeons in this case. Fraser may outrank him, but Fingal was not going to be pushed around simply for doing his job. He held up his arm and pointed at the two broad gold rings with the narrow half ring between. "It's lieutenant-commander now, sir." He heard Sister Blenkinsop's rapid indrawing of breath.

"So it is," Fraser said. "I'll do my best not to forget in future. Now what about this patient?"

Fingal took the chart and was about to start his presentation when a VAD whispered something to Sister, who said, "Excuse me, Commander Fraser, a leading seaman is in the receiving room. There's been an accident."

"You go, Lieutenant-Commander," Fraser said, with emphasis on the "commander." "I'll finish rounds. Do try to be on time for the service." He turned his back. "And this man, Sister?"

Fingal, still smarting, left the ward and headed for the receiving room.

It was on the ground floor near the office of the officer commanding, where Fingal had had his first interview with Admiral Creaser. Fingal was greeted by a junior sister. "Thanks for coming, sir. I've got the patient on the examining couch. He's in a fair bit of pain. It's his hand. I've put an instrument trolley beside the table."

"Let's have a look." Fingal crossed the linoleum floor, past a desk and chair and a wash-hand basin secured to the grey wall. A man in a two-piece blue work overall sat, bent over, on an examining table. The patient was clutching his bandaged left hand in his right and alternating a low moaning with a string of profanity delivered in a thick Yorkshire accent. He looked up as Fingal approached.

"Good God," O'Reilly said. "Henson. Whatever's happened to you?"

"Lieutenant O'Reilly?" Henson said. The man's face crumpled and he screwed his eyes tightly shut before opening them and saying, "You've got to help me. Please, sir. If you don't, they'll invalid me out. Please, sir."

"I'll do my best." As Fingal spoke, he was taking Henson's pulse. One hundred and ten. Either due to anxiety and pain, or blood loss, or both. Fingal remembered how passionately Henson had told Fingal of his desire to make the navy his life, how proudly he'd told Fingal and Deirdre of his progress on his gunnery course. And he recalled the CPO with the ulcer who'd never go to sea again. Was Henson's dream going to go up in smoke because of his injury? Fingal looked at Henson's damaged hand. The dressing was blood-soaked and oozing. "Can you take his blood pressure, please, Sister?"

She didn't waste words but rolled up Henson's sleeve on his good arm, strapped on a blood pressure cuff, and got on with her job.

"What happened?" Fingal asked, partly out of medical need to know and also to distract Henson from the dressing being removed.

"It's one ten over seventy, sir," the sister said.

So there was a degree of shock. Fingal ignored what Henson was trying to tell him. "Bring me a tourniquet and then get plasma ready." There were now two imperatives. Stop the bleeding and replace the fluid loss with plasma.

She handed him a length of rubber tubing and said, "I'll get the plasma drip ready."

"This'll be tight," Fingal said as he looped the tubing round the middle of Henson's forearm and tied it tightly with a half hitch. "I'll get a look at your hand now," Fingal said. "You've lost a lot of blood. I'm sorry I had to interrupt you. Tell me again what happened."

Henson shook his head. "I did something

so fucking stupid I could cry."

Fingal glanced up from unwrapping the bandage that held the dressing in place. The curse seemed to have run off Sister like water off a duck's back. Naval lower-deck patients were not renowned for purity of speech.

"I were showing a clumsy bloke 'ow to close a breech block on a four point seven dual-purpose gun when I got distracted —"

Fingal dropped the soiled bandage into a pedal bin under the instrument trolley.

"And like the daft bugger I am, I slammed it on me own hand."

Fingal flinched. He could imagine the shock, the searing pain of several pounds of steel milled to fit so snugly into the breech that not even smoke would escape when the weapon was fired. Henson might as well have stuck his hand under the blade of a guillotine.

"I couldn't bear to look. The gunnery CPO got stuff and put a dressing on it. There was blood everywhere. The clumsy bloke fainted. Daft duck."

Fingal was working his way through layers of blood-caked Gamgee — cotton wool between two layers of gauze. The last layer was stuck to the wound by clotted blood. He had a choice: rip it off or soak it off.

"The plasma's ready, sir," Sister said. She approached the table pushing a smaller trolley, above which a bottle of plasma hung from a stainless steel gallows. On the tabletop he saw red rubber tubing with a needle at one end for pushing through the rubber cap of the plasma bottle, and a needle for insertion into a vein. One kidney basin held saline, and brown antiseptic was in a small gallipot. There was a sponge holder, swabs, tourniquet tubing, and a splint accompanied by a roll of two-inch bandage. Several strips of surgical adhesive tape hung from a low railing that surrounded three sides of the trolley's top.

"Right," said Fingal. "Henson. I'm going to give you some plasma while Sister gets some saline in a bowl, where I want you to put your hurt paw. It'll make it easier to get the dressing off."

He moved to the sink, washed his hands, and returned.

The sister already had Henson's injured hand in the saline.

"Help Leading Seaman Henson off with his top on his good side, please, Sister." It would be the very devil to get him undressed once the intravenous drip had been set up.

Off came the top of the boiler suit and a white T-shirt. Fingal smiled when he saw a heart pierced by an arrow and containing the word "Elsie" tattooed on Henson's upper arm. Fingal remembered the petite blonde in the Trafalgar Pub. Enough. Time to get on.

In very short order, Fingal had inserted a wide-bore needle into a vein in the hollow at the front of Henson's elbow, the antecubital fossa, and connected it to the tubing from the plasma bottle. The tubing was strapped to Henson's forearm with adhesive strips and the elbow joint immobilised by the splint held on with the bandage. Bending the joint could force the needle from the vein.

"Right," he said. "Sister, hold Henson's left forearm steady."

"I'm afraid this may hurt a bit," he said as he began as gently as possible to remove the last strip of Gamgee.

Henson whimpered but made no attempt to pull his arm away. The Gamgee hit the pedal bin's bottom and Fingal scrutinised the wreckage. Clotted blood obscured his view. He reloaded the sponge holder, soaked the swab in saline, and cleaned away as much of the clot as possible. As best as he could tell, the breech block had mangled the tip of the ring finger to just below the nail and had sliced through the lower middle joint of the middle finger. Only a shred of skin held it on. "Sister, undo the tourniquet for a couple of minutes." He held Henson's hand over the kidney dish, which was now practically empty. "Got to get a bit of blood flow into your hand, Henson, for a minute or two." The cutting off of the blood flow had stopped the man bleeding to death, but depriving the healthy tissues of oxygenated blood for too long would cause gangrene.

"Bloody 'ell . . . sorry, Sister," Henson said,

"but talk about pins and bleeding needles?"

"It's your nerves waking up," Fingal said as his nostrils were filled with the coppery smell of the fresh blood now dripping into the kidney dish. "Henson, I'm sorry, but you've lost a bit of one finger, and the top of the middle one is just hanging on. It'll have to go, but it could have been much worse. The most important thing is that your thumb's fine and so are your index and little fingers. You'll have a working hand."

Henson managed a cross between a grimace and a smile. "That's not so bad, sir. The Andrew kept Lord Nelson on and he'd only got his left arm and one eye. At least it's my left hand what's hurt and I'm right-handed."

O'Reilly nodded his support, but inwardly he wondered. King George VI's regulation-bound navy of today was a very different one from the less restrictive wooden-walled world of King George III's ships. Henson's fate might hinge on a report from his surgeon or some kind of fitness board. But there was no point worrying the man about that now. "Soon have you right as rain," Fingal said, and looked at his watch. "Sorry, Henson, it's time for Sister to tighten up your tourniquet, but I'll make it easier for you. We're going to give you morphine as soon as she's stopped the bleeding. Quarter of a grain, please, Sister."

Henson gasped as the tubing was tightened.

Fingal was gratified to see the bleeding stop.

"I'll get the morphine and then I'll put a dressing on, sir," Sister said. "Then we'll get him up to the ward."

"Thank you, and thanks for all your help," Fingal said. He walked to the desk to fill in an admission slip so the ward staff would know the extent of the man's injuries, that he was being given one unit of plasma, and that he had received one quarter of a grain of morphine. As Fingal sat, he heard through the open window the sweet liquid notes of a lone bugle sounding the "Last Post." He stood to attention, sorry to have missed the service of remembrance, thinking of the words often said after the lines, "At the going down of the sun, and in the morning, we will remember them." He said aloud, " 'Lest we forget.' " He pictured the World War I memorial to the left of the main arcade door. Among Haslar's fallen — 140 surgeons, 9 QARNNSs, and 6 VADs — were the names of 13 Irish naval surgeons who had made the supreme sacrifice. He thought of Deirdre and how vain had been his promise that he'd "do his best" to return to her. And he marvelled at the waste, the suffering, the lunacy that was war.

27

THE EAR OF JEALOUSY
HEARETH ALL THINGS

"Morning, Barry," O'Reilly said. "Making yourself a cuppa? Bite to eat?"

"Not very hungry. Just tea," Barry mumbled, sitting hunched over at the kitchen table. His fair hair was tousled, he was blinking sleep from his eyes, and his shoulders were slumped beneath a plaid dressing gown over pyjamas. If O'Reilly didn't know better, he'd have guessed the lad had a hangover. But he'd been on call last night. He must be just recently risen. And why shouldn't he have a lie-in? It was Saturday and they'd all been working hard keeping up with Ronald's practice as well as their own.

"It's absolutely true that a watched kettle never boils." Barry scowled and inclined his head to where one sat on top of the range. "Going shooting?"

A reasonable question. O'Reilly was wearing his Paddy hat, Barbour waterproof jacket over an Aran sweater Kinky had knitted for him years ago, corduroy trousers, and thigh waders. His slung gamebag held his sandwiches, his binoculars, and a couple of bottles of Harp lager. He shook his head and pulled out a chair, sitting opposite Barry. "I'm on my way to meet Lars in Lisbane. He takes part in the annual bird count on Strangford Lough. I'm no expert at that but I'm going down to keep him company, give Arthur a run."

"At least," said Barry, staring out the window, "it looks like you're getting a half-decent day for it." He yawned and rubbed his eyes.

"Bad night?"

Barry nodded. "And I can forget trying to get an early night tonight. I promised to go up to Belfast to see Jack Mills. He's taking Helen Hewitt to a party in the junior doctors' mess, can't get away until eight, so he asked me to run her up."

It wasn't like Barry to complain about doing a favour for his best friend. "Were you called out last night? I didn't hear the phone."

"Nah. I got a letter from Sue yesterday." As if that explained his mood.

"And?"

He sighed and said, "I miss her, Fingal. I really, really do. I never thought I could miss someone so much."

O'Reilly would have expected a letter to have cheered Barry up, but the lad was clearly down in the mouth. "Aye," said O'Reilly, thinking of the interminable months that he and Deirdre had been apart while he was on *Warspite* in the Med before she had been able to join him in Gosport. "I know what you mean, but take comfort, lad. The time will pass."

Barry fished an aerogram out of his dressing gown pocket. The pregummed piece of lightweight, eggshell blue paper allowed the sender to write then fold the thing up to become its own envelope, thus saving weight. The idea, introduced in the '30s by the Iraqi postal service, had been developed by the British army into the first aerograms or "blueys" in 1941.

"Listen to this," Barry said, his voice taking on a tinge of resentment. " 'Even though it was late October, the sea was flat calm and azure when we went out in an open tourist boat to the Chateau d'If. It's an amazing building, Barry. I can just imagine Dumas's Edmond Dantès tunnelling out of his cell. I'd love to take you here someday and then go to one of the cafés on the Canebière, the High Street of le Vieux Port, the old part of town.' "

"Sounds like she's having fun to me," O'Reilly said.

"Yeah, well, perhaps a little too much fun," Barry said, but whatever else he was going to say was interrupted by the kettle's piercing whistle. He rose, grabbed it, poured boiling water into a teapot, and replaced the kettle on the range top away from the heat.

"Then I got to this bit." He read: " 'I really do want to make the most of my stay here. It's my first trip abroad and there's so much to see. The sixteenth-century fort Saint-Jean was well worth the visit. I wished I had a car because I'd love to go to Aix en Provence. I've missed the outdoor summer music festival, but there are at least five museums there and you know I'm potty about archaeology and old things. I'm told I must see Les Calanques. They're a bit east of the city, a set of mini-fjords, supposed to be very scenic. There's some palaeolithic cave art in an underwater cave in one called Morgiou and there are great spots for lunch in a place called Cassis, it means blackcurrant, and farther east in La Ciotat.' " He inhaled deeply and started to make his tea. O'Reilly would have liked a cup, but it seemed Barry was not offering. And he was scowling again.

"It certainly doesn't surprise me, Barry. Your Sue is not a girl to let the grass grow under her feet. She'd grab every opportunity to expand her horizons. Travel broadens the mind, I'm told."

"Expand her horizons. That's one way to put it, I suppose." Barry brought his teacup to the table, sat, ignored the tea, and laid his forearms on the tabletop. "Sorry, Fingal, would you like a cup?"

O'Reilly shook his head and hid a smile behind his hand.

"Just listen to this. 'Then the answer to a maiden's prayer appeared in the shape of,' " Barry stopped and inhaled through his nose, " 'Jean-Claude Hamou. He's another teacher. I met him on the Chateau d'If trip. He has a Citröen *deux chevaux . . .* ' "

"Two horsepower. France's answer to your German Volkswagen Beetle."

"Thank you, Fingal. I'm familiar with the vehicle." Barry had said it politely enough but when O'Reilly studied his young friend as he bent once more to the letter, O'Reilly could see the concern and frustration in the man's eyes.

" 'And he's going to take me to Les Calanques next Saturday.' That's today." Barry's sigh was deeper than the earlier one and the fire had gone out of his voice. " 'Jean-Claude's an interesting man. A year older than me. Funny as all get out, happy to correct my French — which is improving — and very political. Very' — and that's underlined — 'socialiste.' " Barry looked up and straight into O'Reilly's eyes. "I know it's unreasonable. I know I should trust Sue implicitly, Fingal, but damn it all, I can't stop worrying. A funny young Frenchman, shared politics, exotic surroundings, bottle of wine with lunch, and *voilà.*"

O'Reilly immediately recalled his own

temptation back in 1940. Alexandrine cooking, smells of the Orient, wine taken, an attractive young woman. He cleared his throat and sought for words of comfort. "I —" He frowned, wrestling with how to phrase them. "I'm sure it's all perfectly innocent and aboveboard." At least I hope to hell it is, he thought. Barry took an awful tousling when Patricia Spence went off to Cambridge, found another man, and came back to tell Barry their romance was finished. He'd hurt main sore. O'Reilly decided to confront that probable fear of Barry's head on. "Thinking of Patricia?"

Barry nodded. "There'd be something bloody well wrong with me if I wasn't." He pursed his lips, blew out his breath. "It couldn't happen again," yet his voice lacked confidence, "could it?"

"I'd be extremely surprised," O'Reilly said. "Extremely. Your Sue Nolan's a fine lass. Fine."

"Yes, she is fine, Fingal. She's pretty and outgoing and intelligent. And I'm sure this fellow — Jean-Claude Hamou — is aware of those *fine* qualities."

O'Reilly leaned across the table and put a hand on Barry's arm. "Sue Nolan is no starry-eyed teenager, Barry. She's a mature woman who happens to be engaged to a very sound man of my acquaintance. And she knows all about *his* fine qualities."

"Thanks, Fingal," Barry said, and took the first sip of his tea. "Thanks. I need to hear that. Any suggestions about what I should do?"

"Aye. *Pro tempore,* for the time being, I'd let the hare sit. Don't comment on him when you write back, but be enthusiastic about her sightseeing, her improving French. Don't sound jealous. No leading questions. And you told me she's coming home for Christmas. It'll be here in seven weeks. Try to bide patiently, talk to me or Kitty if you're fretting, and when at last you see Sue when she gets off the plane at Aldergrove, you'll know it's all right."

Barry's smile started slowly.

O'Reilly said, "And if you weren't already going to lose a pound to me when Donal sells his pups, I'd happily wager another fiver on this: that the minute you see her you'll know you've been worried for nothing."

Barry's smile widened.

"But I'm so sure of it, it would be daylight robbery taking another five pound from you, son, so I'm making no bets."

Barry laughed out loud and offered a hand, which O'Reilly shook. "Thank you for listening, giving me lots to hope for. I'm pretty sure you're right, that if we'd bet I would have lost a fiver. Sue is a remarkable woman."

"She is that. And I know she loves you," O'Reilly said. "Soooooo, instead of taking

407

your fiver, I'll meet you in the Duck at five thirty and let you buy me and Arthur a pint." He rose and said, "Now I'd better get my skates on, collect Arthur, and take the short-cut over the Ballybucklebo Hills. These bird count things have to be carried out at the same time all over the lough and I don't want to mess things up for Lars. He's on the organizing committee."

"And his brother is none other than Rever-end Father Fingal Flahertie O'Reilly," Barry said. "I don't remember who said 'confession is good for the soul' —"

"Actually it's 'Open confession is —' "

Barry raised his hand. "And I don't care. I only know I feel better. Thanks, Fingal. Now go and count your dicky-birds. I'm going to fry myself some bacon and eggs."

28
BETTER A FINGER OFF

"Eighty-nine, eighty-eight, eighty-suh . . . suh . . ." Leading Seaman Alf Henson's counting backward from one hundred faded. The 5 percent thiopentone solution that Fingal had injected intravenously was doing its magic.

"Eyelash reflex?" Fingal asked the leading SBA who stood at the patient's head.

"Gone, sir."

"Good." Gentle stroking of the eyelashes no longer led to blinking. That meant Alf Henson was in the second stage of Guedel's four stages of anaesthesia. Fingal injected half as much again as the initial dose of the barbiturate, removed the needle, dressed the puncture wound over the arm vein, and went to the head of the table. The cellar operating theatre with its bright lights and familiar smells of disinfectant and anaesthetic agents had become Fingal's second home.

Captain Angus Mahaddie no longer stood at Fingal's shoulder. Fingal was allowed to work independently and he was no longer terrified that his lack of skill might kill the patient. He could concentrate on giving the best possible anaesthetic while learning as much as he could to take back to *Warspite.*

Fingal picked up the battery-operated Magill laryngoscope with its six-inch-long cylindrical handle, straight blade, and flange on one side set at right angles to the handle's top. It and the rubber endotracheal tube he was about to insert into Henson's windpipe had been designed by a fellow Ulsterman, Doctor Ivan Magill, from Larne. With now-practised skill, Fingal pulled Henson's chin upward and forward, inserting the blade to pull the tongue out of the way. He had no difficulty seeing the man's vocal cords in the illumination provided by a tiny light bulb. The tube slipped in easily and he used a syringe to blow air into a much narrower tube that led to a balloon now tucked beneath the vocal cords. When inflated, this balloon anchored the apparatus in place.

It was the work of moments to attach the tube to the hoses from the Boyle's machine and begin delivering the 10 percent nitrous oxide oxygen mixture. Soon Fingal was satisfied that the patient had reached the third plane of Stage III anaesthesia.

Surgeon Commander Fraser strode to the table. "You again, O'Reilly? How much longer are you going to be at Haslar?"

410

"You can go ahead, sir, and until January."

"Can't come soon enough." Fraser grunted and sat on the stool that Angus had said seven weeks ago had been there since 1910.

Fingal wished for a moment that he was back on *Warspite,* with the marvellously collegial atmosphere of working with Richard Wilcoxson and his crew. But if George Fraser's rudeness was the price he had to pay for these months with Deirdre, he would pay it gladly.

An SBA had already prepared the operative field. An arm-board covered in a sterile towel was clamped to the side of the table, and Henson's arm, hand palm up, with the dressing removed and doused in antiseptic, lay on the board. A leather strap above the tourniquet steadied the limb. Fraser sat on one side, the scrubbed SBA on the other.

"Take off the tourniquet," Fraser said to a circulating SBA who had not scrubbed and was there to carry out nonsterile requirements.

Again Fingal smelled blood as the digital arteries began to spurt. He paid attention to his patient's respiration and the state of his pupils. Everything seemed fine.

As he worked, he heard the single-word commands from surgeon to the assistant. "Clamp." An artery forceps would be handed to him to be applied to one bleeding vessel and then another until all the damaged parts of the fingers nearest the hand would sprout a forest of stainless steel forceps and bleeding would be controlled. The surgeon would deftly tie off each artery and vein in turn with a catgut ligature.

"Cut." The SBA cut the final ligature close to the knot and removed the forceps. "Right," Fraser said. "It's dry. Wash it with saline, then let's have a look."

Fingal bent forward to see and was promptly reprimanded.

"Get your blasted head out of my light, O'Reilly."

Fingal stifled his rage but knew that under his mask the tip of his nose was turning white. He checked Henson's signs. Still fine.

"Scissors."

Fingal heard a *snip* and a *clunk*. Fraser had removed the shattered end of the middle finger, which hit the bottom of a bucket placed beside the table to receive such body parts as fingers, arms, and legs. How little value we really have, he thought, made of pieces to be tossed aside like offal in a butcher's shop.

Henson tried to move. The stimulus of the amputation had penetrated the anaesthesia, and his body was responding reflexively. It was unlikely, though, that he was consciously experiencing pain. Fingal added a small quantity of ether to the mix and Henson lay still.

"Bone nibbler."

Fraser's demands were made in a bored, disinterested tone. This must be routine work for the surgeon, Fingal mused, clearly not a sufficient test for his keen eye and quick, talented scalpel. Without compassion for his patient, the man could only relate to the level of challenge that presented itself on the table. A series of harsh clicks told Fingal the surgeon was now using a steel instrument that had an end like a parrot's beak to cut chunks off the fingers' smashed bones, or phalanges. By shortening them, he created flaps from the overlying skin, which would be sewn together to cover the bone.

"Rasp." The ensuing harsh grating noise was Fraser filing the ends smooth.

"Scissors."

Now he was trimming the skin flaps . . .

"Forceps. Sutures."

. . . and sewing the flaps shut. Once again the command "Cut," rang out — and again as the knot of each stitch was tied and trimmed.

The senior surgeon would be finished very soon and eager to move on, so Fingal cut off the ether and reduced the flow of nitrous oxide.

"Right. Dress that," Fraser said, and stood, pulling off his gloves. "See to the postoperative analgesia, O'Reilly." Not Henson's analgesia, not the patient's analgesia, simply see to *it*.

"Sir. And will we give him sulphonamide?" If the wounds became infected, Henson would risk losing his hand, and that would certainly be the end of his naval career.

"Waste of scarce resources," Fraser said. "There's a war on, remember? Those stumps'll heal perfectly and the man will be back doing a useful shore job in no time." He turned his back to Fingal and said to the SBA who had not scrubbed, "Untie my gown. I've things to do."

"Excuse me, sir."

Fraser didn't bother to face Fingal. "Yes, O'Reilly?"

"I know this man. We served together on *Warspite*. He really wants to have a career in gunnery. So, in your professional opinion, sir, he won't have enough residual function in his left hand to be able to serve afloat again? Ever?" All Fingal could think of was the way Fraser had shown no interest in getting plastic surgery for Flip Dennison, the burned pilot.

"That, Lieutenant-Commander —"

Fingal heard the sarcastic inflection.

"— is precisely what I mean. I do not *have* an opinion on the matter other than professional. Take my advice. Do not become personally involved with your patients. It will cloud your ability to make decisions. And do not try to interfere with mine."

Fingal clenched his teeth. He knew that any reply he might want to make — about how he believed every patient was a human being with feelings and needs — would call down the wrath of God from Fraser. Fingal busied himself shutting off the nitrous oxide and turning up the flow of oxygen as Alf Henson began to stir and mumble. Removing the tube gently from Henson's windpipe and holding a mask delivering oxygen gave Fingal a chance to calm down and then start to think about what, if anything, he could do for Alf Henson's future.

"I'm home, pet," Fingal called as he closed the door of the Alverstoke flat and hung his duffle, cap, and gas mask on a hook in the hall.

The little radio he'd bought was on, and he could hear Tex Beneke of the Glenn Miller Orchestra's amazing saxophone solo in "In the Mood" as Fingal headed for the living room.

"Darling." Deirdre stood up from her chair with a start, and the magazine she'd been reading slid to the floor. He recognized the colourful cover of *Woman's Own* as she picked it up and set it on the chair's wide arm. She must have beaten him home some time ago. She was bathed, her hair combed and shiny, and she wore just a trace of makeup and the perfume he liked. Her Land

Army kit had been replaced with a knee-length dress and cardigan. It had become her routine to greet him as if ready for an evening out. She came to his arms and they kissed. "How was your day?" she asked. "But before you answer, sit down. You look tired."

As he planted himself in an armchair opposite hers, he saw the flower arrangement she'd made yesterday and put on the window-sill: sprigs of white heather and purple lilac berries, bright against the dark blackout curtains. She'd said with a laugh, "Just because everything in here's navy issue and the curtains are dull there's no need for the room to be gloomy." And he'd loved her for her woman's touch.

She sat now, crossed her legs, and leant forward, clearly giving him her undivided attention.

He'd already decided there was no point troubling her with his continuing friction with Commander Fraser, but was willing to say, "Do you remember Alf Henson?"

"The leading seaman who's doing so well on his gunnery course?"

He nodded and said, "I'm afraid he's not anymore. He hurt himself today loading a gun."

"I'm so sorry." And she was. Deirdre never mouthed platitudes. "He seemed such a nice man and his girlfriend was fun. Will he be all right?"

"He's lost most of one finger and the tip of another on his left hand . . ."

She inhaled deeply, hunching her shoulders. "Ooooh, Fingal. That must have hurt dreadfully."

"It did, but that's not what I'm worried about. You saw on Saturday how excited he was about his progress. Gunnery's his life, but it's possible he may get sent to a shore job."

"Would that be so terrible? I mean, it would certainly be safer for him."

"Yes, it would. But it would be awful for Henson. He joined up before the war, planning to make the navy his career. I've seen him on *Warspite*. He eats and breathes guns and gunnery. And he's good at what he does. If he'd wanted a desk job," Fingal said bitterly, getting up and heading to the small Welsh dresser they used as a bar, "he'd have selected the accountant branch. But Alf Henson is a gunner pure and simple."

She took a deep breath. "But why would anybody want to specialise in weapons that kill people?"

Fingal laughed, the sound harsh to his ear, as he poured himself a whiskey. He motioned at the bottle to her and she shook her head. "Nobody would need to if the world was full of pacifists, but it's not. At the battles of Narvik and Calabria, I don't mind telling you it was a great comfort to me to know we have a

417

very skilled gunnery department on *Warspite.*" He remained standing where he was.

She smiled. "If it's protecting you, darling, I'm comforted too. Come and sit down."

He returned to his chair and took a sip of his drink. "And there's something else. I know between the wars it was fashionable for the upper classes to decry the warrior, but men from backgrounds like Henson's still have a very simple but deeply felt patriotism. Serving your country in one of the armed forces is an honourable career, and the only difference between a soldier's rifle and one of Henson's six-inch weapons is the size.

"Behind his guns he's fighting Hitler, defending not so much the world or England as his own little bit of Yorkshire. Winston Churchill has done wonders for the country with his radio speeches urging us all to fight, each in our own way."

" 'We shall defend our island, whatever the cost may be,' " murmured Deirdre. "And Henson's way is on a battleship, manning one of her guns. I do see that, darling."

Fingal looked down and then back up, meeting her eyes. "You do see, don't you? And before one of the eight great guns can even be fired, it takes a whole crew of more than a thousand men to keep the ship working. When a shell from *Warspite* kills an enemy, it's as much my responsibility as the gunners'."

"But you don't like it."

"Like it? No, I don't like it. I hate it. I despise it, but I understand the need. I don't think Henson's a murderous psychopath any more than the young man who joined a volunteer air squadron before the war so he could learn to fly and now has to fight for his life against German airmen. I salute Henson and I want to do everything I can to help him achieve his dream — not just for the war, but for a career doing what he loves after the war is won."

Deirdre leaned forward and took his free hand in both of hers. "I know I'd rather have you ashore, and I'll bet Henson's girlfriend would too, but I do understand. He's got to follow his star. Is there anything you can do to help him?"

Fingal shook his head. "I'm much too junior and I'm not keen to get into another confrontation with Surgeon Commander Fraser. I did try today, but Fraser's already talking about recommending a shore posting for Henson. He didn't want to hear anything I had to say."

She cocked her head. "So there's nothing you can do?"

"I have to be patient," he said, "perhaps try to reason with Fraser some more, but he's my senior officer. I'm not sure. You're too far away," he said softly. "Come here."

She crossed the floor between them and

lowered herself into his lap. "My poor Fingal. All the woes of the world on one pair of shoulders. Can I do anything?"

He smiled up at her, kissed her, and said, "Just listen to me when I moulder on, and love me, pet."

"I do love you, Fingal. So very much." She frowned, sniffed and said, "Oh Lord," then scrambled out of his lap and bolted for the kitchen.

Fingal sniffed too and chuckled. Something was definitely not right.

He heard "Oh blow," and an oven door slam. The smell got worse. Fingal smiled. Deirdre had not been joking when she'd told him she was a rotten cook. Nobody's completely perfect, he thought, but apart from that one flaw, as far as he was concerned, she was in every other way.

She reappeared, shaking her head. "Darling, I'm so sorry. I was so thrilled. I managed to get half a pound of sausages at the Fareham butcher on my lunch break. I think Marge put the word in on my behalf because they're usually kept for locals. I know how much you love sausages. I found a marvellous recipe for sausage and sultana casserole in *Woman's Own* and I was going to surprise you with a treat. But I think I got the oven heat too high and I completely forgot about it when you walked in, and now it's ruined. Everything's all shrivelled up. I'm sorry." She sighed and said, "Will beans on toast do?"

He stood up, grabbed her and kissed her, then, gathering her securely in his arms, began slowly waltzing her around the tiny living room. "Do you remember Al Bowlly?"

"The band leader?"

"It just struck me that one of his songs really summed up your culinary efforts. Listen." He sang,

You may not be an angel, 'Cause angels
    are so few,
But until the day that one comes along, I'll
    string along with you.

She laughed. Deep. Throaty. Then said, "Eeejit. You always make me laugh."

"And you," he said, "always cheer me up. Seeing how you're all dressed up, I'm taking you to the Anglesey Hotel. I'd not mind a pint with my dinner. Now, get your hat and coat."

29
COUNT THE NUMBER

"I'm sorry, sir, but the limit in Greyabbey's thirty miles an hour and you was going like a bat out of hell, so you was. I was doing near sixty just for til catch you." The sergeant, a man in the familiar bottle-green uniform of the Royal Ulster Constabulary, was rather tall around. "Can I see your driver's licence, please?"

O'Reilly tried wrestling his wallet out of his hip pocket but it wouldn't come. "I'll have to get out, officer," he said through the open window. Hellfire and brimstone, O'Reilly thought as he hauled his own not-inconsiderable bulk out of the driver's seat, onto the road, and tugged his wallet free. Here he was, on the fringe of Greyabbey, being stopped by not so much the long arm of the law as the rotundity of the high road regulations. "Here you are." He proffered the maroon document.

The sergeant read it and looked into O'Reilly's face. "Doctor O'Reilly? Excuse me, sir, but would you be related to thon solicitor from Portaferry that grows orchids? It's a common enough name in these parts, but you have the look of him, so you do. Portaferry's part of my manor. I see him sometimes when I'm over there."

"He's my older brother. He's in charge of part of today's bird count and I'm going to make him horribly late."

"The bird count. Aye, I know about that, sir."

"These things have to be done at the same time all over, and I'm afraid I was rushing to get there on time," said O'Reilly. "He's giving the briefing at Davy McMasters's pub at Lisbane."

"Boys-a-boys," the officer said, "small world." He pushed his cap to the back of his head and frowned. "I owe Mister Lars a favour, so I do. He done a great job for me in a fight with my gobshite of a brother over our da's will. So I tell you what," he returned O'Reilly's licence, "just you follow me, sir. We'll need to slow down going through Kirkubbin, but . . ." He grinned and returned to his car.

Lights flashing, siren brassily *nee-naw*ing, the police car shot off like a rocket. O'Reilly followed, often clinging to the steering wheel as the big Rover became airborne from time to time before landing on its springs with juddering crashes.

All the while Arthur, who must, when the car leaped, be experiencing zero gravity, kept up an excited litany of yips, wuffs, and yodels.

In what seemed like next to no time both cars drew up outside Davy McMaster's farmhouse just across a short bridge that spanned a narrow stream. Several other vehicles were drawn up by the roadside. A florid-faced man wearing a duncher, tweed jacket, binoculars round his neck, and old flannels tucked into Wellington boots, looked at the police car, shook his head, and continued crossing the road.

O'Reilly told Arthur to stay, dismounted, and walked over to the police car.

The sergeant wound down his window.

"Thank you, Sergeant."

"Not at all, sir." He lowered his voice. "But a wee word til the wise? I'll not let you off a second time if you roar like a liltie with a supercharger through my patch again."

O'Reilly smiled. "You've my word, Sergeant."

"I'll be running on then, sir," the sergeant said, "but say hello to your brother for me. I think that there's his motor coming this way."

As the police car made a U-turn, Lars pulled up in his maroon Hillman Minx and got out.

"Morning, Finn. Glad you could make it." Lars carried an attaché case in one hand.

"Bloody nearly didn't. Got stopped for

speeding in Greyabbey, but the sergeant found out I was your brother."

Lars laughed and said, "Billy Dunlop's a sound man, the kind of peeler who'll give a kid a clip round the ear and a second chance rather than a criminal record. Wasn't that him I just saw leaving?"

"The same."

"But I thought he stopped you in Greyabbey." He shook his head. "Never mind." He chuckled and then grabbed Fingal's elbow. "Come on, little brother," he said. "Time for me to do that briefing." He held open a door that led into a hall with a tiled floor. To the left was a vast kitchen where a turf-fired black cast-iron range kept the room toasty warm. On the right, a door led to what had been the McMasters' parlour but now served as a small public bar. No one was drinking, although there was the usual tobacco haze, and when Lars followed O'Reilly into the room, seven men left their bar stools and three tables and stood. Two women remained seated. Conversation ceased.

He recognised Jimmy Caulwell, the man to whom O'Reilly had entrusted Colin Brown's pigeon-killing ferret, Butch, last year.

"How are you, Jimmy?"

"Rightly, sir."

Everyone was dressed for the outdoors and all carried binoculars.

"Good afternoon, everybody," Lars said.

"Thank you all for coming out. Before I start on the business of the day, may I introduce my brother, Doctor Fingal O'Reilly from Ballybucklebo?"

A chorus of, "Good day, Doctor," and "How's about ye?" filled the room.

O'Reilly smiled and nodded.

"Now," said Lars, "I know eight of you —"

Fingal listened as Lars mentioned all the names.

". . . were here last year and know what to do, but for the sake of Jimmy — it's his first time — I'll quickly go over the form."

O'Reilly watched as Lars opened his case and distributed sheets of paper. "Here you have sketch maps of the territory for which you are responsible, and the boundary between you and your neighbour's. Our group covers from Gransha Point in the north to Castle Hill in the south. The count starts at twelve thirty exactly, slack ebb, and will finish at two thirty exactly on a rising tide." He handed out new sheets. "These are your scorecards. Each species is indicated alphabetically, starting with 'avocet,' but I don't believe one's ever been seen on Strangford. Write in the numbers of each species that you see in your sector, and, for example, if a flock of ten mallard is on the mudflats when you start and they are joined by five more, the score is now fifteen. Pretty simple. And there is space provided to write in any birds not listed. Last year I was lucky enough to see a garganey teal."

Voices said "Boys-a-boys," and "Dead on," and "Lucky duck." This latter O'Reilly knew did not refer to the little bird with the brown head and chest and broad white stripe over its eye, but to Lars's good fortune in spotting a rare bird. Clearly the counters were experts.

"They usually winter in Africa and Asia, so he must have been blown off course," Lars said, then detailed each counter's area of responsibility. ". . . And my brother and I will take the south bank of the stream here at Lisbane over to a line coming directly into the shore from the Big Craig Lee Island to the south. Any questions?"

O'Reilly noticed that from courtesy the two women had been allocated the gentlest terrain.

He paused. "Right. Off we go. Reconvene here when you've finished and I'll collect up all your notes to give to the central committee. And don't worry, Ruby and Joy. Sergeant Dunlop will be in Greyabbey today, perhaps catching more speeders." Lars gave O'Reilly a penetrating look and the florid-faced man, whom O'Reilly had learned was Guffer Madden from Millisle, chuckled.

"So that's what that was all about, was it?" he said. "Guided you here, did he, to make sure you didn't get into any more trouble?

Our Sergeant Dunlop is a sound man, so he is."

"He is that, Guffer," said Lars. "And he'll not be a whit concerned that women aren't allowed in public bars. Davy'll be serving restoratives afterwards."

"Strictly for medicinal purposes, I'll vouch for that," O'Reilly said, and everyone laughed.

The group left the pub, and as the other cars drove off, O'Reilly let Arthur out of the back of the Rover.

The big dog ran over to a low, whitewashed wall, cocked a leg, and returned to sit at O'Reilly's feet. O'Reilly opened the boot and took out a waterproof camouflaged gas cape, army surplus from World War I.

"Heel," O'Reilly said, and he and Arthur fell in at Lars's shoulder.

"How's Kitty?" Lars said.

"She's well, and she sends her love. I wanted her to take the day off and join us, but she said they were too busy on the ward. I think she's working too hard, but she loves the work and I'll not stand in her way."

"Good for you, Finn. She's doing something she believes in. We don't all have that luxury."

O'Reilly waited until Lars had climbed a low stile, sent Arthur over, then followed. The path led them past a tilting Celtic cross covered in Ogham script and moss, past a small whitewashed church, and through a platoon of weathered headstones. Most were at least one hundred years old. Overhead a few clouds meandered in across a pale blue sky. Man and dog clambered over another stile in the far wall.

"Jasus," said O'Reilly, once again at Lars's shoulder as they strode across springy turf where russet patches of sere ben weeds rustled in a faint breeze. "I've a powerful soft spot for this wee place."

Arthur looked up questioningly at the sound of his master's voice, clearly hoping to be sent out hunting, but today the object was not to disturb the birds.

"Heel, sir," O'Reilly said. "You'll get your run later."

To O'Reilly's right, the grass sloped down to where a stream meandered in its narrow channel past muddy banks. The far side rose to a low, gorse-covered escarpment. Boulders and patches of seawrack were scattered here and there by the sides of the stream.

"Look," Lars said, and pointed.

O'Reilly followed the line of his brother's outstretched arm and saw a little creature — small, high-set ears, blunt nose and whiffling whiskers, ebony eyes, brown glistening fur over a humped back, and a long broad tail.

"River otter," Lars said as they watched the animal run to where the edge of the field curved away to the left.

Arthur stared up at O'Reilly, who muttered, "Stay."

When the otter had gone about its business, they stepped down onto a narrow shingle strand with a tideline of dead seaweed that gave the air its salty tang. Before them, a wide expanse of wet mud was dotted with water stars glistening and reflecting the sunlight.

Lars stopped. "Fifteen minutes to slack ebb, when the count starts." He strode out over the mud and O'Reilly and Arthur followed, boots squelching and leaving footprints that rapidly filled with water. From time to time they noticed spent and barnacle-encrusted brass bullet cases. The skies above Strangford Lough had been used as a practice range for air gunners during the war.

They arrived at a waist-high semicircular wall of boulders and seawrack, a hide thrown up years ago by an earlier generation of wildfowlers. Ahead of it the mud stretched all the way to a tidal island and the waters of Strangford Lough, today living up to its old Irish name, Loch Cuan, the peaceful lough.

"Give me a hand, Finn," Lars said, and together they piled fresh layers of bladder wrack to heighten the rampart that would hide them from any passing birds.

O'Reilly spread the gas cape on the stony floor. "Lie down." It would keep Arthur reasonably dry. O'Reilly unslung his game bag, sat beside his brother, and took out his binoculars. The sun sparkled off the drying mudflats, and for November the day was remarkably mild. "What do you reckon the count will be this year?"

Lars shrugged. "Last year they reckoned, to the nearest round number, Strangford Lough in the winter was home to twenty-five thousand wildfowl — that's ducks, geese, mergansers, snipe. The whole population of light-bellied brent geese winters over. Fifty thousand waders like oystercatchers, dunlin, green and golden plover, and curlew were counted. It's the mud flats. The birds love the marine worms, crustaceans, and the eel grass." He smiled. "I'm glad I joined the Royal Society for Protection of Birds."

"You'll be talking me out of my shooting soon enough," O'Reilly said.

"Huh. I didn't join to try to convert people," said Lars. "But it's good work. As I get older I find I'm not quite as interested in the law as I used to be. But protecting Ireland's natural heritage? That seems like something worth working for. I've become a member of the National Trust as well. Makes sense to preserve the old buildings too." Lars looked at his watch. "It's nearly counting time."

Lars took out his count sheet and a propelling pencil and stared ahead. "Two shelduck," he said. *Tadorna tadorna.*

As the birds waddled along the water's edge, O'Reilly admired their pink bills, black heads, white breasts, an upper chestnut bar and chestnut wingtips.

"See that ball of pale-bellied brent over to the left? How many do you reckon, Finn? I make it sixty-two."

As O'Reilly started his count there was a honking and a cackling overhead and, wings set and paddles outstretched, a second small flock joined the first.

O'Reilly concentrated, muttered, "Stop moving about, birds," and finally said, "Hundred and ten, give or take."

"Close enough," Lars said. "The count is an estimate, but it lets the powers that be set the season's limits, designate bird sanctuaries."

"Interesting," O'Reilly said, and looked out across the lough, past Big Craig Lee Island where a circular stone pen for holding and drying seaweed used to make fertilizer always made him think of a submarine with a central conning tower. He gazed past its familiar shape to the wishbone-shaped Long Island nestled under Castle Hill and on out to the lough's far shore, where the Mourne Mountains bulked purple against a still blue sky. He smiled, thinking of Kinky and Archie on their honeymoon climbing Slieve Donard, the tallest.

A flash of wings caught his eye. A single

snipe jinked across his line of sight. "Did you see that snipe, Lars?"

"No. Good for you." He made an entry. "Isn't it true that two heads are better than one?" he said.

"Unless they're both on the same neck, and then you end up in a bottle of formalin in the pathology museum," O'Reilly said, and they both laughed.

"Fancy a sandwich?" O'Reilly asked.

"Sure. I've noted all the sitting birds. There'll be a bit of a lull in the count now until more fly in." Lars accepted a ham and cheese, but refused a bottle of beer.

O'Reilly munched and drank happily, glad to be out in the open with his dog and big brother in the one place in Ireland that O'Reilly loved the best. He let his mind wander and was struck by two of today's events. Something the police sergeant had said about Lars and the appearance moments ago of the little snipe reminded him of his day out with John MacNeill, snipe shooting at the Kearneys' farm.

"Lars, I don't often ask you for legal advice, but I don't suppose you'd know anything about estate taxes — on big estates?"

"Actually —" Lars said, then, "Hang on a minute. There's a pair of mute swans."

And the majestic white birds rode the sky's highway so close overhead that O'Reilly could hear the air displaced by their slowly beating wings.

"Noted," Lars said. "Estate taxes? Actually I do. The local squire fell off the perch a few years ago and nobody seemed to know much of the law. It's pretty clear on small estates, but quite convoluted for big ones. I really had to do my homework."

O'Reilly took another pull on his Harp. This was promising.

"It worked out rather well for me," Lars said. "One way to escape crushing duties is to give your estate to the National Trust. That's what the squire's family decided to do."

"Give? Give away your estate? Sounds a bit drastic to me."

"I suppose it does when you consider the land had been in the family since the sixteenth century. But you and your heirs can hold on to things like fishing rights and shooting rights, and live in private apartments, provided the place is open to the public for a certain number of days every year. Better than having the place fall down around your ears. I've been doing a fair bit of pro bono work for the Trust recently."

"Have you, by God?"

"Why?" Lars chuckled. "I don't think a country GP's estate is going to give the taxman much of a haul, and Number One Main Street is hardly a stately home."

"True," O'Reilly said, and noticed that the hide was now a tiny island as the tide came in, rolling quickly over the wide low mud-flats. He stood. "Time to move inland," he said, and gathered up his game bag and gas cape. "Heel, Arthur."

Lars stood. "We'll head for the pit hide at the edge of the field," he said, and as the brothers and dog moved away from the mud, O'Reilly said, "I'm not worried, but the marquis of Ballybucklebo is getting heartburn about his."

Lars stopped. "And you think he might need some advising? Surely the estate retains a legal firm? These old families stick with the same firm for generations, Finn."

"Well, that's as may be. All I know is John doesn't seem to be filled with a great deal of confidence and security. I'm sure he would appreciate your help, and not pro bono either. He may be worried for the future, but he's not destitute. He can afford your fees."

"Fair enough. I'd have to meet his estate manager, look at all the land titles, books, have a word with his solicitor."

O'Reilly laughed. "You'll enjoy old Simon O'Hally. He's been advising the family since before I came to Ballybucklebo. Still wears wing collars and a tall bowler hat. He'd be perfectly at home in *Bleak House.*"

"Jarndyce versus Jarndyce. We both had to read it at school, as I recollect," Lars said.

"Put me right off Dickens. Damn near put me off the law."

They laughed together, then O'Reilly said, "I'll give John a ring. If he's interested, you can stay with us while you're working if you need to."

"Love to," Lars said as they crossed the shingle onto the springy turf of the field that ran from the beach to the back of Davy Mc-Masters's farmyard. Lars looked at his watch. "Where did the time go? It's quarter to three. Count's over. Let's head on up to the pub."

"Grand," said O'Reilly, and to Arthur, "Now is your big moment. Hey on out, boy."

And as the big Labrador tore along quartering the field, nose to the ground, tail thrashing, O'Reilly thought, there's one happy dog. And with the prospect of one drink with Lars and his team, a leisurely drive home, a pint or two with Barry, whom he hoped had cheered up a bit, and the ray of light for his oldest friend in Ballybucklebo, he was damn nearly as happy as his dog. And why should I not be? His laugh seemed to surprise Lars.

30
ALL SEEMS INFECTED

"I'd like you to have a look at Leading Seaman Henson, sir," Sister Blenkinsop said.

"Something the matter?" Fingal said. He'd just finished his eight-to-four stint in the operating theatre and had popped onto Admiral Collingwood Ward to collect his overcoat from where he'd left it that morning. "For a man two days postop, he seemed to be doing well when we made rounds this morning. His fingers were healing nicely."

"He's running a fever now of one hundred and his pulse is one hundred and ten."

"Oh, oh."

"The VAD's just made the four o'clock observations. I was going to send for the duty doctor but seeing you're here and I know he's special to you . . ."

"He is special. Lead on."

Fingal followed Sister and a VAD pushing a wound dressing trolley onto the ward. He immediately called, "As you were." Bloody naval nonsense, he thought, all this lying at attention just because an officer was on deck. They went straight to Henson's bed.

"How are you feeling, Henson?" Fingal asked.

Henson's voice was slurred. He was still being given morphine. "Sir, stumps . . . stumps thumping. Dunno what's wrong. Getting worse." The pleading in the man's eyes told Fingal that Alf Henson was less afraid of losing his physical life than of being crippled and losing his future. "Do something," he whispered. "Please, sir. Please."

Fingal put his hand on the sailor's shoulder. "We will. You are going to get better, but I'll have to take a look first." He turned to Sister Blenkinsop. The light shone on her iron-grey hair as she bent her tall frame to look Henson in the eye and murmur, "You'll be all right. You will be all right."

"Can you take his dressing off, please?"

She busied herself with scissors and disinfectant, removing the Gamgee and bandages that together seemed to Fingal to be about the size of one of the sixteen-ounce boxing gloves he and his pal Charlie Greer used when sparring as medical students.

As the last layer was removed, Fingal sniffed at it. Nothing out of the ordinary. Gas gangrene had a characteristic stench and was always a fear when a wound became infected. He saw the gauze was spotted brown from a tiny amount of old blood, but also there were streaks of yellow and that meant pus. Infection. Damn it all, the man should have had sulpha.

Fingal bent to examine the stumps. Both were swollen, red, and no doubt would be hot to the touch and painful. But it would serve no useful purpose to cause more pain to confirm a diagnosis that was plain as the nose on Henson's face. The injured fingers were exhibiting the classic signs of acute inflammation: *tumour,* swelling; *rubor,* redness; *calor,* heat; and *dolor,* pain. Fingal looked at the wrist and shook his head. A thin red line extended from Henson's wrist to halfway along the forearm. Lymphangitis. The infection was spreading. "Just want to have a feel in your armpit," he said, and slipped a hand under Henson's bed jacket. He began to palpate. Nothing out of the ordinary. He'd not expected there to be. The axillary lymph nodes would be the last defence, a string of redoubts, across the path of the invading forces of infection marching up the lymphatic channels. The spearhead of their advance was still in the forearm. When the nodes were involved they would be enlarged and feel rubbery to his fingers, but they would slow up the bacteria — for a while.

Once the nodes were overwhelmed, the microorganisms would have access to the patient's bloodstream and cause septicaemia

— often called blood poisoning — and, frequently, death.

"All right," he said, "I'm afraid you've got a bit of wound infection, Henson. Can we get our hands on some sulphanilamide or sulphapyridine, Sister?"

"Yes, sir." Somehow she sounded doubtful. Why?

"Good." He put a reassuring hand on Henson's shoulder. "We'll have you right as rain in no time."

"Please, sir. Please."

I hope we can effect a cure, he thought, but it still doesn't solve the problem of the man's future. "I think," Fingal said, "we should leave the hand open to the air."

Sister nodded, clearly approving, and, the Lord knew, she'd managed more wounds than Fingal had had hot dinners. She said, "Thank you, Lieutenant-Commander. My nurses will see to the patient, but if you can spare a moment . . . ?" She inclined her head toward her office.

Fingal frowned. What? Had he done something wrong? Damn it, he had a mile to walk to get home to Alverstoke and to Deirdre, and he really wanted to get started. He said, "I'll pop in and see you tomorrow, Henson. I hope you'll be on the mend by then."

"Thank you, sir." With his uninjured hand Henson grabbed Fingal's arm. "You've got to fix it."

Fingal unclasped Henson's hand. "I'll do my very best," he said. "I promise."

Sister was already heading for her office and Fingal followed. Whatever was on her mind, he wanted to get it sorted out.

"Sit down, Fingal," she said.

"Thanks, Elizabeth." After nearly six weeks of working together, they were on Christian name terms out of the hearing of other staff. "What's wrong?"

"Surgeon Commander Fraser doesn't believe in sulphas. He is convinced that the only guaranteed treatment for limb wound infection is immediate amputation." She pursed her lips. "I thought you should know."

"But that's palpable nonsense. Sulphas have been accepted as routine treatment for infection for almost five years now. Ever since President Roosevelt's son was cured of a strep throat back in '36. It was written up in *Time* and reported worldwide, for God's sake."

"I know. I know. But that's not good enough as far as Surgeon Commander Fraser's concerned. Last year he had two patients die in spite of having been given massive doses of sulpha. He's only interested in saving lives, not limbs. And he's the chief of surgery."

"I'm interested in saving lives too. But amputation? That's bloody barbaric. I suppose he uses rum as an anaesthetic too, just like Nelson's surgeons."

441

"No. He'll use an anaesthetist, but I'm afraid it's true about his treatment of choice."

"But . . ." There was no hope of a one-handed man staying in the service. "Henson desperately wants to make the navy his career. He's a very bright young man and his instructor told me the lad has a real future as a gunner in the navy." Fingal's shoulders sagged. He felt his spirits sink.

Sister Blenkinsop nodded, tutted, and grimaced. Then a very small smile flitted across her angular face. "How would you feel about a bit of subterfuge?"

Fingal frowned. "How?"

"The Zymotic block."

"The fever isolation wards?"

She nodded. "We still use them for contagious cases. Look, so far all that is recorded is that Henson has a temperature and rapid pulse. Signs of fever. Commander Fraser is only interested in things he can operate on . . ."

A trait common to many surgeons, Fingal thought. When all you have is a hammer, everything looks like a nail. He had a vivid picture of Fraser's standard opening of the abdomen with a flourish of his scalpel like the coup de grace of an expert swordsman.

"I suggest you make a note that you think Henson is coming down with something infectious, like measles perhaps, something that could sweep through this ward, and have him transferred to the —"

"Zymotic block. Brilliant, Elizabeth."

"It's not entirely without risk to you. If Fraser finds out . . ."

Fingal laughed. "What the hell's he going to do to a younger doctor who made an honest mistake? Court-martial me? Have me drummed out of the service? Hanged at the yardarm? Keelhauled? Elizabeth, you are a genius."

She dismissed his comment with a wave of her hand. "If you're happy, I'll phone over to your opposite number over there. Surgeon Lieutenant Imrie. He's a decent chap, and when I explain I'm sure he'll play along. If your sulpha works. They don't always, you know."

"We'll be sure in thirty-six hours." Fingal felt his spirits rise. "Damn it, Elizabeth, I've been using sulphas since '36. I've lost count of the sore throats, ear infections, urinary infections I've treated in general practice with them."

"I believe you, Fingal. And I want it to work too. And once it has, you can report back to Fraser that Henson's hand's well healed. That's all he's interested in, and that you'll arrange for Henson's discharge and follow up. It's a fair stretch of the legs to the Zymotic block, along the arcade, then down a path that runs diagonally behind Saint Luke's and past the back of the Medical Officers'

Mess. The old designers weren't stupid. They wanted to keep infectious cases well away from the rest of the hospital. Commander Fraser is not one for hiking. If the sulpha works, I'm sure Fraser will never find out."

"It'll work."

"And if it doesn't?"

Fingal shook his head. "There's no need to jump the gun. Either the drug will work or the lymphangitis will spread and his fever won't break. If that happens, Henson will need an amputation, but at least he'll have been given a chance and it still won't have put his life in jeopardy."

"And what about you?"

"Me?" He remembered Fraser snapping, "I'll expect my orders to be obeyed in future."

"You'll have to bring Henson back here. Face Fraser."

"That won't be easy, I agree," said Fingal. "You remember getting the fighter pilot to East Grinstead?"

She smiled. "Best thing that could have happened to him, even if Commander Fraser wasn't pleased."

"Not pleased? That's putting it mildly. I tried to discuss Henson with Fraser yesterday. No go, so I asked for Angus Mahaddie's counsel about how to make sure Henson could stay in gunnery school."

"And?"

"Fraser has lodged a complaint with Angus, my departmental head, about the burned pilot, and has made it clear that anaesthesia is not to interfere with surgical patients again."

"And he is within his rights. An anaesthetist has no authority over a surgeon," she said.

"Bloody departmental chain of command. Ordinarily Angus would outrank Fraser, but some civilian practices have crept into the medical side of the navy."

"And that's usually all to the good."

"Not in this case."

"But despite that warning, you're still willing to chance it?"

Fingal didn't hesitate. "Henson's hand, his future, are a damned sight more important than any bottle Fraser can give me." He saw her smiling at him and realised that she too was taking a risk, and nursing here at Haslar was her career. "I'm putting all my money on the sulpha," he said, "and if I'm wrong, it'll be all my fault, because, Elizabeth, I, as a medic, officially outrank you as a nurse, and if the worse comes to the worst, you can let it be known that you had no choice but to lodge a protest and then obey. Isn't that true?"

She looked him right in the eye and paused.

"Isn't that true?"

"Fingal O'Reilly, when this lunatic war is over and you go back to your peacetime practice, you'll have some of the luckiest patients in Ulster."

He blushed.

"I mean it," she said. "Now if you'll just write the orders for Henson's transfer, I'll call Surgeon Lieutenant Imrie. Make sure he'll start the sulpha M&B 693, sulphapyridine and give Henson aspirin to bring his temperature down as soon as our man arrives." She handed him the chart.

Fingal was chuckling as he wrote.

"All set," she said when she returned. "I'll get a wheelchair and an SBA to take him now." She frowned, then said, "You told me he wants to make the navy his career?"

"Absolutely."

"And you know our job is to get men back to their units as soon as possible. I reckon if the RAF'll let a bloke with two tin legs fly Hurricanes in battle?" Her left eyelid drooped and opened and she grinned.

"Douglas Bader."

"Mmmm. I reckon the navy'll be happy to have a slightly damaged but highly skilled gunner back."

He said, "I'm sure a call from me to Henson's divisional officer would carry enough weight. I'm not a mere lieutenant now but an experienced senior medical officer with the cuff rings to prove it. We'll not bother Angus unless it becomes a court of last appeal situation." Fingal stood, gave her a quick peck on the cheek, and said, "Sister Elizabeth Blenkinsop, I love yah, and Henson will love you more."

"Leading Seaman Henson will never know," she said, "because no one will tell him what we've done. But he seems such a nice young man, and I hate to see anyone's dreams shattered. It's up to your sulpha now, Doctor, and I hope to God it works."

31
A Bargain Dog Never Bites

O'Reilly, with Arthur at his heel, heard the swing door close behind him. The Duck was its comfortingly familiar self: tobacco smoke, beer fumes, laughter, dimly lit. He waited for his eyes to adjust so he could spot Barry. Snatches of conversation ebbed and flowed. "Glentoran over Linfield?" That was Gerry Shanks talking to his friend Charlie Gorman. "Away off and feel your head. Glentoran couldn't beat the skin off a rice pudding."

"I see them Yanks has let off another atom bomb in Nevada the day." O'Reilly recognized Helen's father, Alan Hewitt, and wondered if the lass was busy getting ready for her date tonight with Jack Mills.

"And you mark my words. *You* mark my words." An index finger was jabbed on the bar top for emphasis. "It's them bombs that's buggering up our weather over here, so it is." That was the dour Mister Coffin, the undertaker.

Faces turned to the newcomer and all

conversation stopped as, to a man, the room said, "Evening, Doctor. How's about ye?"

"Evening all," O'Reilly said, spotting Barry at the bar, holding a nearly full pint. O'Reilly moved to join him. "Pint, please, Willie."

"Right you are, sir." And Willie Dunleavy immediately got a pint of Guinness on the pour. "Arthur?"

"He'll get his Smithwick's a bit later." O'Reilly looked round. The noise level of the place, now greetings had been exchanged, had returned to normal Saturday-afternoon levels. The room was packed. Not even much room to stand at the bar. He frowned, then he noticed Donal Donnelly sitting with Dapper Frew and beckoning. "Just a minute, Donal," O'Reilly called, and turned to Barry. "How are you, lad?"

Barry shrugged. "I went down to the yacht club. Your old recipe of keeping yourself busy helped. I'm still worried, but if it can't be cured it has to be endured." He smiled. "I'm going to try to take your advice, believe there's nothing to worry about — and hope to hell you're right."

"Good for you, and" — he inclined his head to Donal's table — "whatever Donal wants to tell us might just prove to be a little more of a distraction for you. Are you up to it?"

"Of course I am, Fingal. I'm not sick," Barry said with an amused smile. "How'd the bird count go?"

"Great afternoon out on the lough. Lars was in excellent form."

"Your pint, Doctor," Willie said, handing O'Reilly his drink.

"Ta, Willie. And we're going to sit with Donal. Bring over Arthur's Smithwick's like a good fellah." O'Reilly turned to Barry. "Doctor Laverty will settle with you later."

Barry grunted, but smiled and said, "Cheaper than the five-pound bet I'd have been very happy to lose at Christmas."

"Just be happy by Christmas and for tonight. Come on, Barry, let's see what's on Donal's mind." O'Reilly moved ahead like a dreadnought through a fleet of corvettes and shouldered his way to where Donal and Dapper were sitting.

"Evening, Doctors." Councillor Bertie Bishop was at a table nearby with a stranger. "This here's a friend of mine from Belfast, Ernie Ramsey. He's with the Belfast Chamber of Commerce."

"How do you do?" Barry said.

O'Reilly grinned. Barry's public school education was shining through. Even after all these years of hearing that greeting, O'Reilly still wanted to ask, "How do you do what?"

"Rightly, sir. Grand altogether."

"Welcome to Ballybucklebo," O'Reilly said. The man smiled.

"I'll not hold youse up, Doctors," Bertie said. "Away you on and sit with Dapper and

Donal. I hear he's getting some kind of rare Australian dogs?"

"News to me," said O'Reilly with a straight face, keeping his promise to Donal not to let on that he was in on the secret. "I'm sure he'll tell us all about them. Enjoy your evening." He led Barry to Donal's table.

Two other men were standing there finishing pints. "Shuey and Sammy's just leaving, so they are," Donal said, "so if youse would like til sit with Dapper and me, sirs, we could have a bit of *craic*."

Barry said, "How's the knee, Shuey?" Barry was treating the ninety-year-old for osteoarthritis.

"I'm still getting about, so I am, but I reckon your man Roger Bannister —"

O'Reilly could remember the excitement when the young physician had broken the four-minute-mile barrier twelve years ago, at the time considered an impossible feat. If Bannister had had Sergeant Livingstone on his tail, he might have gone even faster.

"I reckon thon boy could outrun me now, so he could," Shuey said.

Everyone in the company laughed.

Sammy, Shuey's sixty-seven-year-old son, said, "Youse can laugh now, so yiz can. But you should have seen my da fifty years ago. Even when he was forty, he was still the best runner with the South Down Beagles, and you've til be bloody fit to run cross-country behind a pack of beagles chasing a hare, so you do. That ould saying 'He runs like a hare' isn't because hares are members of the snail family."

While there was a general muttering of assent, O'Reilly wondered if all the exercise — Shuey had been a shepherd and a keen oarsman as well — was the source of his longevity, and if the beagling could have been the cause of his arthritic knee.

"Take it easy, the pair of youse," Donal said.

"Fair enough, Donal," said Shuey, and leant on his son's arm. "Good night all."

O'Reilly and Barry sat. "Under," O'Reilly said, and Arthur lay down beneath the table. *Sláinte.*" O'Reilly drank, savouring the bitter taste.

Donal said in a low voice, "The cat's out of the bag now about the Woolamarroo quokka dogs. Wee Colin told a wheen of his friends at school and they told their mammies and daddies, and now everybody knows."

"Bertie Bishop certainly does," O'Reilly said.

" 'Scuse me." Willie had come over with Arthur's bowl.

Barry paid and said, "So what's the next step?"

"Everybody knows Donal will be getting them on December the tenth," Dapper said. "Now," he lowered his voice, "til avoid any suspicions, like, Bluebird'll come and lodge

452

with me when prospective buyers come over so she doesn't give the game away when people start taking her pups."

Mary Dunleavy's Chihuahua, Brian Boru, the unwanted sire, wandered over and stopped at the table.

Donal, to O'Reilly's surprise, leant down and patted the wee dog's head. "Good boy." He straightened up. "No point bearing a grudge." His voice was barely audible over the pub's din. "The wee man was just doing what comes natural. And if our scheme works, and we make a bundle, he's the one responsible. Bloody good thing he's a long-haired Mexican. Makes the pups look less like greyhounds. In fact, them funny-looking craytures are like no dogs I've ever seen in my whole puff, so they're not."

Brian Boru disappeared under the table to see his friend Arthur, and the sounds of lapping doubled.

"I thought at first it was a disaster," Donal said, "but it's looking better now. Just goes til show that it's a sick wind that blows nobody any good."

"Ill wind, Donal," O'Reilly said.

"Aye, right enough. Ill. Anyroad," and he took no care to speak softly now, "we're just waiting for the news to travel, maybe up til Belfast and some rich people, like the ones who live on the Malone Road or Cherryvalley."

"Have you any notion how to get the word further afield?" O'Reilly asked, but was going to have to wait for an answer because a hush had fallen over the entire pub.

O'Reilly looked over at the doorway, where Lenny Brown stood holding his son Colin's hand. "Willie, I know youngsters aren't allowed in pubs," Lenny said, "but this here's very special, so it is, and all the people we want til thank is in here."

"Sure isn't Colin eighteen?" Willie said with a huge wink. "And isn't Constable Mulligan over in Newtownards the day? No problem. Come on on in."

Lenny moved to the bar, lifted Colin so he could stand there, albeit stooped over because the wooden-beamed ceiling was so low. As usual, one knee sock was crumpled round one ankle.

"Now, gentlemen, *and* Donal Donnelly, who hardly qualifies."

Prolonged laughter in which Donal joined. Ballybucklebo folks were masters of the gentle art of slagging, trading good-natured insults with no malice intended.

"Away off and chase yourself. Sure it takes one to know one, you know, Lenny, seeing as how you're not qualified yourself," Donal said, returning the insult with interest, to more laughter.

"Nice one, Donal," Lenny said, then waved an envelope over his head. "Everybody. This here come in this morning's post." He paused for dramatic effect, then said, "Wait til youse hear this. Wait til youse hear this. My wee Colin's passed his Eleven Plus. He —"

Lenny got no farther. The room erupted in applause, a couple of whistles, several cries of "Dead on."

Colin waved his clasped hands over his head like a victorious prize-fighter.

Lenny waited until a semblance of silence returned. "I want til thank Miss Sue Nolan, who's not here."

O'Reilly glanced at Barry, who was nodding, a melancholy smile on this face. "I'll tell her in my next letter. She'll be thrilled."

"Thank you for that, and with Doctor O'Reilly and Alan Hewitt, who got me to see the light that letting him sit it was the best thing to do for my dead brill wee son."

O'Reilly felt a constriction in his throat. Other people's success, particularly children's, always affected him.

"And Councillor Bishop. I had a wee private word with him this morning to let him know. He knows why I'm saying thanks til him and I think some of youse maybe do too, but he asked me for not til make a fuss about it, so he did. Anyroad, on behalf of my son," Lenny lifted Colin down from the bar, "thank youse all."

Once more the Duck sounded like Belfast's Hippodrome after a headliner had finished their act.

O'Reilly rose. "This should call for Champagne," he said, "but —"

Willie interrupted. "We don't keep any of those fancy French fizzes here, sir."

"And that's all to the good," O'Reilly said, "for I'm not made of money, but I'd like to buy you a drink, Lenny, and can Colin have a lemonade or an orange crush?"

"I'll take a pint, please, Doctor," Lenny said.

"Maybe," Willie said as he started to put a pint on, "Colin would like one of those American Coca-Colas? I've a few in the fridge."

"Wheeker," said Colin. "Sticking out a mile."

O'Reilly rose and made his way to the bar. He was aware that Bertie Bishop was at his shoulder. "Lenny," O'Reilly said, "I'd like to shake your and Colin's hands. It's a great day for you two and Connie, Colin's mammy." He shook with Lennie, but before taking Colin's hand he palmed a half crown. "Congratulations, son," O'Reilly said, winked, shook, and felt the coin vanish.

"Thanks very much, Doctor," Colin said.

"Now," said O'Reilly, "you're going to grammar school. You make sure you work hard and make us all proud."

Before Colin could answer, Bertie Bishop had edged past O'Reilly. "Congratulations,

Colin," he said. "I want you to have this." He proffered a ten-shilling note.

Colin's eyes widened at the money, four times the amount O'Reilly had just given him. "All for me?"

"Every penny."

"My God," Colin said. "I'm getting rich, so I am. Thank you very, very much, Mister Bishop."

Willie said from behind the bar, "Your pint, Lenny, and your Coke, Colin."

"You enjoy your drinks," Bertie Bishop said. He turned to O'Reilly. "Doctor, I wasn't eavesdropping nor nothing, but I overheard something Donal said and I've a wee notion I might be able to help."

O'Reilly's mouth opened. How much had he heard? O'Reilly studied Bertie's face, but there seemed nothing there but genuine interest. Since the man's illness there had been a sea change in the most miserable gobshite in the village and townland. Maybe, O'Reilly thought, Ebenezer Scrooge hadn't needed three ghosts to make him change his ways. A serious illness could have done the trick. "Push your table up fornenst ours," O'Reilly said.

When the seating arrangements had been made, Bertie said, "Donal, it's none of my business and if you want to tell me to take a hike that's all right, but I heard you saying you want rich people in Belfast to know about them there new dogs that's coming. I think I can help."

O'Reilly watched as emotional warfare broke out on Donal's face, judging by his changing expressions: a frown for initial disbelief, a pulling up of one side of his mouth suggesting puzzlement, the lifting of his duncher and scratching of his carroty mop meaning he was wrestling with the dilemma of whether or not to trust a man who not long ago had tried to cheat Donal and his friends out of their shares in a racehorse. Finally, after replacement of the cloth cap, there came a beaming smile, which must mean that greed had triumphed over prudence. "Fire away, sir. I'm all ears, so I am." Donal exchanged a look with Dapper.

"Right," said Bertie. "You want to get the word about your Woolamarroo quacker —"

"Excuse me, sir. It's quokka."

"I stand corrected. Quokka."

Watching Donal, of all people, correcting another's pronunciation required O'Reilly to call on all of his self-control to stop himself guffawing.

"Me and Mister Ramsey here's" — the stranger bowed his head — "in the chamber of commerce up in town. They'll be having our Christmas dinner party on December the seventeenth. Mister Ramsey's having me and Flo as his guests. Would you consider bringing a couple of the pups to the predinner cocktails?"

"Why?" Donal asked.

"Ernie could put the word out beforehand about these amazing dogs, couldn't you?"

"Aye, certainly," Ernie said.

"How much a pup?" Bertie asked.

Donal never hesitated. "Twenty pounds, sir. Them's pedigree dogs and I have the papers til prove it, so I do."

Bertie whistled.

"I know twenty quid sounds like a lot," Donal said, and continued with great solemnity, "but you only get what you pay for."

"Right enough." Bertie clapped Donal on the shoulder and said, "Twenty quid's pocket money to the likes of folks that run Mackie's Foundry, Harland and Wolff's. It'll be a wee doddle getting them til pay up."

Donal looked sideways at Dapper, who nodded once and said, "If you say so, sir."

"I do say so, Dapper Frew," said Bertie, showing some of his former feistiness. He turned back to Donal. "Now, you're the dogs' owner so I'll bring you and a couple of pups to the party. Right, Ernie?"

"Right," Ernie said, "and I'll get you on as a special agenda item before the dinner, during the cocktails."

Bertie said, "You get that pretty wife of yours to tie some red ribbons round the wee doggies' necks. They'll fit right into the festivities."

Donal scratched his head. "I'd like that, sir, but how am I going to get home? You'll be staying for the dinner, but I'd not fit in with all those highheejuns."

"I'll run you up, Donal," O'Reilly said quickly, "and home again." And if I can't finagle my way in to watch Donal pull off the con trick, then my name's not Fingal Flahertie O'Reilly.

"That would be dead on, Doctor," Donal said.

"Fine by me," Bertie said. "Sounds like you've got valuable property there." Bertie clearly believed every word Donal and his friend Dapper were saying.

O'Reilly shook his head. If there was a Nobel Prize for con artistry Donal and Dapper would both be going to Stockholm very soon.

"Do you know, Mister Bishop, Mister Ramsey, I'm your man on this." He leant over and shook hands with each in turn.

"I'll bet," said Bertie, "they'll all be sold in no time flat."

"And speaking of bets . . ." O'Reilly said, and he looked at Barry, who, with a wry grin on his face, was shaking his head in early admission of almost certain defeat.

32
ENGAGE HIMSELF
OPENLY AND PUBLICLY

It was Sunday noon, when an Englishman's place, after morning service in Fareham's 105-year-old Holy Trinity Anglican Church, was in the pub for a predinner pint. With Tony leading the way, Fingal stepped into the inviting semidarkness of the Whitehorse Inn, a pleasant country hostelry on the banks of the Wallington River that had long served as Tony's local when he was home on leave. The war had not curtailed the Sunday ritual and the place was buzzing. The womenfolk, Marge, Deirdre, and Pip, had gone home to prepare the midday Sunday meal. Marge had collected up everyone's meat coupons and had miraculously, Fingal suspected with the connivance of the local butcher, managed to secure a beef roast, which she planned to serve with Yorkshire puddings and parsnips, brussels sprouts and potatoes from her Victory garden.

But before lunch, a pint, and Fingal savoured the thought of both on this precious weekend away from Haslar.

Conversation rose and fell in the public bar and the air was blue with tobacco smoke. Two men were throwing darts with a single-mindedness of purpose, oblivious to the din around them. Fingal could imagine King Henry VIII decreeing that all his archers should play the game every Sunday after mass to hone their aiming skills. At a table nearby, two farm labourers in traditional smocks were playing cribbage.

"What'll you have, Fingal?"

"Pint of bitter, please."

"Coming right up." Tony went to the bar and stood beside a bald-headed, florid-faced gentleman of about sixty in hacking jacket, tweed plus-fours, woollen stockings, and heavy brogues. He sported a drooping moustache and could have served as a model for David Low's Colonel Blimp.

Fingal smiled at the mental picture, imagined the man prefacing his every utterance with "Gad, sir," just like the cartoon character. He fished out his pipe and lit up while he waited for Tony, now engaged in conversation by another regular.

As he let himself sink into the comforting atmosphere of the pub, it was almost possible to imagine himself back in Ireland, that this rare weekend off duty was routine and that he was just a country doctor mulling over his week: the satisfaction of knowing his anaesthetic skills were ever improving; his gratitude to Angus Mahaddie, who'd been a brick, happily coconspiring to get Henson back on his gunnery course. The sulpha had worked, the stumps had healed, and Angus's recommendation that Henson be passed fit for duty had been accepted, with Fraser none the wiser. Alf Henson was now back on Whale Island and expected to be finished with his course by mid-December.

But he was not in Ireland and he was not a country doctor but a lieutenant-commander, due to return to *Warspite* in little more than a month from today, December the first.

"Here you are." Tony set a dimpled pint glass on the tabletop, plopped down beside Fingal, and raised his glass. "Absent friends." The navy's Sunday toast.

"Absent friends," he replied.

"So," said Tony jovially, "good news from the Med the past few weeks. The planes of HMS *Illustrious* sinking that ruddy great Italian battleship *Dulio* and damaging two more of their battlewagons. Still, I don't know how long people here at home can hang on . . ."

They were both silent, sipping their beer. Fingal knew they were probably both thinking of how Southampton had been bombed a week ago and there were rumours that the flashes and sweeping searchlight beams he'd been able to see in last night's northern sky had been the town being raided again — and at only twenty miles away it had been too bloody close to Alverstoke.

In mid-November, the German Luftwaffe had hit Coventry and destroyed much of that city and its fourteenth-century Gothic cathedral. Britain was still taking it, but the price was getting higher. Rumour had it that the Germans had been guided by some secret radio blind-aiming device.

Tony took a long pull on his beer and shook his head. "Sorry, Fingal, I didn't mean to bring up the war." Then he laughed. "As if it's not on everyone's mind. Even here in this little country pub. It's just that I'm thinking of someone," he said quietly. "An absent friend. His parents are Irish like you."

"Any chance I might know them?"

"No, they came from Tipperary, but he was born here, in Fareham. I've known him all my life. Captain Edward Fegen, RN."

Fingal shook his head, sipped his warm, weak beer, and waited for Tony to continue.

"He was captain of an armed merchant cruiser, HMS *Jervis Bay.* She was the sole escort of convoy HX 84 from Halifax to Liverpool." He looked at the tabletop.

"That's your usual run, isn't it?"

"There but for the grace of God," Tony said, and looked up. "Poor old Teddy ran into the German pocket battleship *Admiral Scheer* on the fifth of November."

When Fingal and Deirdre had been enjoying the quiet of the New Forest, Fingal thought, British sailors had been dying in the icy North Atlantic. He shuddered.

"By all accounts he charged the Nazis head on. His six-inch pop guns against the Germans' eleven-inchers. Fought them for three hours and gave the convoy the chance to scatter. *Jervis Bay* was sunk and Teddy was killed." He stopped abruptly and took a swallow of his pint. "But all but five of the thirty-seven ships in the convoy survived."

"Brave men," Fingal said.

"Very brave," Tony said. "And I'm telling you this for a reason, Fingal."

"Go on."

Tony set his glass on the table. He reddened. "Um, you'll keep this in strictest confidence, of course?"

"Naturally."

Tony leant closer to Fingal before saying, "I've been in love with Pip for donkey's years . . ."

Fingal waited. Irishmen could be reticent about discussing personal matters, but Englishmen? Stiff upper lip and all that? The silence between them widened. "Tony," he was eventually forced to say, "I'm your friend, a fellow officer, and I'm also a physician. What are you trying to tell me?"

"I-I can see how happy you and Deirdre are."

"We are that," Fingal said with a grin, and

took a pull on his pint.

Tony held his hands up, palms out, shrugged, and said, "I can't bring myself to ask Pip to marry me. Simply can't do it." His gaze fixed on Fingal's eyes. "It could be my turn on any of the convoys to have to do what Teddy — Captain Fegen — did. See what I mean? It wouldn't be fair to her, leaving her a widow." He sighed. "But it's bloody awful knowing we'll have to wait until the war's over."

Fingal took a deep breath. He hadn't the slightest doubt that if faced with overwhelming odds, Lieutenant Commander Tony Wilcoxson would indeed do his duty, regardless of the cost, and that it was his love for Pip, rather than a lack of it, that was holding him back from proposing. "At one time it looked as if Deirdre and I couldn't get married. When I told her, she said something very sensible. She said, 'We don't need a ceremony.' " He could smell the freshly cut hay lying in the field where she had been working with the Land Army when he had gone to break the seemingly bad news. " 'In our hearts we're as married as any man and woman can be.' " He cocked his head to one side, waiting for a response. When none was forthcoming, he said, "Is that how you and Pip feel about each other?"

Tony smiled and nodded. "Gosh," he said, "I hadn't thought about it quite like that. I thought I was doing the honourable thing. For Pip's sake. But do you think she probably already feels married to me? I realize now that's just how I feel about her."

"Yes, I think she probably does. And if you are killed, if I'm killed — I'm back on active service in January — both Pip and Deirdre will grieve and mourn, and not having had a ceremony in your case won't make the pain any easier for Pip to bear. And you'll have missed a very great deal, believe me."

"So you think — do you think I should pop the question?"

Fingal shook his head. "It's not what I think. It's what you think that matters."

Tony's grin was vast. He finished his pint, stood, and went to the bar, where he had a few words with the publican.

To Fingal's immense delight, the Colonel Blimp type's voice could be heard over the general hubbub. "Gad, sir, if it was up to me I'd —" Whatever he'd do was drowned out, but Fingal was still chuckling when Tony returned and set a small glass of Scotch whisky in front of Fingal before seating himself. Fingal took the last swallow of his pint.

"Just a little something to seal the deal, so to speak, and say thank you. We'll finish these up," Tony said, "head home for dinner. Then if after the meal I might borrow your Austin for a short while? I'll take Pip for a drive. I really ought to speak to her father. Tell him I can support his daughter and all that kind of thing. I already know I have no trouble getting permission from the navy. In fact, the whole thing's been a standing joke between me and my CO ever since he met Pip. He's a good egg."

"Good man-ma-da," said Fingal, laughed, and raised his glass. "Shall we drink to the future Mrs. Wilcoxson Junior?"

"I believe," said Tony, "that would be a splendid idea. Positively splendid."

"Whisky? At noon? I can smell it on your breath." Marge sniffed and stepped back from her son's embrace. "It's not like you, Tony."

"No, it's not," Tony said, "but Fingal and I were celebrating a recent important decision."

Pip and Deirdre, each holding a schooner of sherry, had both half turned and were looking up at the men and Marge. Their chairs were, as usual, separated from the hearth and log fire by a somnolent Admiral Benbow.

"Oh?" said Marge.

"Mmm," said Tony. "Now, I was going to wait until later when we'd be alone, and I know I'm meant to have a ring, get down on one knee, but damn it all —" His words tumbled out, one chasing the other at high speed. "Pip, you know I love you."

Fingal saw her eyes widen, a grin begin. The English might be a reserved lot, he thought, but once the floodgates opened —

"Always have, and in the pub, Fingal helped me to see the light. I've been an idiot letting the war put me off. Philippa, Philippa, will you marry me?"

Pip squealed, spilling her sherry as she leaped to her feet. Nodding, smiling, tears starting, she shouted, "Yes, yes, yes," and threw herself at Tony.

Admiral Benbow let go a basso profundo "Woof."

"God bless my soul," Marge said. "*Mirabile dictu,* wondrous things are spoken."

Deirdre clapped her hands, stood, and kissed Fingal. "I'm so happy for them," she said. "Aren't you?"

"As they'd say in Ulster, it's sticking out a mile, so it is," he said, marvelling at Deirdre's limitless ability to take great pleasure from the happiness of others.

"You Irish," said Marge. "Sticking out a mile, indeed." She laughed. "I like it, and as the news clearly is, it calls for something bubbly. Come with me, Fingal, Deirdre. I want to check on our lunch. And let those two have a bit of time alone."

They followed as she headed for the kitchen, calling over her shoulder, "And don't worry about the spilled sherry. I'll bring a damp cloth when I come back." In the kitchen, pots bubbled on the top of a coal-fired Aga range and roasting smells filled the air. Burnished copper saucepans hung by their handles from hooks in the black rafters above a big pine table on a slate floor. She inspected each pot in turn, then sighed.

"I am so pleased for Tony and Pip," she said. "Now, Deirdre dear, tell me about your lovely day off yesterday."

"It was perfect, Marge. We explored about a mile of the shoreline of the Solent looking out to the Isle of Wight. Then lunch in the Fighting Cocks on Clayhall Road, you know the one where all the staff go, about half a mile from the hospital. They all call it the Pugilistic Pe— Well, never mind. Then we took the Gosport Ferry to Portsmouth and saw *Gone With the Wind.* I cried when Rhett and Scarlet's daughter, Bonnie, was killed."

"Of course you did, dear." The words sounded dismissive, but Fingal could hear the fondness in Marge's voice and the way she looked at her young friend.

"Now, champagne." She went to the Kelvinator refrigerator and opened its left-hand door. "Here," she said, handing Fingal a bottle of Dom Pérignon. He looked at the label and whistled. 1921. "I chilled this so we could celebrate your and Deirdre's first-month anniversary."

"Marge," said Deirdre, looking at the label,

"that's far too kind."

Vintage champagne? Fingal thought. Must have cost a bundle.

"Fiddlesticks," Marge said and, as if reading his mind, explained, "Richard always laid down a few bottles in the year they were produced. Relatively cheap back then, and your first month would have been an occasion worth celebrating. And so now this one is too. We can toast all four of you. Wasn't that lucky I had a bottle ready?"

Lucky, was it? Despite her protestations of cheapness, twenty-year-old champagne for a one-month anniversary? Or, thought Fingal, was Marge like old Doctor Flanagan's housekeeper back in Ballybucklebo, Mrs. Kincaid, a wee bit fey?

"Now, pop it on a tray. There are glasses in that cupboard." She pointed, then busied herself soaking and wringing out a cloth.

Fingal and Deirdre did as they had been bidden.

Marge inhaled deeply, then shook her head, leaning against the sink.

He saw the glint in her eyes.

"I'm so very, very happy for them," she said. "I don't know how you did it, Fingal O'Reilly, but . . ." She had to get on her tiptoes to kiss his cheek. "Thank you. I only wish Richard could be here. Bloody war." She stared into the distance, clenched a fist, cleared her throat, then said, "Come on then, let's get the drinks through, and I want you to do the honours."

He followed her back to the living room and set the tray on the table near where Tony still stood holding Pip's hand, both looking into each other's eyes.

"Do your duty, Fingal," Marge said.

"Right."

Pop. Fizzz. Then Fingal poured five glasses and used the tray to carry and offer them to the company.

"Now," said Marge, lifting her glass, "Lieutenant Commander and Mrs. O'Reilly, please join me in drinking to the health of my son, Tony Wilcoxson, and his beautiful bride-to-be, Philippa Gore-Beresford."

Three voices echoed the toast.

"Thank you all," Tony said, and before anyone else could speak, Deirdre said, "And I have a toast too for us all to drink, and a wish. I'm stealing one of your navy ones to start with," she said. "Confusion to our enemies."

"Confusion to our enemies . . ."

"And you, Fingal," she looked from man to man, "and you, Tony, come back safe and sound to the four women who love you — Marge, Pip, me, and Ma back in Ireland."

As the women drank, Fingal looked at Deirdre, loving her for her understanding, loving her for her love for him and, it seemed —

with the exception of the Germans and Italians — for everyone she met.

33
LEST WE FORGET, LEST WE FORGET

Under a leaden sky the little park near the tarnished pewter sea was crowded. The sombre state of the weather suited the solemnity of the occasion. A small obelisk at one end of the park, the Ballybucklebo cenotaph, was inscribed with the names of the fallen of the Second Boer War, two world wars, and the Korean conflict. As was the case on memorials all over Ulster, the dead of the Great War outnumbered all the others. Ulstermen of the 36th Division had suffered more than two thousand dead on the first day of the battle of the Somme alone.

Surgeon Commander O'Reilly stood at ease with the other Ballybucklebo ex-servicemen in the drizzle of another Remembrance Day, Kitty by his side. He hated to display his medals unless she absolutely insisted, and today she had not. And so he had left them, including his Distinguished Service Cross, at home. It was a small contingent led by its most senior member, "Shuey" Gamble, aged ninety, who had won the Military Medal at the Somme in 1916. He was lucky to be alive. Joseph Devine, who had lost his wife Sheilah last year, was an old World War I Vickers Vimy bomber pilot. Chief Petty Officer Thompson, butler/valet to the marquis of Ballybucklebo, stood beside Declan Finnegan, who had been with the tanks in France after D-Day and had brought home his French bride, Melanie, who stood with him. The man was trembling, but not from the cold. The surgery Charlie Greer had done for Declan's Parkinson's disease had not been entirely successful.

Archie Auchinleck, late of the Irish Guards, kept glancing at the small honour guard from the regiment in residence at Palace Barracks in Holywood. The soldiers were commanded by Sergeant Rory Auchinleck, Archie's son. Kinky stood by his side. Barry was in the almost-deserted surgery and could, if need be, answer the phone, making it possible for her to attend.

The drabness of the day was punctuated by splashes of red from the linen poppies worn by every man, woman, and child.

Today's ceremony, O'Reilly knew, would not have the pomp and circumstance of the service at the London Cenotaph with royalty in attendance, artillery salutes, massed bands, a march past and a flyover by the Memorial Flight, but for the villagers here it was an intensely personal event. In such a tight-knit community, everyone, except for some of the younger children, was related to or had known someone who had served. Just about every villager was here. O'Reilly noticed Roger and Ruby McClintock. The grey-haired old man had a comforting arm round his wife's shoulder. Their only son, Brian, had gone down with the mighty *Hood,* sunk by the *Bismarck* in May 1941.

The service never failed to move O'Reilly to his very core, and Kitty too looked pensive. He wondered if she was remembering the war years she'd spent at the orphanage in Tenerife, how she'd befriended a widowed man and his small daughter, and how much she'd come to love them. O'Reilly would like to have taken her by the hand, but protocol demanded he maintain a military posture.

The war dead deserved his homage. He, who never dwelt unduly on his war memories and was far from being a sentimental man, knew only too well the sacrifices that had been made and the loyalty of those who had made them. He would not miss the simple ceremony for love nor money.

Mister Robinson, the Presbyterian minister, was officiating. Despite Father O'Toole's ecumenism in all matters of faith, it was tacitly understood how difficult it would have been for him to come. He was a man from County Cork, which had been a hotbed of Republican sentiment during the Irish War of Independence from 1919 to 1921. Everyone in Ballybucklebo knew his older brother had been shot down in front of the then-young seminarian, who had not been allowed to give the dying man the last rites. His killers had been the brutal British auxiliaries, the Black and Tans. There was a limit to how far even a man of God could be expected to turn the other cheek. Irishmen had fallen in British wars, but the Republic of Ireland did not mark the day — and neither did Father O'Toole.

"It is now time for the laying of the wreaths," Mister Robinson said.

Sergeant Auchinleck shouted, "A-ten-shun," which the honour guard and all the ex-servicemen obeyed, then, "Present — arms."

Boots slammed, Belgian FN rifles with fixed bayonets were snapped briskly to the "present."

Kinky also came from County Cork and had lived not a mile from Beál na mBláth, where Michael Collins was killed during the Irish Civil War. Her father, however, had refused to become embroiled in Irish politics and Kinky had worked in the north, in Ballybucklebo, throughout the Second World War. She was here to pay her respects to the fallen she'd known as friends and to take pride in her stepson.

As he did every year, the marquis laid the first wreath, on behalf of the British Legion, the white enamel Maltese cross with laurel wreath and crown of his DSO hanging beside his campaign medals. The wreath's artificial red poppies were stained purple in the rain. He stepped back. As he saluted, so did all the other ex-servicemen, O'Reilly included. He sighed.

Bertie Bishop laid a wreath on behalf of the council; Colin Brown, in uniform, one from the Boy Scouts; and Jeannie Kennedy one from the Girl Guides.

Sergeant Archie Auchinleck gave three orders: "Order — arms" and, when the command had been obeyed, "Reverse — arms" when each soldier smartly turned his rifle so the muzzle pointed to the ground, followed by "Off — headdress." Every man's head, military and civilian, was bared.

Over the hushed crowd rang the pure sweet bugle notes of the "Last Post," soaring, floating, and softly, so very softly, dying away.

For two minutes there was not a sound save for the gulls and the susurration of the never-still sea on the shingle and sand. O'Reilly, heels together, arms with hands at the seams of his trousers, gaze fixed firmly ahead, gave his private memories free rein as he knew every adult present would be doing. He remembered gladly those who had returned. Tom Laverty; Richard Wilcoxson, dead of a stroke last year at the age of eighty; Angus Mahaddie, still going strong in Inverness; Patrick Steptoe, now a gynaecologist in England. He recalled sadly those who had not: the countless unnamed soldiers and civilians worldwide of all nationalities, and those of a more personal nature, the fallen sailors of the destroyer HMS *Touareg,* their canvas-wrapped bodies going over the side into the Med. The dead of the Battle of Narvik, including a young German whose life O'Reilly had tried to save. Those dead in the bombing of Portsmouth. The crews of Italian cruisers and destroyers sunk off Cape Matapan. The waste. And he felt a lump in his throat. A quick glance showed that Ruby McClintock had tears running down her cheeks. Lest we forget? How could she?

His reverie was snapped by the traditional ending to the silence by the sounding by the bugler of "Reveille."

When it finished, Sergeant Auchinleck ordered his men to come to attention, on caps, and stand at ease.

O'Reilly replaced his paddy hat and stood easy.

Colin Brown came to the microphone, took a quick look at his mother, then swooped down to pull up one khaki sock that had fallen round his ankle. He must have been very thoroughly rehearsed because his high voice rang out clearly, despite the distortion of the sound system.

In Flanders fields the poppies blow
Between the crosses, row on row . . .

The poem, which always moved O'Reilly, had been written by a fellow physician, John McCrae, a Canadian. Next year perhaps he would ask Mister Robinson if the poem "High Flight," by John Magee Jr., the young American Spitfire pilot who died in 1941, might be included too.

Colin was coming to the poem's close.

We shall not sleep, though poppies grow
In Flanders fields.

O'Reilly sighed again and the stubborn lump in his throat grew.

Dapper Frew, the most talented of the Ballybucklebo Highlanders, stood at attention in full uniform, the great highland bagpipe bag under his arm and the drones over his left shoulder. He needed no microphone as he piped the haunting lament "Flowers of the Forest," a tune only played in public at funerals or services of remembrance. Somehow the harsh notes entwined O'Reilly's heart and squeezed. It was all he could do to hold back his tears. He still could not take Kitty's hand, but from the corner of his eye he managed to glimpse her expression

480

of concern for him and was warmed by it. He was able to stay dry-eyed until Mister Robinson finished with the Laurence Binyon poem called "For the Fallen."

Age shall not weary them, nor years
    condemn
At the going down of the sun and in the
    morning
We will remember them.

The crowd replied as one, "We will remember them."

Archie marched his squad off parade and the old soldiers of two wars stood easy as the crowd dispersed.

O'Reilly still stood, impervious to the drizzle, particularly remembering a Remembrance Day at Haslar in 1940, when a young leading seaman, Alf Henson, had lost two fingers, and Deirdre, only just Mrs. Deirdre O'Reilly, had ruined a sausage and sultana pie. His memory of Alf was fading, but Deirdre he could picture as sharply as if it had been yesterday, though the pain of it had been dulled with time and the return of Kitty.

And there was Bob. As ever, that memory pulled O'Reilly up short. Bob Beresford, best friend of Fingal O'Reilly's medical student days, lying somewhere, as far as O'Reilly knew, in an unmarked grave in Singapore. Killed by the deliberate neglect of his Japanese captors. Lest we forget our fallen? I'll never forget you, Bob.

And as he did, without shame, every Remembrance Day at the close of the service, Fingal O'Reilly let his tears flow for what had been, and what might have been, but had been cut off short. Then he dried his eyes and blew his nose with an almighty honk.

Now Kitty did take his hand and squeezed. "You lost friends," she said, "and I know you're thinking of Bob."

He nodded and knew Kitty was far too tactful to mention Deirdre. "I did and I was," he said. "What a God-awful waste." He shook his head and forced a grin. "No more tears — at least this year."

"Come on," she said. "Home to Number One. A spot of lunch will help cheer you up."

"Eat up however little much is in it," Kinky said. "It is my toad in the hole that you love, sir, and I know you like it too, Doctor Laverty. I'm keeping Doctor Bradley's warm for her, so."

"Yum," said O'Reilly, preparing to attack her Cookstown sausages wrapped in Yorkshire pudding batter and baked, served with carrots, brussels sprouts, and onion gravy. "As any one of the locals might say, Barry, 'Get you bogged into thon.' " He sliced into the first toad, chewed, and said, "Another winner, Kinky. Thank you. And thank you for hurrying back from the service to make it for us."

"Hear, hear," Barry said.

"I thought Rory handled his squad very well today," said Kitty. "You must be proud of him."

"I am, Kitty, and Archie's like a dog with two tails about it. Said it took him back to his days as a sergeant. He's having lunch with Rory now. Making the most of it."

A forkful stopped halfway to O'Reilly's mouth. "Most of what?"

"It does be sad, but is a fact of army life. A month from now Rory's regiment is to be stationed with the Paderborn garrison in Germany. It is a very good thing the Germans and us are friends now."

"I agree, Kinky," said Barry. "And so would my dad. He always used to tell us to love our neighbours, and also to love our enemies, because they were often the same. But I'm sorry Rory will be going."

"Och," she said, "if you look at it on a map it's a powerful way to Germany. But Archie and I do want him to succeed in his career, and these days with all those aeroplanes flying back and forth I'm sure he'll get home leave from time to time, so."

O'Reilly, mouth too happily full of food and too polite to talk with it full, grunted in agreement and smiled at the thought of his old friend Tom Laverty passing off the wisdom of the philosopher G. K. Chesterton as his own. He nodded to Jenny as she came into the dining room.

"Sorry I'm a bit late," she said, "but one of Fitzpatrick's patients' angina was playing up. I think he'll be all right, but I didn't want to leave him until the cardiac ambulance arrived."

"Good lass," said O'Reilly.

"I shall bring your lunch, Doctor," Kinky said, and left.

"I must say," said O'Reilly, "between the three of us we seem to be managing his practice pretty well. But I don't think Barry and I could be coping by ourselves. Thank you, Jenny." He smiled at the young woman, who had not sat down but was still standing, as if waiting for him to finish speaking. "And we're going to need your help for a while longer now that his operation is still on hold. I keep hoping every day when Kitty comes home that she'll have news, but . . ." He shrugged and held out his hands, palms up. The operation that had been planned for last week had run into the kind of day-by-day delays beginning to plague the bigger hospitals. Budget cuts were forcing the emergency cases to shove less urgent ones aside.

Jenny looked down at the tablecloth before looking up and saying, "I've been happy to help out and you've both been very patient, particularly you, Fingal, while I've been making up my mind. Doctor Harley phoned me from the Royal this morning and he wants me to take charge of the well-woman clinic there and —"

O'Reilly choked down a mouthful and leapt to his feet, taking Jenny into a loose bear hug. "That is great news. Congratulations, Doctor Bradley. Richly deserved." He let her go.

"Well done, Jenny," Barry said. "We'll miss you. We really will."

"And you'll miss your lunch if you let it go cold," Kinky said, setting a plate at Jenny's usual place. "Eat up, Doctor Bradley, and keep up your strength."

The phone in the hall rang.

"I'd like to know what all this missing Doctor Bradley is about, but I'd better see to that."

As she left, O'Reilly and Jenny took their places.

"I've had a wonderful time working here," Jenny said. "I've taken the liberty of asking Doctor Harley if he could find my replacement — naturally providing she's acceptable to you two." She smiled. "I said 'she' deliberately. You do have quite a few women who want a woman doctor."

"And they shall have one," O'Reilly said, "if Graham Harley can find one as good as you."

Jenny blushed.

Kinky stuck her head round the door. "It's

your friend Mister Greer, sir."

O'Reilly leapt to his feet again and bounded to the phone. "Charlie? What's up?"

"I wanted to let you know at once. Fitzpatrick, who's nearly going spare with worry and boredom, is about to become an emergency."

O'Reilly gasped. "Is he getting worse?"

"Not at all, but I know how to work the system. Ronald will be declared an emergency and in the operating room next Tuesday, November the fifteenth, or my name's not Charlie Greer."

"Wonderful," O'Reilly said, "and about bloody time. Thanks for letting me know."

"Least I could do for a colleague. We used to call it professional courtesy," Charlie said. "Now I've got to go." He hung up.

"Ha," said O'Reilly, rubbing his hands, "bloody marvellous." He went back into the dining room and broke the news to Kitty and his young colleagues, who seemed as pleased as he. "Now," he said, "Jenny, when will you want to leave?"

"Doctor Harley would like me to start on March the first, but if he can find my replacement sooner?"

"Of course," said O'Reilly, and took a mouthful of toad in the hole. "Bah," he said, "damn thing's cold." He rose, saying, "I'll be back," and headed for the kitchen.

He came back holding a tray with his

reheated lunch and Kinky bearing another tray with a bottle of claret and four glasses. "Here," he said, "you've finished, Barry. Uncork this and pour glasses all round. You too, Mrs. Auchinleck. I want us all to toast Jenny's terrific success." As he watched Barry pour the rich red wine into the glasses, he thought of the poppies in the lapels and on the wreaths this morning. And he murmured, amid the laughter and congratulations, "We shall remember them."

34

To Everything
There Is a Season

"It's a lovely little tree, darling, for our first Christmas," Deirdre said, touching one of its branches lightly.

Fingal caught the wistfulness in her voice as he straightened up from anchoring the four-foot-tall fir in a wooden butter box at the corner of the flat's living room. "We'll decorate it on Christmas Eve. Put the prezzies under it. Angus is going to lend me some fairy lights and glass balls."

"Where did you get it?"

He laid a finger alongside his nose and winked. "What the eye doesn't see the heart doesn't grieve over. There's a stand of small firs behind the hospital near the Paddock. It's unlikely anyone will notice that the stand is now one tree short."

She kissed him. "Resourceful you. Thank you," she said. "It wouldn't be Christmas without a tree. And Christmas Day is only four days away." She shook her head. "Where did December go?"

"I think," he said, thumbing away a single tear that had slipped down her cheek, "I think the winds blew it away."

She brushed away another tear and turned to once again look at the tree. "Those horrid gales, one after the other, sweeping up the English Channel. But we've been so cosy here in our little nest." She looked around and Fingal could tell what she was thinking. In just sixteen days they would be leaving this place where they had been so happy. Now wasn't the time to approach the subject that was on their minds. They both wanted Christmas to be a happy time. The weather was a safer subject.

"I reckon the whole of the British Isles must have suffered," he said, looking out the window. "It's hard to know for sure with no broadcast weather reports anymore. Why give that information to the enemy gratis? Make them send over and risk their reconnaissance aircraft."

"There's been no reports of air raids while the storms were roaring in."

"The gales keep the German bombers grounded. Bloody good thing too."

"I just hope," she said, shovelling slack on the coal fire to bank it, "it wasn't blowing like that in the North Atlantic." The small chunks of low-quality coal, the slack, slowed the rate of burning of a coal fire, but it would still be lit and keeping the flat warmish when they returned after shopping this afternoon. "If it was, heaven help the sailors, both naval and mercantile, and, in particular, Tony Wilcoxson. Pip says he's somewhere between Halifax and Liverpool."

"Look on the bright side," Fingal said. "The U-boats'll have to keep their heads tucked in too. Tony told me that when the gales are screeching the subs can't mount attacks."

"I suppose," she said, giving the fire a last jab with the shovel. But she sounded doubtful. "Anyway, get your cap and coat. I want to change into slacks and then we'll go."

Fingal wandered along to the hall. He echoed Deirdre's question, where did December go? Damn it, the time was going fast. Far, far too fast. He'd be on his way back to *Warspite* on January the sixth. Sixteen days. He lifted his greatcoat from its peg.

Fingal's work had settled into a well-worn daily routine in December. With no enemy actions there had been no "all hands on deck" days and nights like his early introduction in October with casualties pouring in and three operating tables running continuously day and night in each of the underground theatres.

So there had been time for Deirdre, wonderful time. Time for breakfasts together when they were both home in the Crescent in Alverstoke. On nights when Fingal was on

490

call, Deirdre stayed with Marge to be ready to go to their Land Army work the next day. It saved petrol. There had been time to take long walks, go to the cinema, and listen to the BBC, still broadcasting even though Broadcasting House in London had been bombed in October and six weeks later damaged further by a delayed-action land mine exploding nearby. They'd simply moved the newsroom to Maida Vale, just round the corner.

He buttoned his coat and set his cap on his head then took her raincoat down to have it ready to help her into.

Good old Auntie BBC. Wonderful entertainment on rainy shut-in evenings. Neither of them would miss an episode of *It's That Man Again,* better known as *ITMA.* The title referred to the ubiquitous news headline references to Adolf Hitler in the lead-up to the war. Comedian Tommy Handley's skits and songs, such as the antics of Colonel "I don't mind if I do" Chinstrap and Mrs. "Can I do you now, sir?" Mopp, delighted Deirdre. Fingal's favourite comedy was *Much-Binding-in-the-Marsh,* a sendup of the RAF. And while her favourite piece of music was still Beethoven's Ninth Symphony, Deirdre always tuned in to *Music While You Work* if she was home at lunchtime.

Fingal wandered over to the small writing

desk in the corner of the living room to collect his keys and saw the war diary he'd kept during his time on *Warspite*. He'd read excerpts of it to Deirdre since she'd arrived in October. Fingal had stopped keeping it for the past three months. The BBC's *War Report,* with correspondents like Richard Dimbleby and Wynford Vaughn-Thomas, aired immediately after the nine o'clock news, usually read by John Snagge or Alvar Lidell. The report, clearly censored, kept the public appraised of the general progress of the war; the Siege of Malta, the campaign against the Italians in the Western Desert, the fighting in Greece and the Balkans, and the Battle of the Atlantic. He resolved to start making entries again once he had left England so he could tell her of his doings on his next leave.

And war be damned, they'd had time for each other, time to talk, to sit quietly together, to giggle over Deirdre's best efforts at cooking, to have a drink in the pub, to write dozens of the austere, black-lettered "Merry Xmas" cards on plain white paper, and open the incoming ones now sitting on every open surface. Games of Monopoly and Snakes and Ladders had brightened quiet evenings. And there had been time to make love. Lots of time. But now the sands of that time were running out.

Fingal peered along the hall, wishing she'd appear soon. After seven weeks he no longer leant against the door frame to watch her put on her makeup because he resented being away from her even for such a short while, but even now he wanted her close.

"I'm ready, darling." She appeared and he thought how smart she looked in her headscarf, loose navy blue sweater, beige flannel trousers, and sensible shoes.

Today they'd be looking for gifts for each other and buying food. Small parcels had already gone off to both their families back in Ireland and gifts had been wrapped for Marge and Pip.

"Here." He held her coat while she shrugged into it.

She took his hand. "Come on then," she said. "Let's see what we can find in the Gosport shops."

Fingal unlocked the front door of their flat and held it open for her. "Be it ever so humble, there's no-o place like home," he sang, letting the door swing shut. "Where do you want these?" He held several paper carrier bags that contained their purchases.

Deirdre switched on the hall light and was taking off her coat and headscarf and setting the umbrella in its stand. "Just pop them on the dining room table, love, and I'll sort them out once I've done the blackout and poked the fire." She headed for the main room.

"Brrr," he said, and rubbed his gloved

hands together. The room smelled smoky. The little coal fire that they'd banked with slack before they'd gone out was prone to blowdowns if the wind was out of the north-west, and the sash windows, with their fine view over the Solent, could have fitted better. The blackout curtains she'd just closed swayed in the draught.

"That's better," Deirdre said as the poker, an old French bayonet, broke through the crust and cheerful flames appeared. "I'll make us a cup of Oxo," she said, "as soon as I've unpacked." She grinned at him, blew a kiss, and wagged a finger. "And don't you dare peek." She picked up two of the carriers and headed for the bedroom.

They'd shopped for groceries and meat together, but had split up so each could buy the other's personal gifts.

Fingal removed his cap and gloves but kept his overcoat on and hunkered down in front of the fire. One of his gifts to her, a heavy woollen sweater, was lying in a carrier on the table. His coat pockets held a set of pearl earrings, and a silliness. Last week in a tobacconist's shop she'd clapped her hands and chuckled over a crystal ball paperweight containing a miniature village complete with a steepled church and fir trees. Some kind of fluid was shot through with white flakes and when you shook the ball, it looked as if there was a blizzard inside. She said it reminded her of Ballybucklebo in a snowstorm. He wanted to see her face when she unwrapped it.

He took off his greatcoat, hung it in the hall, and returned to the fire. Deirdre was singing Jimmy Dorsey's "Amapola, my pretty little poppy . . ." He smiled. There had been no sign of her earlier tears during their shopping excursion and now she was back to her usual cheerful self. She must get low sometimes, but usually she kept it for times he couldn't see it. When he'd been in general practice, lots of patients would come in feeling run down and wanting a "tonic." As long as Deirdre O'Reilly, née Mawhinney, was around, that was something Fingal O'Reilly would never need.

She came into the room, gave him a quick peck, picked up the rest of her parcels, and headed for the kitchen. "Just be a jiffy," she said. "Enjoy the fire and smoke your pipe."

From the kitchen came the clattering of drawers being opened and closed, the strains of, "I'll get by as long as I have you . . ." and the whistling of the kettle.

He lit his pipe, stretched out his legs, and let a lovely sense of contentment wash over him.

"But what care I? I'll get by . . ."

She handed him a steaming mug of Oxo. "Be careful. It's hot."

"Thank you," he said.

"As long as I have you." She kissed his ear and took the chair beside him. "Now," she said, "it's not very exciting and I know you really like them for breakfast, but how'd you fancy a couple of kippers for your tea?"

"I'd love them," he said, knowing that even Deirdre would have no trouble grilling a couple of the smoked herrings, "and I love you." He sipped his Oxo but let his pipe go out. "Come and sit over here." He set his mug on a nearby table and bent his knees to make a lap.

She came and sat on it, steadying herself with an arm round his neck. His arms encircled her waist and he tasted the beefy tang of the Oxo when she kissed him. He pulled her closer, feeling his pulse quicken. One more kiss then he said, "Oxo is warming, but I think I've a better idea." He inclined his head in the direction of the bedroom.

"Why, Fingal," she said, "whatever can you mean?" And broke into helpless laughter before standing, taking his hand, and leading the way.

He started to unbutton his shirt as she crossed her arms, grasped the hem of her sweater, and pulled it over her head. Her slacks lay crumpled round her ankles. "Deirdre, you are so lovely . . ." was as far as he got when the insistent double ringing of the telephone broke the mood.

"I'll hop in," she said, turning back the

496

bedclothes. "See who it is and get rid of them, pet."

"Right," he said, going back to the hall and lifting the receiver. "Hello? O'Reilly."

"Fingal? Fingal?"

He recognised Marge's voice. It was cracking. "Yes, Marge, I'm here."

"Fingal. It's Tony."

Fingal leant against the wall. "Go on."

"His destroyer was torpedoed off Iceland two nights ago. The Admiralty telegram came this afternoon."

"My God."

"There are no reports of survivors."

Fingal was aware that Deirdre, who had put on a dressing gown, was standing beside him. "It's Marge. Tony's ship's gone down," he told her. "Marge, is anybody with you?"

"Pip's here and Renée Lannigan, one of my regular bridge four."

"Would you like us to come over?"

"Thank you. That is most kind, but no, I shall be all right. I just — I just felt I had to let you know."

"Thank you." What else could he say?

"He's missing, but I'm not willing to believe he's not safe somewhere. Not yet. I'll let you know if I hear anything more."

"Please do." He felt a tugging at his sleeve. Deirdre was pointing at the phone and to herself. "Deirdre wants to have a word." He gave her the receiver.

"Marge, I'm so sorry. Is there anything we can do, anything at all?"

Judging by Deirdre's expression the answer had been "no thank you."

"All right, all right. Look after yourself. We'll come and see you very soon. All right. Good-bye." Deirdre hung up. She went to Fingal and he saw her tears. "Oh, Fingal," she said, "it's too awful. Poor Marge — and Pip."

"We can still hope," he said, but he knew, in the North Atlantic in midwinter, a man's chances were slim indeed. "And while I'm not a good Christian, we can pray."

35

EVENTS IN THE WOMB

"Come on, Lorna. You're next." Lorna Kearney sat primly in the waiting room, gazing at the mural of roses created by Donal Donnelly.

"See that there Donal. He's a quare dark horse, so he is. Imagine him painting such a thing. It's lovely, so it is. Lifts the spirits."

"I'm very glad, Lorna. Now," he said to the seven others, "we'll not be long and then I'll be back for whoever's next."

"Take your time, Doc. No one's at death's door and no one's in a hurry," Shuey Gamble said.

"And if you *are* at death's door," said a pimply-faced youth of seventeen called "Piggy" Hogg, wearing wire-rimmed granny glasses and sniffling into a hanky, "go to Doctor O'Reilly and he will pull you through." He sniggered at his own feeble humour. "He will pull you through. Get it?"

"Or in your case, Piggy," O'Reilly said, "he'll find the biggest, bluntest injection needle and make sure you're cured — of your cold and your cheek, you gurrier."

The others laughed at Piggy's discomfiture as he said, "I'm sorry, sir. I was only joking."

O'Reilly chuckled as he led Lorna along the hall to the surgery. The voice of his senior partner in Dublin's Aungier Place Dispensary in 1936 seemed to whisper in O'Reilly's ear, *Never, never let the patients get the upper hand."* "And don't you worry, Lorna. Piggy won't be having any injections."

She laughed. "No harm til you sir, but you always come on like an ould targe, but don't all of us know that apart from your shooting, and the half of Ulster countrymen like a shot, you'd not hurt a fly?" She wagged a finger. "And thon Piggy Hogg should mind his manners with his elders and betters, so he should."

They went into the surgery and he closed the door. "How are you?" he asked, nodding his head toward the examining couch. Now well into her second pregnancy, she'd be used to the routine of antenatal visits.

"I'm great," she said, handing him a small bottle with her urine sample, and climbing up, "and I had the second set of blood tests done last week at Bangor hospital."

"I got them yesterday. I'll explain them when I've finished the routine work," O'Reilly said as he went to the sink, tested the sample for sugar, protein, and acetone. "All clear," he said, blessing the reagent-impregnated cardboard dipsticks used today for urinalysis. As he went back to the couch, he remembered back to his student days of chemicals, Bunsen burners, and foul smells.

It took only a few minutes to confirm that her blood pressure was 130 over 80, her ankles were not swollen with fluid called oedema, the uterus's size was consistent with the duration of her pregnancy as measured in weeks from her last menstrual period, that a single baby lay with its head toward the mother's pelvis and its back to her right, and that its heart rate was 144 beats per minute. "Everything's spot-on," he said. "Tuck in your blouse . . ." he waited while she did, then helped her down, "and hop up on the scales." He read the result. "You've put on a few pounds since we saw you last, but that's perfectly natural and nothing to worry about. Now have a pew and I'll tell you about the tests, what they mean, and what's going to happen next." He sat in his swivel chair and popped his half-moon spectacles on his nose. There were lab reports to be read.

She sat on one of the wooden chairs.

He made a few notes then picked up a laboratory report form. "All right, we knew that as of three weeks ago, when you had your first set of blood tests, that you're Rhesus negative and that your husband's positive. We also know that at that time you had just a trace of antibodies, the things in your blood that would attack a positive baby's red blood cells. They'd have been left over from your first pregnancy but weren't at a high enough level to worry about in this one."

She frowned. "I understand. But what about the new blood tests?"

He smiled and said, "I'm getting to that. You've been a good lass about taking your daily iron and folic acid because your own blood haemoglobin levels are spot-on. You're not one bit anaemic."

"That's good," she said.

"But, I'm afraid the latest blood tests from last week show that your antibody levels, we call them titres, have doubled from the tests taken three weeks before."

She took a deep breath. "And that means that the wean's being attacked by those antibody thingys?"

"There's no easy way to tell you, Lorna, but yes." He leaned forward and put a hand on her shoulder, fishing out his hanky when she burst into tears.

"I'm sorry, Doctor," she said, and hic-cupped. "It's . . . it's just the shock." She looked down and laid her hand on her belly. "It's hard to believe. I feel fine and the wean seems til be doing rightly."

He handed her the hanky to dry her eyes when she was ready. He waited. There was no point mouthing bromides or trying to explain while she was in tears. Nothing would

502

get through.

She hiccupped, swallowed, blew her nose, and again said, "I'm so sorry, Doctor O'Reilly."

"No need to apologise. You're upset."

She nodded, inhaled deeply twice, then said, "So what's next?" She gave him back his hanky.

"The next thing is to find out exactly —" He'd been going to say "how badly," but changed it to "— to what degree the baby's affected. It'll mean a trip to the Royal Maternity."

"And what'll they do, sir? An X-ray?"

He shook his head. "We try to avoid X-raying babies. No. Doctor Whitfield and his team will collect a sample of the fluid that surrounds the baby in your womb —"

"The waters?"

"That's right, the amniotic fluid, and they'll send it to the laboratory for analysis." He was trying to avoid going into detail about exactly how the sample was collected. It was all very well to tease Piggy Hogg about needles, but most patients hated them, and the fluid was collected through one with a wide bore. The procedure was called amniocentesis. Nor did he wish to try to explain how the sample was analysed. O'Reilly's understanding of bilirubin spectrophotometry was shaky. He'd leave that discussion up to the specialists, but it irritated him that he was getting out of date in his knowledge of modern procedures. "I'll speak to Doctor Bradley about getting you booked in early next week. It's Friday now, but she has friends in high places."

Lorna managed a weak smile. "I'd be very grateful," she said, and rose. "I know there's a lot more patients waiting to see you, sir. Thank you for taking the time to explain."

He stood. "I'm not daft enough to tell you don't worry, Lorna, but the folks at the Royal are getting very good results for the babies of patients like you. For the last few years they've even been able to give babies a blood transfusion if it looks like their blood cell level is low. While the baby's still in your womb. That way the babby can get more mature before it's delivered."

"Honest to God? Boys-a-boys, isn't modern science a wonderful thing?" There was awe in her voice. "I'm sorry I cried back there a wee minute ago, but I was so sure I was going to be fine. It just came as a shock, so it did." She smiled as she started to walk for the door, O'Reilly by her side. "Anyroad, me and Reggie'll be at the service with Mister Robinson on Sunday. We'll just have til pray a bit harder, that's all."

"Do that," said O'Reilly, "and as soon as I hear from Doctor Bradley, someone will give you a call and tell you where and when to go to the Royal Maternity."

She left by the front door and he headed

for the waiting room. He surely hoped the specialists could save Lorna's wean. Time would tell. He stuck his head round the door and called, "Next."

Shuey struggled to his feet. "Just in for a quick oil change, Doctor," he said, and laughed his dry old man's laugh as he limped toward O'Reilly, who offered an arm. As Shuey took it, O'Reilly noticed that Piggy Hogg was nowhere to be seen. Had the silly boy taken him seriously? He felt a brief pang of remorse, but couldn't keep a wide grin from splitting his face. What the hell? No one ever died of a head cold and it meant one less customer to see before lunch.

36
HOPE SPRINGS ETERNAL

"I'll miss you, Fingal," Angus Mahaddie said. He nursed his small Scotch and leaned closer to the coal fire in the Medical Officers' Mess. The Scot would be going on a week's leave tomorrow and wanted to buy Fingal a drink to celebrate both Christmas and the confirmation in the December promotions list of his move from acting to permanent rank. "You'll be going back to the Med in a couple of weeks." With Christmas only two days away, the place was practically deserted. A couple of QARNNS nursing sisters sat together several tables away, drinking tea from porcelain cups. "How do you get there?"

Fingal puffed on his pipe and took a sip of his whisky. "I've to join a cargo ship in South-ampton carrying six spitfires and a Bristol Blenheim bomber in crates to Takoradi on Africa's Gold Coast. Then I fly from there in a convoy of already reassembled Hurricanes led by a Blenheim back to Cairo, then on to Alexandria, and *Warspite*. Much quicker than by troopship round the Cape of Good Hope."

"Safe travels, Surgeon Lieutenant-Commander O'Reilly."

The two men raised their drinks and drank in silence.

Fingal listened to the gentle murmur of conversation from the nurses, the clinking of their teacups, the rattle of rain against the windows, then took a deep breath and spoke. "It's hard to know how to thank you, Angus. I'd not be married but for you. I think I'll be going back to *Warspite* a reasonably competent anaesthetist, and —"

"Wheest, laddie," the little Highland man said, "it was my pleasure on both counts, and you've been a good pupil. You've done well and you'll do well back on *Warspite.* It's a pity about you and Commander Fraser, but that man . . ." he lowered his voice, "could sow dissension in a deserted house. Anyway, you'll be rid of us all in a couple of weeks."

"I will," said Fingal. He looked out through the window as dusk fell over Saint Luke's and the main hospital. "I will miss Haslar."

"Just so, and you'll miss your wee wifey too. The navy, especially in wartime, is a stern mistress."

Fingal grimaced. "I'll miss Deirdre like blue blazes. It's going to be hard to leave her in Southampton on the sixth. But I'll have my memories to take back and maybe I'll get a chance for more leave. This bloody war can't last forever. At least she'll be away from England. Farther from the Luftwaffe bases in France."

"That's true," said Angus, "and I don't think we need worry about a raid on Christmas Day. There's a rumour that both sides have agreed to an unofficial three-day halt to all bombing, so I've arranged another wee thing. I'm afraid I will need you to nip in and make rounds for most of the Christmas holidays, and then be on call, but there won't be many patients. On the day itself, though, there's no need for you to be there. Be with your Deirdre on Christmas Day. It'll be one more set of memories for you both. But be back on duty at nine A.M. sharp on Boxing Day." He grinned.

"I'm seeing her once I leave here. She will be thrilled, Angus. Thank you."

A shadow fell over the two men.

O'Reilly turned to see a red-faced Surgeon Commander Fraser standing behind the chair. "I believe," he said, "I've told you before, O'Reilly, not to interfere with my decisions."

Fingal stood but said nothing.

"The fingers amputation case."

Alf Henson had been back on Whale Island for a week now.

"I had lunch today with HMS *Excellent*'s MO. You returned the man fit for duty. Why?"

"I did." No "sir." It was lucky that rank and

titles were not used in the mess, because Fingal did not feel like according the man any respect. "Because he is a committed sailor. The navy and especially gunnery are his life. Henson's instructor, CPO McIlroy, was in for his follow-up yesterday. He told me Henson's as nimble with a couple of joints missing as he was with a complete hand."

"It's no excuse for disobeying a direct order. I intend to speak directly to the admiral commanding."

Suit yourself, Fingal thought, keeping his face expressionless. I'll be gone in two weeks. Back on *Warspite*. The thought of Tony Wilcoxson drowning in the icy waters of the North Atlantic, oil and wreckage of his torpedoed ship all around him, hit Fingal like a blow to the solar plexus. That life and that possible death were a damn sight more important than getting his knickers in a knot over a possible reprimand following a complaint by a surgical medical officer whose lack of compassion was stunning. In that moment Fingal renewed his vows, first taken as a student, never to allow any institution, even the navy, to stand between him and what was best for a patient.

"Did you hear me, O'Reilly?"

"Yes, I heard you."

"Eh, George," Angus said, "don't be so hasty."

"What?"

509

"Simmer down. Take a breather. Fingal's in my department. Complaints must go through me. You know that."

"I've complained to you once before. Fat lot of good it did."

Angus ignored the remark. "This man, the gunner, he's doing well, Fingal?"

Fingal nodded. The question was rhetorical.

"And the fighter pilot that our sending to East Grinstead got you all tried, George? Any word about him?"

"Pilot Officer Flip Dennison? I had a letter from him yesterday. I brought it to show you." Fingal rummaged in his inside pocket. "Here." He opened the envelope, pulled out a sheet of paper, found the place, and gave the letter to Fraser. "Please read that. From 'Mister McIndoe has . . .' "

Fraser said, "I fail to see —"

"Humour us, George, please?" Angus said.

"Oh, very well." He cleared his throat. " 'Mister McIndoe has done my third operation to give me new eyelids. When they took off the dressing I looked in a mirror and a funny-looking white-faced gorilla looked back.' " Fraser paused. "I don't see what a gorilla has to do with disobeying an order."

"Go on, George. Keep reading." There was steel in the Scotsman's tone.

Fraser raised the letter again, squinted at the writing, and sighed. " 'Great puffy ledges

510

under my eyes to allow for shrinkage of the flesh. Once the grafts have taken, he'll need to trim them and tidy them to finish making proper eyelids, but I can see now, half close my eyes, and the doctors here reckon I'll be back in a cockpit in about nine months. I ___.'"

"I think that's enough," Angus said. "Now, if you wish to lodge a complaint against a young, idealistic officer in my department who is trying to do his very best for the patients, and seems to be succeeding, please come to my office. I'll be in it next Tuesday."

Fraser spluttered and thrust the page at Fingal, who stifled a grin and accepted the piece of paper.

"And, George," Angus said, "do try to remember, it's the season to be jolly. Peace on Earth, goodwill to all men?"

Fraser shook his head. "You're a very difficult man to deal with, Angus Mahaddie."

"Aye, I ken that very well."

"And you, O'Reilly, you are an insubordinate pup. Try to behave for your last few days here." And with that, he spun on his heel and strode out.

Fingal blew out his breath. "Thanks again, Angus. You saved my bacon on that one."

Angus frowned, shook his head. "No, I did not. In my opinion you were absolutely right and he was wrong. Elizabeth Blenkinsop told me about what you arranged for the gunner with the bust hand. In case you needed support if Fraser found out, she wanted me to know." He snorted. "Fraser would have amputated. Bloody barbaric." He looked at Fingal. "And I was impressed that you didn't come running to me for help. The navy values initiative, you know."

"Getting the man to the Zymotic ward was Elizabeth's idea," Fingal said.

"No matter. The gunner laddie's doing well." He sipped his drink. "I have a wee notion Surgeon Commander Fraser might be happier with a posting out of here. Maybe doing less clinical work."

And less harm, Fingal thought.

Angus tapped his fingernail on the rim of his glass. "Aye," he said. "Aye. It might just be time to have another word with my friend in London. I'll say no more." His smile was beatific.

And although he didn't like Fraser, that smile made Fingal shiver.

"It's very good of you both to have come," Marge said, "do come in." She held the front door open. Strands of silver hair straggled from her usually immaculate chignon, there were bags under her eyes, and they were bloodshot.

"Any news?" Deirdre asked without moving inside despite the rain bucketing down.

"Any word about Tony?" Her words were rushed.

"I'm afraid not." Marge shook her head. "Please," she said, "do come in out of the wet. We can talk better when we're comfortable."

Fingal took Deirdre's elbow and helped her into the hall. The two women hugged as Fingal took off his wet coat and cap, hung them, and helped Deirdre with hers.

"Come through," Marge said, "the fire's lit. Make yourselves at home. It's only Fingal and Deirdre," she said to Admiral Benbow, "so settle down. Behave yourself."

The big dog subsided with a throaty grunt in front of the fire and proceeded to snore.

"The kettle's on. Tea?" Marge said as if the rest of her bridge four had just popped in.

"Please," Deirdre said, and sat in one armchair as Fingal took the other.

"I know what you both take," Marge said, heading for the kitchen. "Won't be a jiffy."

Deirdre whispered, "How can she be so calm?"

"It's her way of hanging on. It's the English way," said Fingal, as Deirdre bent to stroke one of Benbow's soft ears. "Try to occupy your mind doing routine things. My own ma used to knit or paint like crazy if she was upset. The day my father died, she sat in our sitting room knitting a navy blue muffler for Lars."

"Dear Ma. I miss her. I can see her doing that," Deirdre said. She nodded to herself and Fingal could imagine her thinking, I'll remember that in case Fingal — and cut the thought off aborning. There was no need to tempt Providence. "I've asked you already," she said, "but please tell me again," she was still whispering, "what are Tony's chances now after two days?"

"Pretty grim," he said quietly. "His ship went down off Iceland. When the *Titanic* sank in similar waters, people only lasted fifteen to thirty minutes because of the cold."

"But surely they'd've had lifeboats on his destroyer? How long did Shackleton and his men survive in an open boat trying to get to South Georgia? I remember learning about it in school but I can't recall all the details."

"I'm not certain," he said, "but I'm pretty sure it was more than a fortnight."

"We'll have to tell Marge. She mustn't give up hope. Not yet. Not until she knows for sure or until it truly is hopeless. He could be safe already and we just haven't heard."

"I love you, Deirdre O'Reilly," he said. "I love how strong you can be for other people."

"What," said Marge, bringing in the tea things on a tray, "are you two whispering about?" She lifted the silver teapot and set it in the hearth. "I'll let it stew for a while." She put the tray on a table and took the third armchair.

Fingal, usually able to invent a story quickly if the need arose, found himself at a loss for words.

"I can guess, of course," she said, "and I believe you're both very sweet. You were worrying about me, weren't you?"

"Yes," said Deirdre, "we were, and Pip, and of course Tony."

"I feel sick with worry. Sick. What mother wouldn't be? I'm afraid I got very little sleep last night. But I've been through it once before with my husband, Richard."

This news about his superior on *Warspite* came as a shock to Fingal.

"I shall tell you about it after I've poured," and with no more ado, as if the only difficulty in her life was the awful rain outside, she prepared and handed out three cups. "Richard, like Tony, was on a destroyer, but at Jutland in 1916," she said, and sipped her tea. "HMS *Turbulent*. She was sunk in the night action."

Fingal was going to explain to Deirdre that Jutland had been a titanic, inconclusive clash between the British Grand and German High Seas fleets in the First World War when he realised that not a child in the United Kingdom hadn't heard about it in school.

"I didn't know for three days, then a telegram said he was missing in action."

Deirdre gasped and stared at Fingal.

"That must have been hellish for you,

Marge," Fingal said.

She nodded. "It was. For five weeks I thought him dead." She swallowed. "My lovely knight, drowned. It was very hard to bear. I tried to be brave, but I'm afraid I cried an awful lot." A single tear coursed down her cheek, then another. She dashed them away. She inhaled, straightened her shoulders. "Then I had a telegram from the International Red Cross. He'd been picked up by a boat from a German cruiser and was in a prisoner of war camp in Germany. He'd lost the tip of a toe from frostbite, but was otherwise all right."

And he'd not said a word about it to Fingal in all the time they'd been together on *Warspite*. It was true most veterans of the Great War kept mum about their experiences.

Deirdre rose and went to stand by Marge. The younger woman put her hands on the older's shoulders. "And now you're reliving it and fearing for your son."

Fingal saw the glistening in Deirdre's eyes and felt for them both.

Marge looked up at Deirdre, but said to Fingal, "I want to thank you, Fingal, for getting my pigheaded son to see daylight about Pip and propose to the gel."

How, he thought, how can she be so calm?

"Pip's frightfully cut up, but when she was here for lunch today she told me how great a comfort it was to her to know that they were going to be married at last. She's treasuring that."

Fingal looked down. Poor Pip. He remembered meeting her on that first day in September. How the girl had launched herself into his arms on the front step of the cottage, thinking he was Tony.

"And," Marge said, "the navy has been very good. They can't send a message directly to *Warspite,* she's somewhere at sea, but there'll be a telegram waiting for Richard when she returns to Alex."

Fingal, no stranger as a doctor to death and grief, wondered how Richard would take the news, although Fingal could guess. Publicly with stoic acceptance, but privately? His only child gone? His son? Privately, Richard would know his own guts had been torn out. Fingal tried to sip his tea, but it had gone cold. "Is there anything we can do?" he asked.

Marge said, "Yes, please."

Which surprised Fingal. She always seemed such a private, self-sufficient woman.

"You will be on duty tomorrow, Fingal, so you'll need to get back to Alverstoke tonight, but I'd truly appreciate it if you could stay, Deirdre. I'd only the animals for company last night and I'd rather not be alone tonight."

"Of course," Deirdre said. "You don't mind, Fingal, do you?"

He shook his head and felt guilty because they had so few nights together left that he'd almost said he did.

"Damn tea's gone cold," Marge said. "I'll get some hot water."

"Let me," said Deirdre, who was already on her feet. She left.

For a while there was silence, then Fingal said, "We really are sorry for your troubles, Marge . . ."

"But I should hope for the best but prepare for the worst, is that it?"

"How did you know I was —"

"I am married to a doctor, you know. I've heard the line before."

"I know it's trite," Fingal said, "but what else can we say?"

She smiled at him. "Do you believe that lightning never strikes twice?"

"It's pretty rare if it does."

"But," she said, "it did once with Richard. I'd waited five weeks. I think I can give Tony a few days more, don't you?"

He was full of deep admiration for the woman's spirit, while still understanding the terrible odds against her son. "Deirdre and I will help you wait for as long as we can, Marge. That's a promise."

She leaned over and squeezed his knee. "Thank you, Fingal," she said. "Thank you very much."

37
FILLED THE TREE AND FLAPPED

"Oh, sir, please can you come at once into the back garden. There's an emergency, so." Kinky, not even waiting for an answer, fled from the dining room.

O'Reilly left the newspaper in a crumpled heap on the table. The story he'd been reading about today's atom bomb test in Nevada would have to wait. He tore through the kitchen, trying to ignore the smell of the halibut being cooked for lunch, and into the garden where Kinky stood, hands on hips, staring up to where the branches of a leafless, fruitless apple tree were etched against a cloudless sky. His gaze followed Kinky's up to the highest branches, where Lady Macbeth was perched on the topmost branch, alternating between spitting and making a piteous caterwauling.

"Bloody hell. Not again." He had a brief recollection of the feisty Brian Boru treeing the little white cat, not once but twice, earlier this year. In that very tree. Then he looked down about four feet. And stared at what he saw. This was different. Very different. "Having fun, Barry?" he called.

"If there wasn't a lady present, Fingal, I'd give you some physiologically impossible advice," Barry called back from where he stood on the first rung of a stepladder propped up against the tree. His shoulders were level with the cup formed by the lower branches, where Arthur lay cradled, all legs dangling in space about six feet above the ground. "I was coming home from one of Fitzpatrick's patients and I saw this." He pointed. "I'm trying to get the poor fellow down. He must have climbed up the ladder."

As if to agree, the big dog made a mournful moan.

"And I suppose Lady Macbeth invited him up?"

"Och, the poor wee dote," Kinky said, wringing her hands. "Can you not do something, sir?"

He could, he supposed, summon the Bangor fire brigade. Firemen were adept at rescuing stranded cats. However, he wasn't sure he wanted the whole village and townland to know that his dog had stranded himself in a tree. And he could tell by the look on Arthur's face that the dog certainly didn't. Shame and remorse were both there in the peak of his eyebrows. Surely between him and Barry they should be able to cope?

"We'll have to get the lummox down first, and there's no simple command to help him." He went over to the foot of the ladder. Gundogs are well trained to heel, sit, lie down, hey on out, push 'em out, and leave it. But in Arthur's training there had been no "turn around backwards and put your hind paws on the top rung of the ladder." Even if it were possible to tell him what to do, the dog's paws could not get purchase on anything. He was stuck. "We're going to have to get him into a position so that he can jump down," O'Reilly said. "He's leaped those kind of heights before."

"Any brilliant suggestions?" Barry asked.

"No," said O'Reilly, "but come you down. I want to get up there and take a gander."

Barry climbed down. "Best of British luck," he said.

"Do you take care, sir," Kinky said. "You are no spring chicken, so."

"Mmgh," said O'Reilly, taking off his jacket and tie, rolling up his sleeves, and starting to climb. "Thank you, Kinky," he said stiffly. He may have been feeling his age lately, but he was still quite capable of climbing a stepladder. Or a tree, if it came to it. Kinky and Kitty were the only people in the entire world who could get away with a comment like that.

He felt a warm, damp tongue on the back of his hand that now gripped one of the lower branches. Arthur was stretching himself as far forward as possible. The sad look in his brown eyes would have melted Pharaoh's hard heart. O'Reilly knew the big Labrador was trying to say, "Sorry, boss. I've been very silly, but that white demon tempted me."

"Aye, you have been gormless, you buck eejit," O'Reilly said, but he kept his voice soft, low. The animal would be terrified. "I thought you and her ladyship were friends?" O'Reilly stepped onto the bough that supported Arthur's chest and surveyed the situation. If he could move Arthur forward far enough, it might be possible to lift his hind legs onto another limb. Then, if his forequarters could be hoisted high enough, his front paws should land on another bough. With a stable platform to push off from, he'd be able to jump down. It was worth a try.

An eldritch howling came from above. "You, madame," O'Reilly said, staring up, "will have to wait your turn. And you're a cat, for God's sake. You're meant to be nimble. The Lord helps those who help themselves. Stop bellyaching and give it a try."

Lady Macbeth had the courtesy to shut up, but merely crouched with her tail wrapped round her.

"Barry," O'Reilly called, "do you think you can get up a couple of rungs and support Arthur's chest if I can pull him forward?"

"I'll give it a go," Barry said, climbed, and

planted his feet on the rung. "Ready when you are."

O'Reilly crouched. "Lie still, Arthur," he said, and could have sworn that the big dog nodded his head. His eyes never left O'Reilly's face. He took a deep breath and, like a weightlifter, neck veins bulging, every sinew straining, managed to haul Arthur forward.

"Got him," Barry said, "and please, Arthur, stop licking my face."

O'Reilly hauled in great lungfuls then stepped onto the next limb and pulled Arthur's hind legs until both paws were firmly on the bough. "Right," O'Reilly said, and with his forearm wiped sweat from his brow as he crossed back. "Can you give him a shove up, Barry?" O'Reilly grabbed two handfuls of Arthur's fur at the scruff of his neck and with Barry's help managed to get the dog's forepaws onto the branch.

Kinky applauded.

"Call him," O'Reilly yelled to her.

"Here, Arthur," she shouted. "Here, boy."

The big dog looked at O'Reilly for permission.

"Hey on out."

And like a massive flying squirrel, Arthur simply hurled himself from the tree, landed with a *whump,* picked himself up, and with a great grin on his face, wagged his tail.

O'Reilly, now back on the ground, said,

"Thanks, Barry, Kinky."

"Huh," Barry said, "I'm sorry, Kinky, but it's like old times. My trousers are covered in moss from the trunk."

"Och sure that's all right. Give them to me after we've got her ladyship down and I'll give them a sponge and a press."

O'Reilly bent over, hands on knees, trying to get his breath back.

"Fingal, are you okay?"

"Fine, I'm fine."

"Dear Lord in heaven, you're not having a heart attack, are you, sir?"

"No, Kinky, I am not having a heart attack. But I wonder, Barry, if you could climb up and get her ladyship. I'm not sure whether those thin upper branches will support my weight."

"Your weight, sir, and the weight of my lunches since you've absolutely refused to eat any more salads." Kinky tutted and shook her head.

O'Reilly was searching for the right bit of repartee when he heard the musical squeak of the back gate opening and Jenny walked in. It must be almost time for her to start her clinic.

Lady Macbeth mewed and everyone looked up. O'Reilly and Kinky "push-wushed" like Billy-oh, but the little cat refused to budge.

"You seem to have a problem," Jenny said, kicking off her shoes and handing her jacket to O'Reilly.

"You don't know the half of it," said Barry. "The other half is right there." He pointed to Arthur.

To their amazement, like one of Nelson's topmen, Jenny swarmed up the tree, gently grabbed Lady Macbeth, and shinnied down again. She handed the cat to Kinky, who scolded the little animal in tones so soft and forgiving that she began to purr.

"I'll be taking her inside, the poor wee pet, and getting the lunch ready too," Kinky said, and left.

"Where in the name of the wee man did you learn to climb like that, Jenny Bradley?" O'Reilly asked.

"Started when I was five. My mother was quite an athlete," she said. "I was on the Queen's team when I was a student. Gymnastics. Comes in handy now and then."

O'Reilly and Barry laughed.

O'Reilly started to retie his tie. "I'd like you and Barry to come in handy about something else," he said.

"Oh?" Jenny said.

"Lorna Kearney was in this morning. Her antibody titre's doubled." He rolled down his sleeves.

"I'll phone Royal Maternity," Jenny said, putting on the jacket of her navy blue suit. "Doctor Whitfield's a good head. He'll accommodate Lorna. When I was being trained to run my clinic, I'd often have chats with him at lunchtime. His team likes to analyse the amniotic fluid in patients like Lorna at thirty-two to thirty-four weeks and then repeat the test in two weeks' time. That lets them see a trend and decide how much longer it will be safe to wait so the baby can be as mature as possible before delivery."

"And is the amniocentesis safe? I've never seen one done. Have you, Barry?" O'Reilly said.

He nodded. "Quite a few, and one of Doctor Whitfield's team, Doctor Ron Livingstone, has found that less than four percent of patients go into labour within five days of the test, so it's pretty safe."

"Thanks, you two," O'Reilly said. "Jenny, I will be grateful if you make the arrangements."

"After the clinic," she said. "I'm going to be running late as it is." She trotted to the kitchen door, waved to Kitty, who had a half day today and was just coming into the garden, and disappeared into the house.

Kitty waved back and called, "Fingal, Barry, I've got great news."

O'Reilly smiled. He would have fun telling her about the great animals-up-the-apple-tree caper at lunch.

"We got Ronald's pathology report today."

"And?" Reilly said.

"And it's a benign meningioma. Charlie

526

reckons that he got it all, so there's only a ten percent chance of recurrence." She looked around. "What are you two doing out here?"

"It's a long story. But that is excellent news. I'm delighted and I'm sure Ronald is too," he said, feeling waves of relief wash over him. He hadn't realized until this moment how much Ronald's illness had reminded him of his own mortality. The chill air was starting to seep through his damp shirt and he shrugged into his jacket.

"He is that and he's getting back a fair bit of function already. His legs are working now and he can feel some heat and pain in his fingers. Charlie's delighted with the progress. Reckons Ronald will be ready for discharge soon."

"I am pleased," O'Reilly said as he bent, patted Arthur's head, and ordered, "Kennel, sir." The big dog, tail between his legs, slunk off. O'Reilly hated punishing an animal, but bad behaviour simply could not be rewarded. "Now," he said. "Lunch," and led the others to the house. As they walked, he asked, "Reckon you could manage on your own for an afternoon next week, Barry?"

"Sure. Why?"

"I'd like to take a run-race up to the Royal, see Ronald."

"He'll appreciate that," Kitty said.

"And," he said, "I could pop over to Royal Maternity and observe Lorna's amnio."

O'Reilly opened the kitchen door. He didn't like this feeling of being behind the times. If another patient needed the same procedure, he didn't want to feel irritated by his own ignorance. Getting older was no excuse for not being up on the latest technology. He stopped in his tracks. "Kinky Auchinleck, what are you doing?"

She was sitting on a chair, little cat on her lap, feeding Lady Macbeth slivers of halibut. "Her ladyship did have a terrible scare, so. It's only a bit of comfort food. I'd be doing the same for yourself, sir, if you'd've fallen out of that tree."

O'Reilly roared with laughter, and sang, "If you're ever up a tree, phone to me."

"What tree? What scare?" Kitty asked, looking from Kinky to O'Reilly.

"Och," said O'Reilly, "Kitty, you'll never believe the adventures we've all just had with the animals."

"Will I not?" she said, and laughed. "When it comes to you, Fingal Flahertie O'Reilly, I'd believe almost anything."

38
WE'LL KEEP OUR CHRISTMAS MERRY STILL

Fingal blinked the sleep from his eyes, shook his head, yawned — the alarm said ten to nine — and looked at the tousled blonde head on the pillow next to his. It was the morning of the second Christmas of the war, but no church bells were pealing their usual tidings of happiness. They had been silenced all over the United Kingdom after the evacuation from Dunkirk last May so that their ringing would be an instantly recognisable signal if the Germans invaded. But bugger the war, it was the first Christmas of his life married to Deirdre, who had been Mawhinney and was now O'Reilly, and he was determined to make it the merriest Christmas ever for both of them.

She wasn't exactly snoring, but rather making little whiffly noises like the ones she'd made when she'd fallen asleep in the pub the day she'd arrived. Then she grunted, opened her eyes, stared at him, and started to laugh. "Fingal," she said, "your hair is sticking up like a haystack after a gale."

"Good morning to you too," he said, and grinned. He ran a hand over his head as she rolled away from him, then rolled back holding a sprig of mistletoe over her head. She was giggling.

Tradition demanded that anyone under mistletoe at Christmas should be kissed, and who was he to ignore tradition? He wrapped her in an enormous hug and kissed her firmly. "Merry Christmas, my love," he said.

"Merry Christmas, Fingal darling," and she kissed him back, then again . . .

They breakfasted very late that morning, and agreed to postpone their Christmas dinner until midafternoon.

While she had her bath and dressed, Fingal happily washed the dishes, then wandered back to the living/dining room. He admired how, despite the war and all the shortages, she had done everything possible to have their flat looking Christmassy. While he'd been at the hospital yesterday, she'd made cheerful coloured crêpe-paper chains and draped them over the frames of the dull, navy-issue pictures hanging on the walls. Sprigs of holly with little balls of cotton wool for imitation snow sat in splendour on the mantel above a cosy fire. A potted pink chrysanthemum was a centrepiece for the dining table.

They'd trimmed the tree last night with the

lights and decorations Angus had lent them, and she'd giggled with delight when he'd crowned the little fir with a golden star and switched on the lights. They'd "listened in" to the radio and the Kentucky Minstrels singing "Bless This House" and "Star of Bethlehem," and before bed, Fingal had put the presents under the tree.

"How do I look?" she said, appearing from the bedroom and doing a pirouette.

He looked at her shining blonde hair, sparkling blue eyes, wide smile, just a touch of makeup. "Ravishing," he said. "You'd be the belle of the Christmas ball — if there was one." He hugged her, pecked her cheek, and said, "And ball or no ball, you'll always be the most beautiful girl in the world for me."

"Thank you, pet," she said. "I hope it makes up for my being such a terrible cook."

"Rubbish," he said. "That meatloaf you made last Saturday was a thing of beauty." He smiled and thought, there's an old saw about love being blind; it should also say love has no taste buds.

She sounded dubious. "I hope I'll do a good job with dinner today. Most of it is ready. I just have to put it in the oven."

"I'm sure you will, so no worrying. Now," he said, bending and picking up two parcels from under the tree addressed to Lieutenant-Commander and Mrs. O'Reilly and marked DO NOT OPEN BEFORE DEC. TWENTY-FIFTH.

Both had Northern Ireland postmarks. "Let's get these opened." He handed her the softer of the two.

"It's from Mummy and Daddy," she said, unwrapping two multicoloured six-foot-long woollen mufflers. The enclosed card read, *To keep you and Fingal warm. Much love and merry Christmas. Mum and Dad.*

She wrapped her scarf several times round her neck. "Toasty," she said. "I can picture Mummy in the green velvet armchair by the fire knitting these in the evening. It does make me feel homesick." But she was smiling as she said it, and fingering the soft wool around her neck. "Do you like yours?"

He grabbed the other one and looped it around his head, almost covering his face. "How do I look?"

"Eejit," she said, laughing.

"It'll be just the job on a cold night on deck." He handed her the second gift. "Go on. What's in there?"

She unwrapped the brown paper to reveal a long, pale, wooden box. "Here," she said. "Open it."

He slid off a lid. The thing was stuffed with colourful silk hankies, but there was something hard beneath. "Mother of —" He cut himself short and lifted out a bottle of Bushmills Irish whiskey. "Mother's milk," he said. "Now we can really drink to a merry Christmas after dinner."

"What's in the envelopes?" Deirdre said.

Three lay at the bottom of the box. The first was a Christmas card from Ma and Lars, the second a war bond for ten pounds from him. The third held another war bond and a letter from Ma.

" 'All our love and a merry Christmas to you both,' " he read. " 'Deirdre, we hope you like the hankies. Life does tend to be a bit drab these days and we hope they will brighten things up a bit.' "

"They're lovely," Deirdre said, picking up a lavender one sprigged with yellow flowers.

" 'I'm sure you'll know what to do with the whiskey, son.' " He laughed and continued reading. " 'There's been a lot of publicity urging people to give war bonds as Christmas presents, and Laura MacNeill and I seem to have become joint chairmen of the local committee, and one must lead by example.' "

"Typical Ma," he said.

"Your mother," Deirdre said, "is definitely one of a kind, and Lars is such a lovely man. I'll get thank-you letters off first thing tomorrow."

Fingal returned to the tree and, bending down, picked up the largest parcel. "Merry Christmas, pet."

"For me?" she said, laughing. In turn, she handed him something that felt as if it were in a box.

"You first," he said, and waited.

She undid the string and carefully unwrapped and folded the paper. "Oh," she said, and gasped, holding the midnight blue sweater by its shoulder seams against her own shoulders. "Oh, it's beautiful, Fingal. Thank you."

"It'll keep you warm back in draughty old Belfast," he said. "Santa Claus brought it."

"I'm very fond of Santa," she said. "He's the patron saint of sailors and I've told him to keep a special eye on you."

"Thank you," he said, and nearly remarked that Tony Wilcoxson could have used a bit of saintly protection. But not wishing to spoil the moment for her, he stifled the comment and handed her another, smaller parcel. "Now this." He waited.

"Pearls? Pearls?" Her eyes widened. She held the two earrings gently in the palm of her hand. One round pearl was attached to a pear-shaped pearl by a delicate gold bar. "I know I shouldn't ask, but how on earth could you possibly afford —"

"Ssh," he said. "Let's just say the navy has bases in Aden on the Red Sea, where the natives are expert divers. A friend had to visit there and did me a favour before I came back to Pompey. A goldsmith in Alex did the rest."

"Oh, Fingal. How wonderful," she said. "You were getting my Christmas present six months in advance. Thank you. Thank you. I'll just be a minute." She dashed off into the bathroom and appeared moments later, wearing the earrings. "They're perfect, darling. Perfect." She kissed him, hard. "Thank you."

Her obvious joy filled him, and he smiled.

She pointed at his gift. "Now it's your turn."

Paper off. Box opened. It was a pipe. But what a pipe. The stem was light brown polished briar and the bowl rough blackthorn. They were joined by a silver band engraved with his initials, and the crowning glory was a conical, perforated, hinged silver lid.

"I found it in an ancient tobacconist's in Belfast," she said.

"So I wasn't the only one thinking ahead," he said.

"That's right," she said, and smiled. "The man in the shop said that blackthorn is sacred to the Irish fairies, the *sidhe*. You've to ask their permission to cut it, and if they grant it they put a protective spell on the wood for whoever smokes the pipe. I want it to protect my Fingal," she said, and for a moment her eyes glistened, but she brightened and said, "And I thought it would stay alight better when you are on deck."

He took her in a bear hug. "What a wonderful girl you are," he said.

"Because I love you, Fingal. Very much."

"And I love you. Now" — he pointed to the two remaining parcels — "let's leave those two until after our dinner."

"All right," she said.

The phone rang. He looked at her. "Marge?"

"With good news I hope," she said, and clenched her fists.

He answered. "O'Reilly."

"Doctor Fingal O'Reilly? Will you accept a person-to-person call from a Mrs. O'Reilly in Portaferry?"

"Yes, please. It's Ma," he said to Deidre, and he saw her relax.

"Go ahead, Mrs. O'Reilly. You have three minutes."

"Fingal. It's Ma. Lars is here, and Deirdre's parents. They've come for the day. We wanted to surprise you both and we've had a trunk call booked for ages. How are you and Deirdre?"

"We're both fine, Ma. And you? And Lars and Bridgit and the Mawhinneys?"

"All fine. Missing you. Merry Christmas, son. And thanks for the presents. A second edition of *Pride and Prejudice*? How wonderful."

"Merry Christmas to you, Ma, and everybody there. Glad you like the book. And thanks for the bonds and the medicine."

He heard her laugh. "To be taken in small doses," she said. "All my love to you both, son. Here's Lars."

"Are you well, Finn? Merry Christmas, and thanks for the orchid book. I've started it already. How's your first Christmas as a married man?"

"I'm a lucky man, Lars. Very lucky. Thanks for the bond. Now, nearly half the time's up. Put on Deirdre's folks. Here. Your mum." He handed her the phone.

"Mummy, is that you? Merry Christmas. We love our scarves . . . and you all liked your prezzies . . . ? Good. I wish you could have come to the wedding . . . It was lovely. You got the snaps . . . Daddy? Lovely to hear your voice."

Fingal listened, smiling, watching her face through her laughter and tears as she spoke to her father.

"Tell everyone we love them and Fingal wants to say — Oh." Her face fell and a buzzing came from the receiver. "Our three minutes were up. But wasn't that lovely?" Deirdre sighed. "I only wish it could be a merry Christmas for Marge and her family."

He nodded. "It'll be pretty grim, I'm sure. But she won't be alone. She'll be with Pip's people. Do you think we should give her a call later?"

"Let's, but right now I think it's time for the king's Christmas message on the BBC."

They listened as King George VI spoke with cautious optimism and promised that the nation's feet were firmly planted on the path to victory.

"By God," said Fingal. "I hope so. I really hope so."

■ ■ ■ ■

The Christmas chicken had been a little un-
dercooked and the small ham overcooked,
but Deirdre had done justice to the vegetables
from Marge's garden. His dear wife must
have scrimped and saved on their rations to
have been able to put rashers of bacon on the
chicken breast and have butter and cream to
make champ. There was a tiny Christmas
pudding — a gift from Angus Mahaddie's
wife, who, like her Ulster counterparts, was
in the habit of laying down next year's puddings the year before, and there'd been no
rationing back then. No crackers, no sweet
mince pies — dried fruit was practically
unobtainable — but Fingal had sweet-talked
Elizabeth Blenkinsop into slipping him half a
dozen of the beers provided to the ward so
they would have a drink with the meal. Ma's
gift guaranteed a nightcap for later.

He savoured the thought of a glass of
whiskey by the fire, curled up with Deirdre,
as he set down his napkin. "I think you've
worked wonders, darling," Fingal said.
"Thank you very much."

"Thank *you,* you old flatterer," she said,
"but I did try." She grimaced. "It'll only be
tinned tomato soup and ham and chicken
sandwiches for tea, I'm afraid," Deirdre said,
"but I thought we might have fun with these

now." She handed him a paper bag. "Spanish chestnuts, for roasting over the fire. We collected them in the forest on our honeymoon. Remember?"

"Indeed I do. We got them on our way back to the hotel the day we saw the deer drinking and we decided to try to have a kid." He smiled at her. "That was a good decision," he said. "I know you'll have to quit your job once you've got good news and tell your matron about it, but I'll be happier knowing you're in the country and out of Belfast."

"It is the rules, I'm afraid. In fact we're meant to retire when we get married, but matron's turning a blind eye. She's the only one who knows, but pregnancy is different. I really will have to go if and when I start to show, then I'll move back in with Mummy and Daddy on the farm in Fivemiletown."

"Could you go sooner? Like once a pregnancy's confirmed?"

She shook her head. "I'll be fine. With you hundreds of miles away I'll be happier working as long as I can. You'll not get to meet your first-born for who knows how long."

"Darling, we've talked about this. I'm not a young man now. I was thirty-two in October. The war could last for years. I don't want to be starting to be a daddy close to my forties. Be sixty before the youngster's twenty. You really want a baby. I really want a baby. It's the right decision."

"Thank you, Fingal," she said. "I do know we've talked about it and agreed, but I wanted to be certain you were sure."

He rose and went to stand over her, putting both hands on her shoulders. "I am not sure. I'm absolutely bloody positive." He squeezed her shoulders and said, "And it was a lovely try this morning before we got up, pet."

She smiled. "Wasn't it?" she said, and covered one of his hands with hers.

He loved how she was no prude.

"And maybe tonight?" Her left eyebrow rose.

He shook his head and laughed. Prude? She was a libertine — and he was a very lucky man.

"Let's get roasting, and while we're at it, I have one more wee prezzy for you."

"And I've a special one for you too. We'll leave the dishes. I'll get the frying pan. You stoke up the fire."

She giggled every time a chestnut popped.

We're like a couple of kids, he thought, and why not?

When they'd eaten the last one, Deirdre went to the kitchen to put on the kettle so they could have a cup of tea when they opened their last presents.

He was so relaxed by the fire he jumped in his seat when the front doorbell started ring-ing. Who the hell could that be? "Bloody blue blazes," he said, getting to his feet and hurrying to the door.

"Marge. Come in." Before she could answer he yelled over his shoulder, "Darling, it's Marge."

"And it's Tony," Marge said. "He's alive."

"Alive. Hooray!" Fingal's cheer probably scared seagulls on the Isle of Wight. "Come in. Come in." He hustled her into the hall, shut the door, and took her on into the main room. "Tony's been found," he said to Deirdre, who was coming from the kitchen.

"Oh, Marge, what a relief." She embraced Marge and said, "Come and sit down. Tell us about it."

Marge unbuttoned her coat as she took a chair. "I heard a couple of hours ago. The port admiral sent an officer to tell me. I've been trying to phone you, but I couldn't get a line so I decided to drive over. I nearly fainted when the butler ushered a lieutenant into the Gore-Beresfords' sitting room, but he was all smiles so I guessed it was all right even before he spoke. And there'll be a telegram sent to Alexandria for Richard too. The navy looks after its own." She beamed at Deirdre then at Fingal. "Pip's over the moon. What a Christmas present for us."

"Thank you for letting us know," Deirdre said. "We've been so worried, and we're delighted, aren't we, Fingal?"

"We are that. Are there any details?"

"He and some of his crew got onto a Carley

float and drifted for a day, frozen to the bone. Some men . . . died overnight," she said, looking down at her hands and fingering her wedding ring. "The survivors, including Tony, were picked up by an Icelandic trawler and taken to a hospital in Reykjavik. They'll be flying him back soon in a long-range Sunderland to the UK."

Fingal couldn't help shuddering at the image that had haunted him since getting the news: the wild North Atlantic seas, the fuel-oil-soaked men clinging to a wood-and-canvas life raft in those icy waters. "If ever anything called for a drink, this is it. We have some whiskey."

Marge shook her head. "Thank you. I very much appreciate the offer, but it's dark out and it's a bugger driving in the blackout. I've no wish to have my family mourning for me because I was a bit tiddly and crashed on my way home. I couldn't rest, because I know how much you care and how it must be spoiling your Christmas, so I simply *had* to let you know." She rose. "But now I'll be running along. Thank you both for helping me hold on, and merry merry Christmas to us all."

"I'll see you to the door," Fingal said, and took her along the flat's hall.

"Good night, dear boy," she said, and went along the landing to the staircase.

Fingal closed the door and hurried back to

Deirdre. "Dear Mother of God," he said, "Such news. Such wonderful news." He grinned from ear to ear. "Marge may not have wanted one, but . . . ?"

"Put water in mine, darling," Deirdre said. "Bring the drinks and hurry back."

When he returned, she was in front of the fire, sitting like the little mermaid, legs tucked up and supporting herself on one arm. He sat beside her and gave her her drink. "I know it's Wednesday, but Tuesday's toast is appropriate. Our men, all of them, and in particular Tony Wilcoxson."

She smiled into his eyes and said, "And Surgeon Lieutenant-Commander Fingal O'Reilly, my only love." And all her relief for Tony's safety and her love for Fingal was in that one kiss. "I'm so happy for them — for Marge and Pip and Tony, of course," she said.

"And Richard. He'll find out soon too if he doesn't already know." For a second Fingal wondered where his old *Warspite* might be. If at sea for any length of time, the first telegram might not yet have reached her. One thing was for sure now. Richard would find out that his son was safe within moments of the battleship dropping anchor.

"Can we do the presents now? And there's something I want to say," Deirdre said.

"Of course," he said and, beating her to the punch, he handed her a parcel.

She unwrapped the paperweight, clapped

543

her hands, said, "Oh, Fingal," and shook the ball. The snow inside fell and she laughed and laughed. "I feel like I'm twelve again. Thank you."

"Merry Christmas," he said. "You can think of me when you make it snow in the glass ball in July."

"And," she said, "you can think of me when you open this." Her voice was serious.

There was a photo album inside the wrapping. He opened the leather cover and lifted the cellophane protective sheet over the first vellum page. A pressed red rose was held in place with a strip of Sellotape over its stem.

"From my bouquet," she said.

He turned the pages; wedding snaps taken by her and of the happy couple taken by Angus. He still thought he looked a right eejit in his formal uniform. "I think I should be in the chorus of HMS *Pinafore,*" he said with a smile.

"Rubbish," she said. "You looked very handsome." She moved closer and turned a page. "Aren't those New Forest ponies little darlings?" Another page. "And those are fallow deer, like the ones we watched drinking."

"Wherever I am, I just have to open this and you'll be with me and I'll feel your love. Thank you, darling." He kissed her. "Thank you."

She smiled and leant over and tickled his ear with her tongue. "You might like to follow up on the promise you made that day," she stared at the photo of the deer, "and even if we don't start a family tonight you'll make me so content that this will have been the happiest Christmas of my whole life."

39
I Am Getting Better and Better

Ronald Fitzpatrick was wearing red-and-white-striped pyjamas and lying propped up on his pillows in the single room on Ward 21. He stared straight ahead. From shoulders to halfway up his neck, he was swathed in a bandage holding a dressing to the surgical wound at the back. That would be where Charlie Greer had made the incision. Two flat aluminium plates, one on the front of Fitzpatrick's chest and another on his upper back, were connected by straps and braces to each other and to a chin support that encircled his neck and lower jaw. "You asked how I am, Fingal? Well, I can tell you that this thing's a bloody pain in the neck." He managed to force a dry, rustling laugh, and O'Reilly realised that for probably only the third time in his life, he was hearing Ronald Fitzpatrick make a joke.

"I'm happy to see you can jest about it," O'Reilly said, and he could understand why. Charlie had explained to O'Reilly that when he had explored the extent of the lesion, he was delighted to see that he would need to incise only one intravertebral disc of cartilage to get access to the tumour and effect a complete excision. The disc must be given a chance to heal, and for that reason Fitzpatrick's neck was supported and immobilised by the brace. Although there would be a great deal of discomfort, he was on the road to what must be going to be an almost complete recovery. Humour, even gallows humour, was often the response when a great fear had been assuaged.

"I am a very relieved man, Fingal," Fitzpatrick said. "I've got the use of both my legs back." To prove it, he wriggled them under the blankets.

"We're all over the moon," O'Reilly said. "Kitty's been keeping me posted. She says Charlie's very pleased with your recovery. You've got a fair bit of feeling back in your fingers too, I believe?"

"I do." He flexed and extended them. "They're not as good as new yet, but I don't think I'll be burning myself on teapots anymore." He had to twist his entire body to look O'Reilly in the eye. "I was a very stupid man back in September, not listening to you and Charlie Greer."

"Water under the bridge," O'Reilly said, admiring the man's ability to be honest with himself and admit it. "What's important is that what ailed you has been fixed. It's been only a few days since your surgery and already you're recovering fast. But it's still going to keep you in here for a while. I know visitors are meant to bring grapes and Lucozade" — both of which adorned the bedside locker, along with a surprising number of get-well cards — "but I reckoned you might be getting bored so I brought you something to read instead. Here." He handed over a book and a glossy magazine.

"Could you give me my glasses?" Ronald asked. "I was reading the newspaper." He sighed and said, "I do wish the great powers would stop testing atomic bombs. Did you know that survivors of the Hiroshima atomic bombing subsequently had a high rate of developing meningiomas? The same tumour that, thank goodness, I don't have anymore?"

"I didn't," said O'Reilly, "but then I imagine you keep up more than I do about things in Japan. You haven't, by any chance, been visiting Japan regularly since the war?"

"No," Ronald said. "I spent a lot of my young life there." He grimaced. "But there was no reason for me to go back, and I never will. Thank you, Fingal. You knew I love to read."

"I did."

He tapped the book. "I tried this chap's first book, *King Rat,* about Japan during the war, a couple of years ago, but I could only get through about half. A little too close to the bone for me. I love the country, its culture, its art, its history. But I've tried to put all things about modern Japan away."

"I'd hoped," said O'Reilly, wondering if he'd made a terrible mistake, "you might enjoy this. It's Clavell's new one. *Tai-Pan.* Set in Hong Kong, not Japan, during the mid-nineteenth century."

"I'll certainly give it a try," Ronald said. "It was thoughtful of you." He looked at the glossy magazine. *"Country Life?"*

"Kitty thought you might like it because —"

"Excuse me, Doctors," a student nurse came into the room, "but it's that time again, Doctor Fitzpatrick. Sorry."

Ah, youth, O'Reilly thought. Blonde, snub nose, green eyes, full lips, and a very trim figure. He wondered if Barry's friend Jack Mills had ever taken her out or if he was still seeing Helen Hewitt, or, and O'Reilly wouldn't put it past Ulster's answer to Lothario, could Jack be seeing them both?

As he mused, she popped a thermometer under Ronald's tongue, took his pulse, wrapped a cuff round his upper arm and measured his blood pressure. Once she had entered the results in his chart she removed the thermometer, squinted at it, smiled, and said as she shook the mercury down, "All perfectly normal." She made a quick note, replaced the chart, and said, "You're coming on splendidly, Doctor Fitzpatrick. You'll be doing handstands next, so you will. Right. I'll be off." She left.

"Cheerful lass," Ronald said. "Does me good. Grew up in a tough part of East Belfast. Working her way through nursing training." He looked at the cover of the magazine that featured a smiling daughter of one of England's landed gentry, one of the famous "Girls in Pearls." "The Ravenhill Road is a very long way from Belgravia. I don't mean to be ungracious, Fingal, but I'd have thought all the huntin', shootin', fishin' stuff would be of more interest to you."

O'Reilly chuckled. "Try the arts section, page fifty-one." He waited as Ronald found the place.

"Oh my." Ronald's eyes widened. "Oh good gracious. 'Netsuke of the Tokugawa Shogunate.' How very thoughtful of her. They ruled Japan from 1603 until 1868. I'm sure I'll find this intriguing." He sighed. "I'm so grateful knowing that I'm going to get better, but I'm afraid it's going to be a long, boring recuperation. Physiotherapy," he pointed at his brace, "weeks in this thing, then a soft Stamm collar for months." He managed a small smile. "Oh well," he said, "I suppose I'll just have to be patient."

"It's what the Latin *patiens* means," O'Reilly said, "suffering or waiting. It's why

550

we call our customers patients."

"Yes, I do know that, Fingal. Now, I wonder if you could help me to move a bit farther up the bed?"

O'Reilly stood, put his hands in Fitzpatrick's armpits, and pulled him up. "Sit forward," and when Fitzpatrick did, O'Reilly fluffed up the pillows. "There," he said, "lie back."

Fitzpatrick made a little huffing noise as he settled. "That's better," he said. "Thank you, and Fingal?"

"Mmmm?" He helped himself to several green grapes and popped them one at a time into his mouth.

"You mentioned patients."

"And?" O'Reilly choked on a grape seed and coughed. "Sorry," he said when the paroxysm had passed.

"I should like to express my most sincere gratitude for all that you and Doctors Laverty and Bradley have done." He picked up a card. "Please read this."

O'Reilly fished out his own half-moon glasses from the inside pocket of his jacket and read,

Dear Doctor Fitzpatrick. Me and Mrs. Duffy was dead sorry to hear you was sick. She seen Doctor Bradley last week for a woman's complaint and said the young lady doctor was very nice and all, but she hopes you get better good and quick so she can come to see you again. Respectfully, Hubert Duffy

O'Reilly smiled. "Very nice," he said.

There was a crack in Fitzpatrick's voice when he pointed at the other cards and said, "They're all like that. It's all very humbling."

If the man had described himself as humble six months ago, O'Reilly would immediately have had a mental image of a hand-wringing Uriah Heep. Now all he could hear was a deep sincerity. "Aye," he said, "it is humbling, the amount of trust we get."

"Yes, that is it exactly. The trust they place in us. I have to make a confession. I was worried that my practice might shrink."

"And it might have. I'd have been just as worried if the tables had been turned."

"Would you really? I can't see why." He produced a small laugh. "Do you remember a radio character in the '50s, Gillie Potter?"

"The sage of Hog's Norton?" O'Reilly said, helping himself to more grapes. "Indeed I do."

"I've always thought of you, Fingal, as the sage of Ballybucklebo."

Fingal's laugh rang so loudly he had to remind himself of where he was, and clapped a hand over his mouth.

"Everybody knows you don't simply look after the sick. You minister to the entire village and townland. I envy your ability. I'd like to be more like that. I'd like really to earn the trust these people have placed in me. And I want to be a better doctor."

For the first time in a long time, Fingal Flahertie O'Reilly was at a loss for words, but there certainly was a lot more to Ronald Fitzpatrick than had originally appeared on the surface.

A stern-looking Kitty walked in. "Doctor O'Reilly," she said, and he could tell that being his wife was entirely secondary to her being the senior nursing sister. "I'd have expected better of you on a neurosurgical ward. I could hear the guffaws of you in my office. You sounded like a wounded heifer." There was steel in her voice.

O'Reilly lowered his head. His "Sorry" was meek indeed.

"And," she said, consulting a round pocket watch pinned to the left shoulder strap of her white apron — all the Royal nurses wore one there — "even if you are a professional colleague, I believe visiting hours are over, and that you have an appointment at the Royal Maternity Hospital with a Doctor Whitfield soon."

O'Reilly rose. "Thank you, Sister," he said as he watched her leave the room. She was right. Lorna Kearney would be at RMH at two thirty today for her first amniocentesis and he was going to be there with her.

Together they'd take another step along the road to managing the incompatibility between her immune defences and her unborn baby.

"You may be right, Ronald, about me looking after the village as well as the sick. Lately, though, I've been wondering if I get a little distracted by it all. Medicine's changed one hell of a lot since we graduated. I've been getting a bit rusty. Not very up on the latest procedures. Take this Rhesus isoimmunisation. Do you know anything about analysing amniotic fluid to predict how seriously a baby might be affected?"

"I was never very good at obstetrics. Pregnant women have always made me somewhat nervous," Ronald said with a shy smile. "And you're right. I don't know anything about amniocentesis."

"I'm going to watch one. Learn a bit. I'll tell you all about it next time I see you." He headed for the door.

"Thank you for coming, Fingal," Fitzpatrick said, "and will you please thank Mrs. O'Reilly for me for the *netsuke* article?"

"Of course," O'Reilly said. "I've got to trot," he said, "but you keep on getting better, and if I can, I'll pop in again." Without waiting for a reply, he left and marched straight to Kitty's office. He poked his head in, saw her sitting at her desk, and shut the door behind him. "Kitty, I really am sorry."

She shook her head. "You can be a great

glipe sometimes, but you're forgiven." She raised one eyebrow. "What was so funny anyway?"

O'Reilly chuckled. "He said I was the sage of Ballybucklebo. It hit my funny bone."

Kitty laughed quietly. "See what you mean," she said. "You know, I've got to know him a lot better since he was admitted. When you get through the armour plating —"

"Sounds like you're trying to sink a battleship," and for a moment he vividly recalled what happened on *Warspite* after the German 250-kilogram bomb had hit.

"You know what I mean. Ronald had built up his protective walls, but inside I reckon there's a pretty decent human being. It just takes a bit of getting through to him," she said.

"I agree. Now don't laugh, but how do you think things might work if we formed some kind of association with Ronald, if only for being on call? He should be back in harness in about another two months, but he'll need to work into it gradually. We could help. And I'm beginning to think I should be starting to make arrangements for Barry and me to go on regular refresher courses. You went to one in London last year, and if we were affiliated with Ronald, he could get away once in a while too."

Kitty frowned, pursed her lips. "There is the business of some of our patients preferring a woman doctor . . ."

"Don't worry about that. Jenny's promised to sort that out, and she's never let us down about anything. There'll still be a well-woman clinic to run, and the customers all seem pretty happy with Jenny. We do need another woman."

She smiled at him. "I'll bet Ronald would be thrilled with the idea now he knows we're not out to pinch his patients. He's told me that being ill helped him to see that he wants to be a better doctor. You should talk to him, Fingal."

"Not now. But soon." O'Reilly felt a pang of something that felt suspiciously like jealousy and yet at the same time he was happy that Ronald had confided in Kitty as well as in himself. He looked at his watch and suddenly felt weary. "Listen," he said, "I have to nip over to RMH, but why don't you and I forget about the practice and Ronald and medicine for tonight? I'll meet you in the Culloden Hotel about six?" The thought of an evening within the solid stone walls of the old Gothic mansion turned hotel felt like good medicine. "We can have a drink, maybe even dinner if whatever Kinky has prepared could wait until tomorrow? I'll find that out when I get back to Number One."

"Sounds good," Kitty said. "Blow the work. I'll drive straight there and see you at six, at least for a drink." And her smile was inviting.

"All work and no play make Jack a dull boy
— and I'd hate to have to live with a dull
Fingal O'Reilly."

He could still hear her throaty chuckle
when he was several yards along the corridor.

40

'Ere the Parting Hour Go By

Fingal had left the flat in the Crescent and taken a shortcut past the Paddock at the west end of the Haslar grounds. To his right he noticed the stand of firs where he'd cut the small Christmas tree, now stripped of its finery and consigned to the rubbish tip this morning, Little Christmas, January the sixth. On this day tradition dictated Christmas decorations should be taken down.

How fast the days had flown.

He realised he was approaching a familiar figure, stiff-backed, neat in her fall, tippet, white apron, and navy blue uniform, who was standing staring over the huge, empty, barren field. He wondered what she was doing. "Elizabeth?" Fingal called.

The woman turned. Senior Sister Elizabeth Blenkinsop smiled a greeting, but her eyes were far away. "Morning, Fingal."

He caught up. "Morning, Elizabeth. Not a bad day for the time of year."

"And it's your last, isn't it?"

" 'Fraid so. We'll be leaving at noon."

"I knew you weren't actually on duty today."

"I'm not. I'm just going to pop in to say my farewells to the staff."

"Nice of you. Let's walk back together."

"Grand, but before we go, if you don't mind me asking, what brings you out here?" Fingal said. "There's not much to see." Which was true.

"No, there isn't. It's a desolate place. But it's not what I see," she said. "It's what I feel." She frowned. "I'm not a superstitious woman, I don't believe in the supernatural. But out here I can sense the sadness of all those interred here and" — she straightened her shoulders — "I get a feeling of England's permanence too."

Fingal frowned. He wasn't quite sure he understood. "Please go on," he said.

She inhaled. "Do you know the history of this place, Fingal?"

"Not really, no."

"I believe it was 1753 they started using these fields, all nine acres of them, to bury those who died in the hospital. Our historians estimate at least ten thousand people are still buried here. The staff used the Paddock until 1859. Until then apparently there were fleets and fleets of headstones, but the tombstones were all transferred to a garden of remembrance at Haslar and the people in charge established a new naval cemetery at Clay-hall."

"Good Lord," Fingal said. It was hard to imagine. All he could see was a large, un-kempt field with a few detached houses at one side, a long redbrick wall at another.

"And," she said softly, "nearly all of them were far from home, lonely, afraid." She looked him straight in the eye. "That's the sadness I feel. Their sadness." She touched his arm. "I've watched you, Fingal, and I know you think the way I do. Every single patient needs to feel they are cared for as an individual, and sometimes when I've been dog tired or we've been rushed off our feet, not able to do that, I come out here, think of all those terrified boys, and remind myself of what I ought to be trying to do."

Fingal swallowed the lump in his throat, said nothing, but realised that for many nurs-ing spinsters, their patients filled the place of the families they never had. Not all, though, felt the same sense of duty as Elizabeth Blen-kinsop.

"A lot of England's history is here, too," she continued, her voice hardening. "A sense of going on. When the *Royal George* capsized in 1782 at Spithead, six hundred drowned sailors were buried here. There are typhus and dysentery victims from Sir John Moore's retreat to Corunna during the war in the Iberian Peninsula, veterans who fought with

Nelson at the Nile and Trafalgar, soldiers from Waterloo." She smiled. "I remind myself what we're fighting for, defending England from that horrid little Austrian corporal and his bullies." Fingal watched as the normally restrained nurse actually stamped her foot. "All of our fighting troops deserve the very best care we can give. That is our duty, and sometimes I need to remind myself of that." She turned and began to walk. "Now," she said, her voice lightening, "you've heard the sermon from a garrulous woman. Let's go to Collingwood Ward, perhaps Angus will drop in, and I'll make us a cup of tea."

"We shall miss you, Fingal," Elizabeth Blenkinsop said as she poured him a second cuppa.

And as she'd suggested he might, Angus had dropped in too. "Just so," he said, shifting his weight on the plain wooden chair, "and we wish you well, and trust you'll keep in touch." Fingal and Deirdre had dined with him and Morag on Saturday night to say a proper good-bye.

The door flew open. "Do you know anything about this, Mahaddie?" Surgeon Commander Fraser stormed into the room, brandishing a letter. "Do you? It has your hallmark all over it. Yours and O'Reilly's." The surgeon did not acknowledge Elizabeth's presence in the room.

"Eh, and a good morning to you too, Surgeon Commander. And what would *this* be, exactly?" The Highlander allowed one bushy eyebrow to arch.

"The most ridiculous order I've ever received." A vein throbbed at Fraser's temple and his face was puce.

"You're not in my department, Surgeon Commander."

While Fraser had dropped both his and Angus's rank, the little Scot was being punctilious.

"And unless you tell me what the order is, it would be hard for me to say if I knew anything about it, now wouldn't it?" His voice was calm, quiet, and held a touch of the sardonic. "You're getting yourself awfully fashed."

"Speak English, for God's sake. Of course I'm blazing. Reykjavik. Bloody Reykjavik. To leave on a Sunderland flying boat from a water aerodrome in northern Scotland next week. I won't stand for this, Mahaddie."

"Well, then, maybe it's the admiral you should be having a wee word with?"

"I fully intend to have more than a 'wee word' with Admiral Bradbury." The man spun on his heel and stormed out, slamming the door behind him.

"Och, the poor wee man. Looks like he's got a posting he doesn't much like." Angus shook his head. "You'll remember we invaded

Iceland on the tenth of May last year?"

"I do indeed," Elizabeth said, "to keep the Germans out. U-boat and long-range bomber bases there would have been disastrous. They would have straddled the North Atlantic convoy routes." Despite the seriousness of the information, Sister Blenkinsop was clearly having trouble keeping a straight face.

"*Warspite* was preoccupied then in the Sea of Norway and at Narvik," Fingal said, remembering how three days later, the great battleship and her escort destroyers had stormed into Westfjord, all guns blazing.

"It seems," said Angus, "we're strengthening the Iceland garrison. They must have need of a naval medical officer. Probably in an administrative capacity. I'm guessing, of course." The hint of a smile flickered at the corners of his mouth. He rose and offered his hand.

Fingal rose and shook it. "I'll write," he said. "And thanks for everything."

"Aye. You'll do fine back on your ship. I can teach you no more about giving anaesthetics, and remember me to Richard Wilcoxson." And with that the little Scot broke the handshake, said, "I'll be off, Elizabeth," and left.

"Sit down, Fingal, and finish your tea," she said, and burst out laughing before saying, "Never play poker with a Highland man. I don't know how Angus kept a straight face.

It's the kind of thing he'd want to keep to himself. No hint that he'd taken any part." She chuckled. "I don't know for certain, but Angus has a very close friend in the Admiralty. A vice admiral, in charge of things like promotions and postings."

And Fingal remembered Surgeon Captain Mahaddie's words in the mess before he went on a week's leave before Christmas. "It might just be time to have a word with my friend in London."

She stopped chuckling. "It doesn't happen often, but Angus had a drop too many one night a couple of years ago. We were having a drink together in the mess. He said he was drinking to old comrades and asked me if I knew what the day's date, April the twenty-third, meant. I hadn't a clue. He told me on that day in 1918, the Royal Navy tried to seal the Belgian port of Zeebrugge by sinking blockships there. The Germans were using the harbour as a U-boat base. We lost more than five hundred men." She glanced down at her desk, then back at Fingal. "I don't think he'd mind me telling you he won his DSO there by saving a man's life." She smiled. "That man, a vice admiral in London now, is the one who got your promotion through and I'm damn certain has arranged a frosty future for a certain surgeon commander of our acquaintance. And he can moan all he likes to our officer commanding, but vice admirals outrank rear admirals."

"I know." Fingal struggled and managed to stay expressionless. "Couldn't have happened to a more deserving chap, could it?" he said.

They were both still chuckling when he finished his tea, pecked Elizabeth's cheek, said his good-byes, and left Collingwood Ward for the very last time. He was glad he'd be seeing Deirdre in a few minutes, but sad at leaving Haslar, just as he had been sad to leave Sir Patrick Dun's Hospital in Dublin, the Aungier Place Dispensary, and the Rotunda Hospital. At least once the war *was* over he'd have his own surgery in Ballybucklebo, and Deirdre, to return to.

"It's been a lovely flat, darling," Deirdre said. "Our first home. I'll never forget it." She was sitting in her usual chair, but wearing her coat, hat, and gloves. Without the glow from the coal fire the living/dining room was chilly. Her two suitcases stood in the hall along with his. Marge had agreed to pick them up at twelve and take them to Gosport Station. Deirdre was to travel to Liverpool to catch the ferry to Belfast. They'd part in Southampton where a cargo ship would take him to Takoradi on Africa's Gold Coast.

"Marge should be here shortly," Deirdre said.

He could see she was struggling to sound cheerful, just as she had last night at Twiddy's where Marge had insisted they come to say good-bye to her and the animals. Pip couldn't join them. She was staying with a school friend in Cirencester to be near Tony, who was convalescing in a rest home there. "Well out of the way of the Hun bombers," Marge had said.

"I've told you this before, pet," he said, "but I'm so glad we decided not to let the Blitz change our plans to have you join me here. I've had the best months of my life since you came. I love you very much, Mrs. Fingal O'Reilly."

"I told you, I'd've come anyway. And I love you, Fingal." She blew him a kiss, which he blew back.

He left the chair where he'd been sitting and walked to the window to stare out across the roofs to the Solent, grey and choppy, and on to the fields of the Isle of Wight. He turned and looked back into the room. Two months and already this place was full of memories; of a ruined sausage and sultana pie, of roasting chestnuts on Christmas Day, her girlish delight over a glass ball and its snowscape. Of lovemaking tender or fierce and always languorous after, lying in each other's arms content, at peace, in love. He knew the Book of Life was a Jewish term for a book where God inscribed the names of all those bound for heaven, but Fingal had chosen to appropriate the expression to describe the place in his heart where he kept his most precious memories: meeting her off the Fareham train and their wedding day had their own pages, as did the coming of the deer to drink from a stream. And today would be in there, a day he'd never forget, even if it was a sad one. There was always the promise of more blank pages to be filled with her — later.

And there was another image. One he really didn't want, but it had been so powerful he knew he would never erase it. This morning she'd used an old copy of the *Daily Mail* for added protection to wrap her glass snow ball. On the newspaper's front page was a photograph of St. Paul's Cathedral nine days ago. The great dome and a spire to its left were defiant islands surrounded by a sea of smoke. Dense black clouds towered in the foreground as high as the colonnades that supported the dome. All around the foul stuff writhed and boiled, and above the dome, brilliantly illuminated even in the black-and-white picture, the undersides of the clouds threw back reflections of the flames raging below. God help the firemen and the heavy rescue squads that night. When would the lunacy end?

He looked over to Deirdre. She was staring into the fireplace, her face in profile. God, but she was lovely.

He took a deep breath, turned, and went to

stand in front of her.

She had to tilt her head back to look up into his face. "I know," she said. "Hanging about waiting's the worst part of saying good-bye, isn't it?" Her chuckle sounded forced, embarrassed. "I never know what to say."

The doorbell rang.

"Marge," they said in unison. "It's open," Fingal shouted.

Marge bustled in, looking from Fingal to Deirdre. " 'Morning, Fingal. Wilcoxson landau service at your service." She bent and hugged Deirdre. "Ready, dear gel?"

"Yes."

"Good." She thrust a parcel at Fingal. "Few sandwiches and some bikkies to eat on the train. I imagine you'll be able to get tea between Southampton and Liverpool, Deirdre."

It was all so matter-of-fact, Fingal thought and, fair play to Marge, good-byes were always miserable affairs.

"I'm afraid one of you'll have to share the back of my Prefect with Admiral Benbow," she said. "The old thing has started getting quite distraught if I go out and leave him alone. Now," she turned and started to head for the door, "I'll trot on down. Give you two a minute." She hefted two suitcases and closed the door behind her.

He stood looking at his lovely young wife. Slowly she rose from the chair to face him.

Neither spoke for long moments, then Deirdre said, "I'm no good at waving a tear-stained hanky from the window as my train pulls away, Fingal. We'll part in Southampton, I know, but let's be sensible about it there." She moved closer to him. "Hold me, Fingal," she said, and he did. Her kiss was long, soft, loving. Then she said, "This isn't good-bye, it's just *beannacht De agat,* God go with you, darling, and keep you until you come back safe to me."

"I will," he said, his voice breaking, and in their last kiss went all the longing in the big man's great heart.

41

HE MIGHT ENJOY THE THINGS WHICH OTHERS UNDERSTAND

The smell of antiseptics greeted O'Reilly as he walked into the long room in the Royal Maternity Hospital. The odour was identical here in the antenatal clinic to the one he'd left behind in the neurological ward of the Royal Victoria, a short walk away. Dettol's overpowering astringency was quickly replacing the outdoor smell of coal smoke and vehicle exhaust in his nostrils. Hushed conversations were interrupted only by the squeaking of the wheels of a midwife's trolley, the rap of her shoes on the linoleum floor, and the rattling of curtain rings as privacy curtains were opened and closed. Pregnant women waiting their turn sat on chairs beneath a row of windows. The place was bright and airy.

The opposite half of the room was hidden by a system of curtains hanging from overhead rails. It divided the area into a series of examining spaces, each equipped with a table and sphygmomanometer.

Like the figures on Munich's town hall clock, doctors in white coats and midwives in navy blue dresses and white aprons appeared and disappeared behind the curtains as patients left clutching lab requisitions or were summoned to be examined.

A midwife weighed each newly arriving patient, noted it on her antenatal chart, then tested the urine sample.

O'Reilly, although impressed with the obvious efficiency of the clinic in full swing, wondered if each patient ever saw the same doctor twice during the course of her pregnancy. He may have been feeling behind the times lately, but he still much preferred medicine his way, where every customer was an individual.

He approached the sister midwife in charge at her desk near the door. "Excuse me. I'm Doctor O'Reilly. Doctor Whitfield's doing an amniocentesis for one of my patients in a few minutes. Can I have a word with him?"

She smiled and rose. "That would be Lorna Kearney. Come with me."

He followed her through a door into a small, more private, windowless room with beige walls, a washbasin against one, and an instrument trolley covered in a green towel. Lorna, wearing a pale blue hospital gown, the kind with a split back that O'Reilly always called the "dedignifier," sat on a chair near a stretcher trolley. She smiled at him but said

571

nothing. She was clearly overawed by the scrum of people in the place.

O'Reilly counted three male and one female medical student identifiable by their short "bum freezer" white coats; two presumably junior doctor trainees, one a young woman; two midwives; and an older physician who turned when the sister midwife said, "Doctor Whitfield, this is Mrs. Kearney's GP, Doctor O'Reilly."

Doctor Whitfield, a man of about forty, with dark curly hair, bushy eyebrows, and dark eyes set above a sharp nose, smiled and said, "What can we do for you, Doctor O'Reilly?"

"I'd like to sit in on Lorna's procedure, if I may. I did a bit of obstetrics in the Rotunda in 1937, but things have changed a lot since then. I'd like to learn more about Rhesus too."

"Happy to have you, and once we've finished with you, Mrs. Kearney," he said, speaking directly to her, "I'll take Doctor O'Reilly up to my office and give him as much information as he wants."

O'Reilly approved. He'd seen hospital consultants discussing patients in front of them as if they weren't even there.

"Then when we get the results sent to him, he can explain them to you. All right?"

"Yes, sir," she said, and smiled at O'Reilly.

"Right," said Doctor Whitfield, "let's get going. Whose turn is it to do the procedure?"

"Mine, sir," a young man answered.

"This is Doctor Sproule, Mrs. Kearney. He's a registrar in training to be an obstetrician. He'll be explaining the procedure to you and the students as he goes along," the senior lecturer said.

"Pleased til meet you," she said. "And it's all right, Doctor Sproule. Youse all have til learn your trade, so youse do," she said. "I understand that."

"And I'll be here," Doctor Whitfield said. "Masks on, everybody." He handed one to O'Reilly, who tied it to cover his nose and mouth. The senior lecturer turned to a midwife. "Can you help Mrs. Kearney onto the trolley?"

Lorna was soon lying on her back, head supported by a pillow, a blanket over her legs, its upper edge at the level of her pubic symphysis.

"Let's have a look at your tummy," Doctor Sproule said, and tucked her gown up to her ribs' lower edges. He stood on her left side facing her feet. It took moments for him to complete his examination and listen to the baby's heart with a fœtal stethoscope. "Your uterus is the right size for your length of pregnancy," he said, "and your baby is in a longitudinal lie, in the left occipito-anterior position. The head is not engaged. Fœtal heart one forty-four."

Doctor talk for the learners, O'Reilly understood.

"That means, Mrs. Kearney, that the wean's in your womb with its wee back parallel to yours, the rear of its loaf is to the right and," he clapped a hand to the back of his own head, "this part of it, called the occiput, is exactly where it should be. The widest part of the baby's head hasn't gone into the birth canal yet, not engaged, and nor should it be at this stage of the pregnancy, and its wee heart is going ninety to the dozen at just the right rate. So we're all set." He turned to the other learners. "You know all about it, but it's important to explain to Mrs. Kearney too. Remember that when you're in practice."

There was a muttering of assent from the class and O'Reilly smiled. He liked young Sproule.

Doctor Sproule put his hand on the right side of Lorna's lower abdomen over the uterus. "It's important to test the fluid in your womb," he said. "The baby's curled up a bit, but just underneath there," he put his finger on the spot where he was going to put in the needle to obtain the sample, "will be a hollow between its legs, tummy, chest, and arms. We'll get our specimen here." He used a ballpoint pen to draw a small X.

O'Reilly watched how her gaze never left his eyes. "All right, Doctor," she said.

"I'm going to go and wash my hands. Put

on rubber gloves. Then I'll come back and I'll paint your tummy here with antiseptic. I'll put in some freezing, wait for it to work, then I'll take another needle and pass it through your tummy and through your womb to where there's fluid, take a small sample, take the needle out, and pop a dressing on the wee hole left behind. It'll only take a few minutes. I'll be back in a jiffy."

"It's all for my baby's sake, isn't it?" Lorna asked.

"Indeed it is," Doctor Whitfield said.

"Then that's all right."

O'Reilly watched as she composed her features and closed her eyes. He had no doubt she was praying.

"Now," Doctor Whitfield said, "while Doctor Sproule is scrubbing, can you tell me, Stevenson, what will be done to the sample when it goes to the lab?"

O'Reilly listened attentively as the young woman said, "The bilirubin content will be measured and the spectrophotometric absorption curve will be plotted."

"Good," the senior lecturer said. "Collins. Why are we interested in the bilirubin?"

A medical student responded. "Bilirubin is a product of broken-down red blood cells. The amount present in the amniotic fluid can only come from the baby's cells that have been destroyed —"

Lorna's eyes flew open and her sharp intake

of breath silenced the young man.

"Continue, please, Collins."

"— by the mother's antibodies, and its properties can be used to estimate," he hesitated before saying, "the amount of red cell affectation."

A good way of avoiding saying "severity," O'Reilly thought. He frowned. He'd have to ask for a more detailed explanation later. Spectrophotometric absorption curves were Greek to him.

Doctor Sproule returned, masked, gowned, and with latex gloves on his hands. A midwife pulled the sterile green towel from the top of the instrument trolley near the patient.

"This is antiseptic," Doctor Sproule said, and he used forceps to grasp a swab, soak it in a brown solution, and paint it on the lower half of her belly over the bulge of the uterus. He surrounded the area with green sterile towels, then lifted a hypodermic, filled the barrel with five ccs of what O'Reilly knew would be one percent xylocaine local anaesthetic, and said, "This will sting for a minute."

"Ouch," Lorna said as the needle slipped through the skin beneath the middle of the X.

O'Reilly assumed that Doctor Sproule would be putting local anaesthetic into the skin, abdominal wall, and uterine muscle, along the projected path of the sample-taking needle.

"While we're waiting for the freezing to take," Doctor Whitfield said, "can anyone tell me what level of bilirubin in the fluid is taken as indicating the requirement for further treatment?"

The other trainee doctor, an auburn-haired young woman, said, "Walker and Jennison in 1962 used a level of nought point two mgs percent, sir."

"Correct. Well done, Stevenson. So do we here at RMH."

The young woman smiled and O'Reilly pulled out a pen and a small notebook from his jacket pocket and made a note of the number so he'd know in the future.

"We'll have all the results in two days," Doctor Whitfield said, "and we'll let Doctor O'Reilly know at once, Mrs. Kearney."

"Can you feel that, Mrs. Kearney?" Doctor Sproule asked as he gently pricked her belly where the local anaesthetic had raised a small wheal.

"No, sir."

Sproule nodded to himself, put down the hypodermic, and lifted a long, wide-bore needle. "Here we go then," he said, "and please do your very best to lie absolutely still." He stabbed the needle vertically through the skin.

O'Reilly watched Lorna's face. She

frowned, presumably because while she couldn't feel the sharpness of the needle's point, she would have experienced a feeling of pressure. Then, as the doctor advanced the instrument, her features relaxed.

He attached a ten cc syringe to the needle and pulled on the plunger.

O'Reilly watched in fascination as the barrel filled with an opalescent fluid.

Doctor Sproule detached the syringe, set it on the trolley, and gently withdrew the needle. A dab of collodion over the puncture was quickly covered with a gauze swab. "All done," he said with a broad smile. "That wasn't too bad, was it?"

If it wasn't, why were there beads of sweat on his forehead? Because, O'Reilly realised, it took courage to thrust a sharp instrument blindly into a pregnant uterus. It would have been entirely possible to stab the baby, its umbilical cord, or the placenta.

"No, sir," she said, "and thank youse all very much."

"We're going to keep you here for a few hours," Doctor Sproule said. "As a precaution."

O'Reilly remembered what Barry had said about the risks of premature labour following amniocentesis.

"Then we'll send you home in the ambulance. If you're worried about anything, let Doctor O'Reilly know at once."

"You do that, Lorna," he said.

"We'll give him your results when they're ready, and we'd like you to come back in two weeks so we can get one more sample, and then we'll be able to let you know exactly what's going to happen."

She nodded. "Yes, sir," she said.

"Right," said Doctor Whitfield. "You students can go back to the clinic, and I'm sure the registrars have work to do." He turned to O'Reilly. "And if you'll come with me, Doctor O'Reilly? I'll explain all about spectrophotometry and prediction curves and action lines." He headed for the door and O'Reilly followed, shaking his head in wonder at the enormous advances science was bringing to the art of obstetrics.

"Cup of tea, Doctor O'Reilly?" said Doctor Whitfield.

"Thank you, but no." O'Reilly glanced quickly round the office from where he sat in a wooden armchair, taking in the overstuffed bookcase shelves, light green walls, filing cabinets, and a big desk covered in papers in front of him. The single window behind the desk where the senior lecturer sat overlooked the lawn and the redbrick main corridor of the Royal Victoria. "And thank you for taking the time to explain, Doctor Whitfield."

"I enjoy teaching," he said, "and it's Charley."

O'Reilly noticed a glass-fronted cabinet in which were arranged an assortment of instruments which he recognised as having been in use back in the '30s for what were called "destructive operations." With no blood transfusions and no antibiotics, sometimes in cases of obstructed labour it was safer for the mother for her doctor to snap the baby's collarbones or crush its head so it could be delivered vaginally. Caesarean section really had been the court of last appeal. He shuddered and said, pointing to the cabinet, "They were still using those things when I was a student."

"Part of my museum now," Charley Whitfield said. "Obstetrics has made great advances in thirty years."

"I know," said O'Reilly. "That's why I'm here. I'm trying to catch up. And it's Fingal."

"Fair enough, Fingal. And you'd like to understand how we manage Rhesus isoimmunisation?"

"Please. I do understand it's a juggling act between leaving the baby in utero until it's mature enough to survive outside and not leaving it too long and letting the anaemia and bilirubin from the broken-down red cells threaten its life or mental capacity. We saw all those things in the '30s."

"I think we're getting better at it," Charley said. "Initially, all we had to go on was the level of antibodies in the bloodstream and the bilirubin level in the amniotic fluid, but recently, in 1961, a New Zealander, Doctor Liley, took things a step further." Charley Whitfield handed O'Reilly a sheet of graph paper. "This is his prediction graph."

O'Reilly saw that the bottom axis was marked "wavelength" and the vertical one "optical density." A straight line ran at an angle of forty-five degrees from the bottom left-hand corner to halfway up the right margin. Above the straight line, a higher curve rose and fell from halfway up to the end.

"When we put a fluid into a spectrophotometer," Charley said, "it will absorb or let light through, and how much it does of either depends on the wavelength of the light being used. Look at the bottom left."

O'Reilly did.

"At a wavelength of seven hundred —"

The figure was clearly marked.

"— nearly all the light gets through, but at three hundred and fifty, look at the right margin, a lot of light is being absorbed."

"I see that," O'Reilly said. "So the shorter the wavelength, the harder it is for the light to get through?"

"That's right, and of course the density of the fluid affects absorption too."

"Water might let a lot through, but milk is more opaque so it would absorb more?"

"Exactly. Now, that straight line on this

graph represents the behaviour of normal amniotic fluid and, quite simply, the shorter the wavelength of the light used, the more of it is absorbed."

"Makes sense."

"The curve above the line is the light absorption qualities of amniotic fluid containing bilirubin."

"So after," O'Reilly followed the lower axis with an index finger, "five hundred and fifty, the bilirubin starts absorbing more light?"

"Correct, and Doctor Liley found he could correlate the height of the bilirubin curve above the straight line at a wavelength of four hundred and fifty with the severity of the disease and the likely outcome for the baby."

"That's bloody amazing," said O'Reilly.

"It gets better," said Charley, handing O'Reilly a second sheet of graph paper. "The vertical axis is marked in units reflecting the values measured from the straight line to the top of the bilirubin curve on the Liley graph. The bottom is the weeks' duration of the pregnancy."

"So you'll plot Lorna's result at thirty-three weeks on this chart?"

"Exactly, and plot it again at thirty-five. The graph is divided by these straight lines sloping down across it, dividing it into lower, middle, and upper zones, and the two top ones are further divided into mild/moderate, moderate/severe, and severe/gross. Depending on the trend revealed by the two measurements, we can predict the probable severity of affectation and pick a date for delivery or, and it's still pretty experimental, actually do a blood transfusion into the baby while it's still in the mother."

O'Reilly shook his head. "Whoever comes up with these ideas?"

"The spectrophotometry and intrauterine transfusion were Liley's." Charley Whitfield blushed, hesitated, then said, "Actually the action graph, the second one, was my notion, Fingal."

"More power to your wheel," O'Reilly said. "I admire you research lads."

"We have our place, but it's the doctors like you, in the trenches day and daily, that do the work."

O'Reilly shrugged. "My best friend at Trinity was in bacteriological research."

"What's he doing now?"

O'Reilly sighed. "He's dead. He was in the army. Singapore." Bob Beresford. He missed him still.

"I'm sorry to hear that," said Charley. "Your friend will have been buried in Kranji Cemetery. It's a very moving place to visit."

"You've been there?"

"I have. I did a spell in the army in Malta and Singapore after the war." He smiled. "I much prefer civvy street."

"Me too," said O'Reilly, rising and extending a hand, which was taken and shaken. "Thank you for taking the trouble to explain about Rhesus. I'll look forward to hearing Lorna's results."

"Young Sproule will phone you." He began to rise.

O'Reilly said, "Don't get up. I'll see myself out." And as O'Reilly left, the academic doctor was already riffling through a pile of papers. Not O'Reilly's cup of tea, he knew. He much preferred GP work.

He left the RMH and strolled to the car park. Quite a day. It was a great relief that Ronald was really on the mend. And watching the amniocentesis had been fascinating. O'Reilly wondered what kind of a mind thought of using a thing like optical density to predict how a baby was doing? A research worker's, that's whose. Poor old Bob Beresford had been fascinated by his work in microbiology. What discoveries might he have made? O'Reilly shook his head. The war had taken some of the very best. Sad. Very sad.

He got into the big Rover, fired up the engine, and started to head for home to see if Kinky could put dinner off until tomorrow. And then, work and cares of the day be damned, off to the Culloden Hotel and, his grin was vast, to meet Kitty.

42
FRETTED WITH GOLDEN FIRE

"Not much longer to Wadi Halfa on Egypt-Sudan border." The now-familiar, accented voice of squadron leader and pilot Ludomil "Effendi" Rayski came tinnily over Fingal's intercom earphones. He was sitting beside Rayski in the nose of the Blenheim bomber, yet, even there, the device was necessary. The constant roaring of the twin air-cooled Mercury engines made ordinary conversation impossible. His oxygen mask had a built-in microphone and smelled of rubber, but at least that stifled the other smells — of sweat and aviation fuel.

To show he understood, Fingal nodded at Rayski.

"After that, one more refuelling stop at Luxor and then to Cairo's Abu Sueir aerodrome. Nearly home for you."

Nearly home. He wondered how long the word "home" for him would mean the flat at the Terrace in Alverstoke with Deirdre. He would not be sorry to see *Warspite* again, though. He was eager to know how Richard Wilcoxson and the SBAs were getting on, how his old friend Tom Laverty, *Warspite*'s navigating officer, was.

Since he'd parted from Deirdre in Southampton Station, the last thirty-two days had been ones of constant travel and an almost persistent ache of missing her. With nothing to do on the cargo ship but sleep, eat, read, and smoke his pipe, there had been little to distract him from his thoughts. She'd be back at work now in the Women's and Children's Hospital on Templemore Avenue, missing him as he was missing her. Elizabeth Blenkinsop had posted a letter he'd written the day before he'd left Haslar telling Deirdre how much he loved her. She'd have to wait for at least a month for the ones he'd written on the ship and mailed in Takoradi where the freighter had docked a week ago and unloaded him and the crated aeroplanes.

He'd been put up in some pretty grim accommodation for two days to await the next flight ferrying aircraft from the coast to Cairo. It cut two months off the time it would have taken to go round the Cape by sea, and Richard had specified he wanted Fingal back by the quickest route once his training was complete. He'd been happy to get away from the hot, humid, smelly Gold Coast, also known as "The White Man's Grave," so prevalent were the mosquito-borne tropical diseases of malaria, yellow fever, and black-water fever. And he'd be delighted to leave this noisy, cramped, constantly vibrating aeroplane.

One thing about being up here, though. It certainly wasn't hot and humid. Probably about minus twenty Farenheit outside. He stared through the front Plexiglas windows of the cockpit. Ahead the empty blue sky stretched limitlessly away to where the earth's curvature was hazily visible and appeared to undulate as the aircraft was raised and lowered by the surrounding air currents. Below he could see the Nile, sunlight flashing from its surface, winding its unhurried way to the Delta. Six Hurricane fighters made up the rest of the convoy. He had to turn in his cramped seat to see three echeloned a little astern on each side of the lead bomber.

There was no radio communication between members of the convoy, so the seven planes had to stay in constant visual contact, the fighters conforming to the course of the leader. The Blenheim's flight sergeant navigator, who had the only wireless in the convoy, sat in his station ahead, stepped down from the main cockpit. He was able to get direction bearings from their next landing field on his wireless and alert his pilot about the course corrections to make to get there. From the ground, the formation must look like a mother goose leading her goslings, strange birds with their underbellies painted azure blue and their topsides in camouflage browns, the official colours of Air Chief Marshall Sir Arthur Longmore's Desert Air Force.

"Bugger it." He grabbed his seat as the plane plummeted from under him. He would have banged his head on the roof of the cockpit had he not been strapped in.

The engines howled as the pilot advanced the throttles, put the plane's nose up, and struggled to regain lost altitude.

"Sorry," the voice said in his ears. "Air pocket. Lots of them and thermals over desert."

"I nearly lost the scrambled powdered eggs I had for breakfast," the flight sergeant said in thick Aussie tones. "Not that I'd miss them. Bloody awful stuff."

Fingal laughed. Whoever had come up with the idea of spray-drying whole eggs to save storage space and preserve them probably thought it had been a clever idea. The things were universally detested in war-rationed Britain and the armed forces. One submarine cook, it was rumoured, had tried to fool his shipmates into believing they were eating real eggs. He'd sprinkled bits of real shells into the reconstituted ones.

The plane levelled off and the engines settled into the usual steady beat that had driven them more than three thousand miles since their journey had begun in a Nissen hut back in Takoradi.

He leaned back in his seat remembering the initial briefing five days ago. An RAF flight lieutenant had stood on a platform in front of an easel on which was mounted a large-scale map of Africa. Over the left breast pocket of his blue/grey battledress blouse he wore the half-wing of nonpilot aircrew and the blue-and-white diagonally striped ribbon of the Distinguished Flying Cross.

Six pilot officers sat on folding chairs. Lord, but they were young. An older flight sergeant sat by himself, looking bored. He'd earlier told Fingal he'd been doing this run since September 1940, when the ferry route had opened: Takoradi to Cairo, then being flown back to Takoradi either in an air force Bombay troop transport or a civilian passenger aircraft. The squadron leader sat on a folding chair on the platform. Fingal noticed that instead of the embroidered cloth wings under a crown of the RAF, the man wore a badge of a silver bird with a laurel wreath in its beak, the insignia of a pilot in the Polish air force.

"Right," the briefing officer said, "I'm the local navigation expert, Flight Lieutenant Bayliss. Smoke if you want to."

There was a small eruption of matches and lighters as everyone except Fingal lit up.

"Beside me is Squadron Leader Rayski, who will be in command of this convoy."

The Pole stood, smiled, bowed, and sat.

"The naval officer Surgeon Lieutenant-Commander O'Reilly will be a passenger on this run. Glad to have you, sir."

Fingal nodded and smiled back.

The briefing officer took a pointer and indicated a ribbon that ran horizontally across the map of Africa from Takoradi in the corner where the continent starts its bulge to the west. The line ran to nearly the far eastern side, where the marker made a right-angle turn due north.

"The run will be made in six legs, with refuelling stops on any leg over five hundred and fifty miles, to accommodate the six-hundred-mile range of the Hurricanes."

There was a muttering, but whether or not of assent wasn't clear to Fingal. Not himself a flier, he reckoned a mere fifty-mile safety margin was cutting it a bit fine, but he must assume these airmen knew what they were doing.

The pointer jumped from place to place on the map as the officer said, "Takoradi to Lagos, to Kano, to El Geneina to Khartoum then turn north to Wadi Halfa and finally on to Cairo. Do try *not* to come down between Kano and El Geneina. There's bugger all but sand marsh and scrub on the ground . . ."

Someone whistled but was ignored.

"Squadron Leader Rayski will brief you before takeoff from each landing field about fuel mixture settings, meteorology, compass headings, ceiling, winds, and your next destinations. He'll also inspect your aircraft. The radial engines on the Blenheim can get buggered up and air filters can get clogged with sand and that's bad for Hurri engines too, so pay attention to what he tells you. Flight Sergeant Park, who's from Brisbane," he nodded to the older man, "will be lead navigator. If all goes according to Hoyle, it'll take five days."

"And if it doesn't?" one of the young pilots asked.

"All the squadron leader can do is get a fix and radio in a report. Each plane carries a desert survival kit. If you get down in one piece, you're going to have a sod of a long, hot walk home."

Fingal squirmed in his narrow scat beside the Blenheim pilot. That had been gallows humour if ever he'd heard it.

He didn't remember dozing off, but Fingal was awakened by a violent roaring coming from the starboard engine. He stared, mouth agape, as a long yellow flame burst from under the cowling and blazed away behind the wing. He had an overwhelming urge to yell "Do something!" but swallowed down the impulse. Ever since he'd had to anaesthetise Flip Dennison, the burned Hurricane pilot, Fingal's morbid fear of being burned himself had gained new life, and this bloody plane's engine was on fire somewhere over the Sudan between Khartoum and Wadi Halfa. He remembered Angus saying, "One thing about Blenheims, if one engine conks out they can keep flying on the other." Fingal stared at the flames and hoped to God the Scot was right.

The Polish voice said as calmly as if the man was ordering a pint, "Extinguisher on."

There must be one built into each engine, because as Fingal watched, transfixed, yet as alert as a cobra facing a mongoose, the tongue of flames shortened and withdrew beneath the cowling. The engine was blackened, the cowling distorted, and the shining disc of the whirling propeller had vanished, only to be replaced by three idly spinning blades.

"Feathering prop."

The blades turned to present their narrow edges to the air and cause as little drag as possible.

"All right down there, Navigator?"

"No worries, mate, but bring your heading to zero zero two degrees magnetic, Skipper."

"Zero zero two. Roger."

The plane banked slightly to port and settled on her new course. Fingal snatched a quick glance to see the six fighters conforming. He exhaled and inhaled slowly. There was a bang, a shriek of tearing metal, the cowling blew away, and he was staring into a blast furnace where the starboard engine should have been. "Holy thundering Mother of —"

"Hold tight everybody. Diving."

Fingal braced himself as Rayski put the plane's nose down and, with the single engine roaring at full throttle, hurtled toward the ground. On the instrument panel, the altimeter unwound at a rate of knots like a child's toy windmill on a stick in a gale, and outside the window the ground rushed up to meet them. And still the fire roared just outside his window until — until, as if somebody had shut a valve, it went out.

He let out the breath he'd been holding, switched on his mike, and said, "It's out." He turned to see the pilot, both hands on the joystick, veins standing out on his forehead, straining to pull the yoke back and lift the aircraft's nose. Fingal found himself clenching his teeth and pulling both fists into his chest as if his extra effort could help. He glanced ahead and the scrub bushes seemed to be moving astern, not rushing directly at him as before.

It was the last thing he saw. A huge hand was forcing him into his seat. He couldn't raise his arms and his face felt as if it was drooping like the watches in a Dali painting he'd once seen. Under the immense G-force, the blood drained from his brain. His last thought — we're straightening up — was left unfinished as he passed out.

"Hello, Wadi Halfa control. Hello, Wadi Halfa control. Woodcock flight leader calling. Over."

"Woodcock flight leader. Woodcock flight leader. Wadi Halfa control answering. Receiving you strength eight. Over."

Fingal struggled to sit upright, shook his head, looked ahead to a small town, and could make out a level sand landing strip, some parked planes, and a few low buildings to the northwest of the place. He listened to the pilot explaining about the fire and the ground controller's instructions giving landing precedence to the damaged Blenheim and putting it in the circuit on final approach.

His ears pained him, and as he'd been instructed he took off his oxygen mask, pinched his nose, clamped his lips shut, and blew. Hard. The pain disappeared.

The undercarriage came down with a pair of *clump*s and in moments the plane jolted, bounced, settled down to taxiing and losing speed. Through the side window he could see a fire engine and ambulance racing along beside them. The plane stopped, and already the heat inside was making Fingal sweat. The single engine was turned off. As Squadron Leader Rayski started to unbuckle his straps, he turned to Fingal and said, "*Przepraszam.* Is Polish. Means I am sorry. Sands, they play hell with air cooling system. It was go and touch for a while." The man's English might not be perfect, but there was nothing wrong with his ability to pilot an aircraft.

"But you got us down, thank you," Fingal said, unstrapping and noticing a fireman in an asbestos suit up on the wing using a foam extinguisher to be certain the fire was really out.

"You know what RAF say. Good landing is one you walk away from. Excellent one is when you can use kite again."

"True," said Fingal, "and it was an outstanding one." They had made it down safely, he wasn't burned, and he would live to see Deirdre again. Life was very good and Fingal laughed and laughed until tears sprouted in the corners of his eyes. He was still chortling as he followed the pilot out of the plane and into the blazing heat of an African noon.

". . . The poor old Blenheim had to stay at Wadi Halfa until a new engine could be flown in, but there was a Martin Maryland that had been left behind for repair and was waiting for a crew and so we took it instead to Cairo. The next day I pinched a ride from Cairo — on another Blenheim I might add, with my heart in my mouth — but here I am," Fingal said to Tom Laverty and Richard Wilcoxson as they sat sharing predinner drinks in *Warspite*'s anteroom. The place was busy. Officers who were not having a run ashore were chatting, smoking. Four were playing liar's dice. The buzz rose and fell. It was as if he'd never left — the ever-pervasive smell of bunker fuel, the steady whirring of fans, the grumbling of machinery, the noticeable roll of the ship.

He'd reported aboard the great vessel as she swung at anchor in Alexandria Harbour not an hour ago and had learned in very short order that since he had left Haslar in January, *Warspite* had seen much duty escorting convoys to Malta and had been bombed on numerous occasions both at sea and in harbour. She had escaped damage until January the second, when a Stuka had dropped a bomb on the starboard bower anchor. No sooner was she repaired than she had been accidentally rammed by the destroyer HMS *Greyhound* on January 31st, but was once again seaworthy.

He had been assigned a cabin, stowed his gear, put his war diary and the photo album Deirdre had given him at Christmas into his desk drawer, and headed for the mess where he'd been delighted to meet his chief and his old friend. Fingal had immediately conveyed messages from Marge and had seen the look of intense relief on Richard's face when it was confirmed for him that Tony was safe and sound. Tom puffed out his chest at the news that Fingal had been able to phone

Carol, Tom's wife, before he left Gosport and she'd said that Tom's son, Barry, was growing like a weed.

Then his friends naturally had wanted to hear about his adventures. He'd kept the story short and to the point.

"Sounds bloody hair-raising to me, an engine fire," Richard said.

"It was," Fingal said, "but everything happened so quickly."

"All's well that ends," Tom said, "and it's," he assumed a Belfast accent, "sticking out a mile to have you back."

"It's good to be back among shipmates, including you, Tom, you Ulster bollix," Fingal said. "Mind you, Richard, your Marge was a tower of strength and your friend Angus Mahaddie is a gentleman of the first order, and a fine teacher. I enjoyed their company. I'm still no Sir J. Y. Simpson —"

"Who?" Tom asked.

"Scotsman who discovered in 1847 that chloroform was a good anaesthetic," Richard said.

"But I reckon the victims will be a bit safer now. Thanks for the opportunity to learn, Richard — and for the opportunity to get married."

"My Marge says your Deirdre is a lovely girl. To both of you." He raised his glass.

Richard and Tom drank.

"I think you both got out of England in

time," Richard said. "Portsmouth was hit on January 10. Poor old Guildhall got it. Gutted, I'm afraid. Just the outer walls and tower standing."

"Lovely old building. What a shame. I first met your son Tony outside the Guildhall in October when he was —"

"Excuse me, sir."

Fingal turned to see one of the petty officers who handled the ship's mail. "Yes, Ingersoll?"

The man handed Fingal a letter. "It come three weeks ago and my officer saw you come aboard, sir. Reckoned you'd want to see it."

"Thank you." Fingal recognised her handwriting. "Your officer was right. Carry on, Ingersoll."

The man left.

"Deirdre?" Richard asked.

"Yes." Yes, yes, yes.

"Don't mind us," Tom Laverty said. "Read your letter."

As Fingal ripped the envelope open, he seemed to vanish into his own world as the conversations, the clink of glasses, the smell of smoke and beer receded into the background.

The letter, a single sheet of paper, was dated November 9, 1940. She'd written it immediately after their honeymoon.

Darling Fingal, darling husband, he read,

I know it takes nearly three months for a letter to reach where you are going in January and I want to be sure you'll get this the minute you arrive. I know this will be read by a censor, but I don't care. I want to thank you, my dearest, for marrying me, for loving me, for caring for me. I want you to know that no woman could love a man as much as I love you . . .

He had to swallow and blink until he could focus on the words. He'd thought by mailing a letter from Gosport hc'd surprise her, but she'd thought of exactly the same thing, bless her.

I love you for the choice we made the day the deer came and pray that soon I'll have the news we both are wishing for.

I don't want to run on. Hearing the same thing over and over can be numbing. I only want you to know that your Deirdre loves you from the bottom of her soul, always has and always will, misses and aches for you and begs you to take care and one day come home safely to me.

I love you, Fingal, and when you look at the rose in the album, think of me and send your love to me across the miles.

Deirdre

He read it twice, put the letter back in its envelope, and slipped it into his pocket. Deirdre. Deirdre. Wonderful girl. Fingal took a deep breath, cleared his throat and said, "Deirdre sends her love." He could hardly wait for the meal to be over and he could rush back to his cabin to write the loving reply that would go into tomorrow's mail.

43
THE MORE
DIFFICULT THE CHOICE

"Come in, Doctor Stevenson. Thank you for driving down from Belfast after a night on call," O'Reilly said as he ushered the smartly dressed young woman into the hall.

"We get the mornings off after, so I'm free until two o'clock," she said. "Thank you for asking me."

He'd noticed her two weeks ago at the Royal Maternity Hospital. She'd been one of the learners the day Lorna Kearney had had her first amniocentesis. He could not deny that the young doctor's thick auburn hair, cut in a fashionable bob, and bright green eyes had made an impression on him. She had the look of a younger Kitty. Something about the slant of her eyes, the curve of her neck. "Here, here, let me take your coat," he said, feeling flustered. The young woman was remarkably contained.

"Doctor Bradley and Doctor Harley both speak highly of you. I spoke to Doctor Bradley after the last clinic here, and to Doctor

Harley on the phone last week." On her professional credentials alone the job was hers — but only if she seemed someone with whom he and Barry could work.

"Thank you, Doctor O'Reilly."

"That's something we need to get clear. It's the usual medical formality in front of the customers, but among ourselves it's Christian names. I'm not good at standing on ceremony. Please call me Fingal." He'd acquired his preference for informality from one remarkable surgeon commander twenty-five years ago. "You are Nonie, I believe."

She nodded. "Nonie. Nonie Elizabeth. After my grandmothers."

"And I believe you know Barry Laverty?"

O'Reilly had told Barry last Friday that she was coming down today for an interview and had asked his young partner to sit in. O'Reilly had been surprised when Barry had been pretty noncommittal about Nonie Stevenson.

"We were together in the same year," she said. "Barry may have told you that we didn't have much chance to get to know each other. We worked in teams of two, four, or six students, depending on the service we were attached to. We weren't assigned teams but chose each other, and that often meant the women worked together because most of the men preferred all-male company."

Fingal noticed a slight lift of Nonie's chin as she said this. He laughed. "In my class at

Trinity, if the women all worked together, they would have made exactly one team of four. I graduated from medical school in 1936. Shortly after Hippocrates."

She laughed. "Things are different now in some ways, and in others they haven't changed at all. Barry and I only did one rotation together in six years. He seemed like a nice enough lad. There were a lot who didn't think women should be doing medicine. Didn't wrap it up either. Sometimes you had to fight your corner, but Barry was never like that. I'd be happy to work with him, Fingal."

O'Reilly had expected Barry to be more interested in a potential new colleague, but the lad still wasn't at himself, still pining for his Sue. He had moments when he'd not shown enthusiasm about anything.

"Come and meet him again." O'Reilly opened the door to the dining room, where Barry immediately rose from his seat. Surgery would be starting a little late, but the patients would be understanding.

"Morning, Nonie," Barry said with a smile. "Nice to see you."

"And you, Barry," she said. "Do sit down."

"Have a pew," O'Reilly said, offering her a chair opposite Barry. "Coffee?"

"Please. Just a bit of milk."

Barry poured.

O'Reilly deliberately sat half-turned beside her, not wanting her to feel as if she were facing the Spanish Inquisition. "You don't mind if we ask you a few questions, Nonie?"

" 'Course not, and I'll have some of my own." Businesslike. No deference being paid from a junior to a senior as was the ingrained custom in Ulster medical circles. He liked that.

"So, Nonie, you've done two years," Barry asked, "nearly halfway to finishing training as a specialist. Why quit now?"

O'Reilly stole a glance at the lad. He looked relaxed but intent. He certainly hadn't wasted any time.

Nonie opened her mouth to speak, but closed it again quickly. Barry apparently hadn't finished his question.

"I mean, I did a year of obstetrics and gynae, but I soon found out I preferred GP so I came here. But to get through two years and quit? Seems odd to me."

She shrugged. "Pretty simple really. I've always enjoyed GP locums so I have some experience, but midder was my first choice. And I'm afraid," her grin was self-deprecatory, "I discovered I can stand the occasional call out at night, but most nights in a busy obstetrical unit you get practically no sleep at all." She yawned. "Like last night. I have to be realistic. I really need my shut-eye. I'm tired of hospital on-call bedrooms, and canteen grub too. I tried to stick it out, but I couldn't see forty years of broken nights. It was starting to affect my — my health."

"I'm sorry to hear that. Nothing serious, I hope," Barry said.

"No, no," she said, shaking her head. "Nothing serious. Just . . ." She inhaled. "If I get too tired I can get a bit . . . you know . . . a bit Bolshie." She gave a little laugh.

O'Reilly made a mental note of that. "But you wouldn't mind taking some call?" he said. "We'd expect you to cover one in four, and the same at weekends."

"I'm single so I'm perfectly happy to help out with call, and live in if you have room."

"There's a bedroom in the attic."

"Suits me, and GP call is usually a lot less onerous. Frankly, one in four will be a luxury." He heard the depth of feeling in her voice. "I've been used to one in three."

"I'm sure," Barry said, "you could get an even better rota in a big group practice in Belfast. Why Ballybucklebo?"

"I'm a country girl, Barry," she said, "from Rasharkin. I like to think I understand country patients. Jenny told me about the well-woman clinic here. I discussed it with Doctor Harley. He advised me to consider that field. It's even more nine to five. He arranged for me to work in that area. So I'd have a good on-call schedule, be doing something I think I'm good at, with patients I can work with."

"So," said O'Reilly, "you've extra training like Jenny?"

"Not as much, but yes."

She seemed personable enough, O'Reilly thought, wants to come for some of the right reasons.

Barry rose. "Fingal, I don't have any more questions. Thank you, Nonie. I'd better get the surgery going." He headed for the door.

"Nice seeing you, Barry," she said to his back.

Barry closed the door behind him.

O'Reilly sat back in his chair. That hadn't gone quite as he had hoped. And yet she had all the right requirements. He liked her. Perhaps she would bring the lad around. "So," he said, "I think I understand why you want to come. You've been honest. I like that. Finish your coffee," he said, "and let me show you round. We'll talk more while you get the conducted tour."

"Lead on, Doctor."

"Waiting room," he said a minute later, and was greeted by a chorus from inside of "Good morning, Doctors."

"Now there's something you don't see every day," she said, pointing to the mural of roses on the far wall. "I like it."

"A young woman with taste." He warmed to that.

"But how does everyone know I'm a doctor too?"

"Excuse me, miss," Cissie Sloan said, "but this here's Ballybucklebo. That nice Doctor Bradley telt Aggie Arbuthnot, her with the six toes, that Doctor O'Reilly was going til get a new lady assistant. Aggie telt Jeannie Jingles, and Jeannie telt Flo Bishop, and Flo . . ."

"All right, Cissie. Thank you," O'Reilly said. "We get the message." He turned to Nonie. "News travels here."

"It's like Rasharkin. Telegraph, telephone, television, or tell, I believe you said, Aggie Arbuthnot?"

"You're dead on, Doctor," said Cissie. She giggled and everybody else joined in.

"Now settle down," O'Reilly said, noting that Nonie was quick off the mark and clearly had a sense of humour. "Doctor Laverty won't be long."

He led Nonie along the hall, knocked on the surgery door, and heard Barry's "Come in."

O'Reilly said, "Hello, Irene. I hope you don't mind —"

"Hello, Doctor O'Reilly, sir, and hello, Doctor Stevenson." Irene Beggs was sitting on one chair while Barry examined her newborn son. The fibroid that had complicated her pregnancy had had no effect on the child. Little Eric was thriving.

"Nice for til see you again. And thanks for looking after me at the RMH."

"I delivered Mrs. Beggs," the young doctor said, "two weeks ago. How's the bairn?"

"Wee Eric's doing rightly, so he is. Me and Davy's tickled pink."

"Great," said Nonie.

"Och," O'Reilly said, "a baby brings its own welcome. Now, I'm sure Doctor Laverty would like to get on, so we'll be off."

"The surgery's well set up," Nonie said once they were in the hall.

"It is."

"I could certainly run a clinic there, but it badly needs a new examining couch."

In his mind's eye, O'Reilly pictured the battered couch. How long had it had that tuft of stuffing sticking out from the top left corner? "We could probably stretch to that. I inherited it from Doctor Flanagan, who'd been in practice here since before the war," said O'Reilly. He was beginning to wonder who was interviewing whom. On the other hand, she had a point.

He and Nonie left the surgery, only to meet Lars coming downstairs.

"Morning, Finn."

O'Reilly made the introductions. Lars had arrived last night. Tonight he, O'Reilly, and Kitty would be having a get-to-know-you dinner with the marquis, and tomorrow Lars would begin working on the legal aspects of the marquis's estate planning.

"Don't let me interrupt, Finn," he said.

"I'm nipping up to Belfast."

"Drive carefully," O'Reilly said as they headed along the corridor.

"This," he said, as they entered the big warm kitchen with its wonderful cooking smells, "this is the nerve centre, and this is Mrs. Kinky Auchinleck, the brains of the outfit, and that," he pointed, "is Arthur Guinness, the sleepiest lummox in all Ulster."

"What a lovely dog," the young woman said, bending to pat Arthur's head. "My father runs Labradors too. Wonderful breed." That put up her stock with O'Reilly. "Kinky, meet Doctor Nonie Stevenson, who may be coming to take over from Jenny."

"I do be very pleased to meet you, so, Doctor."

"Mrs. Auchinleck."

"The clinic may not be your cup of tea, but I warn you, Nonie, tasting one of Kinky's meals will keep you coming back for the rest of your life." He laughed. "It's definitely not canteen grub."

"Will you run away on, Doctor O'Reilly, sir, and not tease a poor Corkwoman? I have an orange sponge in the oven that needs my attention, so. If you'll go into the dining room, sir. I need to hoover the upstairs lounge and I don't want you underfoot. I'll bring you both coffee and a slice of the new cake in a shmall-little minute."

"Don't say you've already had coffee,"

O'Reilly said. "No one should miss out on Kinky's sponge cakes."

Nonie laughed and said, "I'm easy to convince."

As they returned to the dining room, he said, "I assume you are seriously interested in the position. Taking over from Jenny, running the well-woman clinic, helping out with call, taking the occasional surgery?"

"I am," she said. "Doctor Harley and Jenny have already explained the way the clinic runs. Terms of service. Salary. I've learnt all the techniques I'll need."

O'Reilly pulled out a chair. "Shoo, Lady Macbeth." The little cat sprang to the floor and promptly made herself comfortable on another chair. "Have a pew," O'Reilly said. He waited until Nonie was seated and took a chair opposite. "But you don't like working nights?"

She inhaled deeply.

Was she going to bridle? He didn't give her a chance. "Not everybody's a night owl. Brave of you to face it and confess rather than get stuck doing a job you're not cut out for."

She exhaled. "Thank you."

"And it sounds as if your training fits the bill." What he'd seen, he liked, particularly her easy way with Cissie Sloan, and it was imperative to fill Jenny's position. If Barry had had severe reservations, Fingal was sure he'd not have kept them to himself. "I must discuss this with Barry," O'Reilly said, but was happy enough with the prospect of hiring her. "I'll have to wait until the surgery's over, and it's already running late, but can I reach you by phone in RMH after lunch?"

"Call the switchboard. They'll page me."

"If we do offer you the job, it'll be the usual three months' notice of termination by either side?"

"I was going to ask about that, but three months is fine, and I hope it won't be invoked by either side."

"When could you start?"

"I know Jenny would like to get away as soon as possible, so Monday, January the second would be fine," she said. "I'm seeing the new year in with Mum and Dad and my big brother and his wife at the family home in Rasharkin."

No havering. Quick, clean decision. Good. "I'll phone you after lunch."

"I appreciate that."

"That's settled," he said.

"There is one thing," she said. "Charlie Whitfield knew I was coming down. He asked me to tell you that your patient Lorna Kearney was delivered on Friday. The baby had a bit of jaundice, but is doing well. You'll get a letter with all the details. They are expecting to discharge mother and baby on Thursday, so he asks could you make a home visit next Friday? Check up on it?"

O'Reilly didn't like the "it," but understood that hospital specialists, even trainees, grew to be impersonal about their patients. "It'll be a pleasure," he said. "She's Barry's patient so we'll probably drop in together."

Nonie smiled. "Her husband visited her and the baby the next day. Brought Lorna flowers and the wee one a New Testament."

"We're early readers in County Down," O'Reilly said, and they both laughed.

The aroma of coffee and freshly baked orange cake preceded Kinky into the dining room. She set cups before the doctors, and the sliced cake.

"Kinky, Doctor Stevenson may be joining us," O'Reilly said.

"And you'll be as welcome as spring flowers if you do, so," Kinky said, beaming and pouring coffee. "And do you take milk or sugar?"

"Milk, please."

Kinky handed over the cup. "It's hot, and please help yourself to a slice of cake. Now I must run."

"You were right about Mrs. Auchinleck's baking, Fingal. Delicious."

"I warned you," he said. "Now enjoy it." He snaffled a second piece of cake as the two lapsed into a comfortable silence and he tried to picture Doctor Nonie Stevenson around the Number One dining table.

Well trained? Yes. Sense of humour? Yes.

Makes quick decisions? Yes. Approves of rose murals and Labrador dogs? Definitely yes. Hmmm. Doesn't like night call? Gets Bolshie when tired? Barry not overly enthusiastic? Not so good. They'd need to discuss her, but as O'Reilly contemplated another half piece of Kinky's orange sponge, the balance tipped in Nonie Stevenson's favour.

"So. What do you reckon, Barry?" O'Reilly asked from where he sat at the head of the dining table. Surgery was over. "I think she's well trained. Could be a bit thorny."

"I did notice her 'And I'll have questions of my own.' "

"Well, she's honest. Can we work with her? She'd been on call last night and she seemed fine." O'Reilly had already decided he could.

Barry frowned. "I never saw it when we were students, but she had a bit of a reputation of being difficult to get along with, particularly when it came to swapping on-call nights, and you know how important that is for us if something personal comes up."

"Why didn't you say so sooner?"

"Didn't want to give a dog a bad name before you'd had a chance to make your own impressions. And honestly, with four of us, even if she doesn't want to change a night, one of the other two will."

O'Reilly frowned. "We have the three-month clause." He pursed his lips. "Right," he said. "Let's give her a try, shall we? She can start in January."

"Okay by me," Barry said, "and Jenny will be pleased. I'll miss her."

"Me too." O'Reilly rose. "I'll call Nonie right now." He laughed. "And don't let my lunch get cold. I've to phone the switchboard at RMH and you know how long that can take." He was still chuckling as he dialled the number.

"Thank you, Thompson. Please tell Cook we'll dine in half an hour." Now that Thompson had served drinks, the marquis dismissed his valet/butler, a man who had been with O'Reilly on *Warspite* before taking service here. "Is everyone's drink all right?"

There was a chorus of assent from the other four people, Kitty, O'Reilly, Lars, and Myrna Ferguson, née MacNeill, the marquis's widowed sister, all sitting in high wing-backed armchairs around a log fire. One of his lordship's Irish setters lay in front of the grate. Above the mantel hung a portrait of a much younger Captain Lord John MacNeill, smart in his Irish Guards uniform, standing beside his late wife, Lady Laura. It was a decent portrait but it didn't capture the striking woman O'Reilly remembered meeting before a Boxing Day fox hunt just before the war. She'd been gracious and full of life and the marquis had been gutted when she died.

Two adjoining walls were floor-to-ceiling bookshelves stuffed with shelf upon shelf of tomes. Each sat behind a moveable ladder with wheels on a rail above.

"Those are dangerous-looking spears," Kitty said, inclining her head to a display hung on another wall.

"The spears are called assegais and those clubs beside them knobkerries. In African tribal warfare, the assegais were probably the equivalent of the longbow at Crecy and Agincourt. They and that zebra hide shield have hung above that desk," the marquis said, "since great-grand-Father fought in the Zulu war of 1879 at Ishandlwana. He brought the weapons back as souvenirs. Regrettably he neglected to bring back his right hand."

Kitty shuddered visibly. "Bloodthirsty lot, the Zulus," she said.

"Can hardly blame them," Lars said. "Victoria's empire was pinching their lands."

"A bit like bloody Harold Wilson's Labour Government is trying to pinch ours," Myrna said.

"And that's why I'm so grateful to you, Lars, for coming here to advise us," the marquis said. "I do hope you will be able to sort things out."

"I'll do my very best, my lord," Lars said.

"Please, it's John," the marquis said. "We don't stand on ceremony here. Isn't that right, Fingal?"

615

"It is indeed," O'Reilly said, marvelling as always at the peer's innate ability to put folks at their ease.

"And," the marquis said, indicating neat piles of files and ledgers on his desk, "my sister's been getting things ready for you."

"I have," Myrna said, pointing to the desktop. "Books, accounts. Mister Simon O'Hally, the family solicitor, will be joining us tomorrow afternoon, Mister O'Reilly."

Lars used an index finger to stroke one side of his slim moustache. "Please," he said, "it's Lars, and may I —"

"Good gracious, yes. Myrna, please."

"Thank you," he said.

"Good," she said, and favoured him with the kind of smile O'Reilly had last seen on her face the day she'd taken a right and left of woodcock.

Lars seemed to be on the verge of blushing. O'Reilly's big brother had never been comfortable with women, not since he'd been jilted by a judge's daughter on a Christmas Eve back in Dublin.

"And I must say I'm fully confident," she said, "you will succeed in sorting things out for John and help us hang on to the grouse moor and the shooting on the estate."

"Myrna's a crack shot," O'Reilly said. "Lars used to shoot, but he's with the RSPB now. Does a lot of conservation."

"I don't have much time for that," Myrna

said, "at least not for the idiotic folk that get all bitter and twisted about us shooting preserved game birds. The stocks are never allowed to dwindle. The species aren't at risk. The same people don't flinch from eating a steak. Do you know there's even talk about a movement to ban fox hunting? It'll be our shooting and fishing next, mark my words."

"I believe," Kitty said gently, "you've had a couple of tragedies in the field."

"Well, yes, I have," Myrna said. "Lost my husband of twenty years in a hunting accident seven years ago. Bust my own femur jumping last year."

"I'm very sorry to hear that, Myrna," Lars said.

She shrugged. "Thank you. I'm over it all now, and life must go on. Foxes must be controlled. The Celts were hunting them before the Romans arrived in Britain. And the MacNeills have supported the hunt since before the United Irishmen rose in 1798." She made a guttural noise in her throat and shook her head several times. "There's too many bally self-important busybodies around these days trying to tell other folks what to do."

She paused but was warming to her thesis when Lars spoke. He frowned and stiffened his shoulders. While he could be quite loquacious with those close to him, he tended to be shy with strangers. "I don't mean to contradict you, Mrs. Ferguson" — the return to formality was not lost on Fingal — "but many species do need our help." He was emphatic in stressing the "do."

"Until the war, the wild pale-bellied brent geese population on Strangford was being decimated, almost driven to extinction. They represent the only members of the species on the planet. Our efforts are bringing them back. The nene, the Hawaiian goose, was only saved by the efforts of Peter Scott, Scott of the Antarctic's son, and his people at Slimbridge. I'm sorry, but conservation is needed."

Myrna said, "I can perhaps agree there, but keep your hands off our grouse and pheasants, I —"

Thompson appeared, coughed discreetly, and said, "Dinner will be served in ten minutes, my lord."

"Thank you. Everyone drink up," the marquis said, "and we'll head through to the dining room."

Kitty glanced at O'Reilly and he noticed a nearly imperceptible shake of her head. He'd been a fool to mention Lars's conservation work. He'd forgotten how outspoken Myrna could be. "Tell me, Myrna," Kitty said, "how are things at Queen's these days?"

Good lass, Fingal thought.

Not giving her a chance to answer, Kitty went on, "Myrna is actually Doctor Ferguson, Lars. She has a D.Sc. in physical chemistry and is a reader, one step down from a professor, at Queens."

"I'm impressed," said Lars. "Do you know Professor Henbest?"

"He's organic chemistry," she said, "so only slightly." She hesitated. "And," Myrna said with an impish grin, "such a learnèd woman should have better manners than to get up on her high horse with a guest on a matter which might well be of great interest to her but is trivial in the great scheme of things. Lars, I apologise; indeed I apologise to the company."

Lars did blush now and stumbled over saying, "Doctor Ferg — Myrna — I — there is absolutely no apology necessary. None at all. You are perfectly entitled to your beliefs, and to express them."

"Thank you," she said. "And I think if you can argue your case so clearly when it comes to John's estate taxes, we are going to be in very good hands."

"I agree, Myrna," said the marquis, "but he's going to start that tomorrow. Dinner first. Let's go along, shall we? I think Cook has a treat for us." He rose.

O'Reilly's stomach rumbled as he rose, offered Kitty his arm, and followed.

From behind he heard Myrna. "Now. Fingal has told me that you are an authority on orchids, Lars. You must tell me all about them."

44

COME NOT BETWEEN THE DRAGON AND HIS WRATH

Eight a.m. March 28 1941 At sea, somewhere near Crete. The cruiser HMS *Orion* has reported contact with the Italian fleet to the north.

Fingal put down his pen and sat back in his chair. This tiny cabin on the main deck was now a familiar place again, and keeping a record of the war was once again a routine. He knew there was every prospect of a naval battle today, and it would be a battle between two full fleets, with their flagships — Cunningham's *Warspite* and Admiral Iachino's *Vittorio Veneto* — fully engaged. Fingal hoped he would be able to master the anticipatory fear he now was feeling deep in the pit of his stomach. He'd lived through battles before; he would again. He looked at the picture of Deirdre by his bed, glad she was far away and had no idea what might be about to happen.

The first moves had been made yesterday when intelligence reported an Italian fleet at sea commanded by Iachino on the brand-new, thirty-knot battleship.

Admiral A. B. Cunningham, A.B.C. to his men, had gone ashore in Alex, ostensibly to play golf and stay overnight, a fact that would be duly noted by the Japanese consul. Since the signing of the Tripartite Pact between Germany, Italy, and Japan last September, it had become an open secret that the man provided intelligence about ship movements to his country's European allies. Based on his report, the Italians would assume the British ships would be staying in harbour, because Cunningham always accompanied *Warspite* when she sailed.

But Cunningham, true to his name, had slipped back on board after dark, and the battleship had led the fleet from Alexandria last night, March 27th, in the late hours. The plan was a good one, but on her way out the great ship had sucked mud into her condensers. Fleet Engineer Officer Captain B. J. H. Wilkinson and his engine room artificers and stokers had worked frantically four decks below where Fingal sat to make the repairs. But all last night and until noon today, she still could manage only twenty knots. The two other battleships, HMS *Valiant* and HMS *Barham*, and the aircraft carrier HMS *Formidable*, and their escorting vessels all had to conform to *Warspite*'s slower pace. Yet speed was of the essence if an interception with the

Italians was to be made.

Today, March 28th, four six-inch gun cruisers — three British and one Australian — commanded by Admiral Pridham-Wippell, along with their destroyers, had sailed from Greek waters and were south of Crete near the island of Gavdos. Here they had sighted the Italian vanguard to the north.

Admiral Iachino's eight-inch gun cruisers outgunned the British ships, so the Empire cruiser flotilla immediately notified Cunningham and steamed south, hoping to draw the Italians down on the approaching British battleships where, glory be, the repairs had now been effected and *Warspite* could manage twenty-four knots again. The Italians followed Pridham-Wippell and shelled him at long range but scored no hits.

Cunningham's big ships were still ninety miles away.

It would be several hours before the Italians would be in range of *Warspite*'s batteries, but her medical department was at readiness. Richard Wilcoxson had everything set up in the two medical distribution stations so his staff would be ready when action stations were sounded. But for the moment, he was releasing members of his teams in four-hour shifts so they could eat and sleep.

Fingal was not due back for another two hours and had come to his cabin from breakfast in the mess to change his shirt and note the night and day's developments so far in his diary. He was resolved to do his best to keep track of what transpired. He had started the diary so he could tell Deirdre about his doings while they had been apart. Since he'd left *Warspite* last year he'd made no more entries except for a few notes about the journey home on the troopship. As long as he and Deirdre had been together, there was no need to keep a record. Now they were apart, starting the diary again seemed to bring her closer. He pictured them, snug in the upstairs lounge of the house in Ballybucklebo, a peat fire in the grate. He sighed. He was so far from her, far from the pastoral peace of Fareham and the New Forest, far from the Northern Ireland village he had called home before the war. In hours his ship might be embroiled in a fight to the finish with her fifteen-inch rifles roaring and the enemy blazing back. Fingal O'Reilly was well and truly back at war.

He flipped back to the entries he'd made since his return to Alexandria, and to those he had filled in since the beginning of the year.

Jan 1. British attack Italians in Libya as Operation Compass proceeds to drive them out of Egypt.

Jan 2. *Warspite* shells Libyan port of Bardia. Hit by bomb on anchor. Little real damage.

Rest of Jan. *Warspite* shells Libyan ports and escorting convoys. Greeks beat Italians in land actions in Greece and Albania.

Feb 5. Italians defeated by British at Beda Fomm on Gulf of Sirte. Twenty thousand Italians surrender while I am in the Blenheim flying over Africa.

Feb 6. Scary engine fire on Blenheim on way from Takoradi.

Feb 7. I rejoin *Warspite* and old friends.

Feb 14. Afrika Korps under Rommel arrives in Africa.

Feb 22. Seven-a-side rugby football team from *Warspite* (including me) beaten by more than sixty to nil by New Zealanders (we stopped count). Kiwis all ex-internationals.

That entry would make her laugh, he thought.

March 5. British troops sent from Africa to Greece in support of Greeks fighting the invading Italians.

March 22. Leading Seaman Alf Henson, gunnery course completed, rejoins Warspite after a long sea passage from Liverpool. He has been promoted to gun captain of the number-four gun of the starboard six-inch battery.

March 25. Bulgaria and Yugoslavia now part of Axis.

March 26. Italian one-man explosive motorboats attack and cripple HMS *York* in Suda Bay (Crete). Our only eight-inch cruiser. I have to admire the courage of the boats' crews and even if they are the enemy, I am relieved that all six survived.

Another Tannoy announcement seeped through the door of his cabin. "The Italian cruisers have reversed course to the north and are en route to rejoin their battleship. They are possibly heading for home. Admiral Pridham-Wippell's cruiser group is shadowing. We are continuing in pursuit."

So perhaps there wouldn't be a fight after all. He'd not be sorry. "What next?" Fingal wondered aloud. He knew the Tannoy would keep him posted, and he still had free time. He opened a desk drawer, took out the photo album Deirdre had given him at Christmas, admired the wedding photos, the rose now dry and forlorn, then took out a letter, written on the day she'd got home to Belfast in January. The missive had made its weary way round Cape Horn and finally been delivered two days ago.

Darling Fingal,
How sweet of you to write a letter so it would be waiting for me when I got back to the nurses' home.

By now she should have the ones he'd posted in Takoradi too.

I was feeling lonely and reading your lines comforted me. I shouldn't tell you, but I had a wee weep, but I soon cheered up. Your words telling me how much you love me warmed me. And before I say any more, dearest, I love you too . . .

He skipped over her white lies about her journey from Southampton not being too bad — wartime travel was almost always an ordeal — her cheerful gossip about a phone call to Ma, her remarks on the weather, her room, and the awful food in the nurses' home.

I'm going to unpack now and have a nice hot bath before I get an early night. Good thing there's lots of water in Northern Ireland and no rationing. I'll pop into bed and think of our bed in Alverstoke and of being held in the strong arms of the gentlest man in the world. I'll look at his photo on my bedside table and make my snow scene into a blizzard — it's there to remind me of our lovely first Christmas. And I'll think of how you loved me and I loved you and I'll fall asleep and dream of our love and will the days to pass until we can be together again.

Please take care. I love you so much, darling,

Deirdre

He wondered why he'd bothered to look at it again. After so many readings he knew the words by heart.

Fingal, happily smoking his Christmas pipe with its silver lid, felt the wind on his face, the pitch and roll of the deck underfoot. He had to strain to hear the Tannoy's message over the thundering of the screws and the roar of the turbines. "Seventeen hundred hours. After several air strikes from land-based Blenheim bombers and *Formidable*'s air attack group, the Italian ships are retreating at reduced speed. *Vittorio Veneto* has been hit by a torpedo from an Albacore. One Albacore was lost. Our cruiser division is following and maintaining contact."

He noticed that the tompions had been removed from the muzzles of the guns of X and Y turrets. They and their fellows in A and B were ready for their deadly business. Above everything, the ship's thick funnel smoke and that of her consorts streamed astern, vandals' dirty smears on an otherwise perfect azure sky.

"Pity we have to slow down to recover one of our reconnaissance planes," said Richard, as he kept Fingal company on the starboard side of the quarterdeck. "I'm sure A.B.C. hopes to get in among the Eyeties, and he won't be too pleased, but this is going to be something to watch. It's never been done before with our ship still steaming ahead. We usually heave to." A seaplane recovery crane stuck out from abaft the funnel trunking, not far ahead of where they stood watching. Its pickup hook dangled freely.

On the starboard bow, a single Walrus, one of the battleship's spotters, was taxiing at a parallel course on the calm water ahead. It and *Warspite*'s other observation plane had been catapulted off earlier in the day. This one had just returned.

Warspite's bows cleaved the sea.

"Are they seriously going to try hooking onto the recovery ring on the aircraft and hoist it inboard while we're under way?" Fingal asked.

"They are. And they'd better get it right the first time," Richard said. "Scuttlebutt has it that Admiral Cunningham's fit to be tied about having to reduce speed to eighteen knots. You know we catapulted two spotters earlier. They can't land on aircraft carriers, but they can land on land or sea. They were both supposed to fly to Crete, but for some reason this one has come back. We might need to launch it again, so it's got to be recovered. I reckon the pilot'll take a right chewing out."

Warspite's condenser repair this morning meant the ship was now up to her full twenty-four knots. Since then, she, *Valiant, Barham,* and their escorts had strained to catch up with the *Vittorio Veneto.* The torpedo had done its job and the Italian battlewagon had only been able to make fifteen knots, half her regular speed. But that success had cost the lives of the plane's three-man crew. Nothing would persuade Fingal that Horace's famous *Dulce et decorum est pro patria mori* was a truth. It is lovely and honourable to die for your country? Rubbish. And as far as he knew, the Roman poet had not died in battle himself.

Fingal stared down at the amphibious plane's telegraphist/air gunner, a petty officer named Pacey. The man was balancing precariously above his cockpit. "Rather him than me. I had enough of open-water acrobatics in a breeches buoy trying to get on to *Touareg* last year."

Richard smiled and nodded. *Warspite* had

overtaken the little aircraft, and in moments her bow wave would toss it around like a cork. The Walrus's pilot altered course to starboard so his floats were stern to the waves, which passed under without capsizing the small plane. Moments later, the Walrus's aircrewman succeeded in hooking on to the crane.

Fingal, who hadn't realised he was holding his breath, exhaled and yelled, "Bloody well done."

The plane, swinging like a pendulum, was winched on board and respotted on its catapult. Soon it would be refuelled and ready to launch again.

Richard was applauding as the notes of the turbines and propellers bellowed their renewed challenges, the deck beneath Fingal's feet jerked forward, and the great battlewagon raced up to her top speed. The pursuit was still on.

The Tannoy squawked to life. "Twenty-two twentyhours. All sick bay personnel report to your action stations. All sick bay personnel . . ." Bloody hell. Fingal had just got to his cabin after four hours on watch. He'd been looking forward to a few hours of sleep after a restless shift sitting in the medical distribution station twiddling his thumbs, cracking feeble jokes with the SBAs, rechecking that everything was set up correctly, munching on corned beef sandwiches and sipping weak cocoa, listening to the Tannoy, chatting with Richard, and trying to follow the events as they unfolded.

He closed his cabin door and started heading back the way he'd just come: toward the bow along the main deck, up a level for a short walk along the upper deck, then down two levels to the middle deck. Much had happened in the outside world in the past few hours and he'd seen none of it.

Warspite had successfully relaunched the Walrus, and the spotter had reported that *Vittorio Veneto* and several eight-inch cruisers were forty-five miles ahead, making fifteen knots to the northwest. Cunningham, based on the plane's intelligence, had ordered another aerial attack to try to slow the Italians down more.

"Bloody good thing they recovered the spotter and could find out where they were," Fingal had said. "We might still catch up." The excitement of the chase was getting into his blood.

At 7:25 P.M., a cruiser believed to be the *Pola* had been hit and was reported as being dead in the water.

Richard's smile had been grim as they'd listened to the Tannoy announcement. "I don't give much for her chances once our big boys catch up with her."

And now Fingal was on his way back to the

for'ard medical distribution station. Things were going to start hotting up.

As he went down one companionway, the tinny voice continued to narrate. "Twenty-two twenty-three hours. *Orion*'s radar has picked up a single ship six miles from her own position. Our position is ten miles west of Crete, ten miles southwest of Greece's Cape Matapan. Our radar has detected two large cruisers and a smaller one crossing our bow. Range thirty-eight hundred yards."

Where the hell had they come from? Fingal wondered. Had Admiral Iachino detached cruisers or destroyers to aid the stricken *Pola*? The Italian must have been unaware he was being pursued. British intelligence knew the Italian ships had no radar. So now a detachment of the Italian fleet and Cunningham's ships were almost on top of each other.

A full-fledged battle was no longer just a possibility, it was a reality. And things were going to get hectic. He knew he'd be safe four decks down — once he got there. He'd be crossing open deck in a few minutes. At least after his time in Haslar he no longer doubted his anaesthetic skills, and there were sure to be casualties. Lots of casualties, the poor divils.

He was aware of the ship heeling to starboard. The admiral must be turning his line of battle so the great ships' port broadsides were presented to the enemy. Whatever Italian vessels were out there in the pitch-black night would be facing the combined firepower of twenty-four fifteen-inch rifles, each shell weighing a ton, and Lord alone knew how many six-inchers would be firing. Henson would be disappointed. His gun, on the starboard side, might not see any action.

Fingal had seen *Warspite*'s great guns in action in daytime. What would they look like at night? There was only one way to find out. A quick detour before he reported to his post would satisfy his curiosity. He ran up the nearest companionway to the forecastle deck and found he was standing behind the shield of one of the antiaircraft guns. Its crew all wore steel helmets and asbestos antiflash gear. "Hello, Doc. Come to see the fun?" said one of the gun's crew, a man for whom Fingal had lanced a boil two weeks ago.

"Hello, Michelson. What's going on here?" Fingal shuddered with the sudden cold. The night wind of their passage was bitter and he had no duffle coat. He huddled in behind the gun shield.

Searchlight beams erupted from one, then several more British destroyers. Across the water he could see three warships, two large, one smaller, lit up like actors at centre stage. The enemy was steering a parallel but reciprocal course.

"Our officer reckons the Eyetie admiral doesn't know our lot's out here. Poor buggers don't have any radar. He's sent those ships to help out that one that's dead in the water. On our side we're in line astern and *Warspite*'s leading *Valiant* and *Barham*. *Furious*'s been told to bugger off and not risk getting shot at." He pointed out to sea at the enemy ships. "Over there, the silly sods have all their guns trained fore and aft. It's point-blank for our guns. We've got 'em with their pants down this time. It's going to get noisy, sir. We fire broadsides in night actions. Fleet Gunnery Officer Barnard'll give the order to shoot once the big guns are on target."

Movement caught Fingal's eye and he looked ahead. The rifles on A and B turrets were swinging outboard. Death riding smoothly on the well-oiled mechanisms. Fingal could hear voices coming from inside a gunhouse saying, "Ready." Michelson gave Fingal a playful salute, said, "Any minute now, sir," and clapped his gauntleted hands over his ears.

Fingal knew he should leave, but the scene was mesmerizing. The huge guns, the men in their antiflash gear, the night lit up by myriad blazing searchlights.

The *ting, ting, ting* of the firing bells was followed instantly by the blasts from all eight of *Warspite*'s great guns.

His world dissolved into a maëlstrom of deafening basso sound, chest-crushing concussion, blinding light as tongues of dragons' breath seared the air and clouds of mahogany cordite smoke blended with the darkest corners of the devilish night. *Warspite,* all thirty-two thousand tons of her, heeled to starboard.

And from astern *Valiant* and *Barham* were lit up for brilliant seconds in the blaze of their big guns.

All the while, the six-inchers raved away, lethal terriers barking and snarling at the Italian destroyers which were now beginning to appear. And as the huge barrels ran in onto the recoil mechanism, returned to position, and once more hurled their shells, Fingal saw what the missiles were doing. Shells burst brilliantly on the enemy ships and whole turrets and masses of debris were hurled high into the air to splash back into the uncaring pitch-dark sea. In minutes, the three enemy ships were glowing masses, burning from stem to stern.

"Stop it. Please stop it," he whispered. Those ships were defeated. Italians were dying, drowning, being blown to fragments, roasted alive — the worst fate of all — or horribly maimed. It didn't matter that they were the enemy. They were young men. He shook his fist at the B turret barrels. "Stop it," he yelled. But as a tornado doesn't heed a mere human's plea to go away, the great gun ignored him and went on belching its message of hellfire.

To Fingal it seemed an eternity, but only ten minutes after the firing began, the order "Check, check, check," was given. The main act of the Battle of Cape Matapan was over.

Fingal was chilled to the marrow. His ears whistled and rang. He was heartsore from the carnage he'd witnessed, and turning on his heel, headed for his station. There would be Italian survivors. During battles the big ships become floating hospitals for the injured — of both sides — just as *Warspite* had done at Narvik last April.

He descended the last companionway and rubbed his hands over his face, trying to dispel what he'd seen, yet hoping what he'd just witnessed might somehow help to shorten the war. May I and all those like me, he thought as he pulled open the heavy metal door, go home sooner to our loved ones. But what a waste. What a hideous awful waste.

45
IT IS A WISE FATHER THAT KNOWS HIS OWN CHILD

"Right," said O'Reilly, bounding to his feet from a wooden chair as Barry appeared at the back door of the kitchen. "All done for the day?"

Barry slammed the door, cutting off a chilly blast from outside. He nodded and started to unbutton his overcoat. "Mother told me there'd be days like this. If I have to visit one more case of flu I'll — I'll spit. But yes, I'm done." He stopped unbuttoning. "Fingal, why are you wearing your coat and gloves? It's hot as hell in here with the range roaring away."

"I know, but I've been waiting for you. Keep your coat on," O'Reilly said, "I need your help. Come on."

"Help with what?"

"I'll explain in the car," O'Reilly said, "but it's not flu, I promise."

"Bloody hell," Barry muttered sotto voce, but said, "all right."

The stiff northerly breeze was raw on

O'Reilly's cheeks as they crossed the back garden, a back garden quite devoid of Arthur, who was in the lounge, snug in front of the fire where he'd been all week during the cold snap.

"Hop in." O'Reilly let himself into the Rover.

Barry did, and like a grand prix racing competitor O'Reilly took off as if from a Le Mans start.

"Lord, Fingal, where are we going? Is someone bleeding? What's the rush?" Barry clung to the edges of his seat. "The roads are pretty icy, you know."

"I'm used to them," O'Reilly said as the back of the car slewed sideways and he straightened the Rover up. "You remember that Lorna Kearney was being discharged yesterday?"

"Yes. Is she okay?"

"She's fine and so is the baby. Here." He handed Barry a letter. "I got it this morning and I haven't had a chance to get you to explain it to me fully. You read it aloud and I'll try to tell you what it means to see if I've understood what I think I've learned. You can correct me if I'm wrong. I reckon I'm understanding this Rhesus business a lot better now. Fair enough?"

"You hauled me away from a warm kitchen and a chance to put my feet up after a very long afternoon of visiting coughing, feverish, tetchy customers, to explain a letter to you?" Barry shook his head.

"Sorry about that, but I'm in a hurry."

"Why? There's nothing urgent about a neonatal checkup."

"Ah," said O'Reilly with a grin, "but if we get it done quick we'll have time to nip into the Duck before Kitty gets home."

"Doctor O'Reilly," Barry said past pursed lips, "sometimes I despair."

O'Reilly ignored the lad's irritation and reached out to tap the letter in his lap. "Skip the 'Dear Doctor O'Reilly' stuff and all the things we already know like her last period and her blood pressure. Just stick to the Rhesus stuff."

"I want it known that I'm doing this under protest." Barry began to read the report, " 'The results of the patient's first amniocentesis showed that the optical density level was in the moderate zone on the prediction chart. It was decided to wait for two more weeks —' "

"I remember that."

" 'A second uncomplicated amniocentesis was carried out on the morning of Wednesday December the seventh when the pregnancy was thirty-five weeks and five days. Results were received that day. The optical density of the fluid was reported as being point zero six —' "

"So Doctor Whitfield plotted that on the

prediction chart and determined the severity?"

"Right. It showed that the level was almost in the severe zone."

"She was nearly thirty-six weeks by then. Safer to deliver the baby than let the isoimmunisation get any worse. I'd try to get labour started."

"And you'd be right again, that's what they did, and — Jesus Murphy, Fingal, look out."

O'Reilly had not quite judged his line into the crown of the hairpin bend where a lane led to the Donnellys' cottage. This time, despite his best efforts, the car skidded sideways and just missed hitting the road embankment before he was able to get it back on course. "Nothing to worry about," he said. "Go on."

"Nothing to worry about? I thought I was going to be having a chat with Saint Peter. Slow down."

O'Reilly said nothing.

Barry's voice trembled as he read, " 'Labour was induced that afternoon by rupturing the membranes and giving intravenous oxytocin to stimulate uterine contractions. The normal delivery of a healthy female infant occurred at four sixteen on the morning of December the ninth.' "

"Sounds like a fair while," O'Reilly said, accelerating onto a straight bit of road.

"The baby was clearly not in a hurry —

unlike you," Barry said. "Will you please slow down, Fingal? There's plenty of time to get Lorna and the bairn seen to and get to the Duck."

"Oh, very well." O'Reilly let a few miles an hour bleed off the speedometer. "Happier now?"

"A bit, but I think I'd be happier still if I were driving."

"If you were driving, then how would you read the letter?"

Fingal took a sidelong glance at Barry and saw the boy's lips twitch into the faintest of smiles. "Please carry on, Doctor Laverty."

"Right. 'While induction was initially slow, the onset of the active phase of labour began at two P.M. on the ninth.' "

"That's not so bad then."

"Not bad at all. Perfectly normal for an oxytocin-induced labour." Barry shuddered and said, "Did we just pass five men on skis hauling a sledge?"

"What are you on about?"

"I thought we just passed Scott's last expedition on its way to the South Pole. Lord knows it's cold enough in here. Why isn't the heater on?"

"Um," O'Reilly said, feeling a little chastened. "It's broken."

"Well, get it fixed then." And implied in Barry's tone was "you buck eejit."

O'Reilly was about to snap at Barry when

642

he realised how out of character the young man's irritation was. Sue Nolan would be home in four more days. Maybe Barry's mood would take a turn for the better then. For now he was getting a fool's pardon. "I will, but what else is in the report?"

"It goes on, 'A sample of cord blood was taken at birth and a direct Coombs test —'"

"You've lost me."

"Foetal red cells are mixed with an antibody that will stick to globulins, proteins, on cell surfaces. Anti-rhesus antibody is a globulin. If the baby's red cells stick together, that's proof that they have antibody attached to them. The test was positive, so the baby was affected just as the results of the two amniocenteses had predicted."

"How badly affected?" O'Reilly knew that some wee ones were given exchange transfusions. Their own blood contained the breakdown product of the red cells, bilirubin, which caused severe effects like the neurological disorder *kernicterus.* The neonate's blood was removed, taking the bilirubin with it, and replaced with fresh Rhesus-negative blood, which would not be attacked by any residual anti-Rhesus positive antibodies remaining in the baby's circulation.

Barry managed a weak smile. "Clinically, according to the letter, she was mildly jaundiced but exhibiting no signs of any neurological disorder. The baby's bilirubin measured on the same blood sample was less than three miligrams percent, which is below, and her haemoglobin was fifteen grams per one hundred millilitres, which is above the cutoffs for needing an exchange transfusion. They did put her under phototherapy lights for two days. The lights change the structure of the bilirubin and render it harmless."

O'Reilly decelerated, indicated for a left turn, and pulled onto the lane to the Kearney's farmhouse. "I read about that away back in 1958," he said. "A Doctor Cremer published a paper in the *Lancet.*"

"Actually," Barry said, "the effect of light was first noticed by a nursing sister at a hospital in Essex. She thought that sunlight was good for preemies and noticed that it improved jaundice in affected ones."

"Discovery," O'Reilly said, "favours the prepared mind. And there are no better prepared minds in medicine than good nurses'. Smart young doctors cotton on to that early in their careers." He would have expected Barry to comment on the misphrasing of Louis Pasteur's famous doctrine, or the observation about nurses, but given Barry's mood O'Reilly was not surprised when the lad ignored the remarks and simply said, "And by yesterday the paediatricians were satisfied she would be fit for discharge."

The car jounced and quivered.

"If you keep bouncing over ruts like that,

you can add new springs as well as a new heater to your mechanic's bill," Barry said.

"Nonsense," O'Reilly said. "The Rover company builds cars as tough as Sherman tanks." He parked and sat back. "The hospital folks just want us to make sure baby's being kept warm, is established on breast-feeding, not badly jaundiced, and that Lorna knows to take the babby to the follow-up clinic at RMH next Thursday. Come on then. Let's get the job done."

Reggie Kearney answered the door and ushered them in.

O'Reilly remembered the big living room from when he and the marquis had called in for a hot half-un after their day's snipe shooting in October. He wondered how Lars was getting on sorting out John MacNeill's affairs.

Even though the room was overly warm, O'Reilly moved to stand in front of the fire. He rubbed his hands and said, "Jes . . ." He remembered the Kearneys' devoutness. "Brrrr. It's bitter cold out today. I'm half foundered." Barry was right about having the old Rover car's heater fixed.

"Warm yourselves, Doctors," Lorna said from where she sat in a comfy chair beside the hearth. "Doctor Whitfield told me to expect a visit." A crib on rockers stood beside her chair and Reggie, her husband, stood beside her, one big hand on his wife's shoulder.

Barry, whose nose was losing its blue tinge, moved to stand beside O'Reilly.

"You'll be wanting til see wee Caroline," Reggie said, pointing to the crib.

"First things first," O'Reilly said. "How are you feeling, Lorna?"

"Ah, grand," she said. "Grand altogether. Doctor Sproule give me the complete once-over just before I was discharged, so he did. He said for to tell you as far as he's concerned I was A1 at Lloyds and not to worry because they'll be seeing me next Thursday at the postpartum clinic."

"Fair enough," said O'Reilly. "If the specialists are satisfied we'll forgo examining you. Agreed, Doctor Laverty?"

Barry nodded.

"And Caroline?" O'Reilly asked.

"She's still a wee bit yellow, but they said that was to be expected."

"And how's she feeding?"

"Wee Caroline started breast-feeding six hours after she was born, and took to drinking every four hours like her daddy takes to his Guinness on a Friday night." She laughed.

"I like my pint," Reggie said, and chuckled. "We may be good Presbyterians, but we're not teetotallers."

"Good man-ma-da," O'Reilly said, and thought, I'd go a pint myself. Definitely on the way home.

"The only trouble with four-hour feeds is wee Reggie Junior," Lorna said. "I'm sleepy all the time, and Reggie still has a farm to run, so he has. The wee lad was going til get a bit neglected so he's at his granny's until I get better rested."

"Good idea," said O'Reilly. "And you'll have your feet under you in no time." He turned to Barry. "Doctor Laverty, you've had more recent experience with a lot of newborns than me. Would you do the honours?"

"Of course." Barry stripped off his gloves, shoved them into his overcoat pockets, and said, "Mister Kearney, would you hold Caroline for me, please."

O'Reilly watched as Reggie Kearney, all six feet of him, with shoulders like an ox, bent and, with infinite gentleness, lifted his tiny daughter from her crib. He held her tenderly as Barry began his examination by opening the baby's cardigan and pulling up her nightie. Caroline objected.

"Nothing wrong with her lungs," O'Reilly said with a smile as the little one's screeches filled the room. He simply had to speak more loudly. "Boys-a-dear," he said, "that's a powerful bright cardigan she's got on. Some of your handiwork, Reggie? Fair Isle, is it?"

"Aye," said Reggie with pride in his voice, "it is. Fair Isle's a tricky pattern, but not as tough as all the cable stitches in Arran knits.

Anyroad, Lorna said the doctors wanted the wean to have woolly caps to wear all the time so I knit a clatter of them too."

"The doctors advise that," said O'Reilly, "because little ones can lose a powerful amount of heat through their heads and getting cold is very bad for babies, especially premature ones."

"She'll not get cold in this house," Lorna said, rising, taking two big pieces of turf from a wicker basket and putting them on the fire before returning to her seat.

Barry straightened up. "You can dress her, please, Mister Kearney."

O'Reilly was impressed by the nimbleness of Reggie's fingers despite their looking as clumsy as sausages.

"A tiny bit of icterus, sorry, doctor talk. She's still a wee bit yellow, but only from her belly button up, and none on her palms or soles. That's very good."

O'Reilly agreed. It was a rough rule of thumb used clinically to guess the severity of jaundice, but he and Barry had the reliable backup of the figures in the letter from RMH.

"Give her here, Reggie," Lorna said. She had already unbuttoned her blouse.

Reggie bent and handed over his very vocal new daughter and in moments the room fell silent as she latched onto Lorna's nipple and began to feed.

Madonna and child, O'Reilly thought, and

saw how Reggie was grinning and Barry, so grumpy on the drive out and strictly professional here, was standing, head tilted to one side, with a smile best described as dreamy. Mothers' love had that effect. No wonder the great artists, da Vinci, Michelangelo, Raphael, Caravaggio, Rubens, Dali, had all rendered the subject. The moment seemed suspended in time. The warm room redolent with the earthy smell of turf, the intense concentration of the couple on the tiny child held in her mother's arms. The four adults said nothing for several minutes until the steady ticking of a clock on the mantel reminded O'Reilly of the time.

"Reggie, do you mind the day his lordship and I dropped in?" O'Reilly said quietly.

"After you'd been at the snipe?"

"Aye. He said he'd like to give Caroline a christening present. Can I let him know that she has arrived?"

"Go right ahead, Doctor," Reggie said, and immediately turned to Lorna. "I forgot to mention it to you, love. Clean slipped my mind in all the running back and forth to Belfast and wondering if this little one was going to be okay."

"That's all right, Reggie," she said. "It'll be a great honour. She'll be getting baptised in January, and Doctor O'Reilly, we'd like you and Mrs. O'Reilly and Doctor Laverty and his young lady Miss Nolan to come. We hear she'll be back from France for Christmas."

"We'd be delighted," O'Reilly said. "Just let us know the date. Doctor Laverty?"

"I'll need to discuss it with Sue but I'm very flattered."

O'Reilly said, "Right. I think that's about it. I'll let Miss Haggerty the midwife know you're home, and she'll pop in on Monday. See how you're getting on. We need to be heading back. Come on, Doctor Laverty, and if we don't see you before, have a very merry Christmas."

"And to you, Doctors," Reggie said, holding open the door. "And thanks for helping to see wee Caroline into this world. She had us worried a bit, but youse doctors knew the right specialists and they, with the good Lord's help —"

"Och, say no more," O'Reilly said. "I was lucky to have two young doctors who were right up to date and could advise me." And, he thought, to show me that it *is* important for me and Barry and even old Ronald Fitzpatrick to keep up to date.

"Thanks a million for everything, Doctors. And a safe drive home," Reggie said as he closed the door of the farmhouse and O'Reilly and Barry headed for the Rover.

The two men were quiet as they headed back to Ballybucklebo. The car was still frigid inside, but some of the warmth and scent of the Kearneys' turf fire and the closeness of the Kearney family seemed to have taken the edge off the iciness in the Rover. And O'Reilly, now assured that there was plenty of time for a side trip to the Duck, was driving at a more leisurely pace.

"Thank you, Fingal."

"For what," O'Reilly said nonchalantly, keeping his eyes on the road.

"For putting up with my grouchiness on the way in."

O'Reilly nodded. "Apology accepted." He let it hang to see if Barry wished to explain, although O'Reilly was damn sure he knew the underlying cause.

Barry sighed, shook his head, inhaled, and finally said, "I know it's stupid, Fingal, but I still can't stop worrying about Sue. Since you and I talked about it back in November I've tried to take your advice. I've managed to phone her twice, but you know what getting long-distance calls through to Europe is like. The calls have always been cheerful — she's having a wonderful time — and her letters too, but . . ."

"But you still can't shake the feeling that something's wrong?" O'Reilly could sympathise. He remembered only too well the frustration of wartime long-distance communication, when it could take more than two months to get a letter from home.

"Right. Something just feels wrong. As if

there's something I just can't see. As if I'm peering through some kind of fog."

"And is that feeling coming from Sue, or is it coming from inside you? I remember something my brother Lars quoted to me back in September. 'It's not love, but jealousy that's blind.' "

Barry managed a weak smile. "Jealousy. You're right. I am jealous and it's colouring everything. All of my thoughts and my conversations and letters with Sue. I know I shouldn't be, but I'm still worried about Sue and that blasted Frenchman, Hamou. He took her to Aix-en-Provence last weekend to see the cathedral and they had lunch in some famous brasserie, the Trois Garçons or the Deux Garçons."

"I'm no world's authority on conducting illicit affairs, believe me," O'Reilly said, "but do you suppose if, and perish the thought, Sue was being unfaithful, she'd keep telling you about this Hamou?"

"Nooo. But," another sigh, "then why is she going on about him? Does it not occur to her that I might be worried? Does she take my love for granted so much that she doesn't realize how this comes across? I don't know, but seeing Lorna and her baby and Reggie grinning from ear to ear . . . Bloody hell, Fingal, I'm almost twenty-seven. I've had bad luck with girls, but one day, one day soon, I'd like to settle down. We're supposed to be getting married in March when Sue comes home for good. I'd like to start a family. I'm worried, Fingal, and I get cross with myself. I know I should trust her. I know we're engaged but," he shrugged, pursed his lips, "I'm terrified about what she's going to say when she gets here."

"I understand." O'Reilly felt a tiny pang still. "I never did," he said quietly, "never did have a family." Barry didn't need to know why, but maybe one day O'Reilly would tell the lad. "And Kitty and I are just a bit over the hill for childbearing." He laughed.

Barry managed a smile. "I dunno, you're not Methuselah yet, and four years ago Charlie Chaplin was a daddy at seventy-three, and Pablo Picasso managed it at sixty-eight."

O'Reilly decided to try to keep the mood light. He changed down and passed an exhaust-belching Bedford lorry that had chicken coops piled up in its back. "I think," he said, "given Kitty is a tad — em — mature too you might have to invoke Abraham as well."

"Abraham?"

" 'And Abraham fell upon his face and laughed and said, shall Sarah that is ninety years old bear —' "

"Genesis, I believe," Barry said, and laughed.

"Nice to have the old Barry back," O'Reilly said with a smile, "but, frankly if I'd had a

653

son as impertinent as you were before we got to the Kearneys' . . ." And in truth, Barry was the next best thing to having a son of O'Reilly's own.

"What would you do . . . Dad?"

O'Reilly braked outside the Duck and parked the car. "What would I do?" He lowered his voice and nodded rapidly several times. "What would I do? I'd tell him I hear his pain, his worries, that I do understand. I'd tell him to hang on, that she'll be here in Ulster in four days, I'd tell him that the five-pound bet is still open because I know I'd win. I just know." He grasped Barry's upper arm, squeezed and let it go before dismounting and, as Barry appeared on the other side of the car, said, "And I'd tell him, the first pint's on him and maybe the second." O'Reilly realised that there was prickling behind his eyelids and it nearly got worse when Barry looked O'Reilly straight in the eye across the frost-rimed roof of the car and said levelly, "I think, Fingal Flahertie O'Reilly, you'd have made a wonderful father." Then he grinned. "But you'd have had to get used to buying the first round, and I think tonight's as good a time as any to start learning."

46
TO CHANGE WHAT WE CAN

Gulls wheeled and dipped over the small boat–busy waters and the relentless sun shone on Alexandria's palm trees, minarets, domes, houses, bazaars, souks, brothels, narrow lanes, and the broad, ever-bustling Corniche. It looked so peaceful — and would be until the enemy mounted another air raid.

"This report on Matapan makes impressive reading," said Tom Laverty. "Sorry it's taken me more than a month to get it to you, Fingal, but there's been one or two little matters to occupy us."

"Like the Germans coming to the support of the Eyeties in Greece and Rommel's lot running amok in Libya," said Fingal. "Tobruk under siege. Never a dull moment."

The two men were sitting in comfortable chairs in the navigating officer's cabin high up on the bridge structure. By late April, temperatures in Alex were in the mid-seventies and already both men's clean white shirts were damp in patches. The view from the window was out over the big guns where their crews were carrying out maintenance work. Beneath the barrels of A guns, sailors swabbed the foredeck stretching past the breakwater. The huge chains that kept *Warspite* moored started from their cable lockers, ran to the bows, and down into the waters where her anchors, clawing the mud and seashells, held the great ship in Alexandria's harbour.

"You miss most of the fun deep in the ship when we're at action stations," Tom said. "I can see why you need help keeping your war diary up to date. It can get pretty hairy up here; convoy runs to Malta, Luftwaffe units now based in Greece and Libya bombing the bejasus out of us, and us with bugger all air support. We chased Italian convoys and shelled Tripoli a couple of days ago." Tom shrugged then sighed. "You won't know, but A.B.C.'s getting worried. He doesn't think we should have weakened the desert forces by sending troops to Greece. He told us this morning that the situation's so bad now that we've no hope of beating the Germans there, and that the navy's going to have to try to get fifty-five thousand of our men from the mainland to Crete. My guess is we'll be doing another bloody Dunkirk from that island too before long." He tried to force a smile, but Fingal could tell that Tom was concerned.

Fingal said, "We should heed what they say.

'If you can't take a joke . . .' "

" 'You shouldn't have joined.' "

They both laughed, but it was wry laughter.

"I tell you," said Tom, "I'm not sorry to be back in Alex. Maybe get a chance for a decent meal in the Cecil Hotel. And I could do with a couple of Blue Light Ales and a bit of peace and quiet."

"Any word from Ulster?" Fingal glanced at a framed photo of a pretty woman carrying a six-month-old baby.

"Carol's well and young Barry's going from strength to strength. Roll on my home leave. I'd like to see my son while he's still in short pants. I envy you those months in England, Fingal. I really do. How is Deirdre?"

Fingal smiled. "She's well — I think, but the last letters I got earlier this month had been written in January. Those Cape of Good Hope convoys are too slow and too few."

"I hear an airmail service is getting started," Tom said. "The army are already getting letters that way."

"We're not," Fingal said. "Damn it."

"Their lordships in the Admiralty probably still favour carrier pigeons and semaphore, but our turn will come."

"Can't come soon enough for me," said Fingal. He hesitated, then told himself, Why should you be embarrassed about confiding in Tom? He's your friend. "Her most recent letter was dated January the twenty-third.

657

She's — she thinks she might, just might, be expecting." Her normally regular-as-clockwork period had been ten days late on the day the letter had been written. He savoured the words in her letter once again.

I mustn't get too excited, darling, but I do believe I have a part of the man I love to distraction growing in me now.

"Well done, Fingal O'Reilly, you salty old seadog," Tom said, and his voice was filled with happiness. "That's wonderful news."

"It is, isn't it? I literally danced a jig when I read her letter. Swore to myself to tell nobody." But the news had been bubbling in him like steam in a cylinder and the safety valve had just let go. "But I'm glad I told you, old friend."

"So am I, Fingal. So am I. And she's due in . . . ?"

She'd be nearly four months now, but he had no way of knowing. "I reckon late September," Fingal said, "and, I don't mean to be ungracious, Tom, but I am a doctor. I know how many miscarriages happen in the first three months. It's pretty early yet. Could we hold the celebration until we hear she's got past three months? I don't want to tempt Providence."

"All right. We're all the same, us bloody Irish, aren't we? Superstitious as hell."

"We are," said Fingal, fingering the pipe in his pocket that Deirdre had said the *sidhe* had put a protective spell on.

"But let's have a drink anyway," Tom said. "Let's drink to A.B.C.'s pasting of the Eye-ties at Matapan. I've got the facts here." He consulted a sheet of paper. "Listen."

Fingal unscrewed the top of his fountain pen and opened his now dog-eared war diary. "Fire away," he said.

"We damaged one brand-new battleship, sank three — three, mark you — heavy cruisers, *Pola, Fiume,* and *Zara,* and two destroyers. They shot down one torpedo bomber. Do you want the casualty figures too? We lost three men on the plane."

And the Italian losses were probably in the thousands, Fingal thought. He'd never forget seeing those blazing ships being pounded to their deaths, vast chunks flying into the night sky like the pieces in some malevolent ogres' game of tiddlywinks, nor hearing the next morning about the utterly confused melée of opposing destroyer forces that had taken place during the night after the main battle was over. "I'm sure they were pretty grim," Fingal said. "No. No thanks." He hated to think of comparing our losses to theirs like some kind of sporting contest where whoever collected more bodies won the cup. "Dammit, Tom, war's not a seven-a-side rugby match, and for what?" Every single death had been a young man, not an abstract point on a scoreboard. Fingal quoted,

"But what good came of it at last?"
Quoth Little Peterkin.
"Why that I cannot tell," said he
"But 'twas a famous victory."

"Remember learning that at school? Robert Southey. 'Battle of Blenheim'?"

Tom nodded and said, "But I can't spout it like you. And what's come of Matapan is more than just a 'famous victory,' Fingal. It's a complete shift in the naval balance of power in the Med in our favour." Tom wandered to the windows. He pointed to where two other battlewagons swung at anchor. "All our big boys are still intact. Mussolini's had three of his sunk at Taranto, then one badly damaged by us at Calabria. Now add Matapan."

"I'd hope they'd learn. Stop getting their sailors killed for nothing," Fingal said.

"Well said, and if it's any consolation, our side behaved like gentlemen after it was all over. The Italian skipper tried to scuttle the *Pola,* but she was still afloat. Our destroyer *Jervis* went alongside, put a gangway across, and rescued two hundred and eighty-five men. By morning our ships had pulled another nine hundred out of the water, and we'd've got more if the Jerries hadn't tried to bomb our ships. Even then A.B.C. radioed

660

the position of the survivors to the Italians before we buggered off out of range of the bombers. Gave free passage to a hospital ship."

"He's a humane man, Cunningham," Fingal said, "and I'm no pacifist, I just . . ."

"Hippocrates and Mars aren't such a good mix?"

"That's about it." Fingal rose. "Anyway, thanks for the details. Someday when this lunacy is over and we're all back home in Ulster, Deirdre and I will have you and Carol round for an evening, and I'll fish this out," he held the notebook high, "and we'll do the 'old men reminisce' act." He closed his pen. "But for now I want to go to my cabin, write a few letters."

"See you at six," Tom said, "and the first one's on me."

"There," Fingal said, and sealed the final envelope and added the missive to a pile on his desk. Lord knew how long it would take, but in the fullness of time Ma — and he'd been neglecting her dreadfully — Lars, Angus Mahaddie, Marge Wilcoxson, and Bob Beresford all would have letters from him. So would Flip Dennison, the burned pilot who had kept his promise to stay in touch and who in his last letter said he was recovering very well. And last, but most certainly not least, Deirdre would be hearing from him.

He did the letters up with a red rubber band.

He tried to ignore the all-pervasive smell of fuel oil, the humming of machinery. The thrumming of air intake fans underscored the usual sounds of metal on metal as sailors chipped rust, and the occasional bawled order by petty officers. Fingal had been back on *Warspite* for nearly three months and had slipped so easily into the shipboard atmosphere it was as if he'd never left. As if the time with Deirdre, the flat at Alverstoke, even his time at Haslar, had all been a dream.

He grabbed his cap and picked up the letters. He'd drop them off at the outgoing correspondence office on his way to the mess and the drink with Tom. But first he intended to get a bit of fresh air. He closed his cabin door, followed a corridor, then went up a companionway heading aft until he arrived in the open air beside X turret.

A gunnery CPO and — he squinted into a flash of sunlight — yes, it was Alf Henson, were coming the other way. "Afternoon, Chief," Fingal said. He was eager to talk to the younger man, but he couldn't realistically expect any conversation from Henson. Regulations insisted that the petty officer would do the talking unless Fingal asked a direct question of the junior rating. "Henson. A word."

The CPO and leading seaman halted and came to attention.

"Stand easy," Fingal said. "How are you, Henson?"

"Fine, sir."

" 'E's a darn sight better than that, sir," the CPO said. "We've just come from our gunnery officer, Mister Randall, 'im what took over from Mister Wallace 'oo left the same time as you, sir. Leading seaman 'Enson 'ere's getting a mention in despatches and 'e's up for promotion next go round."

"Well done, Henson," O'Reilly said, and thought, That's a step closer to getting married to your Elsie. Good man.

"You saved *Formidable* at Matapan, didn't you, Alf?" the CPO said.

Fingal was intrigued. "You did what?"

Henson glanced at the CPO then looked down.

The chief said, "You remember, sir, that after the battlewagons had pasted the wop cruisers all 'ell broke loose with both sides' destroyers going at it hammer and tongs?"

"I knew something serious was going on," said Fingal, "but couldn't see anything from my station."

"Well, sir, old *Formidable,* wot we nicknamed 'The Ship that Launched Herself' —"

"I was in Ballybucklebo when that happened at Harland and Wolff in August 1939." He remembered because it was a month before he'd proposed to Deirdre. "A supporting cradle collapsed and she took off by herself. Of course," he shrugged and turned his palms, "we built the *Titanic* too."

Both seamen laughed at the black humour.

"Anyway, sir, the night was black as old Nick's hatband, we could see sweet Fanny Adams. The aircraft carrier'd pulled out to starboard. She was about five miles away when our searchlights caught her. Our crew hadn't fired a shot and we was all keyed up and raring to go. We got our guns dead on target when Henson yells, "Mister Randall, that's *Formidable.* Don't shoot, sir. Don't shoot.' You should've seen the officer's face. 'Well done, Henson,' says 'e, and Mister Randall ain't one to give out praise for free."

Fingal said, "I don't like to think what our six-inch shells would have done —"

Bugles blared from Tannoys and the warning bells set up their jangling clamour. An air raid. Action stations. Not again, for Christ's sake. Please. Not in the harbour.

The CPO and Henson led Fingal in the dash for'ard, the gunners heading for their six-inchers on this deck and he for the medical distribution station three decks down. As he ran, he heard the clamour of the anchored ships' antiaircraft ordnance, the thrumming of German aeroengines, the shrieks of falling bombs. From one deck above, *Warspite's* four-inch AA guns bellowed at the foe, and the soft scents of the Levant — palm oil and coffee, animal droppings and garlic, cumin

664

and kumquats — were strangled by the obscene stench of bursting high explosive.

Posting his mail would have to wait.

47
THE STANDING IS SLIPPERY

"Ooops." O'Reilly flailed his left arm and clung for dear life to Kitty's woolly-mittened hand with his right. He regained his balance — just. "Let's stand still for a minute, shall we?"

"Of course, dear." Kitty stopped gracefully, at least as gracefully as anyone could while hauling with both arms to stop the forward and possibly downward progress of such a big man. "Let's get out of the way," she said, and towed him away from a throng circulating clockwise on the frozen pond. She headed toward the rime-covered bank where they'd left their shoes when they'd put on their skates.

It was Saturday and Arthur had had a good run in the morning. A skating rink was no place for a dog, even one as well behaved as old Arthur. O'Reilly was beginning to wonder if it was any place for a middle-aged GP, either.

On the ice, single skaters glided along, their

hands clasped behind their backs. Some, the showier types, presumably imagining they were Hans Brinker on his silver skates, were tearing round the periphery, lapping the slower skaters. A young woman, unknown to O'Reilly, was wearing the full short-skirted gear and doing spins and what Kitty had told him were lutzes and axels in centre ice. Perhaps the aspiring figure skater usually practiced at the King's Hall in Belfast, which had an indoor rink and skating classes.

Couples glided by holding hands or with arms round each other's waists. Breath and body steam rose over the crowd. The shushing of blades on ice was punctuated by children's laughter and shrieks. Most of the adults and some older teenagers were trying to move in time to Waldteufel's "The Skater's Waltz," coming from a Dansette portable gramophone being supervised by Ballybucklebo's resident disc jockey Donal Donnelly. He'd rigged a microphone and speakers too, so he could make announcements.

O'Reilly wobbled but managed to stand panting beside her. "I'd forgotten you did a bit of figure skating in Dublin," he said. "I'm not quite so nimble. And it seems —"

Cissie Sloan, who was skating beside Flo Bishop, squealed, then yelled, "Jasus, Flo, hang on" and flopped onto her backside in time to one of the waltz's famous cymbal crashes. She slithered for ten feet in a flurry of black skirts and white skate boots thrust in the air before coming to a halt with her white fur pillbox hat askew over one eye.

O'Reilly finished his sentence. "— I'm not the only one."

Helped by Flo, Cissie was scrambling back onto her feet. "Don't worry, Doctor. I've not broken nothing so you can quit looking worried, so you can. Nothing hurt but my pride, and truth to tell . . ." She chuckled. "I don't have much of that anyway."

He laughed and said, "I'm glad to hear you're all right, Cissie." He watched as the two women continued down the ice, Cissie still adjusting her hat.

He turned to Kitty. "It reminds me of the Irish judge at a figure skating competition who gave tens to a skater who kept falling down."

Kitty smiled. "Go on," she said, literally putting her tongue in her cheek. "And why would the judge do that?" Kitty adjusted her green crocheted toque and tucked the matching scarf more firmly into the neck of her russet sweater.

O'Reilly adopted a thick Northside Dublin accent. "Why? I'll tell yuh why. Because that there skater deserved tens just for trying. It's feckin' *slippery* out dere."

"Fingal." Kitty shook her head but laughed anyway. "You're a terrible man for the bad jokes. But it's great *craic,* isn't it, to be out on the marquis's lake. Half the village must be here. And look at the Antrim Hills away over there. It's as if someone sprinkled them with icing sugar."

O'Reilly, no longer completely preoccupied with the likelihood of a precipitate descent of his body — and his dignity — started to pay more attention to his surroundings. Half-Mile Water, as the little lake was called, lay in a valley looking down to and across Belfast Lough to the distant Antrim Hills. The sea between reflected the metallic blue of an icy sky. The watery sun was doing its best but there was no heat in it today.

All this week of December the eleventh, snow had threatened and the temperatures had hovered round freezing during the day, dropping to well below at night. John Mac-Neill had telephoned early this morning to say that Half-Mile Water, a lake much beloved by waterfowl that the marquis refused to let anyone shoot, was safely frozen and that, as was the custom on the rare occasions when it did freeze, he had opened it to anyone in the village and townland who might like to skate. The news had travelled fast.

Donal, enterprising as ever, not only was providing the music but had set Julie up nearby with a brazier. Tori was asleep in her pram, wrapped up under a rug. O'Reilly looked more closely. It was a war surplus RAF pilot's fur-lined Irvin jacket. She looked like a tiny smiling brown bear.

Julie was selling toffee apples, Cookstown sausages to be roasted on metal skewers and put into buttered bridge rolls, cups of tomato soup from thermos flasks, and, trusting that Constable Mulligan might turn a blind eye, mulled wine. Blue smoke curled up and O'Reilly found the smell of roasting sausages irresistible. "Let's get a bite," he said.

"In a minute," Kitty said, sitting on the bank. "I want to take off my skates, and so should you before you fall down. I don't think your landing would be as gentle as Cissie's was." She smiled and tugged at his arm.

He plunked down beside her and was faster than her getting his skates off and his brown boots laced up. While he waited, O'Reilly admired the vista.

Bullrushes, their compact summer black heads turned to fluffy grey, lined the lake's far shore. Tall firs flanked the broad grassy banks, the piney scent mingling with the smell of turf smoke drifting lazily from the chimneys of the big house on the hill above. The branches of two nearby cherry trees were dressed in an ivory tracery of glistening hoar frost, and between two twigs the spiral-wheel web of an orb-weaver spider reflected the sun's light and was limned in what looked like silver. He was moved by the beauty of the scene and wishing for a few snowflakes to add a finishing touch when from nowhere he saw in his mind's eye a tiny village in a glass ball with artificial flakes swirling around. He wasn't sad. He was pleased by the memory and pleased when Kitty said, "Come on then, greedy guts. Let's go and see Julie and Donal."

He knotted his skates' laces and slung them round his neck, took her hand, and together they crunched across the rimed grass to the brazier, a rusty oil drum with holes punched in its sides and small pine branches happily crackling as they blazed inside.

"Hello, Doctor and Missus," Julie said. "How's about ye?"

"We're very well, Julie. And you and Tori?" Kitty asked.

"Couldn't be better."

"Two sausages and two buttered rolls, please."

"Right, sir." Julie neatly pricked the sausages to prevent them bursting, spitted them, and gave one each to O'Reilly and Kitty. "The rolls is in a wee wicker basket on thon card table, so they are, and if you like Heinz's ketchup there's a bottle there too," she said. "And would youse like some hot, er — Ribena?"

"Please," said Kitty, and was handed a steaming glass of dark red fluid, which definitely was not blackcurrant cordial, although another steaming canister did contain some for the kiddies. She sipped and whispered, "Not a bad drop at all. A good solid burgundy with a grating of nutmeg. Trust Donal," she said with a laugh.

"Trust Donal indeed," O'Reilly said, and shook his head. He could feel the pressure of a silver hip flask. Purely for medicinal purposes, of course. He paid.

There were folding chairs on a nearby knoll overlooking the lake and John MacNeill, twenty-seventh Marquis of Ballybucklebo, was sitting on one. "Come and join me, O'Reillys," he called.

"We will, John, thanks. Soon as the bangers are done," O'Reilly called back.

The music stopped and Donal's voice, distorted by the speakers, said, "Next up is the 'Hesitation Waltz' introduced by the Castles' dance team years and years ago. When that's over we'll have a fifteen-minute break." And the music with its structured pauses rang out.

O'Reilly led Kitty to the welcome warmth of the brazier where several men were twirling sausages on skewers. Men might not like to cook, but they were first in line when there was anything to roast over an open fire.

"There's room for you and the lady here, sir," Alan Hewitt said. "I'll move over if you will, Gerry Shanks, you great greedy glipe. Sorry, Mrs. O'Reilly, but it can take some coaxing to get your man Gerry here away from the trough."

"Away off and chase yourself, Hewitt, you bollix," Gerry said with a grin, and moved over.

Ah, O'Reilly thought, the gentle art of Ulster slagging.

"Thank you, Gerry, Alan," said Kitty.

The sound of sausages crackling and spitting was almost drowned by cawing as a mixed flock of jackdaws and rooks flapped overhead, heading for their evening roosts. "How are you, Alan?" O'Reilly asked.

"And how's your Helen?" Kitty said.

Alan Hewitt smiled. "We're well. The lass is on her Christmas hollyers. Her and thon Jack Mills, that nice young doctor from the Royal, is away on down til Cullybackey so she can meet his folks."

"There's a thing," murmured Kitty. "Meeting the parents."

"Indeed," said O'Reilly with a glance at her. Perhaps he'd been unkind in his thoughts about Jack Mills and that pretty nurse who had come to take Ronald's vital signs.

Their sausages cooked, the two men moved away and soon Kitty and O'Reilly were following them to the table, where O'Reilly slathered ketchup on his roll before popping the sausage in. "Shall we join the marquis?" Kitty said, pointing the way with a slight bow.

O'Reilly got Kitty settled, unscrewed the cap of his silver flask, which served as a cup, poured, and offered the marquis a drink.

"No thanks, Fingal," John MacNeill said, "but do go ahead yourself."

O'Reilly sat himself down, drank, and took a huge bite of his sausage. Lovely. "Remember visiting the Kearneys last month when we had a go at the snipe, John?"

"I certainly do. That day was a highlight of the season so far for me, Fingal."

Fingal nodded his head. "Well, Lorna Kearney had a lovely wee girl called Caroline last week. Everyone's healthy and the christening's going to be in January."

"Splendid," said the marquis, "and I did promise a present. I'll see to it." He fished out a notebook and a silver propelling pencil and made a note.

"You're very generous about that sort of thing, John," Kitty said, "and about opening your grounds for this."

"Nonsense," he said. "Tradition goes back for more than a hundred years," he leant forward, "and I think I'll be able to keep it going on, thanks to Lars."

"I'm delighted," O'Reilly said.

"He's being a great help. Drives up twice a week from Portaferry. Your brother is confident that there is a lot we can salvage, but initially he and Myrna are listing the things he can't save. The hunters and their groom will have to go, I'm afraid, but I've already found a position for the man. He'll be starting there next February after the horses are sold."

"Brilliant," O'Reilly said. "Dead brill." He drank his whiskey.

"And I'm getting on a bit for yelling 'View halloo,' and tearing over ditches and fences." He laughed.

Someone was tugging at O'Reilly's elbow. He turned.

Donal Donnelly stood, cap in one hand and two leashes in the other, attached to two of the strangest-looking beasts O'Reilly had ever seen. "Excuse me, my lord, I don't want til interrupt, but could I have a wee word with the doctor?"

"Go right ahead. But, I say, Donal, what kind of pups are those? They're like nothing I've ever seen. They're, uh, handsome little fellows, aren't they? Very unusual." John O'Neill bent down to stroke one of the dogs' long ears.

"Thank you, sir." Donal seemed to expand in the marquis's presence. He stood taller and let the pups run around on their leashes so the marquis could see them better. The dogs had grown since last O'Reilly had seen them. They stood about the height of a cocker spaniel and their coats, long-haired and recently groomed, had developed from the original grey and brown into an attractive fawn lighter over the neck and head, darker over the slim back. Stiff long legs, up-curved narrow tail. The most salient features were enormous sticking-up ears and widely spaced, slightly protruding brown eyes.

"They're Woolamarroo quokka hounds from Australia, your lordship. Ten weeks old."

"Well, I'll be damned. Thought I'd heard of every kind of breed there was. But that's a new one on me. Herding dogs, are they? Bet they can gallop."

Colin and Lenny Brown joined the group, Colin immediately putting his arms around one of the pups. "What do you think of them wee lads, Doctor?" Colin asked.

"Amazing," said O'Reilly.

"And you're right, your lordship, they go like the clappers," Donal said. "Of course they're meant for til go charging about all over the place after them quokkas. Doctor O'Reilly and me's going up to a Belfast Chamber of Commerce do tonight to show them off, like. If any of your friends are looking for a good dog, you know where to find me, your lordship."

"I do, Donal. This little chap seems pretty attached to me already." The dog was sitting on the man's polished boots and had snuggled into John MacNeill's corduroy-clad legs.

"I've the ones we'll be taking to Belfast in our cottage, Doctor. Julie's made them wee red waistcoats for the occasion. Everything will be all set, Doctor, sir. I just wanted til be sure you'll pick me up at Dun Bwee at half five?"

"On the button," O'Reilly said. "I'd not miss this for the world. You be ready. I'll be there and —"

His wildfowler's reflexes took over, forcing him to look up. The clipped whistle of beating mallard pinions was as recognisable as the unique roar of a Merlin engine, and sure enough, six mallard, two emerald-headed drakes leading, were coming in low to land. They flared, wingbeats slowing their approach, paddles outstretched in front ready for a water touchdown. But the lake was frozen.

The leading bird made a perfect two-point landing, hotly pursued by the rest. Two beak-planted and slid forward, feathered backsides in the air. One turned a complete somersault. The other three, arriving slightly later, must have seen what was going on. One clawed for height, quacking furiously, and that must have got the quokka dogs' attention. The other two ducks gave pretty good impressions of Cissie Sloan's earlier descent onto her bottom and slid along, webbed feet in the air, to join the other three now all tangled in a sliding, pecking-each-other, quacking heap.

O'Reilly, knowing that no real harm was done and that only their feathers would have been ruffled both literally and figuratively, bellowed with laughter, and everyone crowded around to see what the excitement was about. So he didn't hear Colin's first yell, but only the lad's second "come back here" as the boy bawled through cupped hands. "Daft dogs. Come back here."

Donal had been right. The quokka dogs could shift — until they hit the ice. Then it was all paws heading to the four points of the compass. Both dogs made a peculiar howling, both with their big ears drooping. One hound, legs stretched out fore and aft, flew arrow-straight across the ice, the other was already starting its second complete 360-degree spin, its leash whipping around like a long leather tail.

O'Reilly wondered if Kitty knew a figure skating term for that manoeuvre.

Still, they were catching up with the ducks, and Colin, who had run onto the ice, had fallen onto his backside and was giving a pretty fair imitation of a luger's progress, sans luge.

"Go on, Colin," O'Reilly yelled, and realised that the entire village seemed to be enjoying the fun.

"Ten bob Colin beats the dogs to the ducks," said Gerry Shanks.

"My money's on the ducks," said Alan Hewitt.

But before the bet could be sealed with a handshake one, two more, then two more mallard managed to take off. The dogs stopped sliding, but their endeavours to stand, legs shooting off in strange directions, were not altogether successful.

Colin, propelled by some mysterious law of physics to do with mass, energy, and friction, or lack of same, slid past both animals.

Donal was calling to the dogs, Julie had abandoned her post at the food table, Tori was crying, and a dozen or more people were milling around, on their feet, cheering on boy and dogs. The pups seemed to be mastering the art of walking on ice and Colin, having scooped up their leashes, was leading them off the slippery surface, moving his feet like an ice skater and making steady progress.

"Home," O'Reilly said, taking Kitty's hand and leading her away from the crowd. "I need to get changed for going up to town with Donal and his dogs tonight." He looked down to where hounds and boy had made it to dry land, apparently none the worse for wear. "And I'll say one thing," he said. "Donal told me the dogs could run like the clappers. By God . . . he's right."

Kitty was still shaking with laughter. Eventually she managed to control her giggles. "Only in Ballybucklebo," she said. "Where else could a simple afternoon's ice skating turn into an exhibition?"

"Where indeed," he said, grabbing her hand, and he swung their arms like a couple of schoolchildren might. "And where on

God's green earth would you rather be, Mrs. O'Reilly?"

She smiled up at him, those grey-flecked-with-amber eyes sparkling. "As long as I'm with you, Fingal, not one other place. Not one."

48

ADVERSE POWER OPPOSED IN DUBIOUS BATTLE

"Jasus t'undering Murphy." CPO Paddy O'Rourke was standing in the medical distribution station rolling bandages as the shrill whistle of a bo'sun's pipe came over the Tannoy. "I don't like the sounds of dat. Not one feckin' bit. It means that there's to be no rest for the wicked," he grinned, "and not even us good lads. I wonder what we're in for this time?" His grin widened. "It'll not be a free trip to Galway Races, dat's for certain sure."

Fingal had to smile. Big Paddy's answer to potential danger had always been to joke, but the other sick bay staff, Richard Wilcoxson and three other SBAs, ignored the CPO and instead stared intently at the loudspeaker. The atmosphere in the windowless room was tense. Fingal could sense every man, including Paddy, thinking, What the hell now?

"Something's up for sure," Paddy said as the notes of the ship's turbines increased in pitch. *Warspite* was putting on speed. Fingal had just sat down with his war diary and scratched today's date, May 22th, at the top of a page. He'd been using Deirdre's latest letter, dated February 12th and delivered to the *Warspite* three months later, for a bookmark and he picked up the pages now like a talisman. He'd taken to carrying the letters around with him, a comforter to be enjoyed during lulls in the action.

"Could be almost anything," Richard Wilcoxson said. "It's been three days since the Germans invaded Crete."

"You'd've thought," Paddy said, "the forty thousand British and Commonwealth troops we evacuated from the Greek mainland to the island could've held the Jerries off, but I guess we're losing again."

"Those German paratroops that captured Maleme Airfield made it possible for reinforcements and supplies to come pouring in by air," Richard said. "The defenders are being overrun. And the Axis are trying to supply by sea as well. It's part of our job to support the army."

"Which Tom Laverty says is pretty risky," Fingal said. "The remaining British fighter planes were withdrawn from the island on the nineteenth, and that means no air cover for us."

"The gunnery POs are sayin' dat the Luftwaffe pilots are a damn sight more dangerous than the Eyetie ones," said Paddy O'Rourke.

"Aye," said Fingal, "but fair play to the

RAF. So few fighters were serviceable that they could provide no defence anyway. And poor old *Formidable* only has four planes left so she's no help. She's safer back in Alex."

"So," said Paddy, "that leaves the bloody navy like the little Dutch boy all alone with his finger in the feckin' dyke trying to hold back the flood of sea-borne supplies to the Germans."

"It's more like having a whole hand stuck in," Fingal said. "Last time I was talking to Tom Laverty he explained that *Warspite* was part of a fleet divided into five 'forces,' A1, our force under Rear Admiral Rawlings, and B, C, D, and E all trying to intercept and sink enemy troop and supply convoys and bombard enemy-held positions on the island. Admiral Cunningham's in Alex directing the complex operation and —"

The Tannoy interrupted. "The time is twelve-thirty hours. We are increasing to twenty-four knots and steering for Admiral King's Force C, which attacked a German troop convoy in the Aegean last night. They are running out of AA ammunition and have been under heavy and repeated German air attack for three and a half hours. His flagship *Naiad* has been badly damaged and the *Carlisle*, the antiaircraft cruiser, hit and her captain killed. Force C is withdrawing west."

"Here we go again," Paddy said.

"Our force, A1 — two battleships, *Warspite*

and *Valiant,* and four destroyers — is proceeding east into the Kithera Channel between the islands of Kithera and Antikithera north of Crete to link up with C and provide additional antiaircraft support. Other naval forces will soon be joining. We will keep you informed." The speaker went dead.

Paddy O'Rourke turned his eyes to the heavens, crossed himself, and said, "If you've a minute or two free, Mother Mary, would you keep an eye out for the poor ould British Navy, would you? Thanks. We'd be much obliged." Then his voice lost its bantering tone and he said seriously, "I don't much like the sound of this neither. The Jerries have airfields all over the mainland and on Crete and on Scarpanto now. A pal in signals reckons the brass think the Luftwaffe have more than four hundred bombers and dive bombers at this end of the Med."

"Dunno how much use our fifteen-inch and six-inch guns'll be against that lot. Bit like trying to kill a swarm of wasps with a pistol," Richard said.

The man was right. *Warspite*'s only hope for delivery from air attack lay in her antiaircraft weapons, not her big rifles.

"But I'm sure we'll give them a run for their money." As ever, the principal medical officer exuded calm and passed it on to his subordinates. "With any luck we'll be all right, but to recap what we've planned, if casualties do arrive, the other team in the aft distribution station will deal with lesser wounds, simple fractures. We'll get the serious ones. I'll operate; Fingal, you'll anaesthetise; Paddy, you'll assist."

Fingal and Paddy muttered their assent.

"If two patients need surgery at the same time, then Paddy, you'll take over the anaesthetic from Fingal —"

"Aye aye, sir."

"Fingal, you stun the next patient, hand over to SBA Arthur, and then scrub. Sick Berth Attendant Fletcher will assist you."

It made sense. Inducing the anaesthetic was always the trickiest part, and even if Fingal did the operation, he could then direct his attention to helping the patient recover. Now, thanks to Angus Mahaddie and Haslar, Fingal was quite at ease with what he might soon have to do when the need arose.

So there was no imminent danger, but it sounded as if things might soon start heating up. Fingal opened Deirdre's letter and began reading it again.

. . . and old Doctor Flanagan in Ballybucklebo was sweet. I went to see him yesterday. I didn't want to go to any of the medical staff at the hospital here because regulations say I must retire as soon as they know, but I want to go on working for a bit longer. When I'd finished seeing the doctor,

Kinky insisted on making me a cup of tea and barmbrack just like the day we popped in before you went away after your first leave. She sends her love and says she hopes to see you back in the practice for good very soon. So, darling, do I, because Doctor Flanagan says if the frog confirms his clinical findings you're going to be a daddy in September. Isn't it wonderful?

Fingal closed his eyes. God, but she was a brave girl. He was so glad they'd discussed things again on Christmas Day. She'd not be all alone when she left her job. She'd go home to her parents and how, how he wished he could be with her in September. Perhaps *Warspite* would get a posting to home waters by then? Londonderry would be grand altogether, thank you. He grinned. Well, he could dream, couldn't he?

He was nursing the thought when the air raid warning bells sounded and the Tannoy announced, "The Kapsali Bay Light bears green oh five zero, distance eight miles. There are enemy aircraft approaching the force from both beams and the destroyer screen has opened fire . . ."

He shoved her letter back into his diary.

Even four decks down, Fingal could hear the distant cracks of high angle 4.7-inch guns, the clamour of Oërlikons, the *pom-pom-pom-pom* of Chicago pianos and the harsh rattling of 0.5 calibre machine guns. Judging by the lack of deck vibrations so far, *Warspite* had not opened fire, but the sky over the force would be alive with molten steel. Over the racket of the guns he heard the screaming roar of aero engines rising in a crescendo only to be silenced in a moment. One enemy bomber would do no harm, but . . .

"Three Messerschmitt 109 fighter bombers have burst through the smoke and are approaching our bow . . ."

A machine gun seemed to be *Warspite*'s only riposte, but she heeled violently to port like a boxer trying to avoid a straight left. The skipper must have ordered full port wheel.

From somewhere aft and overhead came the sounds of a vast explosion. The steel of *Warspite*'s hull shuddered and rang like a great tuning fork.

Fingal wasn't sure who yelled, "Ooooh, shit . . ."

Corticene insulation fell in lumps from the deckhead above. He was nearly dislodged from his seat as *Warspite* bucked again, thumped hard twice by nearby underwater explosions. One hit, two misses, but even near misses could spring plates, do underwater damage.

"Bloody hell," Paddy O'Rourke said as he picked himself up off the floor and bent to collect the bandages he'd been rolling earlier.

They were now unravelling across the sole.

"We've taken a hit," Richard said. "We're going to be busy."

"Damage control parties, stretcher-bearers, first-aid men report to your stations," the Tannoy bellowed. "Damage control parties . . ."

Sea-booted feet clattered along a passageway overhead.

There was a deafening hissing of escaping steam.

Fingal dusted his shirt free of corticene fragments and took a deep breath. Where had the bomb hit — and how many casualties had it caused?

"You can go ahead, Richard," Fingal said. The man on the operating table was the first serious victim to arrive. Fingal sat watching his Boyle's machine and adjusting the flow of the anaesthetic gasses while Fletcher soaked the patient's legs with disinfectant before the gowned and gloved Richard and Paddy O'Rourke started cutting off the remains of the man's dungarees. All Fingal knew of the patient was that he was a Scot from Aberdeen. Twenty, blue eyes that had held the fear of death before he'd been put to sleep, ginger hair, a jagged scar on his left cheek. He'd been one of an ammunition handling party when the cordite charges had gone up in flames. His asbestos antiflash gear had protected his hands, arms, and face, but his legs . . .

Fingal cringed. He had met the smell of burned flesh before at Narvik and from a wounded fighter pilot.

At least this man was well asleep. Trying to remove cloth fused to flesh would have been excruciating without anaesthesia, but now the patient would feel nothing as Richard began to clean the burns before using the tannic acid treatment.

It had been less than ten minutes since the stretcher-bearers had brought this patient here. As the SBAs had been getting him onto the table and Fingal was preparing his anaesthetic Richard asked, "Where were we hit?"

"We took it only six feet from the midships edge of the foc's'le deck, sir. Bloody nearly missed us, sir. A five-hundred-pound bomb hit the baseplate of one of the two starboard four-inch guns. Threw it and the crew overboard, made a bloody great hole in the deck, and exploded in the six-inch battery . . ."

"Is there a lot of damage?" Richard asked.

"There was a hell of a fire in there, sir, smoke everywhere, pouring out through the hole in the deck, but the executive officer, Commander Sir Charles Madden's in charge and he's got fire parties in there with hoses and extinguishers. They had to smash a door down with sledgehammers to get into the battery. They seem to be getting things under control, but there's still a man in there and there are tons of wounded on the starboard mess deck too."

"Mess deck?" Richard said. "Of course. It's directly below the battery."

Fingal could picture the blast and flames tearing through the deck where the guns were and down onto the men below. Grim.

A seaman stuck his head into the room. "Begging your pardon, sir, but Commander Madden has sent me. Can you spare an MO? There's a man trapped and the exec thinks if a doctor took off the bloke's hand we could save his life before the fire gets him."

"You've that case to finish, Richard." Fingal stood. "Paddy, take over. I'll go," and he called himself a fool. He was terrified of fire, but the poor trapped bugger would be too. Fingal grabbed morphine, syringes, a bottle of disinfectant, rubber tubing for a tourniquet, a scalpel, a bone saw, Gamgee, and bandages, shoved them in an empty first-aid satchel, and said, "Show me the way."

He followed as the sailor led the way aft while climbing up two decks from the middle to upper deck. A door amidships had separated the port from the starboard six-inch batteries. Smoke irritated Fingal's eyes, made him cough.

"This way, sir." The rating stepped over the door's coaming. The armoured door itself hung drunkenly on its hinges as if great force had been used to open it. Its steel still glowed cherry red.

Inside the battery the heat was palpable even though by looking past the wreckage of number three and four guns he could see daylight and the sea as it seemed to rush past. Fingal sloshed through filthy water from the fire hoses that snaked along the deck. Through a huge hole overhead he could see attacking aircraft. One of the fire crew shook his fist at them and screamed, "Bastards. Bloody Kraut bastards."

Fingal was deafened by the thundering of *Warspite*'s turbines. Her speed hadn't dropped so the engine spaces and steering must have escaped unscathed. He tried to ignore the barking cacophony as her antiaircraft guns blazed defiance at the aircraft overhead, the ship a great wounded beast still hurling her venom at her tormentors.

Although most of the fire in the battery had been extinguished, leaving nothing but blackened debris and, he flinched, charred bodies, flames producing greasy black smoke still sprang up from the remains of number-four gun. Two seamen were playing a hose on a man wearing an antiflash hood and gauntlets who lay facedown on the deck and whose left arm vanished at the wrist under a huge piece of twisted steel.

The flames were creeping toward him. No time to lose.

Fingal tightened his grip on his satchel and steeled himself to advance when a voice said, "O'Reilly. Glad you're here. Anything you need?"

Fingal turned to see the executive officer. "Only a man to help me," he said, but thought, Yes. I need to be anywhere but here.

"AB Phillips. Bear the surgeon a hand. Lively now."

"Aye aye, sir." A young seaman dropped a hose and stepped forward.

Fingal handed him the satchel. "Hold that, keep it open, and stay close to me."

"Aye aye, sir."

Fingal filled a syringe with a quarter grain of morphine. He got on his knees and, shielding his face from the blaze with one arm, crept forward. Steam rose from the gunner's soaking clothes and Fingal, feeling the heat, wished that he himself had something more than tropical rig, shorts and a shirt, to protect him. The flames were nearly beating him back but he gritted his teeth and crept on.

"Soak the doctor and Phillips too."

Fingal heard the exec order and welcomed the relief afforded as cold water hit his bare arms and legs. A hand to the man's throat confirmed that he had a pulse. He was breathing, but unconscious. There was no time for niceties. Fingal drove the hypodermic needle through the gunner's overall sleeve into the big muscle over the shoulder, the deltoid, and injected.

"I'll be asking you for what I need, Phillips. Give me that bottle of brown fluid."

"Aye aye, sir." The seaman passed Fingal the Dettol, which he poured over the wrist of the trapped hand.

"See that rubber tubing?"

"This, sir?"

"Thanks." Fingal slipped it under the arm below the elbow and knotted it tightly for a tourniquet.

"See the scalpel?"

"This it, sir?"

"Good man." Fingal accepted the surgical knife. He couldn't manipulate the arm so he'd have to cut straight through skin and flesh, worry about making proper flaps later back in the operating theatre, deal with the bone, then the flesh and sinews of the underside. The patient moaned and tried to writhe, but was held fast by his hand.

Fingal felt a tugging at his sleeve. "What is it?"

The rating pointed to a small river of oily fluid that was running from the wrecked gun and forming a pool under Fingal's knees. Dear God. Hydraulic fluid. If that went up . . . Fingal took one deep breath, shouted, "Give me the satchel and bugger off."

"Aye aye, sir." The rating did and fled.

Despite himself, pictures of Flip Dennison's charred and scarred face kept flashing into

Fingal's mind. His hand started to tremble.

The executive officer yelled, "Leave him. Save yourself, Doctor. That's an order. Our hoses are useless on hydraulic fluid. And we haven't got enough medical staff. We can't afford —"

Fingal heard the shout as a distant command, a wasp buzzing, distracting him from his purpose of completing the amputation and getting the man to safety. Sod it. He slung the bag by its strap over one shoulder and bent to his work. He willed his hands to behave. Firm scalpel strokes soon revealed the forearm bones. There was virtually no bleeding because of the tourniquet. The saw bit and soon had done its work. From the corner of his eye he saw tiny flames like the ones on a brandy-soaked Christmas pudding begin to dance on the surface of the pool in which he knelt. Every fibre screamed *run.*

He dropped the saw, picked up the scalpel, and severed the remaining tissue. He got the semiconscious man in a fireman's lift and as the fluid erupted with a loud *whoomp* scorching Fingal's face and burning off his eyebrows and the hair on the front of his head, he ran to the far side of the battery to the cheers of the fire-fighting crew and a couple of stretcher-bearers who had appeared.

Fingal set the man down with his back to a bulkhead and ripped off the gunner's anti-flash hood. No. Och, no. Dear God, not Alf

Henson. Not Alf. No time for those thoughts now. Fingal grabbed Gamgee and bandages and fashioned a crude dressing.

He straightened to find himself looking into the eyes of Commander Sir Charles Madden. "That, O'Reilly," the commander said, "was one of the bravest things I've ever seen. You should have run."

Fingal simply shook his head. Tried to stop seeing himself charred into the foetal position like one of the ash-preserved bodies from Pompeii.

"I shall be recommending you for the DSC."

Fingal lost control. "Sir," he said, and his voice was icy. "I don't want your flaming medal. Give Henson back his hand."

Whether from the relief at knowing he'd not been roasted alive or the realisation that all he and Elizabeth Blenkinsop had tried to do for Alf Henson had been futile, Fingal found himself laughing. Hysteria. He brought it under control. "You two," he pointed at the stretcher-bearers, "get Leading Seaman Henson on the stretcher and take him to the for'ard medical distribution station. I need to fashion a stump so we can get him fitted with an artificial hand when he's healed up."

The barking cacophony of *Warspite*'s AA guns almost drowned out the commander's response. "And I shall ignore your insubordination and impertinence and, like it or not, O'Reilly, I *am* putting you in for that gong."

49
AND EVERY DOG HIS DAY

"No," said O'Reilly. "It won't do."

"What won't, sir?" Donal asked as he closed the Rover's passenger-side door. From behind him came a series of high-pitched yips from the excited puppies in the backseat.

"I don't think you served in the Irish Guards, did you?"

"What are you on about, sir? You know fine well I was never in the army, never mind the Guards."

"Then you can't wear their regimental tie in a room full of captains of industry."

"But we're just going to sell some dogs," Donal said, a note of petulance in his voice. He pulled his tie out from under his tweed jacket and examined it — dark red and dark blue, diagonally striped.

"Some retired major is going to have apoplexy if he sees you wearing that thing," O'Reilly said. "You don't know how jealous some folks can be about who can and who can't wear certain ties. And you want to get off on a good foot, don't you?"

"Aye, certainly. I do that. And I sure don't want to give no high heenjin apple plexy."

"Where did you get it anyway?"

"This?" Donal's brows knitted then he smiled. "About a year ago I was doing a wee job for his lordship. Fitting some shelves into his dressing room wardrobe, so I was. My belt broke and my pants near fell down. I asked Mister Thompson, you know, the butler man, for a piece of twine and he give me this instead. Said it was wore out. It had a long tear, but it was right along the seam and Julie sewed it up so's you can't see it anyroad. I didn't know it was special, so I didn't."

"Thompson gave you a regimental tie to hoist up your trousers? He must be mellowing in his old age. Well, go and change it. I'll keep an eye on the dogs. Which two are they?"

"Thon one there with the wee top hat's Boy, short for Wild Colonial Boy of Brisbane. Pedigree dogs have grand names, you know. And the one in the wee bonnet's Mel, short for Melbourne Miss the Third of Carlton."

O'Reilly chuckled. "How the blazes do you think them up?"

"I don't sir. Dapper does. He's quare nor smart, and he wants for the dogs til sell too. Don't forget as well as the stud fees Dapper gets pick of the litter and he wants the do-re-mi when it sells. Anyroad, hang on and I'll be back." He climbed out and both little dogs got up on their hind legs and put their front paws and wet noses on the car's side window. Both, as well as their ridiculous hats, wore scarlet waistcoats that Julie had sewn.

How, O'Reilly wondered, do I get myself involved with Donal's antics? All part of being the kind of local GP I always wanted to be, and let's face it, every time Donal's got himself into trouble hasn't the *craic* been ninety digging him out? He wished Barry was here to share the fun.

O'Reilly laughed loudly enough to stimulate a melancholy howling from the backseat. "Wheest, dogs, wheest," he said, and they quieted at once. Biddable little creatures, and agile too. They might just make good pets.

Donal climbed back in, this time wearing a paisley tie in bright pinks and fluorescent greens.

"Right," said O'Reilly, gasping when he saw the tie. He shook his head. "Off we go. We're late. But the old Rover has lots of horses under the bonnet and I can put my foot to the floor over the Craigantlet Hills as long as they aren't too icy." He roared down the lane fast enough to force Donal to slide down in his seat.

"My God," Donal said sotto voce. "This is quare nor grand, so it is." He stood, duncher grasped in one hand, the dogs' leashes in the other, rooted to the spot at the doorway to

699

Belfast's Grand Central Hotel ballroom. The hall carpet was plush underfoot.

O'Reilly stood at Donal's shoulder surveying the scene. The first guests were beginning to arrive. From the far end came the sounds of the Clipper Carlton Showband as they set up their instruments. Their frontman, Fergie O'Hagan, said into a microphone, "Check, check, check. Microphone check."

The words gave O'Reilly a flutter of anxiety in his belly. "Check" repeated twice more had also been the order for *Warspite*'s guns to cease firing.

The sounds echoed through the room and across a dance floor to where tables and chairs awaited, loaded with white napery and silver cutlery, light blue china and crystal glasses. Light sparkled from chandeliers with false diamond pendants and a multifaceted mirrored ball spun over the dance floor. The chamber of commerce members and their wives were not going to be eating *cruibíns* off paper plates. There would be money here tonight. Lots of money. And, he hoped, lots of good people who would treat the funny little creatures well.

"Do you think Mister Bishop and Mister Ramsey will come soon?" Donal asked.

O'Reilly said, "Bertie told us to be here at six fifteen so we're a couple of minutes early."

"Aye," said Donal, "even though you near put the car in the ditch in your hurry, sir."

"Black ice," O'Reilly said, and sniffed. "The skid could have happened to a bishop. Anyway it's always better to be early in life."

"Right, sir. I'll remember that." Donal bent to the two leashed dogs. "Sit." And to O'Reilly's amazement they did. "I know they're very young yet, but I've been learning them a wee bit," Donal said. "They're sharp as tacks."

Beside the door, a hotel functionary sitting at a trestle table was taking cards with scalloped edges and black copperplate writing from guests arriving like Noah's animals two by two, the gentleman in dinner suits, the ladies in cocktail dresses. One woman bent and patted Boy. "Isn't the little doggy sweet, Henry?" she asked of a moustached, rotund gentleman accompanying her.

He toyed with an unlit cigar. "Strange-looking beast," the man said. "I think it might be one of those rare Australian dogs, Woolama-somethings, that Ernie Ramsey was so keen on. Legs are too long for its body." He handed over his invitation. "Do come along, Sarah. I see the Featherstonehaughs, and Mildred's waving at us."

Sarah gave one last lingering look before following her husband.

"Now there's a thing," said Donal after she'd gone in. "It'll be the women who do the buying — you mark my words, sir. The craytures' big brown eyes bring out the mother in women. My Julie's forever pettin' the wee fellahs."

Had Donal been born into a different social class, O'Reilly was convinced he'd have been a professor of applied psychology. "You could be right," he said, and wondered if it had been the case, to what precisely would Donal have applied his skills? There'd have been a profit in it, that was for sure.

"Right on time, Doctor. Donal," Bertie Bishop said. Flo and the Ramseys were with him.

Donal made a head bob.

"Bertie. Flo, you look —" O'Reilly began. She was wearing an orange flared cocktail dress over myriad taffeta petticoats and was giving a fair impression of a ripe pumpkin. "— wonderful."

"Thank you, Doctor," she said, and smiled. "Cissie Sloan made my dress. She's a quare dab hand at the dressmaking." She looked at the pups. "What lovely little doggies," she patted Mel, "and such a pretty bonnet. Do you think we should buy one, dear?"

Bertie adjusted his bow tie, cleared his throat, swallowed hard, and made no comment.

O'Reilly had the distinct impression that Bertie was biting back a suggestion that Flo should take herself off by the hand, a fine Ulsterism for getting a grip on reality. Perhaps Bertie's newfound humanity did not extend to the animal kingdom.

"Doctor, this is Mrs. Ramsey," Ernie Ramsey said, introducing a slim, dark-haired woman in a black knee-length sheath. "Eileen, Doctor O'Reilly and Mister Donnelly."

"Pleased to meet you both," she said, "and Flo is right. Those big brown eyes are simply adorable."

"We'll go in," said Ernie. "I don't know about you other gentlemen, but my belly thinks my throat's cut. My tongue's hanging out."

O'Reilly was feeling a certain thirst himself.

Ernie Ramsey handed in their invitations, made the explanations, and once inside was ushered by a waiter in tails to a table for six in the front row facing the bandstand.

"This is going til work out very well," Ernie said. "The doctor and Mister Donnelly can sit with us until the sale's over, then they'll be going home."

"That's right," O'Reilly said.

"Harry and Jessica's going to be a wee bit late, so there'll be seats for them with us when you've gone."

A waiter hove into view.

"My shout," Bertie said. "What'll it be?"

All the while, the room was filling. Some guests had taken their seats, others, drinks and canapés in hand, circulated, chatting with old friends. The strains of Kenny Ball's "Midnight in Moscow" flowed over conversations and laughter, and above all a tobacco haze was forming. From time to time, folks would wander over, admire the dogs, and chat to Donal about the forthcoming sale.

A stranger to O'Reilly approached the table. "How are you, Bertie?" the man said.

Very Upper Malone Road accent, O'Reilly noticed.

"Rightly, Johnny," Bertie said. "Johnny Henderson here has a linen mill."

"And a wife who's fallen in love with one of these dogs you were telling us about." He offered a hand. "Mister Donnelly, I presume?"

"I'm your man," Donal said, took the man's hand, and shook it.

"I don't suppose you'd consider a presale offer, Mister Donnelly?"

Donal's face went into its usual deep thought contortions.

O'Reilly could almost hear the man thinking, A bird in the hand is worth two in the bush and, I wonder could I bargain?

"They're twenty . . ." Donal stared into the man's face, "twenty . . ."

That was the price he'd quoted in the Duck. Go on, Donal, O'Reilly thought. Go for more.

"Twenty-two pounds ten each."

"Twenty-two pounds and we have a deal."

"Twenty-two pounds five, Mister Henderson," said Donal, and immediately handshakes were exchanged. "Which one do you want?"

"I'll take the one in the top hat. He looks like a likely little lad." The man bent down and gave Boy a gentle pat and a playful chuck under the chin. The dog responded by licking his hand.

O'Reilly was whisked back to the souks of Alexandria. He was convinced that Egyptian Arabs, renowned for their haggling skills, would have been outdone by Donal Donnelly of Dun Bwee Cottage, Ballybucklebo.

"He's called Boy, sir."

At the sound of his name the little dog looked adoringly at Donal, then back to Johnny Henderson.

"You can have him after the sale, for I need to show them off, like."

"Certainly, Mister Donnelly. Joyce will be overjoyed." He wandered off.

"I think," said Bertie, "you were dead jammy, Donal, chancing your arm like that."

"I don't think so, Bertie," O'Reilly said. "Luck had nothing to do with it. Donal took a calculated risk. One down and nine to go."

The drinks arrived.

"Cheers," O'Reilly said, and took a pull on his pint.

Another stranger wearing a badge of office came over. "Hello all. I'm Sean Brennan, chairman of the chamber," he said. "Ernie, it's time for you to introduce the dog man,

Mister —"

"Mister Donnelly," Ernie said.

"Mister Donnelly," Mister Brennan said, "and get this sale under way."

Ernie got to his feet. "Come on, Donal. Bring the bow-wows."

"Here, Doctor, please," said Donal, handing O'Reilly a notebook and a pen. "You take the money, names, addresses, and phone numbers, and tell them I'll phone on Monday to arrange times for the buyers til come to Dun Bwee."

"Fair enough."

Donal rose. "Come on, pups." Wagging tails curved high over their backs, the dogs followed.

Ernie signalled to Clipper Carlton and the music stopped, then climbed up on the stage and took the microphone. "Drum roll please, maestro."

The snare drum rattled merrily away. Conversation died. All eyes were on the stage.

"Ladies and gentlemen, welcome to our Christmas party and dinner for 1966. Tonight we will be starting the festivities with something quite different. This is the season for giving, and tonight the Belfast Chamber of Commerce is giving a local man from Ballybucklebo the opportunity to sell something very special, some wee dogs so rare I believe one will make the recipient of such a Christmas present the envy of all. May I present

Mister Donal Donnelly and two of his re-markable and unique Woolamarroo quokka herding dogs."

As Donal and the dogs mounted the stage, Clipper Carlton's Showband swung into the chorus of "How Much Is That Doggie in the Window."

The music died and Donal stepped forward. He didn't speak. He gave a quiet order and the two behatted, red-jacketed little dogs rose on their hind legs and each pirouetted, Boy in a clockwise direction and Mel going round the opposite way. Another command and both again stood on four paws.

The room erupted in applause.

Donal now took the mike and, as if to the manner born, said, "Thank youse all, ladies and gentlemen, thank youse all, and Mister Ramsey and the Belfast Chamber of Commerce? Thank you for inviting us — me, Wild Colonial Boy of Brisbane and Melbourne Miss the Third of Carlton." On hearing their names, the dogs each gave one sharp bark.

Laughter and applause.

Begob, thought O'Reilly, Donal certainly knows how to play a room.

Donal squatted with his knees widely separated, commanded, and the dogs jumped up, one onto each thigh, and sat staring at the crowd. He tucked one under each arm, stood and said, "Mister Chairman and Mrs. Chairman if she's here, ladies and gentlemen,

what youse see here is two of the eighth
wonders of the world. These here are two of
the only Woolamarroo quokka herding dogs
north of the equator. All the way from
Rottnest Island off the City of Perth in
Western Australia."

He paused for dramatic effect.

Silence.

"Even in that far and fair country full of
such exotic animals as marsh soopials and
duck billed platty-pussies . . ."

Laughter.

O'Reilly wondered if the Donalapropisms
were accidental or deliberate.

". . . there's only a few Woolamarroo
quokka dogs."

O'Reilly studied the audience. All were paying rapt attention.

"Now," said Donal with a touch of the
conspiratorial in his tones, "I don't need to
tell any of youse learnèd ladies and gentlemen what a quokka is."

O'Reilly counted at least eight heads nodding knowledgeably to a neighbour and having the nod returned.

"And I know youse is all familiar with
Woolamarroo . . ."

More nodding.

"So I don't need to explain. What I can tell
you is that I have for sale nine of these
remarkable dogs, and they're only twenty-
two pounds ten apiece."

A man's voice called, "I'll take one."

"Me too."

"Hold your horses," said Donal. "Doctor O'Reilly, will you please stand."

O'Reilly did, and faced the room.

From behind he heard Donal say, "If youse'll form a queue in front of the gentleman he'll take the names and addresses of and all of the first nine comers, and explain how to collect your new pup."

At least three chairs were overturned in the rush.

While he waited for the queue to form, O'Reilly did some quick mental arithmetic. Nine at twenty-two pounds ten shillings, one at twenty-two pounds five, minus Dapper Frew's pick of the litter, for a total of two hundred and four pounds five shillings, less stud fees and expenses. That would be six months' wages for Donal Donnelly. You're a genius, my friend.

"Now sir," he said, opening the notebook and uncapping the pen, "that'll be . . ."

"Here. Twenty-two pounds ten. The wife will kill me if I don't get one."

And as O'Reilly began to take the man's particulars, he realized, I'm a pound better off myself. I've won the bet with Barry. "Sorry," he said, "I didn't quite catch the street number."

"Sixteen Harberton Avenue," the man repeated.

"Right," said O'Reilly, making a note. One couple were going to be the envy of the Upper Malone Road District, the swankiest part of the city of Belfast. "Thank you, sir," he said with a vast grin, "and a very merry Christmas."

50
THE SURE-ENWINDING ARMS
OF COOL-ENFOLDING DEATH

"How are you managing, Fingal?" Richard Wilcoxson asked, looking up from the operating table where he was removing a splinter of steel from a seaman's thigh.

Fingal had returned to the for'ard medical distribution station and was still getting his eyes used to the brightness of the operating lights. He'd just made rounds of the dimly lit port mess deck, which was now an improvised hospital ward where men, many groaning, lay on the sole and on mess tables, being tended to by first-aid workers under the supervision of an SBA and comforted by their off-duty mates. Much to Fingal's relief, Henson, whose half-baked amputation had been completed professionally, was among the recovering men and on the mend — at least physically.

But seeing to the living hadn't been Fingal's only chore. He'd also been counting the wounded, and — the thought pained him — the canvas-covered dead.

He managed a weak grin. "I've been worse, Richard, but not much. I reckon we're all pretty knackered." He sat on a folding chair, rubbed the backs of his hands against both eyes, yawned, ignored the stubble on his chin, and forced himself to stay awake. *Warspite* had been hit on May 22th and the entire staff of the medical department, doctors, the dentist, and the SBAs had not slept for nearly forty-eight hours.

Now, after two days of incessant aerial attack, she had anchored in Alexandria's West Harbour in the small hours of the morning of May 24th. Belowdecks, the long list of those needing treatment was coming to an end. Above deck, dockyard maties had already swarmed aboard to determine whether the ship's wounds could be treated here where she lay at anchor or whether she should be patched up before being sent to a bigger, better-equipped yard.

"I've got the butcher's bill," Fingal said. That grim naval expression for the list of dead, wounded, and missing dated back to Nelson's day, and from the start of casualties being brought down, he'd been detailed off to keep a running tally.

Richard sighed and said, "Let's be having it."

Fingal produced his war diary. "Twenty-four missing. Some men were blown overboard and the exec reckons it'll be a week before they've recovered the last body lost from the starboard mess deck. Eight dead," he inhaled deeply, "they'll be buried ashore, and I've seen about a dozen I don't think will make it. Sixty-nine wounded, including your patient there, who I am pleased to tell you is the last man who's going to need surgery."

"Hear that, Paddy?" Richard asked CPO Paddy O'Rourke, who was giving the anaesthetic.

"Hold the lights. I'm delighted," Paddy said. "I'm so feckin' tired I could sleep standing up — on a milk bottle."

"We're all pretty done in," Richard said, "but at least we'll be able to ship all but the less-severe walking wounded to the base hospital here." He arched his shoulders and yawned. "Last stitch," he said. "You can start waking him up." He stepped from the table and stripped off his rubber gloves. "Right, Paddy. You're the senior SBA here. Arrange for your crew to clean up and get ready in case we get bombed in harbour, then one of you'll have to stay on duty for a couple of hours. I'll leave the details of the SBAs getting some kip in your hands."

"Aye aye, sir. I'll take the first watch."

"Fingal. I want you to find the exec, give him the figures, then make one last round on the mess deck. The shore parties from the base hospital should be here very soon to get patients evacuated."

"Right."

"Then you're off-watch for eight hours."

"What about you?"

Richard made a kind of grunty laugh. "I'm heading aft to the other distribution station, get everybody organised there, then I'm going to the sick bay on-call cot. I'll be on watch from there for eight hours. You can tell your relief where to find me, Paddy."

Fingal shook his head. Old Hippocrates, what his staff affectionately called him behind his back, was indeed a man of steel.

Fingal waited under the blue Alexandrine skies as the early-morning sun climbed toward its noon zenith. He'd found a haggard, unshaven executive officer, Commander Sir Charles Madden, on the upper deck, deep in conversation with a man in civvies who held a clipboard and was pointing out some figures. They were both staring down the great hole where a four-inch gun and its crew had been until the bomb hit. Wisps of smoke drifted out. An overwhelming array of smells overcame the usual odour of bunker oil: the stench of burnt paint, the hydraulic fluid that two days ago could have turned him into a human torch, scorched metal, and something Fingal recognised, having first smelled it at Narvik, but preferred to try to ignore.

"I'm afraid so, sir," the civilian was saying, "our preliminary examination's pretty conclusive. We can patch her up, but she'll have to go in to dry dock for complete repairs, I'm afraid, and we can't do that here."

"Very well. I'll report that to the captain. Thank you, Mister Robbins."

"I'll send a full written report as soon as I can, but I'll be off now." The man left.

"Yes, O'Reilly."

"The PMO sent me, sir. I have the casualty figures." Fingal handed over the ruled notebook. "I haven't had time to use a proper report form."

"None of us have," said the exec. He scanned the numbers. "Could have been worse, I suppose. I'll let the skipper know." He yawned, stared out over the harbour, and absentmindedly started flipping over the notebook's pages. He looked down, scanned, and frowned. "Keeping a diary?"

"Yes, sir."

"I don't suppose you got much chance to get any info other than the Tannoy reports of what was happening to us over the last few days."

"No, sir."

The man sighed. "They've been bad. We've lost the cruisers *Gloucester* and *Fiji* and two destroyers here in the Med, and we've just got the word from the Admiralty that the *Bismarck* and *Prinz Eugen* have broken out of their Norwegian fjord and are headed for the Atlantic. *Bismarck* sank *Hood* this morning in

715

the Denmark Strait."

"She what? Holy Mother — The *Hood*? That's terrible." Fingal had difficulty coming to terms with the thought that Britain's most powerful warship was gone, and how many of her crew of nearly fifteen hundred?

"I don't know what the news is going to do to crew morale, which I'm afraid is going to get another shock. The skipper's going to make the announcement at noon. The ship bringing our last mail bags from home was torpedoed off Durban."

"No." And he'd been so sure there would be a letter from Deirdre today. The last one had got here on May the fourteenth, ten days ago, and had been written in February. Fingal shrugged. "I'm sorry for the blokes on the mail ship," he said. "I suppose we'll just have to be patient."

"That's right." He smiled. "And it's not all misery and gloom, Doc . . ."

Fingal had wondered why the man was divulging so much information. The "Doc" gave it away. The executive officer's job, as second in command to the ship's captain, was a lonely one. He had needed, just for a moment, a father confessor.

"I do have some good news for you personally, though. I had a word with the skipper about your DSC. He'll endorse my recommendation and pass it on to A.B.C. for ratification."

"Thank you, sir."

The man handed Fingal back the notebook. "Carry on, O'Reilly."

"Aye aye, sir," and with that Fingal left to make one last set of rounds before — oh, the thought of it. Bed.

"The ship will be made seaworthy here and then sail for Bremerton in the state of Washington in the United States . . ."

The whole ship's company, except those whose duties made them indispensible, were fallen in, and Admiral Cunningham's address, which had followed a service of remembrance, was being relayed by loud-speaker. In an act of studied defiance, he had moved himself and critical members of his administrative team back to the battleship the day after she'd anchored. *Warspite* was, once again, his flagship, and the heart of the Mediterranean Fleet.

"The dockyard believe she will be ready to leave in late June."

Fingal tried to pay attention, but the last twenty-four hours had passed in a daze of sleep, work, and meals. He was still groggy.

"And we will be reducing her complement for that voyage, which will mean Blighty time for many of you."

It spoke volumes for the discipline of the crew that not a man cheered. Fingal knew he'd not be one of them, having returned so

717

recently.

"And in conclusion may I say that our losses should not blind us to the magnificent courage and endurance that has been displayed throughout. I have never felt prouder of the Mediterranean Fleet. Thank you."

The exec then did call for three cheers before the crew was dismissed.

Fingal made his way back to his cabin. He wanted to finish a letter to Deirdre. He sat at his desk, rereading a paragraph from her last, and it would be until the next mail ship got through.

Darling. Darling, Darling,
I love you. I love you. I love you. There. That couldn't wait. And I miss you, but I hope the news will bring a smile to the lips I long to kiss. You are definitely going to be a daddy. Doctor Flanagan says the frog is certain . . .

Fingal smiled. The old frog pregnancy test. It was wonderful to have the suspicions she'd raised in an earlier letter confirmed.

I saw him yesterday and he phoned today to give me the test results. I'm so excited . . .

He inhaled and thought of her and home. Someone knocked on his door.

"Come in."

"Sorry to disturb, Fingal," said Richard, "but apparently Admiral Cunningham wants to see us both in his day cabin. It's on this deck."

Fingal rose and grabbed his cap. "Any idea what it's about?"

"Probably your DSC, and I'm your department head."

"Oh. That. Come on, then."

Together they strolled along the corridor, past X and Y barbettes and through a spacious lobby to a door in the aft bulkhead where an armed Royal Marine sentry in his dress uniform standing at ease but on guard slammed to attention.

"Surgeon Commander Wilcoxson and Surgeon Lieutenant-Commander O'Reilly to see the admiral."

The sentry put one hand behind his back and opened the door.

Fingal, feeling somewhat overawed by his imminent meeting with such an exalted figure, followed Richard's lead, took off his cap, tucked it under his arm, marched in beside Richard, and halted at attention before a desk placed amidships, behind which the great man sat.

"Gentlemen, please stand easy and be seated." He indicated two simple chairs in front of the desk.

Fingal remembered the soft Scottish burr

from his earlier meeting with A.B.C. on a platform deck the day Fingal and Tom had watched the fifteen-inch rifles in action.

"Thank you for coming to see me."

Fingal reckoned it was a bit like being interviewed by the headmaster. Schoolboys only spoke when asked a question.

"First, Lieutenant-Commander O'Reilly, let me congratulate you on the award of the Distinguished Service Cross. I have confirmed it today. You must be proud of your young man, Richard."

"I am, sir. Very."

The admiral rose, strode to the far bulkhead, strode back, and stood looking down at Fingal. "Doctor O'Reilly, the Admiralty asked me to inform you of the contents of a cable that arrived when *Warspite* was at sea."

Fingal hunched forward. What telegram, and why not to him if it concerned him?

"I must be the bearer of bad news, and of the navy's apologies for the length of time it's taken to get it to you."

Fingal's eyes widened. His pulse raced. Was Ma sick? Was it Lars?

"No one knew you were married to a young nurse at the Women's Hospital in Belfast. There was an air raid on Belfast Docks on April the fifteenth. Templemore Avenue was hit."

This wasn't happening. It couldn't be. She was injured, but she'd be all right. He inhaled and waited.

"It took quite some time to identify all the casualties — I'm sure you understand . . ."

Fingal did. He only had to think back to the scenes on *Warspite*'s bombed mess deck two days ago.

"You were not listed as next of kin so . . ."

"Please, sir . . ." Fingal didn't want to hear explanations. They didn't matter. "What's wrong?"

Admiral Cunningham looked right into Fingal's eyes. He softened his words. "It seems, and my boy, you have my deepest sympathy . . ." He paused for breath and Fingal, understanding dawning despite his attempts to deny it, felt like a boxer who had dropped his guard, had seen the knockout punch coming, but was helpless and unable to stop it.

"It seems your wife didn't suffer." It took Fingal a moment to recognise that the monotonous low moaning was coming from him. Deirdre. And his child. He felt an arm round his shoulder and looked up to see Richard crouching and looking, with ineffable sorrow in his own eyes, deep into Fingal's.

"I am so sorry, Fingal," Richard said. "So very sorry."

Fingal O'Reilly, his heart in ruins, clutched his arms round himself for what? Comfort? There was no comfort. No comfort. And he felt his tears well and from the depths of his anguish came one aching word, "Noooooo."

51
'TWAS THE NIGHT
BEFORE CHRISTMAS

The traffic was light as O'Reilly drove the big Rover onto Belfast's Albert Bridge across the oily River Lagan. It was Christmas Eve after all, and sensible folks would be with family and friends. The pre-holiday drink with Cromie and Charlie Greer in the Crown Liquor Saloon had been a tradition since 1949, and the boys had been in great form this afternoon. It had been a time of reminiscing, of Dublin memories, of days gone and auld lang syne. And one other memory that had risen unbidden. He'd not told the boys. Now, after his strict ration of two pints, he was heading home. But there was one more side trip to make, one he'd started making at this time of year since 1946 when he'd come home from the war.

O'Reilly left the bridge, headed along Albert Bridge Road, and turned onto Templemore Avenue, now well recovered from its wartime devastation. He didn't intend to park as he had done all those years ago, just drove slowly past the new medical centre on the corner of Albert Bridge Road, past the red-brick houses with their pocket-hanky gardens, past the new Templemore Avenue Hospital where East Belfast GPs and midwives delivered their patients. He swallowed hard as he passed that place — the place where his love had been snuffed out.

He remembered sitting there in his car that first time in 1946, a Christmas Day downpour bouncing off the roof. He'd been surrounded by deserted building sites then, signs that this part of Belfast, like a lobster growing a new claw, was regenerating itself. Could he? Could he rebuild his life? The war had postponed his grief, and that day he had felt the loss as keenly as he had when he'd first learned of it in 1941. No one, even if they'd been stupid enough to be out walking, could see him crying behind the rain-runnelled windows of the car. He'd nursed his hurt, asked the unanswerable, the constant, the gnawing, why? Why his lovely girl? Why his unborn child? Why? He had kept chastising himself. She should have retired after they had married. Matron shouldn't have turned a blind eye. If Deirdre had confessed to being pregnant, she'd have been safely away. Why, why, why had he not insisted she move from Belfast to the country? An imbecile could have guessed that the Belfast shipyards would be a target for the Luftwaffe. And looking back, he knew he'd missed an opportunity to be more forceful on Christmas Day about her leaving Belfast sooner. It was all his fault, and every December 25th would remind him of that. Damn Christmas Day. Damn it to hell.

That had been then.

Over the years the practice in Ballybucklebo, the patients, good old Kinky, and since the early '50s a wriggling Labrador puppy called Arthur Guinness had helped make the hurt less. O'Reilly was now, and had been for some years past, able to smile in fond remembrance, not only of their love in all its shapes and forms, but also of little things about her like her terrible cooking, her wonder at deer drinking from a forest stream, her joyous laughter when his attempt to propose in 1939 had been interrupted by an Irish terrier called, of all things, O'Reilly.

But each year Christmas had come back to hurt him. The hold the ghost of Christmas past had on him had weakened, but the phantom had still been there. Those memories held little pain now, and last year, with the coming of Kitty, O'Reilly had not visited Templemore Avenue.

He waited his turn and nosed out, turning right onto the Newtownards Road that would take him past Dundonald where a brand-new Ulster Hospital had been opened in 1962, a quick left past it, over the Ballybucklebo

Hills, and home, where guests would soon be arriving for the annual Christmas Eve hooley.

I'll always remember you at Christmas, Deirdre, he thought, but with softness now. Not pain.

O'Reilly stood by the sideboard laden with bottles and glasses in the upstairs lounge of Number One. "What'll it be?" he said to the first guests.

"Mine's a Jameson's," Barry said. His grin was vast as, with his arm protectively round Sue Nolan's waist, he said, "and my fiancée will have a . . . ?"

"Vodka orange, please."

She was glowing, and O'Reilly had to admit she looked gorgeous tonight in a red tartan mini-kilt and V-necked, short-sleeved, emerald-green cashmere sweater. She had a slight Mediterranean tan.

Barry had been like a dog with two tails ever since he'd picked her up at Aldergrove airport three days ago, and had that evening confessed with palpable joy to O'Reilly that he, Barry, would've been happy to have lost a ten-, never mind a five-pound bet about Sue being faithful in Marseilles. She had been. Of course, and Barry had been a jealous eejit, but he'd laughed at O'Reilly's "You see? Absinthe does make the heart grow fonder." If Barry had bet, his losings would have joined the pound he'd coughed up to O'Reilly following last week's successful sale of all of Donal's Woolamarroo quokka dogs.

O'Reilly poured the whiskey neat into a cut-glass tumbler. Funny, he thought, it seemed an age since Barry's tipple had been sherry. The boy was growing into his job in more ways than one. He added C & C Club Orange to Sue's vodka. *"Voilà,"* he said, giving her their drinks.

"Merci m'sieur," Sue said, *"vous êtes très gentil. Voici, Barry. Ta boisson."*

He noticed that her French had a hint of the nasal Provençal accent, and that he was being dignified with the formal *"vous,"* you, instead of *"tu,"* but Barry was given the intimate *"ta,"* your. Sue was a polite young woman, even in a foreign language.

"À votre santé," said O'Reilly. "Grand to see you, Sue. Fit and well you're looking, and we're delighted that you can stay the night."

"Barry and I are going down to Bangor tomorrow for Christmas dinner with his mum and dad," she said. "Thanks for putting me up."

"They'll be here a bit later," O'Reilly said. He was looking forward to seeing Tom, his old *Warspite* shipmate, and his wife, Carol. "Excuse me." He inclined his head. "More guests, and I'm on my own up here. Kitty, Kinky, and Archie are in the kitchen getting the hors d'oeuvres ready."

Barry and Sue wandered into the lounge,

Barry to pet Arthur, who lay in front of the fire, Sue to sit and welcome Lady Macbeth onto her lap.

"Bertie. Flo. Good of you to come."

"Merry Christmas, Doctor," Bertie said, and proffered a wrapped present that had the distinct feel of a bottle.

"Thank you," O'Reilly said, setting it on the sideboard. "Now what'll you have, Flo?"

She giggled. "Would you have a port and brandy, Doctor?"

"For you, Flo? Say no more, and as your medical advisor, Bertie, I'm sorry but you're on the bottled stout."

"Can't be helped," Bertie said.

He handed the drinks to Bertie. "Do me a favour, Flo?"

"Aye, certainly, Doctor."

He handed her the wrapped bottle. "Pop that under the tree." He indicated a fully decorated fir standing between the room's corner and the bow window. Parcels wrapped in Christmas paper lay beneath and a gold star of Bethlehem at the tip leaned at an alarming angle to starboard.

"I will, so I will." She trotted off.

"Cheers, Bertie," O'Reilly said, feeling at home now with the portly little man who had, particularly with his promise of a university scholarship for Colin Brown, continued to emerge as a decent human being after all.

"Cheers, Doctor." Bertie drank and said,

"And wasn't that the quare gag, Donal selling them funny-looking dogs?"

"It was indeed," said O'Reilly, deadpan. "More things have come out of Australia than Dame Nellie Melba and the greatest cricketer of all time, Sir Donald Bradman."

Bertie cocked his head to one side, lowered his voice, laid a finger alongside his nose, and remarked, "Or out of a greyhound and a Chihuahua?"

O'Reilly tried to keep a straight face.

"I was having a jar with Willie Dunleavy in the Duck — his gout's well mended now — and I got to wondering. See that there Brian Boru? And Donal with his grue dog bitch? Them Woolamarroo quokkas have the look of a bit of both. And the age of the pups? Makes you think, doesn't it?"

In young human couples it was an Ulster national sport matching the wedding date with the date of birth of the first child. A surprising number of very big "premature" weans arrived every year. It was no surprise that Bertie would do the canine gestational sums. O'Reilly shrugged and said nothing.

"Aye, well. It'll go no farther," Bertie said with a smile. "Them rich folks in Belfast were all happy as pigs in you know what with their wee bow-wows. After you and Donal left that night, two got resold for thirty quid apiece."

O'Reilly whistled.

"I'd be the last man to sicken the buyers'

or Donal's happiness." Bertie raised his Guinness.

There was a time, O'Reilly knew, when doing just that would have given Bertie Bishop a great deal of pleasure. And yet his assurance seemed genuine. "I believe you, Bertie, though thousands wouldn't. Cheers, Councillor," O'Reilly said. "And Merry Christmas."

Bertie laughed and trotted off to give the drink to Flo, who was now chatting with Sue.

O'Reilly had finished his first whiskey and was pouring himself another. He smiled at Kitty as she appeared bearing a tray. "My love," he said, and kissed her.

She smiled and returned the kiss. "Put that drink down, would you, pet? And please put these plates of hors d'oeuvres round the room."

He took the tray laden with plates of sausage rolls, chipolata sausages, chicken vol-au-vents, stuffed mushroom caps, Scotch bantam eggs, cheese straws, and eggs mayonnaise. "Where?"

"Put the warm dishes on the metal tray over the Sterno burners and the cold ones on the coffee tables."

"Right." And he did, having to move aside a plate of marzipan-stuffed dates, a box of After Eight mint chocolate thins, a bowl of cashews, a plate of candied ginger, and a silver cigarette box full of Gallagher's Greens cigarettes strategically placed beside a silver-

and-walnut Ronson table lighter.

"Are Archie and Kinky coming up?"

She frowned. "Archie's feeling a bit shy. He knows the marquis and his sister will be dropping in."

"Bah," said O'Reilly, "humbug. Kinky and Archie are as much family as you and Lars, Arthur and her ladyship, and Barry and Sue." He looked at the youngsters. "You and I would have been proud to have had a son like Barry and a daughter-in-law-to-be like Sue."

Kitty squeezed O'Reilly's hand. "We certainly would and that's a lovely thing to say, you dear old bear," and she whispered, "I love you."

"And I love you, Mrs. O'Reilly. Now go and tell the Auchinlecks to have a titter of wit and if Kinky gets stubborn tell her it's not just me that wants the pleasure of their company. Everyone does."

"Right."

Kitty, leaving with the tray under her arm, passed Ronald Fitzpatrick in the doorway.

"Ronald," O'Reilly said as he moved to greet the new guest, "welcome aboard and a merry Christmas to you."

Ordinarily the man's prominent Adam's apple would have bobbed, but it was hidden behind a beige, spongy, sorbo-rubber high collar. His neck still needed support.

"And to you, Fingal. Thank you for asking me."

"Still on the mend?"

"Oh yes, and looking forward to getting back to work and to our new arrangement. I hear you're hiring a new lady doctor?"

"We are. Nonie Stevens. She's coming on three-months' probation and you'll have your say too if she doesn't seem to be working out, but I'm sure she'll be fine. But we'll not worry about work now. Let me get you a drink. Come on."

They walked to the sideboard.

"Half-pint shandy if I remember from the last time you were here?" O'Reilly asked.

"Oh, blow," Ronald said, "It's Christmas, for goodness' sakes. I'll go the whole hog. A bottle of beer, please."

It was a miracle that O'Reilly stopped himself from slapping Ronald Fitzpatrick on the back. "Good man-ma-da," he said instead, and poured a bottle of Bass Pale Ale, identifiable by the big red triangle on its label, into a glass before picking up his own whiskey.

"I see you've made *Budai* look festive."

O'Reilly chuckled. "That was Kitty's idea. I like the sprig of holly behind him and the cotton wool snow at his feet." The fat little carved man was surrounded by Christmas cards.

One, with a naval motif, was the same kind

O'Reilly had been receiving every year since 1942. It was from the gunnery school in Portsmouth and was signed by Commissioned Gunner Alf Henson and Mrs. Alf (née Elsie Gorman) Henson and family. Alf Henson had recovered, been fitted with a prosthetic hand, and, courtesy of a confidential conversation O'Reilly had had with Admiral A. B. Cunningham, had been appointed as a petty officer gunnery instructor to HMS *Excellent* Whale Island. O'Reilly remembered tending to Alf, doing his damndest to see that he got into the gunnery school, helping him with his loss. That and looking after his other patients had helped Fingal to hide from his own pain, at least for a short time.

"Merry Christmas, Finn." O'Reilly turned to see both Ronald and Lars regarding him with a mixture of amusement and curiosity.

"Been away with the fairies?" said Lars, and grinned.

"Excuse me, Ronald. May I introduce my brother, Lars O'Reilly." He watched as the two men shook hands, and then as Ronald headed to where the others were laughing at something Flo Bishop had said.

"What have you been up to, brother?" O'Reilly asked.

"Queen's University yesterday," Lars said. "Some of the documents about the estate follow *Brehon* law, the early Celtic *juris pru-*

dence. Quite fascinating. It's all written down in a book called *Corpus Luris Hibernici.* The earliest documents are from the eighth century. Myrna's been a help," he said, his voice taking on a slightly strained tone. "She's looked after the family archives for years, you know." He glanced round the room. "Is she coming tonight?"

O'Reilly again heard something in his bachelor brother's voice. Trepidation perhaps. Because of the spat they'd had the night they met?

"She is. She and her brother should be here any minute. Now let me get you a whiskey and water, and drinks for Archie and Kinky and Kitty."

All three had appeared, with Kinky bringing the plates, Archie the cutlery, and Kitty napkins.

"What'll it be?"

"You're sure it's all right, Doctor?" Archie asked. "Us being here, like?"

"You, Archie Auchinleck," O'Reilly said, "didn't marry Kinky Kinkaid. You married her *and* her northern family here at Number One Main. Clear? And any family member of mine is as good as the next man, even if the next man is a peer of the realm."

"Well said, Doctor," said the twenty-seventh Marquis of Ballybucklebo, appearing at the doorway of the lounge. "And, Mister and Mrs. Auchinleck, may I introduce my sister,

Doctor Myrna Ferguson?"

O'Reilly was so taken aback by the marquis's sudden appearance he dropped the water jug in his hand, soaking his trouser cuffs and socks. "Bugge —" Too many ladies. He cut himself off.

"I'm sorry, Fingal. My mother always said I had a bad habit of sneaking up on people. Once, when I was seven, I caused a footman to drop a tureen of cream of tomato soup on Mother's favourite Persian carpet."

"Welcome, John, Myrna. Come in. Come in." The marquis and Myrna were already circulating, shaking hands and laughing. "Och," he said to Lars, "I'll not melt, and this is only water, not soup, but I'll need to change. Look after the drinks, please? Make sure everybody's got one and a plate full of grub by the time I get back?" And he headed for the bathroom to get a towel before going to the bedroom, peeling off his shoes, trousers, and socks. He grabbed a clean pair of pants from the wardrobe and opened his sock drawer with an almighty tug, in his haste pulling the drawer off its tracks. He grabbed it, but not before it deposited its contents on the floor. He looked down. Lying at his feet were two things he had shoved to the back of the drawer, hidden but never forgotten. His ghost.

Kitty wasn't alone in having a ghost from the war years. His wife had laid hers in

Barcelona in the restaurant El Crajeco Loco, the Crazy Crab, when she'd met a girl called Consuela who still called her Tia Kitty.

O'Reilly's ghost hid in a glass ball and a velvet-covered box in the sock drawer, but its outline had softened, its old chill turned to warmth.

He lifted the ball, shook it, and watched the blizzard falling on the little village. He could see Deirdre clapping her hands and laughing like a little girl on Christmas Day twenty-six years ago in a flat in Alverstoke and him saying, "Merry Christmas. You can think of me when you make it snow in the glass ball in July." She never saw another July.

Her mother had given it to Fingal after the war. It was the only one of her personal possessions that had been recovered from the wreckage.

He set the ball on the eiderdown and picked up the box with the medal he hated to wear. His Distinguished Service Cross that Admiral Cunningham had told him on May 24, 1941, had been awarded for gallantry. That had been moments before he had told an unbelieving O'Reilly that Belfast had been bombed.

In O'Reilly's mind's eye, he saw Deirdre wrapping the ball in a page from the *Daily Mail*. A front page with a photograph of St. Paul's Cathedral, the great dome and one spire like defiant islands surrounded by a sea of smoke. All around the foul stuff writhed and boiled, and above the dome, brilliantly illuminated even in the black-and-white picture, the undersides of the clouds above threw back reflections of the flames raging below.

He heard Admiral Cunningham saying, "It seems your wife didn't suffer."

Later in his cabin he'd imagined the Templemore Avenue hospital burning like the houses round St. Paul's and hoped to God the admiral had been right. Every time he'd looked at the ball, he'd seen not a blizzard, but a firestorm.

He hung his head and wiped away a single tear, then he smiled. I miss you yet, Deirdre.

But the years had dimmed the pain. Kinky had been a mother to him since he'd come back to the practice. Old Arthur Guinness was always a source of undying, undemanding love. Lars, solid, humourless, and shy, had been there when he needed his advice. The ache had been numbed, the grief had faded.

And Kitty, wonderful, forgiving, loving Kitty, who had come back to him after twenty-eight years and given him the love, the love deep like Deirdre's, that he had craved in the empty years without her. Kitty has dulled the pain. Made me live again. Kitty, I love you so.

And O'Reilly felt no guilt as he thought,

Deirdre, Deirdre, I'll never forget you, but I know, I know, you'll be happy for me if you can see me now.

He picked up the ball. The storm was over and it was only a child's toy.

Ball and medal went back into the drawer. And the drawer fitted back into the dresser. He'd wear his DSC next Remembrance Day with pride and as a tribute to all who had fallen — like dear Bob — those had had been maimed — like Alf Henson — and those who had served. None must be forgotten.

O'Reilly finished dressing, washed his face, combed his shaggy mop, and with a smile headed back for the party, secure in the knowledge his ghost would not sadden Fingal Flahertie O'Reilly's heart ever again, but live there all his days content as he, at rest, at peace.

AFTERWORD

BY MRS. MAUREEN "KINKY" AUCHINLECK,
LATELY KINCAID, NÉE O'HANLON

Christmas, and it seems that fellah Taylor spinning his yarns come once a year and here I am again back in my own kitchen, pen in fist, putting down more recipes, and not just traditional Irish ones either, though you can't get much more traditional than Dublin Coddle.

Homity pie is one Doctor O'Reilly brought back from the war like his corned beef curry. Crème brûlée was taught to me by an Irish girl who'd worked in the Café de Paris before she took service with his lordship. Eton Mess comes from the same lass. It's very highheejun and served at the Eton and Harrow cricket match. Mind you, I've no time for cricket. Give me a good game of hurling or camogie any day.

And my own ma showed me and my two sisters, Sinead and Fidelma, the making of the orange sponge cake.

Have fun with the recipes and I hope you enjoy the results.

Dublin Coddle

This is a traditional Irish dish and was often made on a Thursday evening to use up all the leftover meat products in the days when Catholics were not meant to eat meat on Fridays. Doctor O'Reilly remembers seeing and indeed smelling it being cooked when he worked for Doctor Corrigan in Dublin in the 1930s, and he tells me that the great Irish writer James Joyce made several references to it in his books.

This is a very simple one-pot meal and can be cooked on top of the stove or in the oven. Just make sure that the pot has a tight-fitting lid.

Here's what you need:

500 g / 1 lb. pork sausages cut into 1/2-inch pieces
250 g / 8 oz. rashers of bacon, roughly chopped
300 mL / 10 fluid oz. chicken stock
2 onions, sliced
8 medium potatoes, cut into thin slices
1/2 stick / 2 oz. butter
Salt and pepper and a good handful of chopped parsley

If you plan to cook the coddle in the oven, preheat it to 180°C / 350°F.

Put the sausage, bacon, and stock into a pan and boil for about 5 minutes. Remove the meat from the pot, reserving the stock.

Spread a layer of sliced onions on the bottom of a casserole dish and continue with a layer of potatoes. Next half of the bacon and sausage mixture, and season well with salt and pepper. Repeat the layering process again, and pour the stock in last. Add half of the chopped parsley and dot the top with butter. Cover with a tight-fitting lid and cook for about an hour. Finish with the remaining parsley and serve with some nice bread. My Guinness bread is particularly good with this (see *A Dublin Student Doctor*).

Homity Pie

This recipe was given to me by Doctor O'Reilly when he came back from the war. He said that Mrs. Marjorie Wilcoxson used to make it and that it was invented by the Land Girls, using ingredients they could grow in the fields.

The pastry recipe is my own. I started using in it 1948 when Doctor O'Reilly bought us a fridge with a shmall-little freezer. He was a terrible man for keeping some of his medicines in the fridge, so.

Pastry
113 g / 4 oz. butter
180 g / 6 1/2 oz. plain flour
Pinch of salt
Pinch of baking powder

1/4 teaspoon cayenne pepper
85 g / 3 oz. strong Cheddar cheese, grated
  coarsely
2 1/2 tablespoons ice water
1 1/2 tablespoons cider vinegar

Cut the butter into small, 3/4-inch cubes. Put into a plastic bag and freeze until solid. Place the flour, salt, baking powder, and cayenne pepper in another plastic bag and freeze for at least half an hour.

I used to beat the pie crust dough with my old Sunbeam cake mixer, but today's cook should place the flour mixture into a food processor and blend for a few seconds to combine. Add the cheddar cheese and pulse for about 20 seconds. Now add the butter and pulse until the butter cubes are as small as a pea. The mixture will be in particles. Add the water and the vinegar and pulse again. Spoon it all back into the plastic bag. Hold the open end of the bag closed and knead the mixture with your other hand until it all holds together in one piece and feels stretchy when pulled. Wrap the dough in plastic wrap and refrigerate for at least 45 minutes, but better if you can leave overnight.

Line a deep 8-inch pie tin with the pastry and leave covered in the refrigerator until needed.

Filling

800 g /1 lb. 12 oz. potatoes, peeled and cut into quarters

25 g / 1 oz. butter

1 tablespoon sunflower oil

3 onions, chopped

2 cloves of garlic, crushed

110 g / 4 oz. spinach or broccoli

175 g / 6 oz. strong Cheddar cheese, grated coarsely

2 tablespoons chopped parsley

Pinches of nutmeg, black pepper, and salt

250 mL heavy cream/1/2 pint/10 oz.

Cook the potatoes in boiling water for 15 minutes or until just tender. Drain them and slice them and set aside to cool.

Melt the butter and oil in a frying pan and fry the onions over a low heat until soft and golden. Add the garlic and cook gently for a couple of minutes, being careful not to let it burn.

Preheat the oven to 180°C / 350°F.

Combine the potatoes, onions, garlic, spinach (or broccoli), half of the cheese, parsley, and seasonings and mix everything together well. Leave to cool. Then place this mixture on the pastry base in the pie tin. Pour the cream over and sprinkle the remaining cheese on top. Place the tin on a baking tray and bake in the oven for 40 to 45 minutes. Leave it to cool for about 5 minutes before cutting into thick wedges. Serve with a salad.

Crème Brûlée

You may wonder what a woman from County Cork knows about foreign geegaws like this. I learned it like I told you from a friend of mine, Emer Cullen, who had worked at the Café de Paris. Himself loves to surprise visitors who think they'll be getting a traditional County Down dinner at Number One. It's fun to make. Give it a try.

50 mL / 2 fluid oz. / 1/4 cup whole milk
450 mL / 16 fluid oz. / 2 cups heavy cream
1 teaspoon vanilla essence or the seeds from
  2 vanilla pods
5 egg yolks
75 g / 2 1/2 oz. brown sugar, plus 40 g / 1
  1/2 oz. more for the topping

Preheat the oven to 150°C/300°F.

Pour the milk and the cream into a heavy-bottomed pan and bring it to almost a simmer, ever so gently. Add the vanilla to the mixture and give it a good stir round. Now you whisk in the egg yolks and 2 1/2 oz. of the sugar, and pour the mixture into a serving dish or individual ramekin dishes. If you don't have time to finish them now, you can pop them into the fridge and finish them later.

When you are ready to continue, put the

dishes into a deep baking pan and pour hot water into the pan until it reaches halfway up the sides of the dishes. This is called a *bain-marie.* Himself explained that this was used in an early form of chemical science to heat things very slowly and gently. But I digress. Now put the pan in the preheated oven and cook the brûlées until they are set. This should take about 30–35 minutes. Now let them cool. You can leave them in the fridge if you do not need to serve them immediately.

Now for the topping. All you need to do is to sprinkle the remaining sugar on top of each dish and caramelise it. I just love to use my blowtorch that Donal Donnelly got for me from Belfast, but if you don't have one you can brown them under a hot grill.

Eton Mess
After you have made the créme brûlèe you will have five egg whites left over. These can be frozen for later use or refrigerated. You could make a simple pavlova, of course, but I think this recipe is more unusual and simply delicious, and dear Doctor O'Reilly with his sweet tooth just loves it. He tells me that it may have been invented by a dog at a picnic, but that's another story. You'll need a meringue to start with.

Meringue
5 egg whites
285 g/10 oz. fine white sugar
1 teaspoon cornstarch
1 teaspoon vinegar

The secret for successful meringue is to make sure that not a single drop of egg yolk gets into the mixture and to ensure that your bowl and beaters are perfectly clean and grease free. I rub a splash of vinegar on a paper towel round the bowl and beaters.

Whisk the egg whites just long enough to see them turn a greenish colour, then, still beating, add 1/3 of the sugar and continue beating for another couple of minutes before adding the next 1/3. Beat again and add the rest of the sugar. Now you should beat until it's as stiff and glossy as can be and then add the cornstarch and vinegar.

Place the mixture on a baking tin which you have greased and dusted lightly with flour. This stops the meringue spreading. Now bake it in the oven at 160°C / 325°F for 3/4 of an hour. Turn oven off and leave for half an hour.

To complete the Eton Mess you'll need
450 g /1 lb. strawberries and raspberries, mixed
2 teaspoons sugar
2 teaspoons balsamic vinegar

2 cups /480 ml whipping or heavy cream *or* a
   mixture of cream and crème fraiche if you
   are trying to reduce the calories
2 teaspoons of vanilla essence

Mash half of the fruit with the sugar and
balsamic vinegar and leave to marinate. Whip
the cream with the vanilla until stiff. Take a
large serving dish and create layers of meringue, cream, and fruit (mashed and whole).
Decorate the top with whole strawberries and
raspberries.

Orange Sponge Cake
This cake is very easy and quick to make using the "all in one" method.

Cake
175 g / 6 oz. butter
3 large eggs
175 g / 6 oz. self-raising flour
1 teaspoon baking powder
175 g / 6 oz. sugar
rind of 1 orange, grated, and 1/2 the juice of
   the orange

Preheat the oven to 170°C / 325°F and
prepare 2 round 8-inch cake tins by greasing
them with margarine and then a dusting of
flour.
   Soften the butter and have your eggs at
room temperature. Sift the flour, baking
powder, and sugar into a large bowl. Add the

eggs, orange, and the butter, and beat with an electric mixer for about a minute. The mixture should now be a soft dropping consistency, but if it is not, just add a little more orange juice. Now divide the mixture between the prepared tins, smooth the tops, and bake for about 30 to 35 minutes in the centre of the oven. You'll need to test to see if they are ready. My ma used to stick her hatpin into the centre and if it came out clean they were ready, but we don't seem to have hatpins anymore so with your finger lightly touch the centre and if it leaves no impression and the cake springs back they are done. Leave to rest for a shmall-little minute. Gently loosen the sides of the cakes with a palette knife and ease them carefully out of the tins onto a wire cooling rack.

Icing:
50 g / 2 oz. butter
175 g / 6 oz. icing sugar
250 g / 9 oz. mascarpone cheese
rind of 1 orange, finely grated

Have the butter nice and soft and beat everything together. Spread on cakes and sandwich together, reserving just enough icing to cover the top.

GLOSSARY

acting the goat/acting the lig: Behaving foolishly.

all ears: Paying attention.

and all: Expression eqivalent to et cetera

Andrew: Naval slang for Royal Navy, also known as the Grey Funnel Line.

anyroad: Anyhow.

arra be wheest: *Dublin.* Hold your tongue.

arse: Backside (impolite).

away off and feel your head: How can you possibly be so stupid?

away off and chase yourself: Go away, or I don't believe you.

away with the fairies: In a brown study, daydreaming, has lost touch with reality.

banger: Sausage, usually pork.

banshee: *Irish. Beán* (woman) *sidhe* (fairy). Female spirit whose moaning foretells a death.

bantam: A miniature chicken (originally from Indonesia) which lays miniature eggs.

beagle's gowl: The beagle dog's gowl (not

howl) or baying can be heard over a long distance. Not to come within a beagle's gowl is to miss by a mile.

Beal na mBláth: *Irish.* Pronounced "Beeuh nuh Blaw." Literally "the mouth of the flowers." A five-road crossroads in West Cork where Long's pub stood in the 1920s. In August 1922 Michael Collins was ambushed near there and shot dead.

beezer: First-rate.

black as old Nick's hatband: Black as the hatband of the devil's hat; very dark.

blether/och, blether: Expression of frustration.

blethering: Talking nonsense.

bletherskite: Someone who never stops talking.

bobby dazzler: *Yorkshire and Tyneside.* Stunningly beautiful woman.

boke: Vomit (noun or verb).

bollix/bollocks: Testicles, or more accurately, the impolite "balls." Used to imply "rubbish."

bollixed/bolloxed: Ruined.

bore (twenty, twelve, ten, eight): Of a shotgun. Calculated by noting the numbers of balls, each fitting exactly into the muzzle, that could be cast from one pound of lead. In American usage, gauge.

bowsey/bowsie: Drunkard.

boys-a-boys/boys-a-dear: Expression of mild surprise.

brave: Very.

bravely: Feeling well.

Brian Boru: Last Ard Rí, High King of all Ireland, who beat the Vikings at the Battle of Clontarf in 1014. He was killed there.

bridge roll: Bread roll longer than it is wide. Ulster's answer to a hot dog bun.

brill: Short for "brilliant," meaning terrific.

British Legion: National ex-servicemen's (veterans') association.

brolly: *RAF slang.* Parachute.

brown jobs: *British forces slang.* Army.

camogie: The women's version of a very fast stick-and-ball game, hurling.

Celtic Twilight: An aesthetic movement celebrating ancient Irish culture, including mythology.

cha: Tea, used as British Army slang, originally from the Gujurati.

champ (thick as): A dish of buttermilk, butter, potatoes, and chives. To be as thick as champ was to be very stupid.

chancing your arm: Taking a risk.

Chain Home: The name given to the string of tall lattice radar masts along the south and east coasts of England to detect and give early warning of German air raids.

chips: French fries.

clappers: Very fast.

clatter: An indeterminately large quantity.

clot: *R.A.F. slang.* A stupid person.

Clydesdale: Huge, powerful breed of plough

and dray horses.

colloguing: Chitchatting.

come 'ere here: Emphatic "come here," often accompanied by "I want ye."

come on, on in: Is not a typographical error. This item of Ulsterspeak drives spellcheck mad.

craic: *Irish.* Pronounced "crack." Practically untranslatable, and can mean great conversation and fun (the *craic* was ninety) or what happened to you since I saw you last? ("What's the *craic*?") Often seen on signs outside pubs in Eire. *Craic agus ceol.* Fun and music inside.

craytur/craythur, a drop of: Creature; a drink of spirits, usually whiskey or *poitín.*

crúibins: *Irish.* Pronounced "crubeens." Boiled pigs' trotters, served cold and eaten with vinegar.

culchie: One who does not live in Dublin. A hick or rube. (See **Jack**).

cup of tea in your hand: An informal cup of tea with a cake or biscuit, as opposed to "tea," which is often the name of the main evening meal.

currency: In 1965, prior to decimalization, sterling was the currency of the United Kingdom, of which Northern Ireland was a part. The unit was the **pound** (quid), which contained twenty **shillings** (bob), each made of of twelve **pennies** (pence), thus there were 240 pennies in a pound. Coins and notes of combined or lesser or greater denominations were in circulation, often referred to by slang or archaic terms: **farthing** (four to the penny), **halfpenny** (two to the penny), **threepenny** piece (thruppeny bit), **sixpenny** piece (tanner), **two shillings** piece (florin), **two shillings and sixpence piece** (half a crown), **ten-shilling note** (ten-bob note), **guinea** coin worth one pound and one shilling, **five-pound** note (fiver). In 1965 one pound bought nearly three U.S. dollars.

daft duck: *Yorkshire.* Stupid person.

dead: Very.

dead brill: Very brilliant. Perfect.

dead on: A strong affirmative, excited acceptance of good news, or a measure of complete accuracy. "I totally agree," "That's marvellous," or "Absolutely correct."

dinna fash yourself: *Scots.* Do not distress yourself.

divil the bit: None. "He's divil the bit of sense." He's stupid.

divil: Devil.

doddle: A short distance or an easy task.

doo lally tap: *Army slang.* Having lost one's mind.

doh-re-mi: Corruption of "dough"; money.

donkey's age: A very long time.

dote (n.): Something or somebody adorable.

dote on (v.): Adore.

doting (gerund): To be wrong because presumably you are entering your dotage.

Dublin coddle: A boiled dish of sliced rashers, sausages, onion, potato, and white pepper.

duncher: Flat tweed cap.

eejit/buck eejit: Idiot/imbecile.

fag: Cigarette, derived from "faggot," a very thin sausage.

fair play to you: To be fair or well done.

feck (and variations): Dublin corruption of the F-word. It is not so much sprinkled into Dublin conversations as shovelled in wholesale, and its scatological shock value is now so debased that it is no more offensive than "like" larded into teenagers' chat. Now available at reputable bookstores is the *Feckin' Book of Irish* — a series of ten books by Murphy and O'Dea.

finagle: Achieve by cunning or dubious means.

fire away: Carry on. Useful except in front of a firing squad.

fit and well you're looking: Good to see you. You look fine.

floors of houses: Numbering starts with the "ground floor," what is known in North America as the first floor. Next above in Ireland and the U.K. is the first floor (in North America, the second floor).

fornenst: Near to.

fortnight: Contraction of fourteen nights, two weeks. A se'nnight (seven nights) is a week.

foundered: Chilled to the marrow.

gag: A joke or someone who is great fun.

gameball: *Dublin.* Terrific.

gander: Male goose, or take a look at.

git: From "begotten." Bastard, often expressed, "He's a right hoor's [whore's] git." Not a term of endearment.

glipe: Idiot.

gobshite: *Dublin.* Literally "dried nasal mucus." Used pejoratively about a person.

Gold Coast: Former British colony. Present-day Ghana.

good man-ma-da: I approve of what you have done or are going to do.

gormless: *Yorkshire.* Witless.

great: An Ulster accolade, or can be used to signify pleased assent to a plan.

great lip for: Dublin. Drinks too much of.

green as you are cabbage-looking: Backhanded compliment implying you are not as innocent or stupid as you look.

gurrier: Street urchin, but can be used pejoratively about anyone.

heart of corn: Very good-natured.

heifer: Cow before her first breeding.

highheejuns: Very important people.

hollyers: Holidays.

HMS: His/Her Majesty's ship.

HMY: Her Majesty's yacht.

hooley: Party.

hot half-un: One-ounce measure of whiskey (with cloves, lemon juice, sugar, and boiling water added).

houseman: Medical intern. Term used despite the sex of the incumbent.

how's about ye? ('bout ye?): How are you? Or good day.

hurling: The fastest stick-and-ball game played on land. A cross between field hockey and organised mayhem.

I'm your man: I agree to and will follow your plan.

Jack or Jackeen: Slang term for a Dubliner, used by natives of Ireland from places other than Dublin, who themselves are called Culchies by Dubliners.

jackdaw: Bird of the crow family but smaller than a crow.

jammy: Lucky.

juking: Jinking. Moving erratically so as to avoid danger.

jakes: Toilets.

jar: An alcoholic drink.

ken: *Scots.* Know.

kite: *RAF slang.* Aeroplane.

knickers: Women's and girls' underpants.

knickers in a twist (knot): Panicked.

"Last Post": Bugle call sounded at day's end or at services of remembrance.

let the hare sit: Leave it alone, or be patient.

lift: Elevator, or a free ride in a vehicle. (If applied to police action, "He was lifted." Arrested.)

liltie/lilty: Irish whirling dervish.

loaf: Head.

lough: Pronounced "logh," almost as if clearing the throat. A sea inlet or large inland lake.

lummox: Stupid, clumsy creature.

manor: *London police slang.* District for which a police station was responsible. Copied from '50's TV show *Dixon of Dock Green.*

matron: A hospital's senior nurse, responsible administratively for all matters pertaining to nursing. In North America the position is now vice president nursing.

medals: The system of medals in the British Army was, with one exception, divided along rank (class) lines. Officers of the rank of major and equivalent or higher only might win the DSO, Distinguished Service Order, although it was occasionally given to more junior officers on the grounds that they had narrowly missed getting a Victoria Cross. Junior officers, captain and below, and warrant officers might win the MC, Military Cross; enlisted men, noncommissioned officers, and privates would receive the MM, Military Medal for deeds of equal bravery. The highest award for valour, the VC, Victoria Cross (akin to the Congressional Medal of Honour), was available to all ranks.

Melton Mowbray pie: A savoury pork and bacon meat pie with a thin layer of aspic between the filling and the buttery pastry. Best eaten cold.

more power to your wheel: Very good luck to you, or encouragement.

M.B., B.Ch., B.A.O.: Basic medical degrees. Medicine was not regarded as a postgraduate degree. The qualification was bachelor of medicine, bachelor of the archaic chirurgerie (surgery) and bachelor of the art of obstetrics.

muffler: Not a silencer for an automobile, but a long woollen scarf.

no harm to you, but: Placatory phrase uttered before contradicting or criticising someone.

no goat's toe: A superior person (usually only in their own mind).

no spring chicken: Getting on in years.

not have a baldy notion: Haven't got a clue.

omadán: *Irish.* Pronounced "omadawn." Male idiot. Contrary to popular belief, men are not the only idiots in Ireland. *Óinseach,* pronounced "ushick," is the female equivalent.

operating theatre: OR.

owner: *Naval.* Captain of a naval vessel.

Oxo: Compressed beef bouillon reconstituted with boiling water.

oxter: Armpit.

oxtercog: Help along by draping someone's arm over your shoulders to support them.

patch: *London police slang.* A police officer's territory. Also derived from the TV show

Dixon of Dock Green.

peeler: Policeman. Named for the founder of the first organised police force in Great Britain, Sir Robert Peel (1788–1846). These officers were known as "bobbies" in England and "peelers" in Ireland.

petrified: Terrified.

poitín: *Irish.* Pronounced "potcheen." Moonshine. Illegally distilled spirits, usually from barley. Could be as strong as 180 proof (about 100 percent alcohol by volume).

powerful: Extremely.

professional medical titles: In Ireland, for historic reasons, GPs and all specialists except surgeons used "doctor." Trainee surgeons used "doctor" until they had passed their specialty exams, when they reverted to "mister." Dentists and veterinarians used "mister" because their basic degrees were bachelorhoods, not doctorates. "Doctor" was also used by anyone with a doctoral degree — Ph.D., D.Sc., D.D., D. Mus., and the like. Professorial rank was reserved for university departmental heads or endowed personal chairs.

puff: Life.

pupil: Schoolchild. "Student" was reserved for university undergraduates. Only those who had successfully completed the necessary university courses and been awarded a degree were said to have graduated.

quare: Irish pronunciation of "queer." Very.

Often succeeded with "nor."

rain: Rain is a fact of life in Ireland. It's why the country is the Emerald Isle. Just as the Inuit people of the Arctic have many words for snow, in Ulster the spectrum runs from "sound day," or "true day, fair weather," to "a grand soft day, mizzling," also described as "that's the rain that wets you," to downpours of varying severity to include "coming down in sheets/stair rods/torrents" or "pelting," "bucketing," "plooting," (corruption of French *il pleut*), "chuckin' it down," and the universal "raining cats and dogs." If you visit, take an umbrella.

range: A cast-iron kitchen stove fuelled by coke, coal, gas, or turf. In rural Ireland it served the functions of heating the kitchen, heating the water, and cooking food.

rashers: Bacon slices from the back of the pig. They have a streaky tail and a lean eye.

redd up: Tidy up.

registrar (medical): Trainee physician, equivalent to a North American resident.

right enough?: Is that correct?

right: Very or real.

rightly: Perfectly well.

rook (n): *Corvus frugilegus* is a black bird like a crow of the family *Corvidae.*

rook (v): To cheat out of money or vastly overcharge.

run-race: Quick trip.

schooner: Glass specifically for sherry, named

for the type of vessels that brought the drink to England.

see you/him/her: An expression of emphasis, and the person referred to may not necessarily be in view.

senior lecturer: Academic rank equivalent to assistant professor.

shed a tear for the old country: Urinate. Usually used by or about men.

shit: (v) The action of defaecation.

shite: (n) Faeces.

sidhe: Irish. Pronounced "shee." The fairies.

Shuey: Peculiarly Ulster corruption of Hughey, which is itself a corruption of Hugh.

sicken your happiness: Really upset you.

sister (nursing): In Irish hospitals at one time, nuns filled important nursing roles. They no longer do so except in some Catholic institutions. Their honorific, "Sister," has been retained to signify a senior nursing rank. Ward sister: charge nurse. Sister tutor: senior nursing teacher, now also obsolete because nursing is a university course. In North America the old rank was charge nurse or head nurse, now nursing team leader, unless it has been changed again since I retired.

skin you: Very cold.

skiver: From scurvy. Waster. Good for nothing.

skivvy: Housemaid of the lowest rank.

slag: Verbally abuse. Slagging can be either good-natured banter or verbal chastisement.

sláinte: *Irish.* Pronounced "slawntuh." Cheers. Here's mud in your eye. *Prosit.*

solicitor: Attorney who did not appear in court, a function performed by more senior lawyers called barristers.

sorbo-rubber: Foam rubber.

sound/sound man: Very good/reliable and trustworthy man.

spalpeen: From the Irish *spailpin,* originally an iterant farm labourer. Now used to denote a ne'er-do-well.

squirt: *RAF slang.* Burst of machine-gun fire.

stall the ball: *Dublin.* Wait a minute.

sticking out/sticking out a mile: Very good/the acme of perfection.

stiver: Tiny sum of money.

stop the lights: *Dublin.* Expression of utter disbelief.

stout: A dark beer, usually Guinness or Murphy's.

stroppy: Bad-tempered.

strunts: Sulks.

sums: Math. Taught initially as counting, addition (the *sum* of two numbers), subtraction, multiplication, and division.

surgery: When used to describe a doctor's rooms, this is the equivalent of a North American doctor's office.

sweet, sweetie: Candy.

sweet Fanny Adams: Euphemism for "sweet eff all" and, dear reader, I'm sure you can work that out. Absolutely nothing at all.

ta-ta-ta-ra: *Dublin.* Party.

take your hurry in your hand: Slow down.

take yourself off by the hand: Please. Get real.

tall around: Rotund.

targe: Foul-tempered person.

telt: Told (corruption of "telled").

tetchy: Irritable.

them there: Emphatic for "them."

thon/thonder: That or there. "Thon eejit shouldn't be standing over thonder."

tip the wink: Inform.

titter of wit: Behave sensibly.

tongue's hanging out: Dying for a drink.

tousling: Roughing up, either verbal or physical.

townland: A mediaeval administrative region comprising a village and the surrounding countryside.

trunk call: Long-distance telephone call.

using the loaf: Being sensible about.

VE Day: Victory in Europe Day. May 8, 1945.

VJ Day: Victory over Japan Day, following the atomic bombings of Hiroshima and Nagasaki in August 1945. In the UK it is celebrated on August 15 (the initial announcement of surrender) and in the USA on September 2 (the signing of the surrender document on USS *Missouri*).

water stars: Bangor term for the way small pools of water in rippled sand reflect the sun.

wean: Pronounced "wane." Child.

wee: Small, but in Ulster can be used to modify almost anything without reference to size. A barmaid, an old friend, greeted me by saying, "Come in, Pat. Have a wee seat and I'll get you a wee menu, and would you like a wee drink while you're waiting?"

wee buns: Very easy.

wee man: The devil.

wee minute: A short time.

Wee North: The six counties comprising Northern Ireland.

Wellington boots (Wellies): Below-knee-length rubber boots patterned on the riding boots worn by the Duke of Wellington.

wheeker: Excellent.

wheen: An indeterminate number.

wheest: Be quiet.

where to go for corn (did not know): At a loss for an answer.

whisky/whiskey: Scotch is "whisky." Irish is "whiskey." Both derived from the Gaelic *uisce beatha* . . . water of life. The earliest licensed distillery (1608 by King James I) is in Bushmills, County Antrim, Northern Ireland.

windscreen: Windshield.

wizard prang: *RAF slang.* "Wizard" was very good, "prang" was a crash, but the full term meant that a very successful outcome had been achieved.

WREN: Acronym derived from the initial letters of the *Women's Royal Navy*. Akin to WAAF (Women's Auxiliary Air Force) or WAVE (Women Accepted for Volunteer Emergency Service — US Navy).

ye: You, singular.

yiz: You, singular or plural.

yoke: Thingummybob, whatsit. Descriptor for something one does not know the name of. Or, aircraft control column.

your man: Someone who is not known: "Your man over there. Who is he?" Or someone known to all: "Your man, Van Morrison." (Also, "I'm your man," as in, "I agree and will go along with what you are proposing.")

youse: You. Plural.

ACKNOWLEDGMENTS

A large number of people have worked with me from the beginning and without whose unstinting help and encouragement, I could not have written this series. They are:

IN NORTH AMERICA

Simon Hally, Carolyn Bateman, Tom Doherty, Paul Stevens, Irene Gallo, Gregory Manchess, Patty Garcia, Alexis Saarela, and Christina Macdonald, all of whom have contributed enormously to the literary and technical aspects of bringing the work from rough draft to bookshelf.

Natalia Aponte, my literary agent.

Don Kalancha, Joe Maier, and Michael Tadman, who keep me right in contractual matters.

Without the help of the University of British Columbia Medical Library staff, much of the technical details of medicine in the thirties and forties would have been inaccurate.

In the Republic of Ireland and the United Kingdom

Jessica and Rosie Buchman, my foreign rights agents.

The Librarians of: The Royal College of Physicians of Ireland, The Royal College of Surgeons in Ireland, The Rotunda Hospital Dublin and her staff.

For This Work Only

My friends and colleagues who contributed special expertise in the writing of this work are highlighted in the author's note.

To you all, Surgeon Commander Fingal O'Reilly MB, DSc, and I tender our most heartfelt gratitude and thanks.

ABOUT THE AUTHOR

Patrick Taylor, M.D., was born and raised in Bangor, County Down, in Northern Ireland. Dr. Taylor is a distinguished medical researcher, offshore sailor, model-boat builder, and father of two grown children. He now lives on Saltspring Island, British Columbia.

www.patricktaylor.ca

Facebook: Patrick Taylor's Irish Country Novels